# KADDISH
# IN DUBLIN

ALSO BY JOHN BRADY

A Stone of the Heart
Unholy Ground

# KADDISH IN DUBLIN

## JOHN BRADY

HarperCollins*Publishers*Ltd

First paperback edition: 1991

---

Canadian Cataloguing in Publication Data

Brady, John, 1955-
    Kaddish in Dublin

ISBN 0-00-647141-2

I. Title.

PS8553.R245K33 1990  C813'.54  C90-095000-5
PR9199.3.B73K33  1990

---

92 93 94 95 96 97 98 99 OFF 10 9 8 7 6 5 4 3 2 1

*For Julia and Michael;*
*Louise, Aidan, Colum and Darragh;*
*Fiona and Laura;*
*Clare, Katie and Alison*

*But who can stand in the way of his soul's*
 *steam tractor?*
*I can say Ireland is hooey, Ireland is*
*A gallery of fake tapestries,*
*But I cannot deny my past to which my*
 *self is wed,*
*The woven figure cannot undo its thread.*

Louis MacNeice "Valediction"
*Penguin Book of Irish Verse*

# ONE

Autumn. A farmer's wife in Tipperary had stabbed her husband thirty-seven times on the previous Saturday night. He had not struggled.

"He was terrible drunk and him coming home from the pub," Kilmartin said. "She might have hit him dead on with the first one. No wonder he didn't stir."

"They have five children. She has, I mean," said Minogue.

Chief Inspector James Kilmartin looked to the front of the report. "Five is right. The oldest is nine and there's an infant just a year old."

"She never reported him at all. Not even to her own family," Minogue continued.

"And that may be what'll sink her in court, I don't mind telling you, Matt. She's in dire need of someone to corroborate the beatings. Even a record of a complaint, a remark to a friend. But sure you saw yourself where they live. A pigsty."

Kilmartin and Minogue had gone the previous Wednesday to Cahir, County Tipperary, where the woman, Marguerite Ryan, was held in jail, and had been driven out to the Glen of Aherlow by two local Gardai. The farmhouse was a squat, whitewashed affair with cement floors. Minogue walked through it, appalled. Clothes lay scattered in the bedrooms, as though a violent storm had moved through the house. The blood had dried to a chocolate colour on the bedclothes. The woman's sister had taken the children. Minogue, a farmer's son, had been unnerved by the filth of the place, the rusted pieces of scrap iron and refuse which had gathered in small mounds by the front of the house over the years.

"She admitted that he just came in and fell into bed: he didn't lay a hand on her," Kilmartin said. He turned two pages and searched for lines he had noted.

" 'He was in a terrible drunken state'—this is her statement—'and he was muttering and cursing and I didn't know what he was saying. He got into the bed and he was asleep almost straight away. I was in a humour of great despair and fear for several weeks, seeing as my husband had been drinking heavily and threatening myself and our oldest, Sean,' " Kilmartin intoned.

"What do you make of that bit—'in a humour of great despair and fear'? Melodrama. It's like an expression out of a book."

Minogue, irritated by Kilmartin's remark, said nothing.

"Or sounds like words someone else would use—a

2

barrister defending her, don't you think? 'My client was in a humour of great—' "

Minogue cut him short.

"Come on, Jimmy. Let's not be picking holes in things."

" 'And I lay awake for many hours that night as had been my affliction these many months, waiting for the first light of day'—aw Jases, Matt, this is nearly too much. It's like a romance book or some class of a thing. 'The first light of day.' "

"What are you getting at?"

"I'm saying that it's a mighty peculiar way of saying things, mighty peculiar entirely for a first statement. It's like she practised it in her mind before saying it, preparing a defence. You know what that is, Matt, don't you?"

"It's florid prose."

"It means she had her mind made up a long time ago. That's how her account comes out so put-together."

"Like she had her speech from the dock prepared well in advance."

"Yep. She had everything planned. That's premeditated murder, if the State has the nerve to so prosecute Mrs Ryan."

Minogue did not want to argue the toss with Jimmy Kilmartin. Mrs Ryan was being held for the murder of one Francis Xavier Ryan, her husband of ten years and the father of their five children. Mr Ryan had farmed seventy-odd acres of good land (in fact his wife had done most of the work) near the village of Newtown in the Glen of Aherlow. Ryan, named after a favourite saint of Irish Catholics, had been twelve years her senior. He farmed poorly, drank most of the money which came into the house and was jealous of their oldest child, frequently berating him and knocking him about for neglecting chores on the farm. Fran, as he was known locally, had been beating his wife regularly and methodically within months of their marrying.

"And prosecuting's exactly what the WAM are daring us to do," Kilmartin added.

"WAM . . . wait a minute. Oh, yes: the Women's Action Movement."

"The same bunch. They sound like bloody paratroops. A crowd of well-fed radicals and students and actresses from Dublin, never did a hand's turn on a farm. They're the ones that don't eat meat and tell the bishops to eff off. Lesbians and what have you."

"They've raised money for Mrs Ryan already." Minogue tried to divert him.

"Sure haven't they plenty of it, isn't that what I'm saying? All well-to-do. They'll make a big thing out of this, so they will."

Both policemen fell to reading paragraphs from the report again.

". . . And see this here, page what is it, page seven, I have it marked, where she says 'Were it not for my children I would not have endured these years.'" Kilmartin paused. "I'll never understand that. Fair enough, I say, but how were the children brought into the world in the first place, I say. It takes two to tango, amn't I right?"

"Jimmy, have you ever heard of contraception?" Minogue murmured. "Can you remember back that far?"

Kilmartin who, like Minogue, was within five years of early retirement, affected to smile.

"Ah, you're not one of those maniacs wanting to put any girl over the age of ten on the pill and turn the churches into bingo halls, are you? Sure, all a woman has to do is say no."

"And if she says no but her husband has his way anyway, that's rape then, isn't it?"

"Here, hold on a minute," Kilmartin temporized with his palms up as he worked on staunching Minogue's attack of logic. "That's not how things are done, Matt. That's a grey area, I mean. There's no plain and simple answers to this business. Let's be reasonable. Marriage is a sacrament too. Man proposes, God disposes."

Minogue held off his sarcasm. "Well, do you think she'll be charged with murder in the first degree?"

Kilmartin frowned. "Well now, it's not my decision, is it? The Director of Public Prosecutions lays the charges. Tell you the truth, I'll be as happy as Larry if this Women's Action Movement crowd concentrate their efforts on the mob in the Department of Justice and leave us Gardai get on with the work. I don't relish the thought of another effort like the Kerry Babies," Kilmartin said, sucking in air through his teeth.

Minogue had had an earful on that topic from his daughter, Iesult. Even Kathleen had prodded at him. A woman in Kerry had been charged with infanticide some time before. The police work had included bullying her during interviews to invent evidence for her trial. Minogue had not seen Iesult so angry since she had been a small child. She had been quite right when she shouted at him that the woman was condemned—what had she called the detectives? Brutal, patriarchal rednecks?—for being some class of a whore and consequently was obviously guilty of the lesser crime of killing her child at birth. "Tried and sentenced before she even got near a courtroom!"

Iesult had shouted down the stairs at him as he headed out the door one morning.

"You're right there," Minogue concluded. He well knew that Inspector James Kilmartin of the Murder Squad had a different reason than he for wishing to ward off such an eventuality.

Kilmartin's secretary, Eilis, drew a draught of cigarette smoke and the smell of paint into his office when she entered.

"Is it yourself that's in it, Eilis," Kilmartin said. Minogue noted the mixture of slight apprehension and irritation in his voice. Perhaps Eilis treated Jimmy Kilmartin thus by way of goading him into asking her to knock on doors first. It was widely believed amongst the detectives who worked in the Murder Squad that Jimmy Kilmartin feared his secretary.

"None other. There's a body lying out on the beach in Killiney. Washed up a half an hour ago. Dalkey station called about it. They have men there now."

"Are they sure it's not somebody sunbathing, now?" Kilmartin winked. He shot a stage glance at the grey sky over the rooftops outside his window.

Eilis blinked once and met Minogue's eyes for a moment. "It seems unlikely. The person in question was shot in the head several times."

At Minogue's suggestion, Kilmartin had Detective Seamus Hoey drop them at Pearse Station. Shea Hoey showed no sign of surprise at being told to drive out to Killiney and meet the two officers there.

The regular, clean, fast service on the new Dublin Area Rapid Transit—the DART—trains still surprised and pleased Dubliners. Its efficiency silenced all but the irredeemable cynics, those inhabitants of the city who enjoyed Dublin the more for being able to find daily reminders of its chaos and decrepitude. Kilmartin had brought a posse of comments aboard the train.

"There's no name for it though, is there?"

"For what?"

"Killing your husband. 'Husbandicide?'"

"Try patriarchicide," Minogue observed. The train hummed out from Ballsbridge Station. "Iesult reminds me about patriarchy every now and then. She's a feminist."

"Mmmm." Kilmartin rubbed his nose.

"She frightens the daylights out of me half the time. I don't know what she'll do next."

"Is she still with that odd fella?"

"Pat the Brain? She is still keen on him. I must say, I like him. He's a droll character."

Kilmartin grunted and looked out the window. The bay, a leaden sheet spread out to Howth, drew suddenly next to the railway line. Dublin Bay was darker than the sky, itself seamless and low.

"She admitted to sharpening the kitchen knife the day before too," Kilmartin observed.

Minogue turned from the window. Kilmartin's face was slack, eyes glassily fixed on the horizon. He too had been hypnotized by the sea. The tide brought ripples and gentle swells obliquely by the train. Minogue felt confused, pleased to be confused, by the motion of the train. What was it about trains that made a body feel removed from the local world?

"Look, Jimmy. She may not have consciously prepared for any crime. It may have been unthinkable, don't you see, so another side to her took over."

"Mad, you mean. She can't plead that."

7

Minogue refused to be drawn.

"She woke up in the middle of the night and she went to the kitchen, got the knife and . . . Bob's your uncle. I hope she doesn't claim she was in a trance or something. She must have been wide awake and calculating to stick him in the heart first time. You know how it is with an amateur—they'll break a half dozen ribs before they get near the heart. But your man was asleep so she could find her spot and . . . Of course she might be used to killing farm animals or that, I suppose."

Minogue imagined the deed. Ryan still in his clothes passed out, drunk, on the bed. Snoring probably. Marguerite Ryan can't sleep. Something wakes her up—A knife in her strong, capable hands, she plunges it—

"Then *thirty-six* more for good measure," Kilmartin murmured. "Seven or eight of those alone would have killed him, too. A tough piece of work, Mrs Ryan."

Kilmartin turned to Minogue as the train pulled into Seapoint station. "Plenty of muscle on her after doing all the work on the farm, I'll bet. And Ryan in the pub all day swallowing pints. Ha ha."

Minogue did not think it wise to let Kilmartin in on the fact that Marguerite Ryan was a heroine in the Minogue household. Even Kathleen had sided with their daughter while Minogue tried to finish his breakfast faster that he might escape further wrath. He felt more than uneasy being held answerable for patriarchy Irish style, as Iesult put it.

"Ah, but did you read the letters to the papers? Jesus wept. People putting pen to paper and saying she should be given the farm and not even charged with manslaughter. Sent back to her children and her house as if nothing had happened," Kilmartin added in an aggrieved tone. He did not take his gaze away from the window.

Neither man spoke further until the train doors opened in Dalkey. A youth with a haircut which reminded Minogue of a Mohican, but with wires trailing from both ears, slouched into the train. He sized up the two policemen, sneering a little, Minogue believed, and flopped as if shot into a seat. He twitched occasionally as he lay there and played chords with gusto on an imaginary guitar.

"Frankenstein," Kilmartin muttered as they stepped onto the platform in Killiney. "Ask him if he can spell haircut."

Minogue and Kilmartin trudged up the steps to the pedestrian bridge which led from the station to the beach. They paused on the bridge and saw again the orange markers, the dozen or so men standing near the plastic tarp. The orange seemed to be the only colour abroad that day amidst the greys of beach and sea and sky. The beach was too soft to allow the Garda cars to drive out on to the sand.

"Never came to a murder site on a train before. Feels sort of classy, I must say," declared Kilmartin. He looked to his watch. "Twenty minutes only. Gob, that's fantastic entirely."

Minogue nodded. The two laboured across a stony part of the beach. Kilmartin started with the two Gardai from Dalkey station; Minogue went to the body. A light breeze was coming in off the water. Sea-smells, the soft lick of the water on sand. A district detective greeted Minogue by name but it took Minogue two tries to remember his surname.

"Gerry. Gerry Sweeny. Now I have it. Who's this victim here, Gerry?"

9

"We don't know yet. He has clothes on but there's nothing in his pockets," replied Sweeny. He hunkered down beside Minogue and drew the heavy plastic back from the face.

Minogue held his breath and let his eyes out of focus. The sound of the sea filled the air around him. He looked to Sweeny's face and found that he too was grimacing. With a great effort Minogue looked to the face again. The wound over the left eyebrow had to be an exit wound: it was too large, too ragged to be otherwise. The dead man's skin reminded Minogue of a fish. The gaping hole was now a lilac, blubbery flower on the man's forehead. At least the water had washed him clean.

"There's two on this side by the ear," Sweeny mumbled. "They came out the neck on your side."

Minogue didn't want to push the ear back to see. "What?"

"This side, Inspector, there's two distinct gunshot wounds here. As well as the one in the back of the head. Hard to miss that one, I'm telling you."

Sweeny rose. His shoes crunched pebbly sand underfoot. He didn't know what to do with his hands. Minogue stayed on his hunkers, already putting up that shield between his own shock and fear and the body which had been a living person. Still, he felt that alertness and dim excitement come to him as his horror gave way. He made a conscious effort to relax his eyes and let them wander about the body.

"Well," he whispered. "I'll stake money that this is a secondary site. I wonder how far away from here he was actually shot, though—"

"Beg your pardon, sir?" said Sweeny, swallowing.

Minogue didn't answer. Already his trained eye

was looking for ligature marks. He allowed his gaze to move slowly from place to place on the exposed skin. The abrasions looked postmortem, he thought. He took out a pencil and poked it under the dead man's shirt, lifted the shirt-tail slowly, and immediately spotted the edge of a lividity which he guessed discoloured the back of the body completely. Minogue breathed out slowly through pursed lips.

"Ow," said Sweeny.

"You're telling me," Minogue whispered. "He was lying somewhere for a while. That's a start, I suppose."

"But he's not long in the water, I'm thinking," said Sweeny.

Minogue nodded. He had seen no marbling on the neck at all. Easing the pencil out from under the flap of shirt, he replaced the plastic over the body, and felt the first currents of discouragement move in on his thoughts. Whatever physical transfers had occurred between the victim and the killer at the murder scene, he thought, had most likely been washed and scraped away by the sea.

"Wasn't bound or anything when he was found?" Minogue heard himself ask.

"No, sir. There's no marks on the wrists. It's an execution, isn't it?"

Minogue kept his gaze on the sea.

"Tell you the truth, I don't feel up to checking the body proper this minute now," Sweeny whispered. "I'll leave it for yous professionals on the Squad."

"Thanks," said Minogue.

A doctor, to judge by the BMW he had left moored next to the squad cars, was walking down the beach towards the body. He was youngish, earnest and grim, swinging his bag as he hurried with a Garda in tow. Minogue didn't recognize either man. He stood and looked inland. Cliffs: the steep hill of Killiney above, a few feet short of the official status of mountain. The sky felt close, almost malicious.

A van drew slowly on to the beach. Seeing he could go no further, the driver reversed towards the squad cars. Minogue knew one of the scenes-of-the-crime policemen who stepped out of the van and began donning boiler-suits. Kilmartin left the group of policemen and began walking towards the van. Minogue found it impossible to remember the dead man's face. His concentration had been stolen by the wounds, and he wondered what kind of a gun or a bullet had caused that. Three shots at least. Revenge? For what? How had the body turned up here? A pair of seagulls scratched the dull midmorning with their screaming overhead.

Kilmartin was standing next to him now. "All right," he grunted. "I'm as ready as I'll ever be. Let's go, Matty."

Kilmartin scrutinized the pebbles and sand next to his feet before he knelt down heavily and turned back the plastic.

"Are yous gentlemen involved below?" the waiter asked them.

Minogue and Kilmartin had walked back up the beach and into the lounge of the one hotel opposite the station. The beach and its events were out of sight to the two policemen seated as they were by a picture window. Kilmartin had eaten most of the chicken sandwiches and downed a pot of tea. The sea air, he claimed as he stifled a belch, wasn't it great? Minogue was working on a second Bewley's coffee.

"If we're not now, we will be," Kilmartin replied. "Did you make this tea with bags or with real tea leaves?"

"Bags."

Minogue refused more coffee which the hotel offered black, to be doctored with cold milk by the customer. He far preferred his Bewley's coffee *in situ*, in a Bewley's Oriental Restaurant, complete with scalded milk, a sticky bun to play hell with his dentures and a deafening noise of plates and loud conversation.

"Terrible business. Never happened since I started at this place. That's fifteen year ago next November," the waiter observed. He too had been immobilized by the sea, Minogue noticed. The sea looked tranquil from here. The waiter stood over the two policemen, his tray against his chest, gazing out the window. Minogue wondered if everyone near the sea today looked as if they had been summoned by a hypnotist.

"Tell us, do you work here every day?" Kilmartin asked.

"Weekdays three till half-eleven. I do a Saturday or Sunday if they're short. I don't have to. We have the union now, thanks be to God," the waiter replied slowly from his trance.

"Thanks be to James Connolly and Jim Larkin, you mean," Kilmartin said.

"And that Marx fella too," Minogue added.

"Hah," said the waiter. The humour had broken the sea-spell. He looked to Minogue and then to Kilmartin. "I heard the poor man was after being shot."

"Who told you that?"

"Danny the barman. He seen the commotion with the Garda cars and he went over. Before the man was covered up, too. A terrible gruesome sight, says

13

Danny. What's the country coming to, do you know what I mean?"

Minogue recognized the futility of a reasonable question asked in an unreasonable environment. He offered an honest appraisal. "An unnerving maturity, I'd say."

"What?" asked the waiter.

"Is there more tea?" snapped Kilmartin.

The waiter drifted away through the empty lounge, drumming on his tray. Kilmartin stretched out his legs and reached for his cigarettes. After blowing out the match with a cloud of smoke he tapped his finger on his watch.

"Look at that, would you. Hoey's still in the bloody traffic, I'd swear."

"He may be down on the strand. Detained or looking things over," said Minogue. "The traffic doesn't be that bad this hour of the day."

Kilmartin coughed. "Boys oh boys, if the buses and the trains go on strike there'll be convulsions as regards the same shagging traffic. There's rumblings on that score too. We might as well stay home if there's a bloody strike, I'm telling you. I wish they'd legislate that crowd back to work. Just once, anyway," he said.

"Aha. So you're not really a follower of Marx," Minogue noted, as though he hadn't known Kilmartin for twenty and more years. "Half my crowd at home have turned sharply to the left. I feel the breeze by times myself."

"It's that Pat Muldoon, your daughter's fella, if you ask me." Kilmartin's tone took on an ominous, schoolmasterish tone.

"As for the busmen, I say we let the Army come in

and either drive the bloody buses or use Army lorries. Remember when they used to do that?" asked the philosopher-king.

"I do. Don't you think that seeing Army lorries and uniforms on the streets here would make us look like the banana republic we are rapidly becoming?" an indelicate Minogue advanced.

Kilmartin laughed without sparing a smile. "Jokes aside, there are plenty of people in the country who wouldn't mind seeing the unions get a rap on the knuckles. Maybe having Army lads on the streets would improve general morale."

"Getting the trains to run on time, is it? Then maybe we should take over the Isle of Man and call them the Malvinas."

"Fine and well for you to be laughing about it, Matt. I'll tell you this and I'll tell you no more." Kilmartin leaned closer to Minogue to shield his wisdom from the returning waiter. "There's men well up the ladder, well above us little pissers," he whispered, "men who'd like to put the unions and their Leftie hangabouts to work and get the country back into the civilized world. Leadership is what we need, let me tell you. All you have is ad-hoc-itis, floating fluff until election time."

Minogue did not care to listen to the remarks of high-ranking policemen which Kilmartin might have overheard at the boozy conferences he liked to attend. He believed their political vagaries to be less antic than threatening. "I tend more towards the hangabout position rather than the alternative," he murmured.

Kilmartin grunted. "Tell you what. If there was a new party introduced tomorrow morning and it wasn't full of lunatics, there'd be plenty of people'd come out of the woods and support it. Every dog and divil is ready for a change. What do you think?"

The waiter laid the teapot on the table. Kilmartin flipped the lid, looking for the tea-bag.

"I took it out," said the waiter. He turned and sailed back to the bar.

"*Plus ça change*, Jimmy—"

"I heard that Gorman would like to get out from under the Chief and get things going," Kilmartin rejoined.

Minogue remembered Gorman, the Minister for Defence, fervidly denying rumours that he was anything but 110 percent loyal to the Chief and the Party. To Minogue, the Chief looked like a crooked Caesar in profile. The Party Whip meant precisely that in Irish politics: the Chief had a tribe, not a political party.

"See him on the telly the other night, telling the reporters about rumours started up by the media? Ha ha, butter wouldn't melt in his mouth, that Gorman," Kilmartin concluded.

"I understand that Gorman hasn't a brain in his head at all, at all," Minogue offered mildly. He saw Hoey stepping around a table next to the entrance to the lounge. Kilmartin looked up from his ministrations with the tea as a man with the face of a Toby jug followed Hoey into the lounge.

"Jases," Kilmartin said. "Not Hynes."

Shorty Hynes was a reporter for one of the two Dublin evening papers. He was a prodigious drinker, a gregarious and disarming character well known in the pubs and clubs of the city. Hynes could not wholly conceal the fact that he was as tenacious as a badger with a bone between his teeth. He specialized in lurid descriptions of murders and violent crimes, wringing

out the most minute and morbid details to gratify the
tastes of the citizenry of Dublin and the island generally. Kilmartin had had Hynes barred from the headquarters of the Murder Squad after a spat between
them. Hynes had been speechifying that the people
had a right to know. Like any speechifier, Kilmartin
did not take to competition in this line and he had told
Hynes that, generally speaking, "the people" were
iijits. Hynes did not dispute this fact but still argued
their right to be privy to details of a murder investigation. His insistence on this point had landed him out in
the street. Still, Hynes had not taken it badly, and Kilmartin and he maintained a relationship which occasionally bordered on the civil. Hoey's tight lips
suggested that Hynes had refused to be put off looking for Kilmartin on the beach.

"Ha ha, men," Hynes shouted, rolling his *bonhomie*
across the room ahead of him. "The very men I was
looking for. I was told that yous were at the scene but
minutes before I arrived."

Kilmartin glanced at Hoey.

"Are we just in time to have a nice little pick-me-
up?" Hynes beamed.

"A kick-me-out-on-me-arse, you mean," muttered
Kilmartin.

"Landlord, landlord!" Hynes cried spiritedly. The
waiter reappeared, looking more the ascetic monastery
novitiate than before. Hynes ordered a Johnnie Walker
and flipped a finger at the three policemen.

"No drink here," Kilmartin declared.

Hynes shrugged and sat down, his hands on his
knees.

"A few words, Chief Inspector, for attribution? And
Sergeant—whoops, Inspector—Minogue . . . fresh and

well you're looking." The reporter smiled again.

"We were sitting down here discussing how nice it is to be nearer to retirement, Mr Hynes," Kilmartin drawled. "To have able and expert policemen in the Technical Bureau to go over the ground for us. To be looking forward not to be straining to be polite to certain members of the public, to certain organs in society."

"Which organs, now?" Hynes guyed.

"Arra, don't be offering me occasions of sin now, Mr Hynes, if you don't mind. My colleague here has a refined sensibility. I meant the media, specifically the press. There were times when journalists didn't run berserk with the smell of blood to titillate their readers."

Minogue doubted that the bibulous Hynes had sought Kilmartin out merely to torment him. The reporter must have heard less than he wanted down on the strand.

"What's with your man down on the beach?" Hynes asked brightly.

"Apparently the man is dead, Mr Hynes."

"Ah, but the world and his mother knows that, men. But sure that's only the beginning, isn't it?"

"Mr Hynes, I'm going to be briefed as soon as there's an officer comes here to brief me. There's more than enough expertise and feet plodding over the scene below. You'll doubtless have heard as much, and perhaps more, down there as you'll hear from me," said Kilmartin.

Minogue met Hoey's eyes. Hoey looked to heaven.

"I thought as much," said Hynes. He lit a cigarette from the butt of another and ground out the expended one slowly as though choking a hen. Minogue began calculating: he has a cigarette in his gob the minute he wakes up. Seven o'clock, say. A cigarette in his gob all day, then, so an average of five every hour if he takes them easy—up until the pubs close. Seventeen hours at—

Hynes was squinting up through a thread of smoke at Kilmartin, his fingers holding the butt pressed into the ashtray. "But my readers would still like your reactions." He spoke around the cigarette.

"To what?"

Minogue liked Kilmartin's pose. He even looked aloof, leaning back in his chair across from Hynes, as if trying to keep him at a distance.

"Someone phoned his paper, sir," Hoey interrupted.

"Garda communications lagging behind the press, is it? We passed it on to your crowd a half hour ago," said Hynes.

Kilmartin blinked.

"Your reaction to the murder of Billy Fine's son," Hynes added.

"Chief Justice Fine?" Minogue asked. The waiter laid a double Scotch languidly in front of Hynes.

"None other," the reporter replied earnestly. He looked over his glass at Hoey and winked.

"Someone phoned the *Irish Press* claiming responsibility, sir. We couldn't get through to you, what with the train and everything. I got it on the radio, but the Guards on the beach don't know yet," Hoey said quietly.

So it is a paramilitary thing, Minogue thought. But Fine?

"Paul Fine," Hynes said.

"Who called and said they'd done it?"

"Are you ready for this one?" Hynes said, flourishing his glass. "'The League for Solidarity with the

19

Palestinian People.'" He downed another gulp of Scotch.

Kilmartin stood up and motioned to Hoey, who followed him out to the foyer of the hotel. Minogue did not get up immediately, preferring to leave Kilmartin to vent his unjust anger on Hoey in private.

"I never heard of that mob, did you?" said Hynes, his eyes a glaze of wily smugness. He swallowed more whisky and slipped a notebook out of his pocket.

"Maybe you can have your say instead of Kilmartin, now," he continued. "Give him time to find his feet." Try as he might, Minogue did not detect any sneer on Hynes's ruddy face.

"When he finds them he may plant one of them on your arse, I'd say," Minogue offered.

"Oh, comical entirely. Is it my fault that the newspaper values its correspondent enough to put a space-age phone in his car? You're well known for your ways yourself, Ser—Inspector Minogue," Hynes replied without trying to hide the ambiguity now. "But this isn't a home-grown effort, with the mention of Palestine, is it?" Hynes probed.

Minogue extemporized by saying nothing.

"And I don't just mean that the man's daddy is a Justice in the Supreme Court."

Hynes finished the Scotch and looked down the glass at Minogue.

"The Fines are Jews, Inspector dear. One of our own, to be sure, but Jews nonetheless."

# TWO

Minogue's thoughts kept returning to Hynes's "nonetheless" while Hoey drove back into Dublin. Instead of going back to the beach with Kilmartin, Minogue was now on his way to Justice Fine's home in Rathgar. He was very nervous but too agitated to stay annoyed at Kilmartin. It was not so much that he resented being stuck with going to Fine's house; what galled him was Jimmy Kilmartin's method of inducing him to go with Hoey.

Kilmartin had heard from Hoey that Fine had been in his chambers when he was told about the murder of his son. No policemen had been to the house yet. Minogue had seen and heard the old Kilmartin then, the gritty Mayo giant who had been lost to the cattle-dealing or horse-racing professions in becoming a policeman; the Kilmartin who still defied the tailors of Dublin to encase him in suits which lessened the comic

21

incongruity of city garb for him. When Jimmy Kilmartin had been recuperating after an operation, Minogue believed he had discerned a more thoughtful Chief Inspector, but the cajolery and cattle-fair persuasion now seemed to have returned in full force. "That bloody snake Hynes in there knew before we did, for the love of Jases," Kilmartin had grumbled. "We'll nearly have to be thanking him for not notifying next of kin before we get our hands on a case. I don't like looking like an iijit."

Uncharitably, Minogue wondered if the Chief Inspector was fretting less about the dead man's next of kin than about Hynes making him look flat-footed. It was more likely that Kilmartin's agitation had ballooned at the realization that he would be dealing with one of the leading members of the Irish judiciary. If Justice Fine were to but raise a ripple on his forehead about this investigation, Kilmartin might expect that ripple to be a tidal wave of disapproval by the time it reached him.

Kilmartin used a radio patch to phone from Hoey's car. Fine was home by then, he found out, so Mrs Fine knew now. It was at this stage that Minogue had had the first snare tripped on him, by his own agency in part. He had mentioned to Kilmartin that he knew Justice Fine peripherally. Kilmartin lost his chokehold on the microphone as he waited for a message from dispatch and squinted at him. Minogue knew then that there was something afoot. He believed that had he looked closer he might have seen the horns sprout from Kilmartin's calculating temples.

"How peripherally, Matt?"

"Um. I was in the Jewish Museum several months ago and I saw him there. Very peripheral entirely."

"'The Jewish Museum?' In Dublin, Ireland? Europe? Go away out of that, there's no such place. Sure there's hardly a Jew in the country," declared Kilmartin.

"You might not see it as you drive by. It's also a synagogue too, by times. It's part of a terraced row of houses in up near the canal. A galloping horse would miss it."

"Go on, anyway," said the galloping horse.

"Visitors sign their name in a book by the door. There he was, sitting there, reading the paper. I recognized him. Very ordinary-looking fella."

"No robes?" tried Kilmartin.

"They don't sleep in them, Jimmy. It's only Special Branch men and defrocked Jesuits sleep in their clothes."

"That's it, then?"

"Well. He said something to me as I was signing the book."

"What?"

"He didn't look up from the paper, that's what made me laugh. 'And how's tricks with the bold Inspector Minogue this fine day?' he said."

"Go on with you, he did not." Kilmartin's jaw slackened. Hoey was staring too.

"I was surprised, to say the least of it. I signed me name anyway and I asked him if we had met. He said no. I asked him how he knew me so, and he said my name came up in a dinner conversation, in connection with that Combs thing."

"Ho ho, bejases and I'd say it came up, all right." Kilmartin shook his head. "And you minding the shop for me. Wanting to give External Affairs and every other public servant on the island heartburn, bad luck to you."

23

"All I wanted was to get them to drop their immunity for Embassy staff so we could interview some of them."

"And all the tea in China. So he knew you were a bit of a—" Kilmartin rubbed his chin.

"A crank?"

"Did I say that? Did I even think that? I was going to say 'topnotch-Garda-officer.'"

The former Jimmy Kilmartin was indeed back. There was that challenging sincerity on his face, daring Minogue to suspect that he was being buttered up.

"Fine's on the committee that runs the Museum," said Minogue.

"So you'd know the man to say hello to and pass the time of day with," Kilmartin burrowed.

Minogue had paused then, while Kilmartin spoke into the radio, knowing the battle was lost but wanting to let discomfort settle on Kilmartin too.

"You're not going to be asking me to pass the time of day with him, though, are you, Jimmy?"

Hoey was through Terenure now. Fine's house was but minutes away.

Paul Fine had been married until two years ago. His ex-wife was English and she remained in London. *"One of our own to be sure, but a Jew nonetheless."* Did that "nonetheless" sum up the fact of being a Jew in any place but Israel? Kilmartin would definitely be worried by the mention of "Palestinian." A question still hung around the edges of Minogue's thoughts: how had the telephone call from this group come within an hour of the body's being discovered? Had the group planned to phone anyway, knowing that he'd be found? Yes, Kilmartin would not like this mention of Palestinian one bit.

To stem his own anxiety, Minogue turned to Hoey. "Do you know any Jews here at all, Shea?"

"Not a one, sir. I wouldn't know one if I saw one."

"Do you know how many Jews there are in Ireland?"

"I don't."

"There's about 2,000, so there is. North and south. Fewer every year, too, I'm thinking."

"Is that a fact? I heard a joke there a while ago. Maybe now's not the time, though. Ah . . . harmless enough, though. It's about a roadblock with a gang of thugs up in Belfast. Doesn't matter if they're Catholics or Protestants for this one. They stop this fella driving his car and they stick a gun in the window, like. 'Are you a Protestant or a Catholic?' they ask. 'Neither,' says the man. 'I'm a Jew.' So that sets them back a bit. They have to think about that one, you see. Finally one of them asks: 'Are you a Protestant Jew or Catholic Jew, though?'"

"I think that'd be a good one another time," Minogue allowed. "Do you know Abrams, the jewellers down in Dame Street?"

"Beside the hat-shop? I do."

"They're Jews. I bought Kathleen's ring there. It didn't fit properly so I brought it back. She thought I had bought it for another girl. Or so she said. Bernard Abrams was in it then. He fixed it. I was by the place there a few months ago and the son was selling out. To go to Canada, I think."

"Hold on a minute. There's a Dr Lewis up in the Rotunda: he's a Jew, isn't he?" Hoey asked.

"To be sure. If you hadn't been a Galwegian, you'd

have been one of the thousands that Lewis delivered. It was him who landed Kathleen and meself with our two. Three actually—" Minogue felt a tingle, all that was left after the years had cauterized the memory of their first child, an infant, Eamonn. They had been told at the time that the child had forgotten to breathe.

"Well, the Lewises go back a long time. A family of doctors," Minogue added.

He took a deep breath in an attempt to calm himself. Damn and blast that Jimmy Kilmartin, the sleeveen: all that talk about Victor Hugo and loaning him books to read in the hospital hadn't changed him an iota. Damn him the more for infecting me with his own anger and anxiety, thought Minogue as the car turned into Fine's street.

"There's a funny thing, now," Hoey began as though talking to himself. "Hold on, is it 147 we're wanting?" He leaned over the wheel looking for door numbers. "There it is," he muttered.

"'Yep. A funny thing," Hoey murmured as he turned off the ignition. "I don't know what words to use when we're talking about this. I hear meself saying 'Jews,' then 'Jewish,' and I don't like the sound of either. I don't mean the words themselves. I don't know what it is."

"Like 'a Jew' is not an Irishman too? Or is it a declaration?" Minogue suggested.

"Something like that maybe." Understanding flickered in Hoey's eyes before he lapsed into the preoccupied frown. "And 'Jewish' doesn't sound strong enough, like someone's only tending to be a Jew. Ah, I'm not making any sense. It's just words. "

"Did Fine ever send away any gunmen?" Hoey asked.

"I don't think he did. The nearest he would have come to the Special Criminal Court might have been an appeal on a sentence that got to the Supreme Court."

"So they wouldn't have been trying to get at him through the son for that. But it's the Palestinian thing that gives me the willies, so it does," Hoey whispered.

Minogue walked ahead of Hoey to Fine's large Victorian house. The half-dozen stone steps up to the door seemed a penance to Minogue. Damn and damn Jimmy Kilmartin again. He knocked. Hoey was licking his upper lip nervously as he looked to the scroll on the door-frame.

"You take a few notes here if we can talk, Shea, all right? I'm jittery, I don't mind telling you."

Minogue heard the latch being pulled back inside. His apprehension crested as the door opened slowly. He breathed out and felt his body root him through leaden feet to the step, while the September sky pressed down on him.

Fine stood in the doorway. Minogue identified himself. Fine beckoned the two detectives inside and they followed him into a parlour. Fine walked slackly to the fireplace and leaned his shoulders on it. Minogue heard him breathing through his nostrils.

"We can come back—"

"Stay put now," Fine said, looking beyond them to the window. Minogue feared the worst but Fine did not pounce.

"I'll look into the matter of how my wife got to hear of this from the neighbour and not from the Gardai some other time. I expect there's some reason, some excuse," Fine said. "I had a call from the Garda Commissioner five minutes before you came. I'll take the matter up with him. It's nothing for you, for you personally, to feel awkward about."

"Justice, I might as well—"

"It'll be better if you call me Mr Fine."

"Mr Fine," Minogue began again, "I'll give you as much as I know, as much as we know, if you want to hear it."

"I do, inasmuch as I need to hear it sooner or later," Fine replied.

"Your son was shot three times. Where he was shot suggests some kind of a punishment killing, an execution. There are no signs that he was otherwise abused before he died. It's very likely that he died instantly. From what our forensic technicians tell us, and this is in the absence of the State Pathologist's work yet to be done, Paul was shot at very close range."

"He was shot in the head," Fine said, as though addressing nobody. Minogue's stomach coiled in anguish. He heard Hoey draw a breath and hold it as he perched on the edge of the chair.

"Yes, he was," Minogue replied hoarsely.

Fine blinked several times. His eyes looked out on nothing local to the room or the men in it. Minogue believed that he saw Fine grow smaller, become a different man in that minute's silence. Hoey's jittery animal eyes darted to the ceiling when the cries sounded upstairs again. Footsteps skipped quickly down a staircase. A bearded man in his middle years opened the door, glanced at the two policemen and gestured to Fine. Fine left the room. Minogue noted the skullcap, the yarmulka, as the bearded man turned and drew the door closed behind Fine.

Hoey blew his breath out between tight lips. "Jesus, I hate this. I really hate it. I'm not cut out for this at all. Christ, I'd give anything to be out of here this second. I'm not up to it."

The doors opened and Fine returned. The bearded man followed him and laid a tray on a set of nesting tables. Minogue busied himself making unnecessary way for the arrival of the coffee, the better to allow Fine to take out his hanky and wipe away the tears. Hoey had noticed too and he co-operated by standing up and fussing about awkwardly.

"Ah, that's too kind of you now, Mr Fine. Our tongues were just hanging out for the want of a bit of something in this line. We'll have this down and be out of your way in a flash," Minogue said. He looked up at the bearded man, seeing a face perhaps familiar.

"You may know Johnny Cohen here, Inspector. He's a cantor up at the temple in Orwell Road," Fine sighed as he dabbed his eyes.

Minogue stood and shook hands with Cohen.

"Johnny is a relation of my wife, Rosalie. His wife, Carol, is upstairs with her, along with Rabbi Silverman. I expect there'll be a gaggle of people descending on the house any minute so let's get started," Fine said, sitting heavily into an armchair.

Minogue sat down gingerly, anxious not to spill any coffee into the saucer. He felt an odd relief at Fine's words. Fine had a Dublin accent, soft and nearly ironical, so unlike the contorted blends which Minogue heard regularly in the suburbs. A real Dubliner, a Jew, one of the great legal minds on the island, and he still used expressions like 'a gaggle.' Fine's face now seemed bigger, open.

"You know," Fine said slowly, the cup next to his lip as he stared out the window, "Johnny and I, the first thing we said when he came to the house an hour ago."

Cohen paused by the door at the mention of his name.

"If I recall, it was Johnny actually got the words out first. 'I hope and pray that Paul is not dead because he is a Jew,' you said, Johnny."

Fine's eyes stayed fixed and vacant while he sipped at the coffee. Cohen's head dropped and Minogue could see the eyelashes batting rapidly. Hoey's body seemed to scream as Minogue noticed him squirm. Cohen looked to Minogue's eyes once as he closed the door. Minogue had to break the contact and stare down at his cup, his mind raging with shame and helplessness.

"I hope the same, Mr Fine," Minogue said to his cup.

Minogue thought about Hoey's question before he slammed the car door.

"Peculiar because he's so ordinary? What did you expect, Shea?" he asked.

Hoey shrugged and started the engine. Minogue took his notebook and flicked through the pages.

Paul had been born on 12 July 1956. Fine even remembered the time: a Thursday morning around three. Fine had last seen his son on Friday, in the restaurant of the Art Gallery in Merrion Square. Who would make the formal identification of the body, he had asked. If he was up to it himself, Minogue had replied, they could bring Justice Fine to the hospital now. Fine had said that he couldn't go then, not before his wife's sister showed up at the house.

"Your handwriting is gone as bad as mine," Minogue murmured. "But go on: what did you expect?"

"I don't know. Something different, I suppose."

Minogue remembered his own pleasant bewilderment when he had first visited the Jewish Museum.

An older man who had been sitting at a desk had
looked up at Minogue as he entered and asked him if
he had been to the Museum before. Minogue replied
that he had not. The man rose from his seat, introduced himself as Stanley Davis—he was called Stan—
and led Minogue on a tour of the synagogue. Where
Minogue had expected the rich accents of Eastern
Europe or the Middle East, he heard only the practised diffident stoicism, the tones of men ever ready to
disabuse a non-Dubliner of any presumptions about
Dublin. He heard in Davis's voice something else too,
an easy mix of earnestness and resignation.

Stan had pointed out his son in several of the pho-
tographs housed in the folders which he had been
working on when Minogue arrived. The son at sports
events, the son at garden parties (did people still have
them?), the son rigged out in tennis gear and shaking
hands with a tennis star. No detail of genealogy
escaped Stan Davis and he had a story to go with
every face in the albums. Where was Stan's son now?
Oh, he had done very well in the insurance, and he
had up and gone to London. Stan's wife had died two
years ago. Stan didn't want to take up the son's offer
of his own flat in London yet, he said, but he didn't
look at Minogue as he said it. He wanted to see the
Museum off the ground before he left. That'd be his
legacy if he did leave, Stan had said. Minogue remembered Stan Davis's wan face, a man in his seventies
but with the clear and grave countenance of a child,
looking at him as if to say: Well, that's my story and
what do you think?

Minogue continued glossing over Hoey's notes.
Hoey lit a cigarette. The coffee had killed Minogue's
incipient appetite, leaving him with a smouldering

space in his belly. Fine had anticipated the questions and the details which the detectives sought. He had left the room twice during the interview, both times to answer the phone. He took the first call before the lumbering Johnny Cohen had made it down the stairs at a run. Cohen had pounced on the second ring with the second call.

"He must have had a row with Paul somewhere along the line," Hoey murmured. "And they sort of kept their distance, if you follow me."

"Um. I remember the way he mentioned about Paul dropping out of the uni after two years, all right," Minogue agreed.

"Not to say there would have been bad blood or that class of thing. God, no. Just the usual family thing," Hoey emphasized. Minogue heard the caution behind Hoey's qualification: he was giving himself, not the Fines, the benefit of any doubt as to whether Jews were also mired in "the usual family thing."

"I mean to say, look at the other two children in that family," Hoey continued. "One a dentist, the daughter some type of a research scientist. Careers and families, the whole bit."

Both policemen watched the taxi stopping in front of their own car. A middle-aged woman emerged hurriedly from the back seat, her eyes red from crying. She ran to the gate and pushed it open. A younger woman stayed to pay the taxi-man and then she too hurried up the steps to the door, which was already opening. Fine stood in the doorway, his arms by his side, the shock clear on his face now. Both women embraced him. It seemed to take an effort more than he could summon for him to embrace them in return. He stood with his eyes closed as they drew him back into the house between them.

"Jesus, Mary and Joseph," Hoey whispered tersely. His fingers jabbed at the packet of Majors in his haste to get another cigarette. Minogue felt the stab of grief keener this time.

"For the love of Christ," Hoey mumbled, his hands shaking with the lighted match wavering at the end of the cigarette. "Will this day never end?"

"That's the sister-in-law he's been waiting on, I'd say. He'll be out in a minute," Minogue said. His chest heaved once, twice. He wondered if Hoey felt the same ache of shame as he did, the same confusion after realizing that it was shame.

It was five minutes before Fine reappeared at the door. Johnny Cohen was with him. Both men were wearing black hats with modest brims. Hoey was out of his seat and holding the back door open by the time the two men had walked to the gate. Fine was very pale now.

There was no talk in the car. Minogue stared out the front window all the way to Vincent's Hospital. Cohen had his hand under Fine's arm when they stepped from the car.

Minogue heard Hoey's "Jases" under his breath before he himself saw Kilmartin and God Almighty, Garda Commissioner Lally, in the hall. God Almighty was in a civvy suit. Kilmartin danced attendance on him, seconding his nod to Minogue before they advanced to meet Fine. Minogue saw Kilmartin's signal to stay back. The Commissioner took Fine's hand. Fine nodded but seemed dazed. He did not look at any of the policemen's faces. Cohen seemed to be trying to get closer to Fine, his hand firm under Fine's elbow now. The Commissioner's head bent close to

Fine's and Minogue heard "condolences . . . family . . . sincere . . . outrage . . ." Kilmartin followed with a briefer handshake. Minogue heard an "everything possible . . ." at the end of Kilmartin's whisper.

Minogue went to the toilet. He took his time washing his hands. He washed his face then, and checked that his hairline had not scampered back another inch or two since that morning. Then he stooped and took a drink from the tap. He recalled the doctor kneeling by the body on the beach, shaking his thermometer, and shivered at the commonplace indignity of death. Kilmartin barrelled into the toilet just as Minogue was ready to take more stock of the face looking back at him from the mirror.

Kilmartin stepped to the urinal and fumbled.

"That's the boy, all right. At least we got that part right."

"Did he give God Almighty an earful about not hearing it from the Gardai first?" asked Minogue.

"No he didn't. Relief all around, let me tell you. Jases, I would have given out the pay about that if I were him."

"I'll wait outside," said Minogue.

"Don't be running off on me now, do you hear me, Matt? God Almighty wants to see the pair of us after you've seen Fine home."

Minogue did not try to hide his unease.

Hoey drove stiffly, with almost ostentatious care, as though carrying a delicate or explosive cargo, Minogue thought. Billy Fine's slack, pale face didn't turn to meet Minogue but stayed, directed towards the window. Minogue did not take notes: he knew that Hoey was soaking it all up too. Hoey steered the car up through Ranelagh on the return journey to Fine's home, while Johnny Cohen held Fine's hand on the back seat. Minogue had watched Cohen dart occasional angry stares at him during the drive, and had returned them several times. All right, be protective, Minogue was ready to tell Cohen, but don't get in the way of any scrap of information that'll help us to catch Paul Fine's killer.

"Lily couldn't stand Dublin," Fine murmured. "That's the long and short of it. And I don't blame her for that, not one bit. The heartbreak was that Paul couldn't stay away from Dublin, probably for the same reasons that Lily couldn't stay in it."

Cohen coughed; a sure sign, Minogue decided, of anger that he was trying to control. He sensed that Cohen was the prickly guardian of a community which did not welcome prying Gentiles.

"How long were they married?" Minogue asked.

"Two years," said Fine tonelessly. "She tried, you know," he said then and glanced momentarily at Minogue. "Even with our community here she still felt like a stranger."

Minogue watched Cohen scratching behind an ear, and wondered if Cohen could hold off making a remark.

"'Strangers in a strange land,'" said Fine. He let out a sigh and his free hand went to his eyes. Minogue looked away as Fine's head went down. Cohen leaned close to his friend and whispered in his ear. Fine nodded several times and relaxed against Cohen's bulk. Hoey's frown had deepened, and he seemed to be squeezing the wheel very tightly as if willing the car to move. Minogue waited.

"Anyway," Minogue heard Billy Fine say, "that's

our lot, maybe. Paul wasn't as thick-skinned as our other children. David's set up as an orthodontist in London. Never come back, I imagine. Julia's engaged to an American fella she met at a conference on plant genetics—"

Minogue stole a glance at Fine and noted the wry expression.

"We'd given up on her getting married," Fine added with the beginnings of a faint smile. He met Minogue's cautious eye and smiled weakly. "Tough piece of work, the same Julia."

"Great," said Minogue. "The only way to be, I'm thinking. We have one like that. She'd frighten the wits out of lesser mortals."

Fine's weak smile rallied, but then dropped off his face. He turned to looking out the window again.

"I gave you that woman's name, didn't I?" said Fine. Minogue looked from Fine to Cohen. Fine seemed to sense the tension immediately, and he sat up and looked at Cohen. "Oh, it's all right, Johnny. For God's sake, it's not dirt or anything. Everything counts in this line of work. I gave you her name, didn't I?"

Minogue nodded. Paul had had a girlfriend, Mary McCutcheon. She was a journalist.

"Although he never talked to me directly about things like that." Fine paused as though to weigh his words. "He never introduced her to us. I think he was ashamed. Yes. But I believe he was very fond of her."

Minogue felt the acid sting of tears on his own eyes and he turned back in his seat, blinking, while Billy Fine wept in the arms of his friend.

# THREE

"**D**id any of ye hear of these lunatics before?"
Kilmartin and Minogue shook their heads.

"The League for Solidarity with the Palestinian People. Not a foreign accent either. Mother of Jases, as if we didn't have enough to be going on with," the Commissioner declared. "I have a lot of faith in you fellas. So does the whole country too, let me tell you. Yous have the nose for getting convictions."

Minogue stole a glance at the neck stretching the collar, the farmyard face. Gardai had always had a measure of suspicion for their Commissioners since the force was founded in 1922. There had been auto-crats and weaklings, Napoleons and incompetents in the post. It didn't take a Leftie to declare publicly that every Garda Commissioner was too much under the finger of his political overseer, the Minister for Justice. Too political.

"You can't imagine the pleasure I had putting me name to last year's Report on Crime," said the Commissioner.

Minogue's gargoyle within sniggered: did he mean the 450-odd crimes in which firearms were used? The seizure of four rocket-launchers by accident, perhaps? Maybe Lally meant the overall detection rate of 32 per cent, published in black and white for the public to get the willies over? Maybe the state of community-Gardai relations in Dublin, the one county with half the country's population—?

"Yes, indeed. Every blade out there on the beat knows that if there's a person murdered in this country then the perpetrator has less than one chance in twenty-five of getting away with it—"

Must be going to ask for something big, thought Minogue. Kilmartin listened with an apparent gravity, nodding his head for emphasis.

". . . I threw that 95 per cent success rate at policemen in that bloody conference in Stockholm last month and bejases if they were nearly calling me a liar." The Commissioner shook his huge head for emphasis. He's like a horse settling on the bit, Minogue thought. A finger came out of the fist which the Commissioner had been raising and lowering on the table.

"'Oh, but in Ireland we hear there is much crime of violence,' says one of them, a shagging Frenchman, I think. Well, I cut him short then and there, so I did, in short order too. And I was thinking of Jimmy Kilmartin and yourself, Matt, when I settled this Frenchman's hash. I wouldn't mind but the ones that were bragging about little crime were iijits like the Swiss and the Norwegians, races without the brains and the vim to do a bit of divilment anyway. All they do is sit at home and count their money or commit suicide. Pack of shites . . . Anyway, all the lads on the Squad have the creative approach as well as the hard work. Do you know what I said to this Frenchman, do you?"

"No," Kilmartin whispered.

"I nearly told him to eff off. They think they're the bee's knees, that crowd. Well, I happen to know that they have dracul—"

"Draconian?" said Minogue.

"Exactly. Draconian laws to be harassing their citizens, so I do. The French are savages in their own right. Anyway, I says to this upstart, 'You're addressing a policeman whose Murder Squad is an example to the civilized world.' Do you get the hint about civilized? Themselves and their Algeria!"

What civilized world, Minogue wondered. The Commissioner, more fully inflated with that happiest of Irish emotions, the fearless rebuffing of any suggestion that things Irish were not the equal and better of anything on the planet, became even more animated. Minogue did not like this man one bit.

"That's the way," said Kilmartin. Minogue winced at his sycophancy. The Commissioner dropped both fists dramatically on the table and his whole demeanour changed in an instant. His face was now a mask of stern determination.

"So that's the confidence I had under me hat when I was able to say to Chief Justice Fine that all the resources of the Garda Siochana would be brought to bear on this dastardly crime."

Did he really say "dastardly crime" to Fine, Minogue's gargoyle asked.

"Most particularly, the proven record of the Murder Squad." The Commissioner sat back in his chair, satisfied with his oratory. "And do you know, men, that Justice Fine knows you, Matt?"

"A fleeting acquaintance, I'm thinking," said Minogue, his suspicions returning in full.

"Maybe so, but evidently the man has the same faith in you as I do and as Jimmy Kilmartin does. You're not an Inspector for nothing, I can tell you."

Kilmartin must have known this would come out, Minogue realized then.

"He asked me if you'd spearhead the investigation," said Lally.

Minogue did not trust himself to look at Kilmartin now.

"So naturally I told him I'd speak to Jimmy Kilmartin about that. To see how the land lies, if you follow me." God Almighty turned to Kilmartin.

"Absolutely, sir," said Kilmartin guilelessly.

"Great stuff, men," said the Commissioner, rising. "Can I have a call on it every day? The Minister has asked me for a briefing every evening: that's the kind of priority it has. He's expecting to be prodded during Question Period as to security. Oh, and lookit . . . I had the Branch, er, see if they had any file on this Paul Fine. He was by way of being a journalist. The name sort of struck a chord, like. He was a bit of a Leftie when he was in college, that sort of thing. Mild; no record of trouble with the law."

Lally swept an arm over imaginary protestations and squinted at both policemen. "That's all water under the bridge, so it is. Trotskyist, Leftie, journalist, Jew—none of that matters a damn to us, isn't that the way to approach it? Fair play and justice for all."

Then why mention it, Minogue wondered.

"I've greased the wheels with the Branch already,

seeing as I had that titbit of information about Fine. There's a Gallagher in the Branch, Sergeant Gallagher. I believe that he and another few under him monitor these foreign fanatics here."

Fanatics. Minogue sat down again when the Commissioner left. Anything to do with the Middle East meant fanaticism, apparently. There were no Irish fanatics, of course.

"Looks like you're elected, Matt," Kilmartin said from the door. Minogue hoped it was a trace of relief he detected in Jimmy's voice.

"Can I have Shea Hoey and Keating too, then?"

"To be sure," said Kilmartin remotely. He held his hand on the door yet. "Look. A few things. The Commissioner in his haste may get a hold of you to find out how you'll be doing on this case—instead of getting his brief from me. You heard him say he wants to hear from us every day?"

Minogue nodded.

"All I'm saying is, don't leave me in the dark on anything. I don't want him telling me what I'm supposed to know. I know what you're thinking: 'Ah, he'd never do that.' I'm not saying he would, but you can see he's jumpy about this. And another thing. I don't want any of the hooligans in the Branch knowing too much about what we're up to. Take whatever you can off this Gallagher fella, but don't be giving him so much as the steam off your piss in July. Don't be surprised if you-know-who is about to give the identical little speech to the Branch, telling them to keep their own investigation under their hats."

Kilmartin arched an eyebrow and winked. Neither gesture dispelled Minogue's bafflement. "You're still a bit of an innocent, Matt. That doesn't mean you or I should be taken for a gobshite, though, does it?"

"I'm not so sure I want to know more at this point," murmured Minogue.

"Here, so, think on this: God Almighty has no choice but to go along with Fine's request to have you running this. And don't be worrying about me and me pride. I'll be more than happy to take the credit from you when the time comes. But don't forget that you have the name of being a class of a wild rozzer."

"I do?"

"Don't be an iijit, of course you do. You nearly managed to make a diplomatic pig's mickey out of the Combs business. God Almighty was expecting you to march down to the British Embassy and break down the door looking for any more involved in that Combs case. You don't think you'd be drawing an Inspector's pay today if the Commissioner was the sole captain of the ship, do you? It came down from Justice, right from the Minister too, as a signal to the Brits that we done right here and we support our police, no matter what the politicos might say. That sort of political weather spoils our gallant Commissioner's humours, don't you see. He just wants to run his shop like any other yo-yo high up on the State payroll."

Minogue had heard it before. He had no sympathy for the Commissioner's humours.

"Perhaps I should be grateful to have you keep me from falling under a bus too?"

"Don't be getting uppity, Matt. Just be looking over your shoulder when you're working on this."

Paul Fine's flat was in Ringsend, close by the new city-centre bypass route. His flat was the upper storey of a house which backed on to Ringsend Park. The house, standing at the end of a terrace, was removed both in architecture and original function from the houses on the terrace itself. Minogue guessed that it had been an official billet or quarters for a functionary who had worked on the docks around this part of the Port of Dublin.

The air was thick with seagulls and pigeons. Sulphurous, fishy smells on the air reminded Minogue that the Liffey Basin and docks were on the far side of the bypass road at the foot of the terrace. He could see the upper decks and cranes of moored cargo-ships when he looked in that direction. A young woman holding an infant stood in a doorway half-way down the terrace watching the two policemen. The snout of a Garda car showed from a lane next to Fine's place.

Ringsend had had the name of being the toughest assignment for Gardai but that was twenty and more years ago, Minogue reflected, as he stared bleakly down the grimy road. Pitched battles outside and inside the pubs on Saturday nights had been routine then. Innumerable gangs and family racketeers fleshed out the crime figures in Kingsend and Irishtown. As with the newer working-class areas such as Inchicore and Crumlin and, more recently, Tallaght, much damage had been done to Garda work by Gardai themselves. Young Guards, countrymen fresh from training, had been thrown into areas like Ringsend and had been backed up and directed by Gardai also overwhelmingly from the country. Over the years, those old hands had distilled their native dislike for Dubliners into a cynical and heavy-handed contempt. Time, not training, had settled the matter. Ringsend and Irishtown had become quieter as the first generation born into the flats and terraces had married and moved out. The Garda Press Office still liked to point out, to nuisances who asked why Garda-community relations were so bad, that crime rates in places like Ringsend had plummeted because Garda foot patrols had solved the problem.

"They used to say that a sign you were a real Dubliner was if you knew where Raytown was," Minogue observed. Hoey took note of Minogue's melancholy tone, of Minogue examining the grey sky over the docks. "Yep," Minogue added. "Raytown's over there by Ringsend village."

"Seems like a rough spot still to me," Hoey said.

"Ah, it is and it isn't. Is this the house?"

A cramped glass porch had been built around the front door. Two Guards were sitting in the kitchen drinking tea. The middle-aged woman who had admitted Minogue and Hoey fussed with the teapot for the new arrivals.

"Miss Connolly has keys for the flat upstairs, sir," one Guard said, rising from the table.

Minogue declined tea, and took the keys.

"When was Mr Fine here last?"

"Let me see. This being a Monday . . . It would have been Sunday morning. Late morning. I was doing a bit in the garden there, and I saw him come out. About eleven o'clock."

"In the morning?"

"Oh yes. We all go to bed early here, we do. The whole street does be as quiet as a graveyard at nine o'clock at night."

"Sure it was him?"

"Certain, I am. A very nice man, Mr Fine. I'm still not able to believe it. Lovely young man. Of course I knew he was a Jew, seeing as I see the mention of his father in the papers and so on. Lovely family, I'm sure."

Minogue staved off his discomfort. He was less irritated than nervous at people telling him that Paul Fine was a Jew.

"Did Mr Fine speak to you at all recently?"

"Oh, precious little. 'Good morning' and 'Good evening.' Very much kept to himself and always polite."

"Any chat with him at all?"

One of the Gardai started in on another piece of sponge cake. Minogue didn't care that they were all seated around the table listening. She might say something different to them and that would be good for starters.

"Nothing. I'm alone here, you see. I never married, as I was saying to the lads here." She smiled wanly towards the two Gardai. "But I don't like to be putting conversation on people. If I met him at all, it'd be: 'How's it going, Miss Connolly?' and 'Grand weather.' Oh, a lovely young man."

She looked entreatingly at all the policemen and shook her head.

"Any visitors, Miss Connolly?"

"Let me think . . . Very, very occasional . . . very odd . . ."

"Do you mean odd visitors, is it?"

"A very odd time, I meant. It was only people he'd arranged to come and visit, I'm sure. There was one fella, I remember his face, used to call by sometimes. Familiar-looking, a fella with a beard. They'd sit in the garden of a nice day. Have a little wine and all that," she said with an air of casual insight. "Having a little wine and all that" might constitute glamour or bohemian living in these latitudes, Minogue guessed.

"A fella with a beard?"

"Matter of fact I saw him on the telly once. Fitz-pat—"

"Fitzgerald?"

"That's it. He's a bigwig in RTE," said Miss Connolly, referring to the head office of the Irish radio and television stations. "But he's a bit of an atheist too, I believe. I brought them out tea once and I was introduced. Mr Fine said that Mr Fitzgerald was his boss and he was trying to soften him up for a bit more pay. A nice sense of humour, I'd say. Terribly nice lad . . . There were a few others too, all in the same line of business, I'm sure. You know how you can tell, what with the trendy clothes. Have a cup of tea or a bottle of stout maybe. I'd hear them upstairs, but never late at night, never."

"Did you ever meet his girlfriend?"

"No, I didn't," she replied. "Sure you wouldn't like more tea?"

Minogue glanced at the two Gardai whose car was blocking the driveway outside. One had crumbs in the folds of his uniform. A nice easy few hours' work holding Fine's place until the Murder Squad came by. Minogue gestured for the younger Guard to step out of the kitchen.

"We're going up to his flat now. Go over what she remembers again, would you? How long he had been here, any irregularities? Did he ever come home drunk, was he ever having rows that she knows of? Arguments with people on the phone? Did he ever tell her anything about his work or personal life? Any strangers on the terrace this last while, callers looking for Fine?"

"Like Arabs with headgear?" the Garda asked.

Minogue fixed him with a stare.

"It's just that we heard there was something to do with Palestine . . ." The Garda tried to regroup with a careful smile.

"Did she see any letters addressed to him? Don't worry about her saying she never noticed such things—just probe. She's not a woman to be missing things, I'm sure."

Minogue phoned Kathleen after an hour. The last ten minutes he had spent seated on Fine's bed with Hoey, going over what he had recorded in his notes. He had told Hoey to get hold of Gallagher in Special Branch for late afternoon. They'd be wanting all Gallagher had on extremist groups. Hoey was to phone the television station, RTE, and insist on seeing Fitzgerald as soon as possible.

Kathleen answered after two rings. Minogue told her that he'd be late. "I'm sorry. You'll have to watch *Die Nasty* on your own."

Daithi was in the States these five weeks past. Iesult was out on a date with Pat the Brain. Psychology and philosophy lectures over a glass of beer?

"I won't be able to understand it without you there to take it to pieces for me," Kathleen replied.

Minogue grinned. "It'll be gone ten o'clock, I'm sure."

"Fine and well, Inspector. I heard it on the half-one news, and I might have guessed you'd be in the thick of it. Just don't be taking too much on yourself."

Was that a resigned rebuke?

He told her about Fine wanting him on the investigation.

"That's a great compliment, I suppose. Why you, though?"

"Remember that time in the Jewish Museum, just after it opening up? He was there then and he spotted me, apparently. But tell me," he interrupted himself by asking his wife of thirty years, "how's life treating you, anyway? Taking into account it's a Monday and we're not in Honolulu or lollygagging on some island in the Mediterranean."

"True for you. I'm grand anyway. There's a letter from Daithi, by the way." The change in her voice, the late attempt at cheerfulness bit sharply at the edge of Minogue's mind.

"Ah. Anything new with him? Is he behaving himself?"

"He sounds fine. Read it yourself when you get home."

Minogue replaced the receiver. He looked across at the half-empty bookshelves. Paul Fine had read—or at least collected—books on a wide variety of subjects. One shelf held *Quotable Quotes* next to a copy of *Church and State in Modern Ireland*. Hoey had found folders of clippings from British and Irish newspapers as well as a dozen and more cassettes with labels which neither man could make out. They'd be a job for the painstaking Keating. Recordings of interviews? There were seven video-cassettes, again of unknown content, marked only by dates and numbers. No video-cassette recorder, but a colour telly and a Sony radio with shortwave bands. Fine had kept his paraphernalia tidily, even his clothes. One of the two bedrooms was by way of being an office, apparently. Tidy but smelly from ashtrays and closed windows. The whole house was damp. A single picture of Fine's father (was that his mother too?), himself between them as a teenager, standing by a heap of stones in some sunny place.

His belongings had not been disturbed, by the look of things. A drawer full of odds and ends, from disposable razors to a photograph of a dog. Had he spent all his nights here? Neither Minogue nor Hoey had found any notebook or diary. There had been nothing in the pockets of the light tweedy jacket on the body.

Minogue recalled the Commissioner's confidences about Paul Fine's past involvement with fringe groups. Fine's father had not even hinted at any wild side to his son, but that was natural: the son was dead. No parent would recount the failings of a child to a policeman. Minogue would have to burrow around such boulders before trying to hoist them and get an accurate picture of Paul Fine.

Mary McCutcheon. Fitzgerald from RTE—he had Fitz's name before. Fitzgerald was an acerbic producer of current affairs programmes for the radio, a man who seemed to be at his happiest when inflaming the Catholic hierarchy enough for them to write a letter to the papers complaining about bias in broadcasting. Minogue seemed to remember Fitzgerald also maddening the Special Branch with a programme on one of their many failures; something about a raid on a farmhouse, waving guns about, without finding a trace of the subversives they were expecting to bag. Was Paul Fine cut from the same cloth as Fitzgerald? Hardly. Fitzgerald and the other hyper-educated apostates on the island would have necessarily gone to Mass and confession, necessarily been beaten by Christian Brothers and necessarily been sickened by the posturings of their politicians before looking for their vengeance. Fitzgerald and company, the bishops and the politicians who doffed their hats to the clerics yet—they were all part of a family squabble. Fine was outside that fold.

Minogue heard Hoey trudging back up the stairs.

"Sergeant Gallagher says McDonald's in Grafton Street, about three, if that's all right," said Hoey cautiously.

Minogue wanted to laugh away the sudden irritation. "You're not serious."

"He says to phone him if that doesn't suit. That's the Branch for you, staking out their territory. He says he works out of a car most days anyway, but he carries the stuff in his head."

"What about the Fitzgerald fella, our television guru?"

"His programmes go on the air at five, and he says he needs to be at the controls for some of the live interviews. He'll be there all afternoon."

Minogue didn't know what to do about Gallagher. Would he have to take him in hand already?

"How did you get Gallagher?"

"I phoned Branch HQ here and they radioed him. He phoned from somewhere, to the phone below here, I mean."

"I see, says the blind man . . . Well, would you get him for me on the phone, Shea? Tell him I want to talk to him myself."

The beginnings of a smile pushed at Hoey's cheeks.

Minogue gathered the video-tapes and cassettes awkwardly under his arm. Keating could go through the folders of clippings. Maybe the bulk of Fine's work would be in his office in RTE. Closing the door, Minogue hoped that his assumption was not leaking too badly yet: that Paul Fine's work had had something

to do with his death. He did not want to believe that
Fine had been singled out as a Jew alone, a cipher for
some group, to be murdered for being a Jew. But an
Irish Jew . . . what would that group want with killing
him for that? To prove that no Jew the world over was
immune from Palestinian wrath, that the Palestinians
had allies all over the world? Minogue's mind lurched
into crackpot associations.

He made his way down the stairs. That madman in
Libya . . . a favour in return for guns to the Provos? It
could be a message to the State's judiciary too, the ones
who had reluctantly ruled that the Offences Against the
State Act, the most powerful and abused legislative
weapon against the IRA, was constitutional. Madness.
But hadn't there been several prominent British Jews
assassinated in the Seventies? No wonder Jimmy Kilmartin had waved him on with this one, bad 'cess to him.

The Garda who had been questioning Miss Connolly met Minogue in the hall. "You were right, sir,
she doesn't miss much."

Hoey reached for the telephone as it rang.

"Run that through a typewriter, like a good man,"
Minogue said to the Garda. "And shoot it up to John's
Road for my attention. Investigation Section."

Hoey held a hand over the receiver and waved it at
Minogue.

"Get it hand-delivered before tea-time this evening
too, if I can put you to that trouble?"

The Garda hid his resistance well.

"It's a tall order, I know, but the matter could be
urgent in the extreme."

Minogue took the phone and listened. A bus or a
lorry passed close to where Gallagher was making
his call.

"Sergeant Gallagher? Matt Minogue. Yes, yes, and how are things with you, now? I'm running an investigation on this murder of the judge's son, Paul Fine. Did you know about it, a possible connection with some Palestinian group or the like here? You did? Oh, the Commissioner's office, were they?"

Minogue listened to Gallagher while Hoey leaned against the door-frame, his arms folded. Minogue winked at him and Hoey's smile broadened. It was seldom that Gardai, even the crime ordinary detectives from the Central Detective Unit in the Castle, could twist arms with the Branch. Such was the guile within Minogue's Trojan Horse of charm—and no small store of charm it was, in an island where charm was a currency both inflated and squandered—that he had made an informal liaison with Special Branch officers to crack the Combs case.

"Is that a fact . . . ? Well, you know how it is when they get a fire lit under them. Lookit, are you a Gallagher from Gweedore? You are? From Falcarragh, go on, are you? God, there are terrific hurling athletes being bred in that little Eden, amn't I right? Well. I'm in a considerable hurry with this information and I have to be in the RTE studios within the hour . . . Is there any chance you could sit in on a meeting here, say, five or so? Yep, our HQ's in John's Road. Good man, so."

Minogue took Miss Connolly's key to Fine's flat before he left.

"Essential it remain undisturbed until we go through the effects in detail, Miss Connolly. Now if you remember anything which perhaps you hadn't thought of in your chat with the Garda or myself here, phone this number immediately, if you please."

Minogue handed her a card which said *Investigation Section*. "Be it ever so small, it may still be important. There'll be a policeman by with this key, probably in the morning. Be sure and ask for his identification if you're in any doubt. A youngish fella, Detective Officer Keating, and he'll be making a detailed examination of Mr Fine's effects. He looks a bit like . . . how would you describe him, Shea?"

"He's a bit like that fella, what do you call him . . . Heston. Charlton Heston," Hoey said earnestly. "Did you ever hear of—?"

"The film star?" Miss Connolly asked.

"That's the one," Hoey concluded without a trace of humour.

# FOUR

**H**oey bought fish and chips in Ringsend village, and they ate them while driving out on the Coast Road. Hoey turned up through Sandymount and landed on the Merrion Road within sight of the television mast which marked RTE but two miles away.

"Little enough in the flat, so," said Hoey.

"I didn't find what I was looking for in the line of pads of paper and appointment books. I'm hoping his desk has more of that class of stuff," Minogue replied. "Plus there are those tapes. God knows how many hours of stuff is on them. He might have kept memos on tape."

"No word-processor or magic computer in the flat," Hoey added. "I thought they all had them now. Anyone in touch with his wife, his ex-wife? She's in London, isn't she?"

Justice Fine said he'd have to phone her," Minogue

replied slowly. "But I was just wondering to myself . . . how the hell we can get started on this."

"Motives, you mean?"

"Yep. I can't see the killer. I just can't. We need something a lot more direct than some phone call from a group of I-don't-know-whats. Any iijit can make a telephone call. Did you get the text of what was said?"

*"'This is the voice of Free Palestine. We are the League for Solidarity with the Palestinian People'* . . . Hold on, what did they . . . Oh yes: *'Let the world take note. No—'* Hold on a minute, they mentioned Fine at the end . . . *'No spy or aggressor who works against the cause of Palestinian freedom and justice is safe from retribution. Fine has paid the price.'* Some mouthful, that."

The "freedom and justice" soured Minogue more than most clichés.

"But, just for the sake of argument," said Hoey, "don't fanatics get very het up if one of their members sorts out his head and leaves them? Say if Fine was a Leftie back in university, but now he meets his old cronies, Palestinian sympathizers even, and antagonizes them with common sense?"

"Go on," said Minogue.

"Well, Fine might have rubbed shoulders with radicals back then, maybe stayed in touch with them. Say he meets up with some of them again and says he'd like a contact to someone who knows anything about links between, I don't know, Libya and the IRA . . . So they look him up and down, thinking to themselves, well this Fine boy is gone very, let's say middle class—"

"Bourgeois."

"That too. And the nerve of him, coming back and trying to mine us for touchy info that could land us in trouble," Hoey continued.

"And being as they are very put out about back-sliders, and paranoid by nature—"

"A hothead says that Fine is now an agent of the imperialist running dog whatever, by way of being a traitor too, I suppose. What do you think?"

"I have little enough insight into the paranoid mind, but you may have something. When did they call the press?"

"Close on half-ten."

Half-ten, Minogue echoed within. Last seen by Miss Connolly on Sunday morning. No more than twenty-four hours in the water.

"How do tides work, Shea? I mean, if you threw something or somebody into the water, would it be washed up in the same place it was thrown in, if the tide was coming in, like?"

"I haven't a clue. I believe that a tide will do different things depending on the lie of the land around the coast. It's a shocking complicated business."

Hoey turned off Nutley Avenue and into RTE.

"Do you know what, though?" Hoey murmured. "Aside from this crap about 'working against the cause' or whatever—I mean to say, that's a mystery until we find out more about what Fine was up to that might have rubbed someone the wrong way—I wonder why they didn't call until the Monday morning, and him being murdered already on the Sunday? Maybe they had some crooked reason, I don't know. Do you think they knew the body would be washed up?"

"You have me there," Minogue replied.

Beyond the barrier and the security guard at the entrance to Radio Telifis Eireann, Minogue phoned to confirm a five o'clock pow-wow on the Fine murder. As the murder appeared to have been committed in

Dublin, the State Pathologist could autopsy the body.
Minogue had not seen a coroner out on Killiney strand
before he and Kilmartin had left for the hotel. They
might not have bothered to have him come to the
scene: gunshot wounds on a body, along with "clear
signs of wounds from the effects of an explosive deto-
nation" were at the top of the list for mandatory postmortem examination. By five o'clock today Minogue
would have something from the Technical Bureau's
forensics, those incongruous boiler-suited men who
had inched and kneeled their way over the beach.
These scenes-of-the-crimes examiners knew of, but
didn't much like, the name which Minogue most often
heard them referred to: bagmen.

Mickey Fitzgerald had to be paged from the security
desk which met the visitors to the RTE radio building.
Minogue spent the two minutes' wait gawking at the
employees who entered and left the building. Hoey
jabbed him in the arm once and nodded towards a
duo of stylish men leaving.

"That's your man, what's-his-name. Reads the
news most days."

"Him?"

"Yes. The one with the baggy suit that looks like
wallpaper."

"The up-to-the-minute Italian suit that costs three
hundred quid, you mean. Sinnott?"

"Yep."

Fitzgerald was a tall, skinny man with a beard. A
few strands of grey stretched out to the fringe which
almost touched the rim of his wire spectacle frames.
Minogue thought of John Lennon. Fitzgerald shook
Minogue's hand.

"I know you," he said, and turned to Hoey.

"Detective Officer Seamus Hoey, also of the Investigation Section," said Minogue.

"Ah, what a relief it is," Fitzgerald said without any evident humour. "At least yous're not part of An Craobhinn Aoibhinn."

Minogue rather liked the sarcasm. This nickname for the Special Branch had little to do with the mythical "Sweet Branch," the fount of turn-of-the-century irredentist poetry with the mists of the Celtic Revival swirling about it.

"Were you expecting a bust of some type, Mr Fitzgerald?" Minogue probed.

"We police ourselves here, lads," Fitzgerald replied with more cynicism than coyness this time.

Minogue did not take up the bait. He would be no match for Fitzgerald as he, Fitz, presumably knew every in and out of the Broadcasting Act. A section of this Act forbade RTE from airing interviews with members of proscribed organizations. Successive Irish governments had consistently subscribed to the notion that what didn't appear on television could not exist in the minds of television viewers.

On this issue, executives in RTE were uncertain how to react. They were partly flattered by the implication that television was such a powerful medium of communication; they also took it for granted that, unlike the U.S., their Irish fellow citizens knew there was life outside television. Rather than have a Minister slap an order on the service over any particular item, therefore, RTE had undertaken to keep its censorship in-house.

Fitzgerald led the two policemen through the building and towards the current affairs workroom. His department consisted of a huge room held in by walls of glass. Minogue decided not to make a comment about glass houses. The room was sectioned off by cloth-covered room dividers and desks stood in cosy spaces created by the high squares of orange and blue. It was all very modern, very dynamic, Minogue believed.

Less than half the desks they passed were occupied. A cluster of people sat at and around one desk, smoking and talking in low tones. They fell silent and looked to the policemen as they passed. Typewriters clacked at a distance. A radio was playing reggae music. Posters extolled visits to Madrid and an exhibition of Escher drawings which had come and gone at the National Gallery six years previously.

Fitzgerald stopped by one desk.

"That's Paul's. I put all his stuff in the drawers and that vertical cabinet there and I locked them. That was yesterday when I heard the news."

He looked blankly to Minogue who was aware of the group still staring at them.

"And you have the keys?"

"I have. I swept his stuff off the desk and stuffed it all into his drawer and cabinet. The newsroom heard it first and a fella came over to us. We were terribly shocked here, just couldn't believe it. Even with my expert knowledge of police procedure from watching the telly, it took me ten minutes to get me head together and fix up his desk. Hardly anyone here locks their desks. I turned the keys and put 'em in me pocket."

"Good man. I'll be wanting to look at this stuff later, Mr Fitzgerald," said Minogue.

"And I'll be wanting a list and a receipt detailing anything you take," Fitzgerald replied.

Minogue looked back to the silent group and met their gaze for several seconds.

"I have me own private cell over here," said Fitzgerald.

Seated in Fitzgerald's office, Minogue took in the furnishings while Fitzgerald phoned for Brendan Downey. When Downey appeared, Minogue recognized him as one of the group huddled about the desk outside.

"What did Paul Fine do here, as regards his job?" Minogue asked then.

"He was a reporter/researcher: that's his job description. He was one of eight people who works for the producer, i.e., me. He was a journalist and a reporter. Basically he would have called himself a journalist. He had been on the afternoon programme—"

"*Day by Day*?"

"Good for you, Inspector. We squeeze in segments of between five and ten minutes' live time. It's a magazine format that takes us to news-time on this channel."

"To the Angelus, you mean," said Minogue.

It was hard to tell what went on behind the beard, Minogue realized, but he believed that he saw Fitzgerald's amusement push his glasses up slightly. Fitzgerald had made no secret of his opinions on institutions like the Catholic Church. Minogue struggled to recall when it was that several bishops had jointly written an open letter to the newspapers, complaining about a sinister anti-clerical undertone to many current affairs programmes on RTE radio. To the credit of the Director General, he had asked them for proof. In a religion which regards the notion of "proof" as an upstart provincial relative to horned heresy—stigmata, moving and bleeding statues excepted—this was an impertinence. Fitzgerald, a tenacious weed, still held his job.

"True for you. Sort of sets the tone for the news, wouldn't you say?" said Fitzgerald.

Minogue almost smiled. Fitzgerald was no more than forty. He'd have allies, a common passion, support now. Minogue could remember the dull bells of the Angelus broadcast forty years ago in that pious, somnolent Ireland, summoning people to prayer at midday and at six. Fitzgerald and his generation could jibe now: he was educated and tough. It had taken Minogue thirty and more years to know that within the vague narrative which made up his life was retained the precise anger of his own rebellion. There had been few Mickey Fitzgeralds then. Minogue was now almost content that his anger had been blunted into detachment; Fitzgerald had made no such concession, he was sure.

Downey smiled tightly as though anti-clericalism was but an exchange of pleasantries. Hoey looked lost. Minogue stretched.

Fitzgerald's teeth showed for an instant. He took off the Leon Trotsky intellectual glasses and rubbed his eyes.

"Bren here did some stuff with Paul," he said.

"Before we go into whatever stuff you or he was working on, can you tell me if there were any peculiarities about Paul Fine recently?" Minogue began. "I mean if he was under stress or under some threat? Losing his job, a dangerous assignment, something of that nature? Did he behave in an unusual manner recently, make any odd comments?"

Fitzgerald shook his head.

"Anybody come looking for him here, asking after him here?"

Fitzgerald looked inquiringly at Downey, who shrugged.

"Appear worried about anything? His personal life?" Minogue tried again.

"No," said Downey.

Downey was well able to talk. Minogue interrupted him several times. The first time was when Downey mentioned Libya.

"No, nothing to do with the, er . . ." Downey looked to his boss to share the quip. "'Proscribed organizations' and all that. No, it was off-the-wall, we were talking over a pint one night, you know, talking up possible projects for the programme. We knew there's a fair number of Arab students here on student visas. We were just wondering if there was any story in that, you know—if any of the Arabs had connections with members of the, er, you know."

Minogue looked to Fitzgerald rather than Downey. "Lookit, lads, can we stop this pussyfooting around with the terminology? 'Proscribed organizations' and the rest of it? Call them the IRA or the Provos or whatever you like. My colleague here is not a tape recorder or a lie-detector either, in case you're wondering. He's only jotting down notes. If I want a statement out of ye, I'll ask ye. So can we talk like we're citizens of the same planet?"

Fitzgerald's arched eyebrows gave way to a shrug.

"Like I say," Minogue added. "We're not the mind police or anything. We can only do good work if people are co-operative with us. Now, this is a murder investigation so don't spare our sensibilities. We tend to like getting straight to the point. We're tough nuts the pair of us, aren't we, Shea?"

"We're awful tough, so we are," Hoey obliged.

"Matter of fact I can safely say that I don't even go to Mass and I suspect that Detective Hoey here doesn't go to confession either. So can we hurry it up here?"

Downey resumed. "He said he'd do a bit on that, just to get a feel for it. We just decided off the tops of our heads to start with any Libyan connection first, seeing as Gadhafi's very much in the public eye. He's on record as supporting the IRA."

"Ever heard of that group, the League for Solidarity with the Palestinian People?"

Fitzgerald shook his head too. "I know from reporting on stuff like that that some other outfit will invent a name to cover some incident, just to keep it at arm's length and see what public reaction will be," he said.

"What outfits?"

"Well, in this case I don't know," Fitzgerald said emphatically. "There's no Palestine Liberation Organization or Popular Front for the Liberation of Palestine in Dublin. And there's no jihad that I can tell. I bet that yous know them or at least your Branch does. There are none of the madmen from Lebanon here either, the Hezbollah crowd or other pro-Iranian groups. That's not how those organizations work, as I understand my reading. They don't send members here as students to be farting about with the IRA in secret. Sure, there are sympathizers and militants amongst any group of students from Arab countries. I'd bet there are even informal groups where PLO sympathizers give a speech here in Dublin. That doesn't translate into guns and bombs, though."

"The links are organized on the Continent," Downey added. "You know, Paddy Murphy from Belfast goes to Amsterdam or Copenhagen and meets So-and-so. They don't come here offering guns."

"We knew all that but we still thought it was worth a second look. The situation changes. Libyans might be interested in causing a commotion here," said Fitzgerald. He began polishing his glasses with a paper handkerchief. Idly Minogue wondered if Fitzgerald had more in common with the keen, cerebral pugnaciousness of a Jesuit than he realized.

"Did Paul Fine actually get to the stage of going out and meeting these students?"

"I don't think so. We were just starting up, catching up on background at this stage. It was his story basically, he was just picking my brain a bit. Same as we all do here," Downey added a little defensively. Minogue caught Fitzgerald's eye for an instant. Had Fitz powers of mind-reading, from that look on his face after Downey's mention of picking one another's brains? Minogue had instantly thought of a family of apes grooming themselves.

"Do you keep a notebook, Mr Downey? Could you tell us the names of persons you or Paul Fine were to meet with in this regard?"

Downey blinked. Fitzgerald continued cleaning his glasses, taking excessive care with his handiwork. Hoey tapped his pencil lightly on the pad and glanced at Minogue.

"Such names would be a great help to us, Mr Downey. They would in no way incriminate anybody," said Minogue.

Downey looked to Fitzgerald but had no guidance there. Fitzgerald breathed on the lenses again.

"It's not the custom for policemen to be asking journalists for their diaries or notebooks. Excepting places such as Chile, perhaps," Fitzgerald observed.

"I didn't know you for a man who revered customs," replied Minogue. "I rather like novel approaches myself."

"Thanks but no thanks," said Fitzgerald conclusively. "I appreciate your appreciation. A free press does not involve policemen following up names in a journalist's notebook and questioning them on what they may or may not have said to that journalist."

"I don't much care what they said to Mr Downey here. I want to know what they knew of Paul Fine."

Fitzgerald put his glasses on, curling them around his ears carefully. Minogue saw a brain-warrior girding his loins.

"Seeing as we're talking man-to-man here, Inspector, let me ask you this: is it because Paul's da happens to be a Justice of the Supreme Court that you are so pushy?"

"Not principally," Minogue answered.

Fitzgerald rested a languid gaze on Minogue for several seconds, then he turned to Downey. Downey left the room. Must have known and made their minds up before I ever actually asked, Minogue thought.

"It's because Paul Fine is a Jew, isn't it?"

"That could well be," said Minogue slowly. "But I don't like to say it out loud. Every victim of a murderer gets our best. I may look like a superannuated culchie cop to you but I am in fact a lunatic—a lunatic in the sense that I am a stubborn weasel when I get to grips with the murder of a person. My bite is very bad indeed, Mr Fitzgerald, and I'm at the age where I don't much care for jaded slogans like 'the freedom of the press.' Not that I'm not a democratic person. It's that I tend to lose track of public rituals when I seek out fairness for someone like Paul Fine. We're his advocates, in a sense. Now if you want to get on your high horse and find my superiors' ears in order to have me taken to task, fire away. But you'll be surprised. This is a very personal business. You get to know who was treated so unfairly that they end up on a slab in the pathology department of a hospital and turn into a heap of reports on your desk. Frequently you get to like those victims and the people they were stolen from: you even get to like some of them inordinately. And it tears at your stomach and it can make you sick in yourself, this grief and madness. Do you know what I'm saying at all? Let me know when I'm trampling on your civil rights, won't you?"

Minogue heard Fitzgerald breathe out heavily through his nostrils. He looked to his watch.

"Tea?" said Fitzgerald. Minogue believed he had won something.

Downey brought the tea. He sat next to Hoey as they doctored their tea and pointed to names in his notebook. Hoey began copying them.

"If you think that Paul was by way of being very religious, you'd be wrong there," said Fitzgerald. "I don't know if there are lapsed Jews like there are lapsed Catholics but he didn't wear his religion on his sleeve. I asked him when he came to me with the bit about the Arabs, the students, if he hadn't an interest to declare there. He laughed it off, treated it as a joke."

"A joke," Minogue echoed with a leaden emphasis.

"Yes. Because being a Jew he'd necessarily be expected to have it in for any Arab. Stereotyping. Get this, now: Paul was an unashamed progressive, like a lot of people here. Your mob call it Leftie, I don't doubt. Let's just say that Paul wasn't a gobshite. We have to fight our corner here on this programme. There'll always be complaints, and dinosaurs from the bog wanting to put us off the air and have more 'entertainment,' less looking at the Emperor. Paul wouldn't have been working here if he was a bread and circuses man. It was a personal challenge to him to go out and meet these students, he said. He actually had a lot of sympathy for Palestinians. We think there are no shades of opinion in Israel, you know, and we assume that every Israeli—and therefore, every Jew the world over—supports what has happened in Israel over the last ten years. Not so."

"It's getting a bit murky for me," Minogue murmured. "It seems odd to me that he should be murdered for being a Jew who was apparently taking an interest in Arab goings-on as regards Ireland."

"That's putting it a bit crudely. I don't think any of those students would do that, even if they knew Paul was a Jew. Remember that he was an Irishman, a Dubliner. Would you have known him for anything but that if you'd met him in the street?" asked the rhetorical Fitzgerald. Dead with a hole the size of a tenpenny piece in his forehead, Minogue wanted to reply. The back of his head pulped too, Mr Smart-arse Fitzgerald.

"Point taken. What if there are more militant students coming here now? Like you were wondering about, ones with some brief to be involved with our crop of IRA? What if one of them knew precisely that Paul was a Jew?"

Fitzgerald shrugged. Minogue drained his cup and he watched as Fitzgerald rummaged in a drawer of his desk. A grainy newspaper photograph of Daniel Ortega fluttered to the floor by Minogue's feet. He picked it up and laid it on Fitzgerald's desk. Fitzgerald smiled then and laid a key by Minogue's cup. Minogue couldn't suppress a snigger.

"There: now you know for sure. Don't tell the bishops," said Fitzgerald.

"I didn't think you kept pictures of the Sacred Heart in there, Mr Fitzgerald. Don't be worrying about shocking me."

Fitzgerald announced that he had to get back to work. He had allotted nearly an hour to the Gardai, holding off calls and conferences for this interview. Now he had to get on top of this evening's programme.

Minogue asked him what other stories Paul Fine had been working on.

"Bren will tell you those. I knew some of them. He did a story on chemists down the country refusing to stock contraceptives. Em, he trimmed something we got about Thatcher's own constituency, you know, how the locals view her. What else? The Arab student thing, of course. Oh, I forgot: it was his turn to hunt for some scandal."

"Scandal? Journalists?" said Minogue, not quite carrying it off.

"We're always interested in what sulking backbenchers might be bellyaching about. Especially with the Ard Fheis, our glorious governing party's convention, coming up in a week and a half. Not a lot of Party members will talk to our programme, you see—before the Ard Fheis, I mean. We have the name of stirring up trouble, making mountains out of molehills because our format pretty well dictates that we can't give them a half an hour to gab. Still, we try. There's always a grumbling TD out there, a fella who would like to air his notions."

"I take it you mean a bit of muck-raking." Fitzgerald affected shock. "Seeing as we're talking man-to-man here," Minogue added.

"You're not a bishop in disguise, are you?"

"I'm merely a pawn," replied Minogue.

"It's not muck-raking. It's called accountability and scrutiny of public officials and it's rather popular in textbook discussions on democracy. I mean that we might want to check how many holidays a Member of Parliament or councillor takes and if the State purse is being devoted to projects a little too close to home for these boyos. Recreations, expense accounts, that sort of thing. See how they vote on certain issues, who they're rolling around in the sack with. Who's on the up-and-up, what Cabinet decisions do to whom. Squeeze all that into a quickie magazine format for tired motorists, and you're a better man than I. There are the obvious limitations."

"Sounds mighty exciting," Minogue fibbed.

"I'll tell you what I like the most about it," said Fitzgerald. He rubbed his hands together theatrically. "Aside from raising the wrath of the curators of culture and family life here, it's knowing that the whole mob listen to our programme so they can get any dirt on their rivals. Then they pretend to condemn us for finding something isn't quite square. I love it."

"Did Paul do much of this stuff?"

"No he didn't, actually. He hated it, if you really want to know. I rotate staff through that job. It's a constant issue, potentially anyway."

"Did he do well at it?"

"Well . . . he didn't, I'd have to say. His strengths were in other areas. He didn't have the killer instinct really—"

Fitzgerald stopped.

"What a stupid thing to say, after what has happened," he murmured. "What I meant to say was that

Paul found this part of the work pretty distasteful."

"What did he like to cover in the line of his work, then?"

"He liked fairy stories."

"I don't follow."

"That's what we call them here. Sort of like good news, news that has or could have a happy ending. A new centre for adult education, more money for battered wives' shelters, something progressive in the schools. Paul wasn't a hungry bollocks like the rest of us, keen to tear at the vitals of those who misgovern and undo us. A bit nice, was our Paul."

Fitzgerald's demeanour changed with the last sentence, said slowly as if considering something foreign to him. His eyes were now less alert and guarded, Minogue believed.

"That doesn't get anyone very far, does it?" Minogue said.

Fitzgerald looked glum when he left them with Downey to open Paul Fine's desk. Minogue had twenty minutes to look through its contents. He found two card indexes, a half-dozen school copybooks, some used, a small cassette-recorder you could shove in your pocket. No cassette in it, none in the drawer. Over a dozen hanging-file folders. Minogue left the files in the cabinet and looked through the copybooks. Fine had apparently kept notes. Minogue could read most of the pages, some home-made shorthand excepted. The most recent date appeared to be almost three weeks previously—notes from an interview which concerned agricultural fertilizers turning up in rivers.

One card index held names and addresses, listed alphabetically. The other, also bound with a rubber band, detailed lists of subjects. Minogue made sense of most of the topics. Fine had dated previous broadcasts on some items. Opening to P, Minogue saw "*Papal Visit—expenses*," followed by references to radio and television broadcasts. An idea for a future story on the radio, probably. Minogue checked "*Israel*" and found sub-topics too: "*Irl—Isl.(dpltc.)*," "*Isl.—S. Africa*," "*Isl.—West Bank.*" Fine's system also noted related subjects and programmes with some references to print media: "*I.T.*" for *Irish Times*, "*Gdn.*" for *Guardian*, "*Ind*" for the British *Independent*. The different media references were colour-coded, yellow for radio programmes, black for newspapers, red for television. Nothing under A for Arab. Stupid to expect that. No "*League for Solidarity*" either. Minogue found entries for the IRA and Intelligence Services. Methodical fella, Paul Fine. If he was bored some day or short of a topic he could go to his index and even whet his appetite further by looking at some previous treatments of topics. None of his sources was dated earlier than two years back. Maybe he skimmed off the older entries at the end of every year and started new cards to stay up-to-date—

Hoey was fingering through the file folders in the drawers of the desk. Fitzgerald had indeed stuffed what he had found on the top of the desk into the drawers. A packet of Carrolls cigarettes, a telephone message on red paper to call Mary. Minogue took the number to check against Mary McCutcheon's. A small internal phone directory was pinned to the partition in front of the desk with postcards and cartoons next to it. There were several receipts and credit-card flimsies in the drawer, none less than a week old, and pens, pencils and biros in profusion. Minogue noted the Access card number to check for attempted uses since Fine's death, and found a slip of paper with two names on it. He was able to read one of the names directly: *H. Ali.* The other looked like *Khatib.* Sounded Arabic too. Surnames? He copied them.

Minogue pocketed the copybooks and flattened them in the inside pocket of his jacket. He handed the two card indexes to Hoey, who promptly stuffed one in each pocket.

Minogue locked the desk. He found Fitzgerald behind the glass wall of a studio with his head encased in headphones the size of polite teacups.

"I'm holding on to the key," said Minogue. "It's out of your hands for the moment, but thanks very much for acting promptly and securing what may be valuable clues. It may prove useful, I don't know. There'll be a detective back to go through the stuff properly. Phone me if you have something, would you? Questions, recollections, anything you hear. Complaints too, if you want."

Fitzgerald nodded without removing the apparatus. As Minogue turned away, Fitzgerald beckoned to him and he pried one of the headphones away from his ear.

"Do you have anything to do with that Ryan business down in Tipperary?"

"I did," replied Minogue.

"We're going to be having a WAMmer here for a live interview about twenty after. Do you know of the Women's Action Movement?"

Minogue nodded but didn't take the bait. "I'd better make haste, then," he murmured.

"Aha, I see. I just wanted a detail cleared up. Someone suggested it to me last night and it stuck in my head. You know how everyone has an opinion on this—whether it should be considered murder and all that?"

"All we do is give our evidence to our department up in the Park. They process it, file evidence, word it and then they throw it to the Director of Public Prosecutions. The DPP lays the charges on behalf of the State."

"OK. I know for a fact that this woman from WAM is going to be talking about the case being a psychological watershed."

Minogue thought of incontinence. "What's a psychological watershed when it's at home?"

"The Ryan woman killing that husband of hers, fighting back. All the claims about wife abuse in holy Ireland. The line you'll hear this evening will be about a revolution in Irish life, women not taking it any more from Church or State or husband."

Minogue fixed on Fitzgerald's "line." Everything was a "line" in this racket, then. Minogue knew the fascination which the Ryan case seemed to hold for many people all over the country and he was suspicious of it. Jimmy Kilmartin himself, that distant look in his eye, was that a portent of "a psychological watershed?"

"It's the whole bit about the strong woman figure in the Irish psyche, I was told last night. That's what strikes a chord with everyone," Fitzgerald continued. "So tell me, do the Gardai recognize any significance in how Fran Ryan was killed?"

"He was stabbed to death with a kitchen knife," Minogue replied cautiously. "Not on any altar of sacrifice or anything. No incantations or signs painted on the wall—"

"Yes, but how many times?"

"Ah, I bet you know yourself, Mr Fitzgerald."

"Thirty-seven, am I right?"

"You are," replied Minogue.

"So yous don't see any significance or ritual thing about that?"

"To do with where the planets were, is it?" Minogue tried.

"No. Fran Ryan was thirty-seven when he died."

# FIVE

**M**inogue and Hoey were five minutes late for the meeting. Minogue guessed Gallagher for the one who looked like a graduate student, subtly raffish and smart, mustachioed and denim clad. Kilmartin was whispering with a sergeant whom Minogue recognized as a forensic technician who was always trying to organize golf tournaments which were a cover for lengthy booze-ups.

He walked to Gallagher and introduced himself. Gallagher's accent was the faintly interrogative earnestness of Donegal.

"You don't mind guiding these fellas here through your stuff too, do you?" asked Minogue as he glanced around the room. "We're all off the Squad here. Keating. That's Shea Hoey there I came in with. The world and his mother knows Jimmy Kilmartin, I'll bet. 'The Killer' himself. The one he's talking to has a preliminary from the scene and we're waiting for anything from the autopsy. It's early days yet with the pathology, though, so we shouldn't be expecting anything proper until later this evening."

Gallagher stroked his moustache. "I can give you the broad picture, but this League crowd . . . I might as well tell you now, I never heard of them."

"Well, tell us about the overall situation, then, will you?" said Minogue. He felt drowsy now.

Kilmartin lumbered over as Minogue took his seat. "You have a green light," he confided. "God Almighty was on the blower to me an hour ago. 'Results!' says he. You know what that means. Steam-roller. The pressure is on, man."

Kilmartin glanced quickly in Gallagher's direction. "If that Gallagher drags his heels or sulks a bit, I'd bite him," he said slowly.

Gallagher stood and nodded at Minogue.

"We'll start, so," said Minogue.

Minogue drew several circles around "9 mm." He drew squares around ".30/.32—7.62/7.65 mm."

"Whatever calibre it was, the gun was fired from between one and two feet away. Few particles in the scalp, a radius of nearly four inches. Very little scorching within that area. Em—" The assistant to the State Pathologist was reading from handwritten notes in a binder. "The first shot killed him. Instantly. A subsequent shot took a piece of vertebra here. A shot to the neck blew out the artery. The blood loss has to be a consequence of how the body lay after the shooting."

He turned to the overhead projector and used his pencil to home in on a point on the diagram. To Minogue he looked like a younger Vincent Price. The upward glow from the apparatus highlighted his face and the smoke being drawn like a silk scarf towards the fan beneath the projector. The smell of hot plastic and cigarette smoke mixed with the odour of stale clothes—his own? he wondered—had made Minogue sleepy. He looked to the probable height of the killer, an estimate of the angle of entry for the first shot. Fine was five foot ten in his socks, the angle no more than thirty degrees before the bullet went slightly awry. The one who fired the gun had to be no smaller than five foot eight . . . if he or she was standing in ordinary shoes, on a spot level with Fine. Sitting, though? If Fine had been sitting down? Minogue's mind reeled.

"How about him being shot as he sat down?" Hoey said.

The assistant turned to the projector again and waved his pencil over shaded areas on the figure.

"We can't tell from the bruising here if—do you see those bruisings there over the forehead? Well, the drawing, I mean, obviously—he banged his head after being shot and falling to the ground. In a chair, say, he'd pitch roughly forward, then to one side when his upper body'd meet with his knees and . . . it'd take us a while to suggest probabilities. One thing worthy of mention, as I was saying earlier, was the degree of bruising. With the possible exception of that bruise near the hairline, the bruises were occasioned after death. None is severe and that is important."

Occasioned. I like that verb, thought Minogue.

"It's safe to say that the victim was not intentionally clobbered or abused at all. The motion of the water and the nature of the materials on the water's edge account for the abrading and slight bruising which forms nearly all of what we're talking about."

Tides, thought Minogue. Time and tide wait for no man. Time of death (he remembered the feeble attempt at humour on that: "Ah now, lads, no miracles, please") was between eighteen and twenty-four hours of the time of discovery. The body, cruciform, drifting in the darkness as the moon drew and released tides around the island.

Kilmartin flicked the venetian blinds open and Minogue rubbed his eyes in the glare. Gallagher waited until the assistant had left and his audience was all commissioned Gardai. He began with the file which the Special Branch had maintained on Paul Fine. With a sense of decisive deliberation, Gallagher said the file was inactive. The last entry had been three years previously.

"What status was Fine's file?" asked Minogue.

"Status?" Gallagher resisted.

"Was he regarded as a high priority?"

Gallagher didn't reply immediately. Minogue caught sight of the mild warning in Kilmartin's glance. Fine and well to bite Gallagher if he was surly, but not in front of other policemen.

"Er, no. Fine was a student in Trinity College for two years, studying Political Science. His name came to our attention a few months after he started college when he appeared on a membership list for a certain organization, one we routinely keep track of," Gallagher lisped, without looking up from the sheet he had drawn out of his jacket.

"Hardly the Legion of Mary, ha, lads?" said Kilmartin. The policemen grinned obligingly.

"You may know the organization," Gallagher rode in on Kilmartin's attempt to head off awkwardness. "Eco-Al. Let me give you a sketch on this group. *Eco* is just eco, the way it sounds. It can mean economy and ecology. *Al* is for alliance. Say it quick and it sounds like 'equal.' All intentionally clever. We have reason to believe that Eco-Al got some funding from unusual sources on the Continent. There's common stuff between Eco-Al and other movements: the Green Party, CND in Britain, Greenham Common women, Animal Rights movements. Take it as understood that Eco-Al has received money from an organization in Paris called Accord International. It's by way of being a quartermaster for cash which is thought to originate in Eastern Europe and probably the Soviet Union. There is no doubt in the wide world that Eco-Al has been infiltrated by persons with other priorities, secret or otherwise, including Trotskyite groups and ex-members of RS."

"RS?" asked Kilmartin. "If you say that quick, it's 'arse,' isn't it?"

Even Gallagher laughed at that.

"Not intentional this time, but you might be on to something there. I'll pass it along."

More laughs.

"Revolutionary Struggle. They're nearly all students. The ones that aren't are hangers-on trying to get off with rich girls who have fallen in love with the proletariat. They're not all the ideologues and screamers they look. One of 'em turned up at a post office robbery last year in Castlebar with an assault rifle under his armpit. He's number two on our list since. We think he's in Amsterdam. Anyway—"

"Any cross-over between this mob and the IRA?" asked Kilmartin.

"No," answered Gallagher. "That Eco-Al thing fell in on itself. The organization still exists in name but is pretty well defunct. You couldn't keep a coalition like that together in Ireland. It was a hothouse thing. All that's left of Eco-Al is a small group of university graduates who meet over pints and write letters to the paper about acid rain and the state of the nation's water resources."

"Right enough, I know that crowd," said Kilmartin. "They let their children run around with no nappies. Want to give fish and sheep the vote and outlaw flush toilets and motorcars."

"Let's get back to the other business," said Minogue, struggling against a sluggish afternoon mind. "Palestinians and their sympathizers."

Gallagher stretched his arms and began fiddling with a pencil. Minogue deduced that Gallagher was restive at having to explain basics to crime ordinary detectives. Hoity-toity Special Branch: Supermen with their own liturgy.

"The Palestinian thing is not a cut-and-dried affair in Ireland. It's an odd business. Palestinians find common cause with Republicans here. Then there's a lot of people saying that Irish nationalism has so much in common with Zionism and that results in support for Israel."

"So you're telling us that it's confused."

"No. A good rule of thumb here is that Lefties here tend to stick to the Palestinian side. You and I know that IRA personnel have trained and travelled and received munitions from various places in the Middle East."

"Wait a minute, Pat," said Minogue. "Sooner or later we have to consider the possibility of some *quid pro quo* thing, a favour done by our local gunmen in return for arms or money."

"It could well be a Provo loaning out a gun or two," added Gallagher. "They're still at the rent-a-gun for bank jobs, I grant you. But"—he paused—"why not take the line of a paid-up contract murder? A professional killer or terrorist, in and out from the Continent or someplace."

"All right so," said Minogue, still scrabbling for some hold. "You've brought the meeting to that contentious point, Pat. We're trying to profile a killer. Trying to see him clearly. I've given the matter some thought, the possibility of a professional killer being responsible, for whatever motive. I think we can't be distracted by thinking about some international hit-man or hit-men: that would be discouraging. Let's plug away with the lines we have. Stay flexible. Even if we are chasing a pro, we need to find the locals who set it up. A pro doesn't just walk in and pick anyone. What we can try to focus on is some small cell, one fella even, who's a cross-over between IRA or Left-wing and other groups with strong interests in the Middle Eastern business. Not just in Palestinian matters but militant Muslim groups."

Gallagher nodded and continued stroking his moustache as if trying to drain something out of it, looking towards the ceiling as he listened.

"But like I said," Gallagher murmured finally, "if it's a pro or semi-pro floated in for this, paid for the job and gone already—"

"Shite," said Kilmartin. "The hell kind of a chance do we have if the killer got a gun and a passport and a fistful of money out of a diplomatic bag and he's back in Paris or Beirut or whatever?"

Gallagher shrugged. "Then we have our work cut out for us," he said. He continued mulling over the question and then shook his head slowly.

"We can usually pick names out of our heads for certain jobs. If you said: 'We're looking for someone who knocks off post-offices using assault rifles and works with two others and steals four cars for one job,' I could reel off three or four names. But right now we can't point to anyone in or out of the groups we monitor who is fired up enough and savage enough to do this murder. Three shots in the head suggests expertise to me, that's all I can say. Our militants are a fairly tight family bunch, to tell you the truth. The home-grown real hitmen don't care a damn for anything outside the IRA-Brit side of things. They wouldn't do freelance stuff like killing Fine for an Arab cause. Very, very unlikely."

"Humph," grunted Kilmartin, shifting himself in his seat. "Don't forget the call to the newspaper was an Irish accent. Let's say some foreigner, some fella from the Middle East, did it but had an Irish mate to do the phoning. They're cut-throats out there in the Middle East, you only have to watch the news to know that."

"You may have something there," Gallagher allowed cautiously. "It'd also make it look like there was an organization here, some support for their cause."

No-one spoke for several moments.

Gallagher's quizzical glance towards Minogue brought him out of his thoughts and he suppressed a yawn. "Yes, Pat. Sorry. Yes. Will you carry on with the student thing now, if you please? Middle Eastern students and groups and what-have-you here in Ireland?"

Chair legs scraped and policemen rearranged themselves while Gallagher prepared his notes again. Minogue lapsed into his chair, retreating within.

He had been lucky, if luck was the word. After the nightmare of carrying the body through the bushes and briars in the early hours of Monday morning, the panic and fear and sweat like a fever gripping him, he had hefted and dragged, rested with then wrestled with the corpse for an hour, getting him down off the damn hill. His body remembered the dank night air off the sea enveloping him like a clammy cloak.

He had seen dead bodies before, plenty of them. Those villagers shredded in the Bekaa Valley, the dust of their pulverized homes still settling on their faces where the flies fed. Never so close, though: close enough to see the head jerk, hair part suddenly as the shot spread shock through the skull, the body drop like a stone, as though thrown to the ground. Had to make certain then, and not think: shoot and hold and shoot again, quickly before you scream yourself. Must watch too, as the head hopped and the legs twitched.

He shuddered as he changed gear for the first traffic lights on the outskirts of Bray. His armpits prickled. He couldn't remember getting this far, just following the rush-hour traffic south on the Bray Road. His face felt swollen with the sweat. He munched third gear, missing the gate. The car felt strange to him still. Could the drivers next to him imagine what he had been going through, what he was still going through? He had found the shell casings, scrabbling in the grass and briars; he had rolled the body into the bushes. A dog barking somewhere, rustling in the foliage. People used this park, of course they did. Not of his choosing at all. Panic had burst like a flare in his chest, leaving every part of his body aching. Dog barking again, breaking the tremendous weight of silence of a warm autumn afternoon. Dull echoes of the thumps as he had fired still pulsed in his mind. Then looking up and seeing the child watching him. Luck? Paralysed, beyond any thought or action. Couldn't touch the child. A boy dressed up in his Boy Scout uniform, stick in hand: there had to be more of these youngsters nearby. He remembered trying to smile at the boy but something was shouting inside his head, knowing he couldn't control his facial muscles. The boy had moved off. Luck?

He accelerated with the green light and turned down towards the wasteland of rubble which girdled this corner of the town. He passed a metal foundry, long abandoned, where teenagers drank and pelted bottles against the few remaining walls. Bonfires scarred and blackened the stones, and rats scurried in the dock-weeds and scattered bricks and rubbish. It was tea-time, the lanes were deserted. Rusting hulks of cars stood in the nettles by mounds of rubble. He eased the car over bricks and burst plastic bags full of refuse and steered towards a roofless building. Small shapes moved around the debris. The tyres spun as he worked the car over a concrete parapet in which steel rails were still embedded. More car wrecks, many burned too.

Seize the chance, just go through with it. That's how war is. War? He swore at the burn of confusion and anger which erupted around his heart. Struggling with a dead man down a hill in the hopes he'd never be found; clammy with loathing and disgust and weariness, embracing the stubborn body of a man he had killed as though it were a penance. Cursing and praying, nearly in tears, stumbling with his load while everyone slept. Dark night of the soul, he had wondered later. The life of one man for the greater cause. One man—it was as though another voice had said that aloud next to him in the car. Panic and rage made a tremor race up his back. He cast a glance towards the covered body. Now it was two.

He stopped the car and switched off the engine. When he tried to move he found that he couldn't. He bowed his head and prayed but the hands on the wheel remained as fists, tight and tighter as he struggled. Lucky, he thought again with savage irony. Lucky because he was still sane enough to get this far. He checked his watch again. He imagined the body moving, rising, casting off the blanket, going for his throat. Less than an hour ago he had killed the other man who now lay huddled across the seat. The man had shouted once but the bar had thudded into the side of his turning head before he got his arm up. Hit him again, this time on his knees, putting him out. The film of yellow light had seemed to pulse and brighten as he had stood over the man, listening to the deep breaths whistling in his nose. He had fumbled the cord out of his pocket, finished him. Desperate then, feeling this could not be real, he had heard himself sob as he tightened the cord, his hands cramping with the strain until he let go at last. A blot of blood had issued from the man's ear.

He had watched the street then, but no-one had passed. He had opened the garage door, driven in the car, and swung the door down again. It had taken him ten minutes to wrap the body, drag it to the car and bundle it into the back seat. Then he had gone through the kitchen, cleaned the blood from the lino and latched the door. After that, he had driven away with his cargo, out into the beginnings of the evening rush-hour traffic towards the comfortable suburbs of Dublin's south side—

He skirted the buildings and debris carefully, stopping to look back at the car. This needn't have happened, he knew. He might have had an option, some hope of avoiding it, if that body hadn't drifted in on the tide. He choked off the remorse with anger and looked about the site. Joyriders set fire to the cars they had stolen around here, he had heard. Beer cans lay heaped beside half-melted plastic cider bottles. He listened to the clacking of the suburban train, the DART, in the distance. The nearest houses were almost a quarter mile off. He looked back at the car again. People'd see smoke but the most they might do would be call the fire brigade. Even at that, the petrol would have done its work. Couldn't wait, anyway.

He uncapped the petrol and doused the upholstery. The petrol soaked the blanket and began dripping onto the floor. He let the string into the can and drew it out slowly, looped one end around to the underside of the front seat and tied the other end to the top of a reinforcing bar which stuck out obliquely from the rubble nearby. Before lighting the cigarette he squeezed the string to make sure it was moist enough. Then he cupped clay and dirt into a small mound under the string. Slowly he plugged the cigarette into the clay. He left an inch between the smoking tip and the string. Four, five minutes, he thought. When he stood, the scene seemed to gather itself around him, crushing him. He felt his stomach stir with nausea. Dizzy too, he breathed in deeply and rubbed his eyes hard. A funeral pyre, he thought, or a sacrifice. He forced himself to utter a short prayer. Through the fear and the unbelieving, as he heard his own heart beat loud, he knew that he had held fast. As grotesque as this was, as clumsy as it was, he had been lucky—blessed, perhaps—and he had held fast. He jogged across the acres of rubble and the derelict shells of factories, and he headed for the train station.

The briefing ground on. Minogue could feel the bafflement, the tiredness of the detectives hanging in the air. While he waited for a pause in Gallagher's delivery he watched a detective yawn.

"Will you run up a list of likelies from what ye know about extremists here who are interested in matters Middle Eastern?" Minogue asked finally. "Students and citizens not necessarily affiliated with Republicans here too?" he added.

Gallagher blinked and studied the table-top.

"I can put the request through the Park to cover you," Minogue said. He could think of no less ominous way to remind Gallagher that the request could have the Garda Commissioner's scrawl on the end of it after going through his office in Garda HQ in Phoenix Park.

"Ah no, it's not that," Gallagher said awkwardly. "I know we have to get the lead out, and free up personnel and info if ye want it. I was just thinking ahead, trying to figure an easy way. We don't have the files cross-indexed, you see. We go by names, we go by organizations. Then we have files from the Aliens Office for resident foreigners. I can run up a list, all right, but it'll take time—"

"And the Ports of Entry data, to follow up on an in-and-out killer from abroad?" Minogue probed gently.

"To be sure," Gallagher replied quickly.

Somebody's belly rumbled, Kilmartin's. "Jases! Did you hear that war-cry, lads? I could eat the cheeks off a Jesuit's arse through the confessional grille."

Whether planned or not, Kilmartin's grumble loosened the tension which Minogue had felt settling after he had made his request for Branch material.

"How many students are we talking about?" asked Kilmartin.

"Students from the Middle East? I don't know for sure. There are upwards of 200 Lebanese students here. I only know that because I heard it the other day. The Lebanese are very keen on university education. I don't know what religion the Lebanese here are, even. I'd bet a lot of them are Maronites, Christians."

"Libya. Syria. Places with big Muslim populations."

"Iraq too? Do you want to know about Iran?"

Kilmartin looked exasperated enough for Gallagher to skip any answer.

"Here's a rough guess, then: 450. That's a generous estimate. Included in that are militants and ordinary people who don't beat any drums. You might find a PLO member and then you might find a member of the Irish Arab society—both ends of the spectrum."

"Right so," said Minogue. "Let's get on to specifics with this League for Solidarity with the Palestinian People, then."

Gallagher sat back in his chair and tugged at his moustache.

"I'm afraid I don't have anything on them. I never heard of them—and I'm the expert." Gallagher shrugged. "Are you sure you got the name right—the girl on the switchboard, I mean."

"Shite," said Kilmartin.

It was seven o'clock.

"Sandwiches?" asked Minogue.

"Hamburgers and chips," Keating said.

Minogue caved in. "Let's give ourselves a few minutes before we get down to brass tacks as to what we're going to do here," he murmured. He asked Hoey to copy the names from Fine's index cards onto the blackboard. Gallagher stayed in his chair and watched Hoey scrawling on the board.

"Now I might be able to plug into that," said Gallagher, nodding towards the board. "Where'd you get those names?"

"An index of Paul Fine's. We found it in his office."

Minogue walked by Gallagher and out into the hallway. Kilmartin, there ahead of him, turned to the Inspector.

"I phoned the lab for an update just now," he grunted. "They're ready to put it in writing that Fine was shot somewhere else than the beach. We've had men up and down the beach since the middle of the day."

Minogue thought about the manpower which Kilmartin had suggested calling in. He'd need at least fifty men: Killiney Bay stretched miles down to Bray. The body probably hadn't made it more than a couple of hundred feet offshore before the tide had drawn it in. Minogue didn't want to think about Fine being shot aboard a boat and being dumped over. Fifty Gardai to do the hotels along the promenade in Bray, all the entrances to the beach . . . the railway stations for a sighting. Fine hadn't owned a car. Go on the radio news tonight, at least. Wait until tomorrow for the telly, get a good clear recent snap for the papers too. Door to door? There couldn't be more than a handful of older houses directly adjacent to the beach, houses built before the State decided that the foreshore was State land. In every place along the beach that Minogue could think of you'd have to be right down on the strand to see anything happening at the water's edge. And who'd be down on the beach at night, anyway? Gurriers with cans of lager and joints and their mots for a wear. Model citizens: the least likely to step forward.

"I think we'd better set about it, all right," Minogue concluded.

Kilmartin could call in detectives from the Central Detective Unit in Harcourt Street as well as other crime ordinary detectives from District Detective Units around the country.

"Let's start by posting a car at every and any car entrance to the beach. Stop anyone going down to the beach and ask if they were around on Sunday or Sunday night. I'm sure there are regulars who drag the dog out and what-have-you every day there. Then to the beach accesses for pedestrians only. As for ourselves here, we should look at possibles from Fine's card index for one thing."

"Be more than fifty, Matt. Tell me a hundred."

"Can we do it?"

"According to the phone call I got this afternoon from You-know-who, we'd better," Kilmartin replied sardonically.

"I see. Let's put men to yacht clubs and boat clubs, then, and boaters out of any harbours south from Sandymount," said Minogue. "All the way to Bray. Anything stolen in the line of boats, people seen tampering with boats, boats going out after dark. DART stations, in case he got on or got off on the south side. Leave a photo at every ticket office, for starters."

Minogue heard his assumptions creak insistently as he widened the net which he knew was in untried waters. Who was to say that Fine hadn't been shot anywhere in Dublin and then left on the beach or in the water after dark? So far they hadn't met anyone who could tell them where Paul Fine might have been on Sunday after he'd left his flat. Minogue mentally underlined Mary McCutcheon's name again.

He walked out into the yard and took in some of Dublin's stale air. Kilmartin sauntered out after him.

"I called God Almighty and I got the Assistant Comm instead," Kilmartin muttered. "Are you ready for thirty men tonight? Give them your mind after we set them up at a meeting tonight and then we're off and running already."

Minogue wanted to be away from Kilmartin, away from this swell of impossibility rising towards him. Fine's friends—someone—must have been with him some time over the weekend. Kilmartin flicked his cigarette away and spat expertly.

"I don't see myself as the one to bang the drum for this crowd tonight, then," murmured Minogue. "Will you give them the rundown and I'll sort out individual assignments with Shea Hoey?"

"Fair enough," said Kilmartin brightly, chastening the surprised Minogue. "Do you have an idea where you'll want to start?"

"Six men to go over cassettes and videos we found in the flat. I'll earmark another six experienced interviewers for whoever Gallagher thinks is worthwhile off Fine's index. Those are my main ones for now anyway. . . . I don't know if the Branch will insist on using their men for any suspects they pull out of their own files."

Kilmartin nodded, looked to the sky and yawned long. Minogue thought he heard Kilmartin's dentures click when they dislodged during the yawn. Age, he reflected dully.

"Here's something I was thinking about just now," said Minogue. "Do you think that whoever shot him knew that the bullets would go clean through?"

Kilmartin didn't look away from the skyline.

"You're the crafty boyo, aren't you now? I know what you're getting at."

Minogue felt guilty stepping into the pub with Kilmartin. It was ten to eleven.

"That's what I worked all these years to set up, Matt. Don't be looking like a whipped pup. Hoey probably knows the ropes better than I do now, and Keating is no slouch either. Murtagh just looks stupid; he's actually a sly bollocks with plenty of brains, just a bit lazy. Don't be worrying about no skipper at the helm. No-one is indispensable, they say."

Kilmartin knew the barmen in Nolan's. Minogue declined whiskey, settling for a pint of stout instead. Kilmartin had a Powers whiskey and a bottle of stout.

"Here's to retirement. The golden years and all that," Kilmartin toasted ambiguously. The stout was too heavy and chilled for long gulps. "Let's not be fretting about some international gangster. We'll come up with some Provisionals link yet, wait'll you see."

Minogue thought about the work which was afoot already tonight. Gallagher had settled on the names of eleven students which he believed might help. One of the detectives had asked if they should Section 30 any students. Reluctantly, Minogue had assented, and told the detectives to throw the Offences Against the State Act at people on the list if they dragged their heels.

"I'm not happy sending them out to interview those students with nothing under their belts to poke at them with, no way to see if they're being entirely truthful," said Minogue reflectively.

"No other way around it, Matt," countered a defensive Kilmartin.

Was this what rank did, Minogue ruminated. Another pint of stout was slapped on the counter in front of him.

"Ah, Jimmy, I can't."

"You can't leave it behind you, that's a fact."

He watched Kilmartin scoop the change from the *fait accompli* off the counter.

"Lookit, wait and see what turns up on these tapes. Maybe Fine had a diary on him and it was lost. Stolen? Maybe they took it, whoever did him in, don't you see. No sign of a wallet or anything, am I right? So he may have had vital things on him when he was killed."

Kilmartin was right to keep doors open, Minogue reflected. For himself, he needed a night's sleep, to be away from this.

Minogue re-read the letter, posted nine days ago somewhere in New York City. At least the boy wasn't writing from the bridal suite of some dive in Las Vegas. Kathleen buttered more bread. It was half past seven. Minogue had managed to steal into bed without disturbing anyone last night. He awoke to the alarm, lying in the same place as he had when he first stretched out in the bed. He felt dull, bunched.

"Cathy with a C. I don't know. I can't tell from this letter, I'm hardly an expert," Minogue tried.

"Your own son, mister. Don't you see what he's getting at?"

"I don't, I suppose."

"He's interested in her, that's what. To my way of thinking he's not telling us the half of it. 'Irish,' he says. As if that's supposed to impress."

Minogue believed that Kathleen was more nervous than angry.

"Everybody's Irish over there, I suppose, if they want to be. You see he's after meeting her family and everything," she added.

Minogue folded the letter and placed it under his saucer. Hopefully the saucer might devour it.

"He's testing us out. A fella can be very nervous when he meets a nice girl," said Minogue. Listening to himself he heard the stupidity of the remark.

"Nervous, is it? He's there in New York without a visa, working on the sly for some computer company and he's nervous? What about his poor parents?"

"Cathy . . . same name as Kathleen, basically. A very nice name, that. He has the same good taste as his father. I was nervous when I met you," Minogue tried to divert her.

"Pull the other one, it has bells."

"We said we'd give him the fare, so that was that. The boy is enjoying himself a bit. He knows he can't stay there forever."

"That's what I'm getting at," Kathleen said. "Don't you see? He may have it in the back of his head to marry this Cathy girl and stay there."

Minogue returned to his egg. It looked up from the plate at him, begging not to be slashed. For a moment he remembered nearly emigrating to the States thirty years ago. Did genes act like that, wait and ambush the next generation?

"So will you drop him a line and make him see sense."

Not the time to be asking her what "sense" she meant, Minogue knew.

"I will."

Iesult slouched into the kitchen in a dressing-gown.

"You're only missing the curlers and a cigarette in your mitt," welcomed Minogue.

Iesult stopped and sneered theatrically.

"When's the wedding? I hope it's one of those vulgar parties with everyone decked out in iijity clothes," she fluted.

# SIX

Kilmartin was lying in wait for him. Hoey rose from the desk and brought what looked like statement sheets with him, as the three policemen sat at Kilmartin's table.

"Any one of these fellas jump out and say 'me' to you?" asked Minogue.

Hoey shook his head. "One we didn't find was a Syrian fella. The other Syrian knew him, though, said he was in England visiting his sister since last week," said Hoey. He placed the statement sheets—photocopies, Minogue saw now—on the table and began sorting them.

"Let's start with this one, Khatib. He's Iranian."

Minogue's eyes ran beyond the Judge's Rule, the caution given to the person making the statement. Hoey read his copy again.

"It's clean, the whole thing. We got to see this Egan that he mentions and Egan confirmed that

Khatib and another student were up on some mountain in Kerry over the weekend with him. Clean living. Why can't they go drinking like everybody else, I ask myself. Khatib never heard of Fine. Didn't know of any murder."

"Now, this one here, Ali. He has a Jordanian passport but Gallagher says he is or was Palestinian. We had to put him on a Section 30 to shut him up. He's a hot lad entirely."

Hoey did not read this one. Minogue looked up from the half-page statement once to see Hoey's lack of interest.

"Ali more or less dared the detective—who is it? O'Reilly from Store Street—to charge him. 'What possible offences could I have committed against the Irish State?' sort of thing. Knows his law," said Hoey.

"Resist at all?" asked Kilmartin.

"No sir. If he had shut up he would have been home in bed by eleven o'clock instead of walking home at half-two in the morning. He's a member of the Irish-Arab society. Quite legit. More of an intellectual than anything else. He has a tongue like a rasp on him. He knew a lot about Irish politics, if that's any consolation. Never heard of or knew anyone called Fine. He spent Sunday afternoon studying in his flat and he gave two names to corroborate."

Hoey turned to the next statement. Minogue knew that they had nothing to help the investigation along, with these three students. They read through the remainder slowly. Keating sat at the table quietly without announcing himself.

"Did you put in a 'want' to police where this Ebrahim fella is supposed to be visiting, in Nottingham?" Minogue asked.

"Yes, sir. There was a reply on the telex this morning. He is there, and his sister is married and living there too."

Gallagher's lists, Minogue thought: have to go back to them and widen the net.

"Only one admitted to knowing about the murder. None said anything to suggest that they knew Fine at all or knew that he was a Jew," Hoey went on. "None professed to know of any organization called the League for Solidarity with the Palestinian People. One of them, the Mahoud fella three statements back, said he'd like to hear more about them. Smart-arse. Later on, as you'll see if you read the end of his statement again, he says that if anyone'd know of such a group, he would."

"Bit of a spoofer, is he?"

Hoey shrugged and looked around the table as if to invite optimism.

Kilmartin coughed. "If we're going to follow along with this line," he began slowly, "I see two possibilities."

He paused to light his cigarette.

"The outfit we want is a splinter, maybe a whole new group. Its baptism of fire, if you like."

"Like a declaration to take them seriously?" said Keating.

"Yes. I can't see IRA involvement here at all, beyond maybe renting out some guns to this group. These people are likely young and have some contact with groups who have guns. A new crowd arriving here doesn't have that contact, but a splinter group would. As for the IRA, they wouldn't have anything to do with killing a Jew. Pardon me putting it like that. If they wanted to take a swipe at the judiciary here, they wouldn't have picked Fine's son. And if they did, they would admit doing it, am I right?"

Minogue nodded.

"So you have educated or semi-educated people with heads full of theories about how the Irish are in the same boat as the Palestinians maybe," Kilmartin went on. "Fringe people, maybe did a bit of university, enough to get themselves confused."

"Where ignorance is bliss . . ." murmured Hoey.

"Now you have it. Learned just enough to stay stupid. Definitely not for the man in the street. He doesn't give much of a shite what's going on in the Middle East—until some of the UN troops start getting shot. The IRA will take the guns and talk about the Palestinian cause but bejases—" Kilmartin concluded with a scornful pull at the cigarette.

"Gallagher says that the IRA wouldn't touch Muslim fanatics with a ten-foot pole, sir," said Keating. "On account of how the Ayatollah and his mob hate anything to do with socialism."

"Oh, does he now?" said Kilmartin.

"But there might be another kink in this, sir—if you'll pardon me saying so," rejoined Keating. "Remember that Fine used to be enough of a Leftie for the Branch to have a file on him. Could we be talking about some class of a falling-out here?"

"We need to know where he was killed," Minogue interrupted. "I think we're jumping the gun here. What was the other possibility you thought of?" he asked Kilmartin.

"Just that it might be a group we know who did the murder—except that they don't want to get a bad name on the head of it. "

The policemen fell silent.

"The timing of the call to the paper," said Minogue. "That's something I'm having trouble with."

"We up and left for Killiney after the call came through from Dalkey station," Hoey joined in. "While ye were on the train out, that's when the call came in to the press."

"Ten twenty-nine," said the exacting Keating.

"And that was only twenty minutes or so after the body was first sighted and reported to Dalkey station. That's odd. Why call then to claim responsibility?"

"Maybe they were going to call that time anyway," suggested Keating. "We can't be sure right now that it wasn't coincidence."

"The world treats persons who rely on coincidences rather harshly," said Minogue. "I think they knew that Fine was to be found shortly or had just been found."

"Couldn't have anything to do with the oul' lad who found the body, though," said Kilmartin. "Seventy-odd years of age. He's nothing to us at all, at all."

"Yes, but why call if there's no body? I mean, if they dumped Paul Fine in the sea so as he might float out and not be found. They must have known that the body would be found. Leave the motive for killing him in the first place: what does it say about the planning that went into the killing? They attempted to make the body disappear, to all intents and purposes. So why would they want to call and claim responsibility for a murder, when they didn't want the body found?"

"Unless they saw, or knew about, the oul' fella finding him Monday morning," said Kilmartin. He was beginning to enjoy himself, Minogue realized, speculating out loud, prodding discussion. Maybe Jimmy Kilmartin had longed to play second fiddle for a long time so that he could throw ideas around and not have to feel silly if they came to nothing? Or was there a little malice in it, seeing how much Minogue could stay on top of an investigation which looked like it could become an intractable mess?

"Or it means that the body wasn't dumped that far away from where it was found,"said Keating vaguely. "It could have been pushed in from Killiney beach itself, and the tide didn't do the job they hoped it would."

"There'd have been people on that beach until dark," said Hoey. "They'd have seen any body floating even fifty feet offshore."

"But the point is"—Minogue tried to recover his thread—"if they had planned this killing and they really wanted to have the body disappear, they could have arranged that. So, the timing of this killing was not of their choosing, I think. It may be that there was no elaborate plan to kill Paul Fine at all."

The policemen took turns scrutinizing the walls.

"What word from Pat Gallagher on the Ports of Entry lists?" Minogue tried.

"Em, nothing yet," said Hoey quietly.

"Where's this Mary McCutcheon one?" asked Kilmartin. "Someone has to know what Fine was at over the weekend."

"She's up in Sligo doing a story, sir," said Hoey. "She's to come down to Dublin on the train this morning first thing. She only heard about it last night herself. She's a reporter for the *Irish Times*."

"Is she his girlfriend or intended or what?" asked Kilmartin.

Hoey shrugged. "Paul Fine's da knew of her but never met her. Mickey Fitzgerald says that she was more or less Paul's girlfriend. Ten-ten, the train schedule says, in Kingsbridge."

"She's not a Jew, though," Kilmartin observed. No-one answered him.

"Nobody else know where he was over the weekend? Downey or Fitzgerald out in RTE? This man had no friends, is it?" complained Kilmartin.

"Still looking, sir. He seems to have kept to himself since he came back from London," said Hoey.

"All right. We're taking a radio car up to Kingsbridge, meet this Mary McCutcheon. The first thing you hear off anyone at the beach today, contact us. And get a hold of Gallagher: try and get him over here by half eleven, we'll meet him here. Tell him we'll be wanting to go through the universities today. Get every name off C3 lists for Republicans and Lefties with any connection—even rumoured—to Arabs or Muslims or Palestinians. Cross-check against students and radicals, look for any match-ups. Even for travels to any part of the Middle East. See if there are any gunmen after being released from Portlaoise prison this last while, any fellas that ever did freelance stuff."

Minogue paused. "Do we have the manpower this morning, at the beaches and the coastal points?"

"Yes, we do," Keating answered.

"So how does it feel to be in charge of a hundred Gardai? Didn't I tell you that Hoey and Keating can do the brunt of it? How will they ever learn if they don't get to do the real McCoy?"

"Right, Jimmy. "

Kilmartin slammed the door while Minogue extricated himself from behind the wheel. Minogue would not tell Kilmartin that it was he, not Kilmartin or

Hoey or Keating, who had to answer finally to Justice Fine and a jittery Commissioner.

The Sligo train was not in yet but it was suggested that it was running on time. Kingsbridge station would have been a jewel of a building had it been kept up on the inside over the last fifty years. Its Victorian mass had recently drawn filmmakers to use parts of it, Minogue remembered. The station lay next to the Liffey within sight of the Phoenix Park. It was not near enough to the city centre for travellers' comfort. Neither was it sure of itself in an age which did not make much of the ceremony of train travel. The quays next to the station were suffused with the sulphurous stink of the Liffey, long an open sewer, and the tangy hop smell of the Guinness brewery. Minogue, climbing out of his sleep even yet, did not welcome the characteristic Dublin stink.

"Are we going to hold a sign up with her name on it, like at the airport?" asked Kilmartin. The noticeboard clicked overhead.

"Is that the Sligo job on the way in?" Kilmartin asked a passing porter.

"Sligo and Donegal," the porter drawled, content that he was addressing a policeman from the provinces—a culchie—who might not yet know that no trains went to Donegal.

Mary McCutcheon walked straight to the two policemen.

"Are we that obvious?" Kilmartin asked astringently.

"I'm a reporter," she answered. Minogue introduced himself and Kilmartin, skipping the ranks. She looked as if she hadn't slept and didn't care that she hadn't. She smoked, inhaling the smoke deeply as though to still her darting eyes. There was something mannish about her, Minogue believed. Stayed up late, no stranger to a gin and tonic? She wore cord jeans and a blouse which looked like a shirt.

Mary McCutcheon hoisted her bag better on her shoulder and walked between the two men. "It hasn't sunk in with me yet," she said to neither of them. "That much I'm sure of."

Her eyes were yellowed but still intense, with dark bluish marks under them. Middle thirties, Minogue guessed, glancing at her again. Runs herself hard.

"Thanks for coming down so quickly," Minogue said. "Will you tell us where you last saw Paul?"

"Last week. Wednesday. We met in Gaffney's pub about eight."

"Was it a date, like?"

She smiled grimly up at Kilmartin. "To anyone else it might have been. We're old friends, put it like that. We work in the same business, more or less."

It took considerable probing from Minogue to get by Mary McCutcheon's edges. She seemed to lose her caution when Minogue told her that yes, Paul Fine had been shot to death. She shook herself abruptly once more after that news, when Minogue mentioned who had claimed responsibility in the call to the press. "I heard that," she murmured, stabbing her cigarette at the ashtray: they were in the buffet now. "Who or what the hell are they? My first reaction is not to believe it," she said.

After a challenging look to both men she lapsed into an account of herself and Paul Fine. She was separated from her husband, who still lived in London, just like Paul's ex-wife, Lily.

"We met over there, two peas just out of our pods.

There was a crowd used to go to the navvies' pubs where we could expect to find Irish people. He was trying to sort out what he wanted and I was trying to forget my fella. Hilarious, you're thinking. What was funny was that we both admitted that we missed Dublin terribly, more than we ever expected. You've seen what the city has turned into here: the back-biting and the knocking and the booze and the poverty . . . all that. This damn town is rotten with journalists and only a few are worth not slamming the door on. Sounds pretty flimsy, doesn't it? Like a bad cliché—'You don't miss the place until you leave it.' I don't know."

She looked around the buffet as if targeting something to comment on.

"Neither of us really knew what it was that dragged us back to this place. I took a drop in pay for the privilege of living here and getting taxed to hell and back again. That's what seemed funny to us then. We didn't believe in that emigrant nostalgia shit, but it happened. Dublin. He was Dublin for generations, a Dublin Jew. Me, I'm Wicklow about fifteen years back. Paul had been to Israel and the States."

Minogue remembered the picture of Paul Fine standing with his parents in front of a pile of stones in some sunny, dusty place.

"He said he'd like to try Canada. A lot of his friends from school went there. But he admitted that even there he'd probably still want out. Back to Dublin."

"So you kept in touch with him when you came back here?" asked Minogue.

"'Yup. Let's get down to basics here now. For a while we thought there might be something for us. Together, I mean. For starters, I'm a *shiksa*."

"A what?"

"A Gentile. A non-Jewish woman. A non-starter for marriage prospects. Well it didn't work out, as you probably can guess. Paul was on the rebound from Lily. He was very hurt, very guilty. Lily is a tough piece of work. Tough but fair. He always said she was right to stick with her career, that he had agreed to try London, that her job was more important. No, it didn't take with us and we knew it wouldn't. We took the unusual step of staying friends. I actually got even more . . . fond of him. Me and my mother stuff. I wanted to help him, I think. That was two years ago."

Did she know anything about Paul's work in RTE, Minogue asked. Very little. He liked RTE but said that some of the other people there were hatchet-men. Meaning? Too keen for any story, ones with dirt, vendettas with the church and politicians. She didn't mind that one bit, she said: it was about time. Had he mentioned what stories he was working on recently? No. What did he do at weekends? Another few seconds' scrutiny of Minogue this time. Visited his parents sometimes, met her for dinner if she was in town. A film, a concert. Sometimes went away for a weekend to bed and breakfast it in Galway or Mayo. He liked the west.

"Didn't he have school-friends or pals he went to university with? Wouldn't they stick together socially?" Kilmartin risked.

"'They?'" she asked acidly. "You mean Jews?"

Kilmartin blinked. Minogue heard his feet moving under the table.

"Paul Fine was a Dubliner. That's not to lay claim to anything glamorous, I know, but maybe that was part of what I saw in him, my mothery business. The difference between him and my hus—my ex-husband—was

that my ex expected me to mother him when he
wanted it. Paul didn't. If I don't bowl men over and
intimidate them, I seem to mother them to death. Paul
didn't fit so well. I think he slipped through the cracks
here and there. Some people might call that backing
away, but I wouldn't. He wanted to escape a few
things, not in a cowardly way, though . . . I know he
didn't attend synagogue. His friends? I don't know.
They moved away. I'm talking about educated people,
doctors and accountants and dentists and engineers.
To the States and Canada, London. Paul stayed. That's
all. I suppose it was stubbornness and being one of the
oldest Jewish families in Ireland. I'm sure that counted
for something."

Kilmartin asked about Paul's Left-wing aspirations.
Her face showed she was mastering the temptation to
cut at Kilmartin again.

"It was an intellectual commitment. He was caught
in a lot of ways. For example, he could agree intellec-
tually about Begin and the Right-wing in Israel being
racists themselves. But you felt that if you pressed
him, he'd want to say or feel something else. Do you
know what I'm saying?"

"I think I do," Minogue said.

"Maybe it was being Dublin more than, or as much
as, being a Jew too. Ideologues don't do very well in
this city. There's that saving grace of scepticism, isn't
there?" she said morosely. "So Left-wing and Right-
wing is diluted here, maybe even dissolved. The tribal
stuff predates it, the territorial bit too.

She seemed to gather herself in a frown of concentration.

"What I mean is that nobody that I remember
pressed him or took him on as regards his opinions.

110

You can tell your Special Branch pals that Paul was very uncomfortable with extremists."

She glared at Minogue. Her anger fell away across her face then, as speculation and remembrance took over.

"One doesn't argue the toss with an Irish Jew, you see," she said resignedly. "And I think he knew that people would never bite him for his opinions the way we bite one another here. Yes, it is a 'we' and a 'they,' isn't it."

"'Strangers in a strange land,'" Minogue murmured. He didn't care that Kilmartin would take umbrage at his fraternizing with the enemy she had proven she was with her sarcastic remarks.

Mary McCutcheon blinked. Ash fell from her cigarette. "He used to say that too. As a sort of a joke. Where did you hear it?"

"I heard his father use the expression the other day," replied Minogue. No one spoke then. Minogue mustered some energy to draw himself out of the swell of pity he felt approaching.

"Tell us, Mary, if you can, any conversations you had with Paul about the Middle East or Arabs. Any connections he drew between the Middle East and Ireland, say. Did he know any Arabs or the like here?"

Mary McCutcheon did nothing to ease Minogue's discomfort at the vagueness of his fishing expedition. She smiled, as though disbelieving the claims of a suitor.

"Right now I can remember nothing. Nothing," she replied slowly.

Kilmartin mimicked speaking slowly into a microphone and left to check in with Hoey on the radio.

"I'd go for a dose of tea," Minogue said. "How about yourself, then?"

Her gaze told him that she had slipped into another domain, behind a curtain which the steady vein of cigarette smoke seemed to mark. She chewed distractedly on her thumbnail, the cigarette but inches away in the clasped hands she was now holding to her mouth.

Kilmartin was back before Minogue had settled down to the pot of tea. He motioned Minogue away from the table.

"Leave the tea and cakes routine now. They're after turning up something in Killiney," said Kilmartin.

"On the beach, is it?"

"No, up the hill in the park. An oul' wan phoned in this morning and said she heard something there on Sunday evening. You know Killiney Hill, the park and everything, don't you?"

Minogue did. Hundreds of acres of park, woods and bushes stretched from Dalkey Hill across to Killiney Hill and then down into the village of Killiney. Parts of the park were precipitous and densely wooded, almost alpine. Minogue remembered tripping over courting couples in glades when he had strolled on the Hill previously.

"A bit wild, yes," he said.

Minogue drove through the older part of the city, the Liberties, and joined the traffic swirling around Stephen's Green. He dropped Mary McCutcheon at the top of Grafton Street.

"Can we reach you at work if you're not at the other number?" he asked her.

"Sure," she replied listlessly.

Her face was showing that blankness which Minogue recognized as the first tentative and incomplete understanding that someone she knew and was close to was dead. He did not like leaving her on the street-corner with the crowds of shoppers with their busy-ness and smiles to hammer home her shock.

"It's all right. I'm going to the office now," she rebuffed his stillborn words.

As neither Minogue nor Kilmartin had a handset, they became lost in Killiney Hill Park. Minogue strayed from the path and was rewarded by the sight of a uniformed Garda standing against a tree having a clandestine smoke. The Garda directed them to a small clearing. Keating and Boylan, from the Technical Bureau, were standing to the edge of the clearing. A man wearing white cotton gloves was squatting under brambles to one side.

"There's a sample gone already, sir," said Keating.

"Was there a lot of blood?" Kilmartin asked.

"A goodly amount soaked in here," Boylan said. "There are signs that someone dug into the ground here looking for something. It wasn't any animal either, it was someone looking for a particular thing." Boylan pointed to the dark maroon patches which showed under the brambles. "A penknife or a stick or something, see?"

Kilmartin tiptoed a few steps in. The forensic expert obliged with a long white-gloved finger. He reminded Minogue of a magician or a Parisian waiter.

"Looking for the bullets, hah?" Kilmartin whispered close to Minogue's ear.

"He must be an expert, then. He checked to see if they went through and then scuffled around to get them back," said Keating.

"It's unlikely that the shot in the head was done with Fine being obliging enough to lie down. So the killer wouldn't be so damn perfect about that first one. Sure enough, if Fine got the other two after falling dead already, the killer could look in the clay for those two bullets easy enough . . . cool, calculating bastard," Kilmartin murmured.

Minogue looked around the glade. It was easily fifty paces from the nearest path. A silencer would have done it handily. What the hell had Fine been doing here? Sitting reading a book? Had he come in here with the murderer, an acquaintance?

"All these bits of bushes and leaves and things here, signs that the killer tried to cover him up. Fine was shot here, fell there." Boylan's arm swept down slowly, finally. "Got two here in the neck. He was rolled here in under the bushes and hidden. Someone dug out the two slugs then, I'd say."

"This is where he was shot," Minogue repeated.

"No sign he was dragged in here, sir. He walked in."

Minogue thought for several moments. "A detector here . . . on the way?"

"There is," Boylan answered. "The third slug might be around."

Minogue was irritated by the "slug," less because it belonged on American television than because it sounded crude and blunt.

"How'd he get Fine down on to the beach, then?" asked Kilmartin. "We're talking about a 'they' now, aren't we?"

"More to the point," Keating said, unconscious of any impertinence, "why?"

Kilmartin turned to the voices coming in from the path: four forensics, two of them carrying fat briefcases, the others lugging stakes and plastic shelters. One of the latter two unloaded nylon cord and orange stakes from a plastic bag.

"What time was this oul' wan out with the dog?" asked Kilmartin.

"Half-five, sir. Just before her tea. She said it sounded like someone slapping something off a tree trunk; like a whip, she said, or a piece of rope against the bark," Keating replied.

That'd be a silencer for sure, Minogue pondered. A hollow crack, a thud.

"She doesn't remember how many she heard exactly. Two or three, with a few seconds between one and then the other or others. 'A few.' She thought it was youngsters farting about in the woods. Her dog barked and ran into the bushes, barked and barked, and she had to call it back several times. She put the lead on him and went off home and thought no more about it."

Close to eighteen hours before the discovery of Fine's body, Minogue thought.

"Planned?" Kilmartin squinted at him.

"There's the question, all right. I don't rightly know."

"A hell of a difference between being planned and being systematic," Kilmartin growled. Minogue liked to believe then that what he heard in Kilmartin's voice was disgust at how Paul Fine had been murdered.

"The elements of clumsiness and a definite hint of expertise as well . . . I don't understand it. On the one hand he had the neck to hang around and recover the bullets. He may even have picked high-velocity bullets so he *could* get them after. How did he get his hands on a handgun and a silencer, not to speak of the

ammunition? I don't like the cut of this stuff: I keep on
having these visions of diplomatic bags. Not in our
league at all, at all. Something else, too, that I don't
much understand is, why the effort to recover the bullets unless he believed we had a chance to trace the
weapon from the bullets?"

"Maybe he plans to hold on to the gun, or has to
give it back to whoever he got it from, clean as he
can," Kilmartin suggested.

"We don't even know if it was an automatic," murmured Minogue.

"I'll tell you this: if he was such a cowboy as to stay
and get his bullets back, you can be damn sure he
picked up any casings if it was an automatic. We can't
afford to say no to that," warned Kilmartin.

"I know. But identifying the gun loomed big
enough in the killer's mind for him to stay around
and tidy up for fear—"

"Get up the yard, Matt," Kilmartin interrupted
Minogue's speculation. "We never get a ballistic
match on a third of the firearms we recover for com-
mission-of-crime weapons. If it was the Provos renting out guns to a freelance, they'd move the gun
around afterwards. We'd never get to look at it, you
can bet your bottom dollar."

Kilmartin held his palm out and looked up at the
greyed sky. Minogue saw a leaf shiver as a raindrop
landed on it.

"For the love of Jases! Lads, lads." Kilmartin turned
to the men in the clearing. "It'll be pissing now in a
minute, can ye get a bit of shelter up quick?"

The detective wielding the cord nodded.

The rain hit Minogue and Kilmartin full before
they were half-way back to the car. They shuffled

under a chestnut tree. Minogue noted the brown edges on the leaves. Already, and it only the middle of September? The rain whispered through the undergrowth, creeping around the two men. A sparrow flitted by with a hoarse twitter.

"Whatever Fine was doing here, it must have taken a couple of people to carry him down to the beach. That has to be a quarter of a mile," said Kilmartin.

"Clumsy, you're saying," Minogue suggested vacantly. The rain pleased him, that he should be marooned under a tree.

"Someone with enough nerve and training and motive to shoot Fine. He shoots Fine and then the panic sets in. It happens to anyone, no matter how expert, I can tell you. He tries to cover up the body. He's in a hurry to get out of there. Off he runs. But later on he says to himself that maybe he should move the—"

"Or someone else says to him that the body can't be left there," said Kilmartin.

"Fair enough. It might even be a different fella or group who moves the body. I can take on the idea of a conspiracy, then. But why can't the body be left up on the Hill?"

"Too easy to find?"

"Maybe so, but—"

"People are always walking their dogs up there or taking their mots up there for a bit of you-know-what," said Kilmartin.

"The oul' wan on Sunday evening didn't have the nerve to go into the bushes after the dog," Kilmartin continued.

"But why would the killer care if the body was found up there?" Minogue tried again.

"Jases, I don't know. Yet, I mean. Maybe he didn't want Fine found at all. So he goes back after dark and drags him down to where they can sling him into the water and hope the tide carries him out. High tide was eleven o'clock Sunday night, so the tide was on the way out at midnight until two o'clock in the morning. Maybe he knew that."

"'They,' 'he.' I'd like to settle on one or the other. Try this one." Minogue looked up towards the flickering leaves overhead. "He or they decided that Paul Fine mustn't be found up there because he'd have been seen by other people up on the Hill before he was killed. Say he's up walking around the park, he was to meet someone. Naturally we'd be appealing for any possible witnesses who were also up on the Hill taking the air that afternoon. What if he was with someone else, a someone who lured him into that spot where he was shot? Say the person he was with who did the killing?"

"Go on, so," Kilmartin muttered.

"It fits so far, doesn't it? The killer could have been close to Paul, so it could have been someone he knew or trusted. Now the killer doesn't want us to find a Sean Citizen who can tell us he saw Paul Fine walking around with someone who looks like X. But if Sean Citizen sees us on the telly asking for anyone who might have seen Paul Fine whose body was washed up on the beach, he'd say to himself that he was up on the Hill, not on the beach, so what would he know?"

"They don't want us knowing who Fine was with, the someone who might have killed him?"

"Or helped to kill him, Jimmy. The trouble is the intent, clear intent. Leave aside the motivation for a minute. The killer brought a gun, a handgun, and not to pick daisies with it. He or his cronies intended to kill Paul Fine. But he hadn't planned on how to dispose of the body. So it was incomplete, the planning. That's what bothers me. It was inopportune for them, time *and* place. Something must have happened to make the killing necessary."

"What if the murderer is a real expert entirely? He could have been waiting his chance a long time and just picked Killiney Hill," Kilmartin protested.

The rain was easing. Minogue realized that he had no answer to Kilmartin's alternative. He could not now distinguish between raindrops and rainwater draining from the leaves overhead.

"You could say that the killer didn't get the opportunity he was hoping for: the right time and the right place. So he up and did it there, thinking he wouldn't get his chance again," Kilmartin said.

"You think Fine was followed, stalked?"

"Now lookit, Matt," Kilmartin said as he squinted up through the branches. "If it was some crackpot politico, he must have followed Fine around the place."

"Why follow him all the way out to Killiney on a Sunday afternoon to kill him? Why not shoot him one night when he's coming home to his flat?"

Kilmartin affected to whistle. "OK, Matt," he said then. "Let's take the shagging bull by the horns. Fine may have been killed by someone he met out here, or someone he came out here with. He sets up a meeting with one of these Arab fellas to chat him up for a story he's going to do for the radio. Maybe it all starts up nice and gentlemanly, but the Libyan or the Palestinian or whatever trick-of-the-loop he is pulls out a shooter and kills Fine. For poking his nose into this business."

119

"We're assuming that Paul Fine found out, or could have found out, that there really is something going on between the Libyans and the IRA, aren't we? C3 and the Branch don't think there's anything to that," argued Minogue.

Minogue's reluctance pushed Kilmartin to snappishness. "Don't be giving me that professor look, Matt. I'm only throwing ideas around, the same as you do yourself. Keeping our options open, man dear."

So Kilmartin was gaining some hidden satisfaction from having him head the investigation, Minogue realized. I'm only doing to you what you did to me with all your notions, Kilmartin might yet say. Now how do you like being in charge? would surely follow quickly on that remark too.

"Listen," Kilmartin said in a milder tone. "Listen, listen, the cat's pissin'. Where, where, under the chair . . . What I'm saying still fits because people walking around the park would remember seeing an Arab lad. He'd stand out, complexion-wise, can't you see? If Fine came out to meet the Arab here and it was the Arab that killed him, then he'd be terrible keen to get the body away to hell from where a witness might place the Arab with poor Fine."

Minogue nodded, hoping to give Kilmartin the impression of a sage considering worthy comment. The air was cooler after the rain. The ground was yielding up rich scents from the undergrowth. They walked quickly back to the park gate. Minogue saw the rain out over the sea now, a grey curtain moving off beyond Killiney Bay.

Kilmartin phoned the Squad office. Eilis gave a little whinny of amusement when he announced himself.

"There's telepathy for you now," she murmured. Kilmartin heard her shuffle papers. "Wait a minute," she added. "Right," she said then, and spoke as though recording private thoughts for a diary. She told Kilmartin that Gardai had found remains in the back seat of a burned-out car outside the town of Bray. Bray was eight miles south of where Kilmartin now stood.

"Shite," said Kilmartin.

"Pardon?" Eilis asked archly.

"When?" Kilmartin grunted.

"The car was set on fire yesterday evening. The brigade took their time. It's a dump kind of place. Vandals, they thought. They towed it away after the fire, not knowing, and left it in the yard by the station. Someone had a good look in this morning and decided it was a body, not a bit of the back seat down on the floor of the car."

"Do they know who it is, at all?"

"No they don't. The car was an inferno entirely when the brigade arrived."

"God never closes one door except he slams another," Kilmartin grumbled and turned to Minogue. Minogue was studying the patterns of the clouds as they swept over Killiney Hill. "Here, you. You'll have to do without the benefit of my companionship on the Fine case for the moment at least," he declared to Minogue. "Bad luck comes in pairs."

"Tell them I'll go myself for starters, Eilis," Kilmartin said finally. "Give me some directions. It'll take me a half an hour from here, I'd say."

Minogue drove Kilmartin down to Killiney station. "You can arrive in style on the train again," he said.

"That'll impress them no end," Kilmartin said grimly. "Do you know what I'm going to tell you?

121

Bray is one town I hate the sight of. A town full of knackers and hurdy-gurdy men. Chancers. I'll beg a lift back later on in the day."

Kilmartin left a curse on Bray and its inhabitants dangling in the air as he entered the ticket office.

# SEVEN

**D**aithi Minogue's letter almost cost the State purse dearly in Merrion Row where Minogue came within inches of hitting the car ahead. He had been practising phrases for putting in his letter to Daithi. None satisfied him. *"It's not for me to . . ." "Your mother and I would like to think that . . ." "Although it may not seem quite apparent to you now . . ."*

The brake lights on the bus were grimy. Minogue's tyres howled and he stopped within six inches of them. Three youngsters turned around in the back seat and laughed at him. He thought of urging Daithi to take time to think things over. Maybe, Kathleen had suggested, he should send clippings from the papers to show that there were plenty of engineering jobs available here in Ireland. Daithi might repeat his protest that there was no point to working here because the income tax got you in the neck. *But there are good jobs, Daithi* . . . Bribery of sorts. The boy didn't want to be here.

How odd, bitterly amusing nearly, to hear a boy of Daithi's age complain about the state of the country. Was he using that as a way to criticize his own family? Minogue began to believe that he should have headed off this problem years ago when he had first noticed the challenge from Daithi. He should have tried to stand up for Ireland then. It had to be more than that, though: the boy wanted attention from him, answers. Did Daithi like his parents too much to be able to get angry with them?

Attention, answers, someone to defend the island. Minogue couldn't do that and not feel foolish. It might have been better to have been stricter with him, to have had prescriptions and advice, to have been the paterfamilias more. How had Minogue come adrift from the role which other men his age found so satisfying and so natural and so damned easy? Little to offer Daithi now, beyond some assurance that he could not put in words. The Oedipus stuff is rubbish, he thought. Were parents supposed to resist their children so much? It wouldn't be any help to tell Daithi to trust his own experience. The boy was but twenty-three now. Did he want to be summoned, scolded perhaps, worried over? These were signs of love, apparently. These were things parents were supposed to do?

Detective Garda Seamus Hoey was indeed as capable as Kilmartin had told Minogue—even more capable than Kilmartin thought. Kilmartin used him as a feather in his cap (how shrewd Jimmy Kilmartin was to have held on to Hoey when he had arrived as a trainee) but Shea Hoey knew to fit Kilmartin's measures. He gave every sign of being calmly diligent. At home, in his bachelor life in the flat he had in Sandymount, Minogue could guess at a Hoey who might even play a piano for pleasure, who should marry and make someone happy.

Minogue's gaze fled to Eilis when Hoey looked over, aware that Minogue had been looking at him. Kilmartin had that knack of spotting talents, all right. Eilis was permitted to be offhand. Her cool but unaffected Garboisms hid the fact that she was brainy, not merely distant. Eilis's eccentricities were part of the price which intelligence paid in a world gone mad with convention and system, Minogue believed. Her job was to conduct the symphony of inquiries, meetings and reports which formed the day-to-day business of the Investigation Section.

When the mandarins in the Department of Justice decided that the Investigation Section should also deal with other serious crime, Kilmartin had stood his ground. Why not a proper paid-up Emergency Response Unit system? A Special Task Force with regular armed teams on patrol in Dublin? More resources to the Hold-Up Squad? With conniving, alliances and bull-headed shrewdness, Kilmartin had helped effect all these. There was little that Kilmartin would not do in pursuit of his passion to keep the Murder Squad together as a separate unit, if not in name then in function.

Nonetheless, Jimmy Kilmartin was not unaware of Chief Supers and Assistant Commissioners grumbling that their respective divisions should shortly have enough trained personnel for murder investigations and that they'd be needing Dublin-based expertise infrequently. This was so because Gardai circulated through the Investigation Section as trainees, learning the trade and returning to their divisions. Kilmartin had been canny enough to spot trainee talent and thus promptly appropriate detectives like Seamus Hoey, a yawny and sometimes moody Galwegian who had been stationed in Athlone, the most boring town in Ireland. Hoey soaked up information like a sponge and listened to everything. Kilmartin and Minogue had learned to be alert when Hoey began his sentences with the roundabout bashfulness of "Well, you may think this is a bit odd of me to be bringing this up here and now but—"

Detective Garda Keating was more obviously methodical and he liked to bear the cross of filtering through enormous amounts of data. Keating was so enamoured of the new age that he had bought an expensive computer for his own use and had taught himself many things in his spare time at home. He had unwisely mentioned his purchase to Eilis in one of their almost sibling squabbles. Keating, a bachelor younger and less understanding than Hoey, had some vague notion that Eilis was to be fenced with because she was unmarried and not unattractive.

"A computer, is it," Minogue remembered Eilis saying. "Can't you go out and throw yourself at girls and disport yourself like a normal buck and not be sitting at one of those things getting a humpy back and a low sperm count with the radiation?"

Keating liked to be given impossible tasks with large amounts of information to immerse himself in: Photofit and Identikit features, car registration plates, clothing manufacturers' weaves of synthetic materials, bank account transactions from ten years ago—all brought a frown to his features until he was actually in the search and enjoying the impossibility of his task, away from superiors who expected him to admit it would be easy for him.

Minogue saw that Hoey had not shaved, and he guessed that he had kipped down for part of the night on a couch in the First Aid room on the ground floor. Hoey had his feet up and was smoking. If this was co-ordinating a task force of policemen, Minogue wanted to be thus trained.

"Well, Shea. You heard there may be another out in Bray?"

"Yep. The Killer phoned a minute ago to say it's 90 per cent sure it's a murder. The fire was started with petrol sprinkled inside the car, he thinks. Or the firemen in Bray think so."

The Killer: Kilmartin. Minogue had heard that his own nickname, very infrequently applied because it had never caught, was Moonie.

"Have we anything from the men posted at the beaches?"

"No. There was one oul' lad complaining about teenagers interfering with one another and drinking Johnny-jump-up on the beach all summer. Nothing at all off Killiney beach proper. I've heard nothing from Killiney Hill Park, the site, either. They hit a few bits of metal with the detector but all they have is hairpins and bits of things. How do you like that for news?"

"And Paul Fine's tapes?"

Hoey picked up a page with a handwritten list inscribed on it. He handed it to Minogue.

"Keating has three fellas now doing the videos and the cassettes again. He's out in Fine's flat himself, fighting off pots of tea from her nibs, Miss Connolly. I think maybe we were fibbing about him looking like Charlton Heston in the Moses film. Maybe she expected him to arrive out in one of those short little skirts the men used to wear then. I'm going by the pictures from the Catechism, do you remember?"

"Will I ever forget?" Minogue murmured the stock answer as he looked down the list. Interviews with politicians about the upcoming Ard Fheis, the party-in-government's convention. There was almost one hour with members of the Irish-Arab society. There were no interviews with Arab students. A ten-minute telephone interview with a David Thornbury, chairman of Middle Eastern Studies at Sussex University. Scatty interviews, taken on the hoof apparently, with bus drivers and conductors in Dublin about what they thought of the forthcoming strike. A half-hour with a self-help group of former psychiatric patients in Limerick. That'd be what Fitzgerald called his fairy stories, the good news.

"Thirteen hours in total. There're no interviews with any of those Arab lads Gallagher was interested in after he saw Fine's index. It looks like they were on the level about not knowing Fine. He must have been just starting out, getting names like we keep on being told. Still and all, he must have done some research or reading up on his topics, though, because . . . remember the newspaper references on his index of topics and stories?"

Minogue nodded.

"He must have made notes. Keating might find 'em out in the flat. Or Murtagh, in his desk over in RTE—"

"Did we have any call-ins from the radio and telly appeal last night?"

"Let me see. I think there were three or four only last night and . . . upwards of ten so far today. We've followed up on seven of them altogether. There was a fella worked the ticket office in the train station out in Dalkey on Sunday. He thinks it might have been Fine that came through the turnstile, he says, but he's not so sure. He saw the photos that were dropped off at all the stations. It was his missus that phoned us up; he didn't think it was worth bothering about because he was dithering. The rest are people to do with places along the coast. Walking on the beach on Sunday evening, some of them. Fella in Bulloch harbour saw a boat going out late that night. Nothing yet."

"So we still can't place Paul Fine after he left his flat Sunday morning," Minogue said gloomily.

"Not yet, sir. One of the callers—called in last night about eleven—asked for 'the Investigating Officer.' Switchboard gave out your name but when we couldn't give you to him on a plate he put down the phone."

"What about those other tapes, those videotapes from the flat? What's on them?"

"Right,"said Hoey, swinging his feet off the desk. "I nearly forgot. They're all off the telly. RTE programmes too, current affairs and news. Bore the arse off you, it would. The economy, unemployment . . . discussions off talk-shows with bigwigs out of different parties. There are—hold on, I'll get the sheet— four segments on the last Ard Fheis, last year's, with Chief whipping up the party faithful and promising the world."

Minogue could imagine the scene on the video. Ireland's Taoiseach, the Prime Minister, the Chief with his hawk face to match his manner and his past—a buccaneer Nero—taking the applause of sycophants.

"I watched some of them myself last night," Hoey continued. "Had a bit of a laugh, I can tell you. There was one good one, actually; maybe I shouldn't say good one. Do you remember that series, last year, on the security situation?"

Minogue did. Having met Mickey Fitzgerald since, he could imagine Fitzgerald's hand in such a series, even though it was on the television. A memo had been circulated right to each Garda and clerical worker in the Force after that series. The memo cautioned them that information and opinions about security and policing were not to be given out to members of the press or the public. The programmes had made much of leaks from disgruntled Gardai doing Border duty and oblique grumbles that the Army felt ill-equipped to detect and deal with incursions by British Army units into the South.

"Well, you had the Minister for this and the Minister for that, the Opposition shouting blue murder and the rest of it. Maybe Fine was trying to resurrect the issue again—that's what the media do, isn't it? Keep things on the boil and come back to heat up the same issues if they're in danger of cooling down too much."

"I suppose," replied Minogue. "Still nothing on video to do with Arabs or students?"

"No, sir. I had a fella go to the archives in RTE. He's to see if Fine was looking through any material to do with his stories. I found out they keep records of requests, you see."

"Good for you. It's as well one of us is wide awake, Shea," murmured Minogue.

Minogue perused his copy of the autopsy report from the State Pathologist's office. Entry wound was consistent with impact and penetration by a high-velocity bullet. Gun could have been discharged up to two feet from the head—

Minogue then tried reading between the lines of the appended comments from the ballistics section of the Technical Bureau. The commentary seemed to have a strained, reluctant tone. Minogue wondered if this was an elaborate way of saying they had nothing with which to direct the investigation from a forensic viewpoint here. Most probably a .38 or .30/.32 calibre. What was that in the metric again? Minogue flicked the page and consulted the small box-chart for conversion: .38 was 9 mm, .30 was 7.62 mm, .32 was 7.65. The bullets were almost certainly of fully jacketed construction. For the bullet to penetrate two bone barriers, it would in all likelihood have had to be round-nosed as well. There was no mention of metal traces from the bullet's passage. Whoever wrote the ballistics report would have looked at the pathology report first anyway. No fragments of the casing which could have pinpointed a manufacturer. The Continentals tended to favour brass or even copper jackets, the Yanks went for steel or cupronickel, Minogue recalled vaguely.

Fully jacketed round-nose bullets: high velocity, high energy but low stopping power because of the penetration. Minogue wondered what Thatcher Scale meant in the report: the Iron Lady herself? For penetration of two cranial bone barriers, the bullets had to have a Thatcher value of at least fifty—

A flitting notion stirred in Minogue's mind again. An attribution of deadly expertise, of intent, had crept into even the bland prose of the ballistics report—a report which had been cautious from the start because it was only a commentary on the pathology work: ballistics had had neither weapon nor ammunition to examine. It was a gun for working up close, not a cannon. It was very rare to find calibres larger than .38s bothering with fully jacketed ammunition. Those handguns were designed with stopping power in mind, their bullets chosen to leave their mark, to gouge, to dredge, to flatten ... to damage quickly.

Minogue shivered. He turned the page and looked below the conversion table. A hand-drawn box followed, with a summary of ammunition in use by Gardai and the Army. The Army used 7.65 mm for their sub-machine guns, but not of high-velocity manufacture. The Garda Special Branch units and squads had access to and training in machine pistols which used 9 mm ammunition, a fit with the Walther PPK automatics which had rapidly gained favour over the last decade as Gardai used firearms more. The report noted that it was likely that both Army and Gardai held some stocks of high-velocity ammunition which could be used with a handgun ... but such rounds would almost certainly be employed for evaluation and comparison purposes, in a restricted environment such as laboratory testing.

Great, thought Minogue darkly as his eyes wavered down over the point-form conclusions again. Barrel-length of a handgun had to be at least four and one half inches to effect high-velocity at all ... He retrieved a ruler from his drawer and spread his fingers along it. You could still carry an automatic handily enough in your jacket pocket ... A reminder that automatics were much easier to secure good silencers on.

There were the more punctilious conclusions then, the writer of the report glad, and even smug about showing command of his material ... There were several licensed copies of the popular parabellum designs like SIG-Petters, Walthers and Berettas, but there were also over a dozen known unlicensed copies of perennials such as Walther PPKs and .38s being mass-manufactured in Hungary, East Germany, Czechoslovakia . . . Consideration should be given to the large numbers of Soviet Tokarevs (formerly Mauser 7.63 pistols) in circulation since unrest in the Middle East had become more widespread after 1967. Tokarevs were arguably the automatic pistol best suited to use with high-velocity ammunition . . . *Diplomatic bag*, Minogue's gargoyle muttered within: *This was an assassin's gun.*

Minogue snorted with exasperation. He laid the sheaf of papers back in a wire-mesh tray on his desk. He would phone Gallagher within the hour if the same Gallagher hadn't phoned by then to tell him what the yield was from the Special Branch files. There had to be somebody close to Paul Fine, Minogue's thoughts protested, someone to whom he chatted, or at least mentioned what he was planning for the weekend. He stood up from the desk. All the tables and desks in the squad room were occupied and two blackboards on wheels had appeared overnight. One was used for schedules of assignments, the other was mostly blank, with entries for what they knew of the last days and hours of Paul Fine.

Minogue looked at the faces of the dozen policemen on the task force. He recognized more than half of those in the room. The ones he knew were detectives from the Central Detective Unit, rafted over from the Puzzle Palace. Kilmartin had ordered detectives drafted in on the case to squeeze into the squad room yesterday evening to listen to Hoey. Twice as many ordinary Gardai, mostly from stations in the Dublin Metropolitan South Divisions, would receive their instructions in turn from the policemen who had attended this meeting.

With the discovery of the murder site away from the beach, Minogue would now have to make a new media appeal to persons who had been taking the air on Killiney Hill on Sunday. Two full days ago—

Hoey was on the telephone now. Even Eilis looked busy as she rattled on a typewriter. A short detective with a gaucho moustache (Minogue wondered how lax the codes were becoming, as he saw an incarnation of a Venetian boatman in the detective's face) stopped by Eilis's desk. He held out a video-cassette to her but she nodded towards Hoey. The detective stood by Hoey's desk until Hoey put down the phone. After a brief conversation, Hoey smiled. The detective said something else and Hoey laughed outright. He took the tape and removed it from its case. The gaucho Venetian (Minogue thought he remembered him as a Sullivan) shrugged, smiled again, and walked away. Hoey noticed Minogue sitting on the edge of his desk, and ambled over.

"You look like you're ready for Honolulu."

Minogue shook himself out of his reverie. "Uh. Like yourself. I'd like to be sitting in Montparnasse with an espresso burning a hole in the table in front of me. Here, Shea, why don't you go out yourself and get yourself a bite? A cup of tea or something."

"I might, at that. We're at the hump, I suppose," Hoey answered.

Minogue nodded his assent. "The hump" was Hoey's word for the doldrums which inevitably afflicted investigators as they moved beyond the beginnings of a difficult investigation. Minogue had heard Kilmartin call it "the fuckin' Sahara stage." One evening in a pub he had gone through the plot and events of *The Lost Patrol*, a favourite film of his because it starred Victor McLaglen, as a way of illustrating the trials of a murder investigation. Minogue had forgotten what Kilmartin had likened the unseen snipers of the desert to, by way of comparison with the course of an investigation, but the memory of the whole had stayed with him.

Any murder that wasn't committed by a friend or relative of the victim, any murder that had no witnesses, was difficult. After the initial flow of information, the setting up of assignments and statements, the piecing together of a picture of the victim, came the lull. In this lull occurred the really dogged police work. Sometimes this Sargasso stage lasted for months.

"Plenty of time before anything breaks, I suppose," Hoey added wearily. "Maybe I'll go and watch that video again. They missed a bit the first time around. A few minutes of something sandwiched into another clip. It might have been there from the time the tape was used for something else, though, because it starts suddenly and ends suddenly."

"Anything of interest?"

"It could have been Fine on the gossip trail. Remember Fitz said it was Fine's turn to go through the laundry basket, to see what shenanigans our elected representatives had been up to."

"The same Mickey Fitzgerald calls it accountability, if I recall," said Minogue.

"Hah. The Ard Fheis is coming up, so maybe they were in a hurry to find some dirt on anybody. There's a bit of an interview with what's-his-name, Gorman, on *Meet the Press*. You know that programme that does be on after ordinary people go to bed? Fifteen minutes before they shut down for the night, fellas off the newspapers poking at different politicians every week. Gorman was on; 'the Man in the Wings' they call him. They were trying to bait him about who'd step into the Chief's shoes."

"As if the same Chief is ever going to let go his grip," said Minogue. Hoey smiled wanly at the uncharacteristic vitriol in Minogue's tone.

"Exactly. Everyone over the age of six months knows that Gorman'd love to wake up one morning and find himself running the country. 'Ireland in the new age' and 'new economic realities,' that's his line, isn't it?"

"You know a lot more than I do about him. The brain goes dead on me as regards that stuff. I can't tell one of them from the other when they talk like that. All I know is that he was shuffled into Defence last year, a new Minister."

"Ah sure, it's only the fact that Gorman is a distant relation on my mother's side. He's Galway, is Gorman. A lot of people at home think he's the cat's pyjamas entirely. He's off the farm but he lectured in economics at the university. Speaks French, but knows how to handle a hurley stick and even swallow pints, I heard. But don't think the Chief doesn't know about Gorman. They have to be sort of civil to one another. Gorman is on the tape saying something about 'unquestioned allegiance' to the Chief. Maybe Fine was going to interview Gorman, and he wanted to be able to quote him from that television show—"

Minogue decided to leave Hoey to his cynical pleasures with the tape. He'd have to be thinking of a dinner himself soon. He looked to the blackboards again. The conference and assessment was set for half-two today: that'd be to give God Almighty time to conjure up a weighty press release for the tea-time news on the

telly. Minogue turned away from the cacophony of
phones and typewriters, settled himself in his chair,
and tried the pathologist's report again. His eyes followed the print but took in nothing beyond an odd
word. He turned to the photocopies of the notes which
the policemen on telephone work had made. Some
had still to be typed. Thirteen calls in all, with officers
dispatched to get statements on seven. Minogue lost
his concentration again.

*Strangers in a strange land . . .* Fine had used the
phrase with an unmistakable irony. It might have
been true for those Jewish families who had fled
Russia and Lithuania to come to Ireland after the
Tsar's May Laws in eighteen-eighty something,
Minogue guessed as he tried to recall more from his
visit to the Jewish Museum and his own reading. Fine
must have meant it ironically. The Fines had been
here for nearly 200 years; Justice Fine was a Supreme
Court judge—

Paul Fine had never wanted to leave Dublin, it
seemed. It was his city. Married to a Dublinwoman,
Minogue had cracked some of the code which might
explain Dubliners' attachment to their shabby capital.
Maybe needing to return to Dublin had cost Paul Fine
his marriage. His father didn't know the names of any
of Paul's friends beyond his schooldays, and several of
these had emigrated. He knew Mary McCutcheon and
Paul's boss whom he misnamed as Fitzpatrick. Had all
Paul's school-friends, the friends he'd met at temple as
a youngster, the friends he'd spent summer holidays
with—had they all emigrated? Or had he wanted some
breathing space after returning from London, and
avoided them? A lapsed Jew, like a lapsed Catholic,
Mickey Fitz had said. In other words, there was no

such thing: once in, never out. It was in your marrow, in your dreams, even fifty years after you had renounced it. Only a fool could think his life was being run by what his thoughts suggested to him on a fine sunny day. Gallagher, phone Gallagher.

Minogue was switched three times before he heard Gallagher.

"Yes, I have a tentative list of, let's call them sympathizers. Irish, I mean. I have thirty-eight." He sounded pleased with himself, Minogue believed. "I pulled in even the marginal ones. There are others, of course, members of groups we don't monitor because they're harmless."

Minogue jumped in with both feet. "Will the Special Branch be wanting to conduct their own interviews themselves, Pat?"

"Oh, I'd say there's be interest in that here, all right. We work through our own contacts here, you probably know. On the inside, you see," Gallagher added awkwardly. "The Chief Super knows about my assignment here and . . ."

Minogue remembered that Chief Superintendent Farrell of the Special Branch was rumoured to model himself after J. Edgar Hoover. The Branch was his personal army against subversives and criminals, and no-one would tell him how to do his business.

"I'll ask to clear it, then, so that Branch officers can follow up on your list and we don't be tripping over one another," said Minogue.

Minogue liked to think that he noticed the relief in Gallagher's voice after that. Gallagher would not miss the hint either, he was sure. When the press release went out this evening, few would pause to wonder what the phrase "joint Murder Squad and Special

Branch task force" meant—beyond apparent co-oper-
ation, that was.

Kilmartin was back at his office minutes before
two o'clock. Spotting Minogue, he wavered in his
path and walked towards him. "Honest to God,"
said Kilmartin, looking over his shoulder, "there's a
mountain of paper inside on my desk. I don't doubt
but that I'll have a pain in me head like the kick off a
horse if I have to read all that today. Did you have
your dinner?"

"I had a bowl of soup and a sandwich," Minogue
replied.

"That's what I should have had meself, I'm telling
you. I ate something in a pub in Bray and bejases I still
don't know what it might have been. Steak and kid-
ney something. Came out of a tin with a snap of
Lassie on it, I bet. The heartburn is bad after that. Bray
is the back of the neck."

"What's the story in Bray, then?"

"There's someone burned to a crisp in the back of a
Volkswagen Golf. Looks like a man, but I wouldn't
bet too much on that. The fire was so hot that bits of
the damn car went and melted themselves. Metal, I
mean. How do you like that?"

Minogue was tempted to reply that he didn't think
it was so hot.

At half-past two, Minogue counted eighteen policemen arrayed about the squad room. Gallagher sat with
an untidy-looking Special Branch colleague. The room
was soon full of smoke. The typewriters were silent.
Two detectives were sharing a joke. Hoey was back in
time and Minogue let him have his lead. Hoey asked
to hear from the scenes-of-crime examiners first.

The blood had tested positive as Paul Fine's type. No bullets had been found on the site. An area of forty by forty metres square had been examined so far. A dragnet of the beach had produced nothing pertinent to the murder. The detective remarked that a prophylactic had been found on the beach, and Minogue did not twig what he meant until he looked up to see several policemen smiling.

Three interviews with citizens responding to the media appeals were still in progress. The remainder had elicited no direct knowledge of anything to do with the murder. The best information to date had been the call from the woman which had led to the murder site.

These not unexpected results still moved Kilmartin to some testy rhetoric. "Why did these busybodies phone up then, I ask you? Have they nothing better to be doing?"

"All is not lost," Hoey replied sententiously. "There is one fella, a ticket man at Dalkey station, the one whose wife phoned up. He says he's no more than fifty-fifty sure he saw Fine coming through the turnstile sometime Sunday. Just after dinner-time, he thinks. Not very solid at all."

"Alone?" Hoey asked.

"Yes. Seeing as he must have got *on* the train, if it was Fine who was there in Dalkey station, we'll get in touch with the men who were on shifts on Sunday at the train stations. We have the snapshots in all stations now, anyway."

"Is there anything worth holding our breaths over with these calls that are going on at the moment?" Minogue asked.

"Maybe one of them, sir. He's having a bit of trouble remembering his times on account of him having a few jars on Sunday night. He went to the beach, not actually onto the beach, but into the car-park after he came out of a pub in Ballybrack. He was courting his mot in a car. He says she was driving, if you don't mind."

"Maybe he's the boyo who left the frenchies on the beach," Kilmartin said.

"That's a good one," the detective lied. "Fact is he took the trouble to phone. I think that the public in general is very taken aback with this. That the victim was shot three times in the head and him being a, you know, a Jew. This fella anyway, he phoned us before he realized he didn't really have anything of substance to offer us. He said there were two other cars parked in the car-park, maybe three. Up to the same trick-acting, maybe. But there was one car there before he came and still there after he left. He was sure there was nobody in the car while he was there. That's as much as we got out of him."

"Type, age . . . colour?" said Kilmartin.

"Sorry, sir."

"Ye'll be ready for calls tonight to do with the site out on Killiney Hill instead?" asked Minogue.

"To be sure."

Hoey read a précis of the autopsy. He pointed to the blackboards then and worked his way through the questions which several of the policemen put to him.

"Are these all the stories Fine was working on?" one asked him earnestly.

"All we know of so far. See this one here, the one on the Arab students? He didn't get that far on this, not to the stage of interviewing the students he had on a list. He'd read up on some material associated with this work he had planned. Look over at the items here listed from one of his indexes . . . Video-cassettes on stories he was supposed to cover or dig up. This list here . . . that's of the audio-cassettes we found."

Hoey nodded to Keating. Keating stood, moved to the blackboards and talked his way methodically down the lists.

". . . So far, going through the stuff in his desk, there's nothing standing out. He kept paper files on these stories and he had odds and ends in another general file. Clippings he did himself, a note about some programmes done before. We're still going through programmes he put material together for in the past year, to see if he made himself any enemies. The nearest we've come is a story on a fertilizer plant polluting part of the River Barrow. He was on to that story first and it went down very well. That means the press took up his story and used his report after it came on the radio. Fine was interested in what-do-you-call-it, ecology—"

Eco-Al, Minogue remembered—Paul Fine's involvement in what the Special Branch had decided was not merely ecology but a Trojan Horse for godless communism to turn the Irish on their heads. Minogue had not felt the need to fence with Gallagher on that issue of surveillance of Eco-Al, to ask what exactly the Branch's "good reason to believe" or "substantial links" meant as regards Eco-Al's being a stalking-horse for the Bolshevist hordes.

Hoey returned to the blackboard. He looked comical to Minogue, who didn't know why. The term *demonstrative* did not fit Shea Hoey but there he was, rapping a forefinger on the board like a teacher.

"So we know that Paul Fine did not bump into any gunmen, political or just over-the-wall thugs, in the course of his journalistic work. It looks like he didn't get the opportunity to rub such parties the wrong way at all," Hoey repeated. "Such that they might want to be after shooting him."

The atmosphere in the room was now sweaty, airless. Yawns were spreading around the room, followed by stretches.

". . . nothing we've discovered yet in his personal life so far," Hoey went on. He paused and pointed to the cluster of names around Paul Fine's.

"His wife, his ex-wife, is an English girl. She's the same religion as he is. They parted and she's living beyond in London. No disputes there, except she didn't want to live in Dublin and that was that. No rows with his brother or sister . . . Two years in college, then London . . . then he got married, stayed on in London, didn't like it . . . Into RTE when he came back to Dublin."

"Do we have all his bits of paper and what-have-you?" asked a young detective. Minogue recognized the face of the blow-in from the Central Detective Unit. Doyle? Yes, Doyle.

"For his work? Yep," Hoey replied. "Insofar as we have gone through his belongings at work and in his flat."

"Was he carrying anything with him when he left his flat Sunday morning?" Doyle asked.

"The landlady didn't see anything. He may have had some little pocketbook or a notebook."

"Tape-recorders," Doyle said. "Don't them journalist types carry them around?"

Minogue liked Doyle's persistence. Jimmy Doyle, was it? No, Kevin . . . Danny?

"We haven't found one yet. And you're right, he would probably have had some class of a recording device too," Hoey allowed.

"But aren't they full of themselves with those things, word-processors, these days?" asked Doyle.

"Computers?" said Kilmartin.

"No disks or diskettes," said Hoey cautiously. "And he didn't have a computer."

That seemed to stay Doyle's speculation. Hoey waited for a rejoinder. Hearing none, he turned to the board where a time line had been drawn to represent the last few days of Paul Fine's life. An asterisk stood beside 5-5:30 p.m. Sunday, followed by a question mark in brackets. Hoey cleared his throat and began at the top of the board. Minogue's eyes stayed fixed on the asterisk while he listened wearily.

"Excuse me now for interrupting again," Doyle said. "I have this mental block about this man's work, the journalism thing. I know it's radio and all that, but doesn't every journalist have to know about computers and the like, these days? That's how the newspapers are done now: I saw it on the telly. You even have correspondents sending their stuff in on telephone lines, off their own little computers. Surely to God RTE has something like that?"

"Phone 'em up, then, like a good man," said Kilmartin, interrupting with an irritable scratch of his head.

Hoey resumed after Doyle had gone to find a phone in some privacy. Minogue's eyes returned involuntarily to the asterisk, the probable time of Paul Fine's death. There was still no entry for the last Saturday of his life. Mickey Fitz had called Paul Fine the equivalent of a lapsed Catholic. He'd hardly have been at home observing his Sabbath, so.

Minogue's mind slipped free of its moorings again. Paul Fine, the son of a prominent Irishman, an Irishman who was also a Jew. A Jew who practised his religion, a son who did not. Friction. A man who was a legal scholar, an authority with a mountain of accomplishments behind him: a son who seemed unsettled, who hadn't found his own path. Paul Fine's brother was a dentist in London, his sister a research scientist. Minogue imagined the talk around the Fines' tea-table. Would Paul have recoiled when his father mentioned how Paul's sister had made an important breakthrough in her work, or how Paul's brother had had to move to bigger offices because his practice was getting so large?

A mood of irony settled on Minogue then as he realized that Paul Fine had wanted to return to Dublin, while his brother and sister, successes, had left. Did Dublin beckon to those who would be failures elsewhere?

Doyle reappeared towards the end of Hoey's description of what clues could come out of the murder site.

"There," he said in the pause which Hoey made for him, "I knew they had to have something there. I don't watch the telly for nothing, you know. RTE has a big computer that the staff can use." He glanced at his notebook. "It's called a Newstar computer. It's wired up to a cable from an international press agency. The fella I was talking to says that not many of the staff bother to use that part of it but it might be that Fine did use it for typing stuff up. People have their own bits of the computer, like their own filing cabinet, on board the contraption."

"Is there anything under Fine's name on it?" Kilmartin asked.

"Wouldn't tell me. 'Need an authority to do that,' says he to me. I told him I was a Guard and he could call Harcourt Street and find out, but no go. Users have their own codes anyway, like their own little keys to their locker."

"So there could be some of Fine's stuff on this computer, stuff we haven't seen," Minogue joined in.

"Could be, sir," Doyle replied. "Why don't you send me over there with a bit of something to wave at them so as I can find out?"

# EIGHT

**F**our o'clock brought Minogue beyond temptation and he fled to Bewley's Café. He was through the door and fumbling for his car keys when he heard Kilmartin calling behind him. He pretended not to hear him over the traffic but Kilmartin outpaced the slowing Minogue. Minogue wanted to be alone in noisy and contented solitude, in the ruck which made up Bewley's, but he didn't want Kilmartin, stricken with a heart attack from running, on his conscience.

Minogue was in a bad enough humour for not having thought of other places Fine might have stored his work. He had phoned Fitzgerald, hoping to short-cut Doyle's work by finding out whether Paul Fine did use the computer. Fitzgerald had told him that he didn't know and Minogue had had to believe him.

"Here's your hat, what's your hurry?" wheezed Kilmartin, falling into step with Minogue. "Jases, you're out of there like a blue-arsed fly. Take your time, man dear. I know where you're off to, anyway."

"How so?" said Minogue.

"I asked Her Nibs," said Kilmartin, referring to the Delphic Eilis.

"'His honour is making a bee-line for Bewley's,' says she. 'By the look in his eye.' Wait till I tell you—I just heard that Ryan woman was released without bail. She's home with her children."

Minogue didn't believe Kilmartin at first.

"I swear to God. She was charged with manslaughter, given her dinner and put out on to the street. That's not the half of it. There was a crowd of Women's Action heavies with her, having a hooley and dancing in the street. Bedlam. They took her back to the farm, bejases, and there's a crowd of them staying to help her with the farm work and make sure nobody comes around that might blackguard her."

Kilmartin began to laugh. It was the laugh of a Hollywood castaway gone mad from thirst in the Sahara, Minogue believed.

"It's a bloody commune on the farm. WAMmers milking the pigs and feeding grain to the dog. A pack of lesbians in a commune, a revolution. They might declare a republic and what would we do then? Ha ha," Kilmartin continued. Unbidden, he sat heavily into the passenger seat.

While Minogue piloted sourly down the quays, Kilmartin repeated bits of his news and views all the way to George's Street. The newspaper headlines on a stand by the entrance to Bewley's cut him short. He stopped and grasped Minogue's arm. Minogue looked to the papers for more about Marguerite Ryan, the new heroine of Ireland.

"Look at that, would you," Kilmartin hissed. "The busmen are going on strike. Isn't that the last straw entirely?"

Minogue did not think so. He carried his large white coffee to a table near the window. Normally he would have tried to avoid this rather moribund branch of Bewley's by loping on down to Westmoreland Street, another five minutes away. With Kilmartin in tow he had decided to cut his losses. Kilmartin sat down opposite. He could not stop shaking his head every few minutes when he returned to the subject of Marguerite Ryan. Minogue wondered if that was how erotic obsessions showed themselves.

"She's actually getting away with murder. We did all the paperwork and sewed it up tight. The next thing you know is the Director of Public Prosecutions throws out the murder charge and . . . Maybe we ought to phone up and tell them she gave him one stab for every year of his mortal life."

"Let the hair sit, Jimmy," said Minogue acidly. "It's not proof of premeditation. Stress can drive a body to episodic madness. That's the be-all and end-all of it for me."

Kilmartin was agog at his colleague's dismissal.

"The urge might have been so strong that she couldn't stop herself. Possessed," Minogue added.

"The assessment says she's the full shilling, Matt. There's nothing about temporary insanity. Didn't I read some rubbish in the papers about the WAMmers saying it has to do with a woman's monthlies?"

The coffee had boosted Minogue into sarcasm.

"Anybody do a psychiatric assessment of Francis Xavier Ryan?"

Kilmartin made a face and sipped at his coffee.

"As for the premenstrual syndrome, I haven't had it myself," Minogue added. "I do be feeling sorry enough for myself when I have a little headache, even. Menstruation is no lark, I understand."

Minogue enjoyed Kilmartin's shock as he noted a face turning from the next table. Kilmartin bowed lower over the table and whispered like a schoolboy whose blasphemy might be overheard: "You mean to say that if your wife or mine gave either of us a clout one day and then said it wasn't her fault on account of her you-know-what, that'd be fine and well by you?"

"It may be that I actually deserve a clout every now and then. It's to your own head you should be looking, Jimmy. "

"Thanks very much."

"Let me say this: Marguerite Ryan is no Tipperary Joan of Arc, but sooner or later she might have had to defend her life with that husband the way he was. Maybe she was the victim of a crime we paid no attention to."

Minogue hid behind his coffee cup then. He expected Kilmartin to send a taunt his way about being bossed around by Kathleen and Iesult at home, now that Daithi was in the States. Kilmartin changed the subject instead.

"I say we sack the busmen and be done with it. People are fed up with them hooligans dictating to the public and causing hardship to everyone just because they want a few bob. They're robbing us blind with the fares anyway."

"*Sic transit*—" murmured Minogue.

"You're telling me," said Kilmartin quickly.

"Are you going to run for election on it?"

"Easy for you to laugh. I was half tempted several times to do something in politics: I couldn't do much worse than the shaggers and shoneens we have now. Leadership is what we badly need if the country is to get going again," declared the statesman Kilmartin.

Going where, Minogue wondered.

"Do you have anyone in mind?"

"There's the fly in the ointment, Matt," Kilmartin said earnestly. "I can't see anyone on the scene right now. It breaks my heart to see the government gearing up for the Ard Fheis with the Chief and his cronies working up to an election after they've wasted some money on their constituencies. It's a machine at work, not democracy, isn't it?"

"You're quite right."

Kilmartin looked around the restaurant as though to glean more pleasant topics to raise with Minogue. Minogue's thoughts drifted towards Paul Fine. Fine had been assigned to work on digging up dirt on these office-holders which even Kilmartin had consigned to the large domain of yobbos and chancers. It was an assignment which Paul Fine hadn't been thrilled about. Was it because he was by birth excluded from the tribal in-fighting which Irishmen like Kilmartin revelled in?

"What about that Gorman, would he be to your liking?" Minogue asked Kilmartin.

"There's an interesting one. Mind you he's part and parcel of what has the country going to pot now. That's not to say that he's a completely lost cause, though. Maura at home was telling me the other day that Gorman is by no means a yes-man. He's a good Minister, if you toe the line and keep up with him. It's not an easy bed to lie in, being a Minister for Defence and you not being forty years of age, you know. But Gorman's popular and he's been to school too. Still and all, if he's anybody worth thinking about why is he with that crowd of hill-and-dale robbers that're running the country into the ground right now?"

"Maybe he didn't want to be a voice in the wilderness," said Minogue coyly.

"Me bollicks. I don't know if he has the belly in him for real leadership, though. When it comes down to the wire he'll be lining up at the trough with the rest of them—wait'll you see. The Chief has his hatchet-men out all the time listening to see who might be getting too popular or who might be getting ideas of stepping out of line. They'd give Gorman the chop—very rapid like—if they found he was slipping the leash on the Chief."

"For a man who doesn't like the current government, you know a lot about them."

"Ah, go on, I don't know more than the next man. You know yourself that the fella who's belly-aching about this or that party is the fella who'll vote for them come the election. 'Tis the bane of our existence here, voting for personalities . . ."

Minogue marvelled privately at what Kilmartin had just conceded. Even Jimmy Kilmartin, middle age on him like a volcanic crust, was displaying that enduring paradox of cynicism and hope, that cardinal Irishism that Minogue had learned late he could not escape himself: professing to be aloof while sitting on an overwhelming desire.

"Do you hear me at all?" Kilmartin was saying. "When we find out who was in the car in Bray, we won't be sitting here running the world. We'll be earning our pay these next few days, I can tell you."

Hoey put Doyle on hold and walked over to Minogue's desk.

"Doyle, sir. He nosed around with the computer thing in RTE. Something interesting, do you want to listen in?"

Minogue pressed the flashing yellow button while Hoey returned to his extension.

"Minogue here now. Shea Hoey says you are inside a computer or something."

"I went to Fine's office, that big room with all the desks, and I asked a man called Downey if Fine made much use of the computer for his work. Some people use the computer for word-processing and what they call internal mail. Downey says yep, that Fine used to use the computer. Journalists file stories on them. There's a room with eight terminals in it for the staff to use them as they wish. Some bigwigs have terminals all to themselves. Anyway. Paul Fine used the computer in the past, to type up reports. He had a user number and a password like the others. The idea is that you do your bit of whatever on the computer and then you save it. There's a print room too, and you can go and collect your stuff, depending on whether it's your turn on it or whether the printers are taken up."

"Did you get into the computer and look?"

"That's what I was saying to Shea, sir. There were no items in Fine's file on the computer. I got the manager of the Information Services to get the password and get in. Downey thought it was a bit odd that there was nothing because he was always slagging Fine about using the computer instead of his own brain. I was told they scrub the files every now and then but they give you lots of warning to save your files or to let them know they're still active."

"Is there any other way to check and see for stuff he may have had in his files there? Stuff he had a while ago?"

"I asked him that. There is. They do tape backups every day in case there's a power loss. The computer does the taping automatically every evening. Some of the stuff they keep, like payroll, in case they find there was a mistake later on. They always keep a week's worth of everything on the computer but only selected stuff stays on tape for longer than that. He's gone to find the tapes for me now."

"To all intents and purposes a person working under his own password would not have people looking over his shoulder, would he?" Hoey asked.

"God, yous're very devious. Matter of fact I asked him that. Who would know other people's passwords, like," Doyle replied. "He told me that it was no big secret with passwords at all. He keeps the passwords in his files but it's not a question of anybody knowing another person's password after snooping around for it in his filing cabinet. It's that the passwords are quite easy to figure out. Often it's a bit of someone's name. He knows that some users even loan out their passwords to others so they can work on the same material."

"Are there other ways to eavesdrop, so to speak?" Minogue broke in.

"There are, apparently," said Doyle. "If you know another person's password there's a way to look at what he's doing, if he's working on the computer at the time."

"Phone us when you get through that tape thing, so," said Minogue. "And dazzle us with more of that verve and acuity."

Eilis turned from emptying her second ashtray of the day. She looked from the becalmed Hoey still cradling the phone to the semi-reclining Minogue who was also mulling over Doyle's discoveries.

"Verve and acuity," she said as she lit up a Gitane. "There's no knowing what a person will hear from parties working around here. It'd make a girl think twice."

Kilmartin emerged from his office, scratching his ear and looking for Minogue.

"Time for evening prayer," Kilmartin said with a leaden irony.

Minogue flipped a folder on his desk and uncovered his summary for Kilmartin to feed the Commissioner with.

"There's a little something to add to this and bring it up to the minute," Minogue murmured. "Doyle went out to RTE and chased up something on the computer there. Paul Fine used the computer but there's nothing in his file. Doyle's working up a copy of what might have been on the computer in Fine's name a while ago."

"Fair enough," said Kilmartin vacantly as he read down the page. "That's all from the Gardai on the beaches today?" he asked, looking down to Minogue.

"The best we have is from callers-in, I'm afraid. That woman who put us on to the site. The lad with his girlfriend in the car-park late Sunday night, we're stuck with him . . . he still can't put a make on the cars he saw."

Kilmartin couldn't hide his disappointment. "Jases, that's not much. With seventy-odd men?"

Minogue shrugged. "Don't forget the better parts. There's the ticket man who can tentatively place Paul

Fine in Dalkey station around one o'clock. He might have gotten out of a train with time to spare and walked up over Dalkey Hill to Killiney Hill Park. It's a nice little jaunt. "

Minogue watched Kilmartin's head waver slightly from side to side as he went down the page again. "And remember the appeal tonight will be on Killiney Hill, not the beach. I put Gallagher's plans in point form because I don't know any more than what you see. Thirty-eight names, he told me. It'll take time. Not something we can rush him with," Minogue added.

Kilmartin nodded distractedly and yawned. He slapped the file folder against his thigh.

"I didn't even want to be thinking about this fella who was toasted out beyond in Bray. The remains are in poor shape but we have an engine block number. A Volkswagen. I was to get a phone call a half an hour ago."

Kilmartin had been gone ten minutes when Eilis directed a call to Minogue. The car in Bray had belonged to one Brian Kelly, thirty-four, of Leopardstown Gardens, civil servant. Mr Kelly was a Principal Officer in the Department of Finance. He was unmarried. He was not answering his phone. Gardai from Cabinteely were at the house. Mr Kelly had a brother, a priest in Finglas. His parents lived in County Carlow. Had any effects been left intact for identification after the fire? A watch with an expanding strap was partially intact. Clothing had been burned off completely. Remains of a leather wallet, melted plastic (probably bank cards), some change on the floor of the car.

Minogue asked for the details again. This time he wrote them down. It was a matter of ferreting out his dentist's name to light on an X-ray identification. Minogue saw five o'clock looking back down off the wall at him. He watched Keating about to begin typing from his notebook.

"How would you like to be Jimmy Kilmartin for a while?" he asked Keating.

"I wouldn't mind the pay and the perks," Keating answered cautiously. "I was just about to type up me summary of Fine's office stuff."

Minogue headed Keating off at the pass. "Is there anything that'd change what we're at now? Diaries or notebooks?"

"No," said Keating as he flicked his notebook shut.

"We will most likely have to set up a team for another case, that's what I'm getting at."

"The man out in Bray?"

"Yes. It may well be this man here," Minogue replied, handing Keating the sheet.

"You'll have to pick up an X-ray from the pathologist's. They did 'em this afternoon. There's a fella looking through Kelly's house for receipts. Now phone here the minute you get a match off the dentist's charts."

As Keating was leaving, Eilis was moving from desk to desk with small bundles of photocopies. She tendered Minogue's share into his hand. They were copies of statements from members of the public who had telephoned the help-line in answer to last night's media appeals. Hoey, his copies in his hand at the blackboards, wrote in the sighting at Dalkey train station on Sunday. So the ticket man was sticking by it now, enough to sign a statement on it, Minogue thought. Paul Fine's last Sunday now had two placings before the asterisk and the question mark next to it. There was still no writing under the Saturday.

Kathleen said that she had heard the appeal on the half-five radio news.

"Killiney Hill Park," she said. "That's creepy, I'm telling you. I always liked going for a stroll there. It'll be a while before I'll be wanting to walk around that spot again."

Minogue told her that he didn't know what time he'd be home tonight. There could be another investigation being launched. It was up to Kilmartin to put a team together for that but he might be foraging for experienced detectives who were working with Minogue at the moment. That could mean that her husband might be taking over the Fine case directly, without Shea Hoey there to direct traffic for him.

"You are coming home some time tonight, I take it?" said Kathleen. "At least you're not relying on the buses. There are some walkouts already. Aren't they divils entirely?"

"It may be late enough, but I'll be home, all right," replied Minogue. He did not sound as decisive as he had wanted to.

Claustrophobia seized him as he looked around the squad room. Have to get out in the open air, he thought. His thoughts ran to the Fines: what would they be doing now, a day and a half after their son had drifted in off the sea? Gone. Murdered. Never to see again. Can't shake his hand, can't look at him across the table and share a joke. He should at least phone Justice Fine and tell him how the investigation was going. Sooner or later he'd have to interview the Fines again, this time to get in touch with another Paul, a son with whom a father and mother had had differences. The stuff of family life: arguments, bickering, friction. The

Paul Fine who was hidden under the biography Minogue had built so far.

Loss swooped low in Minogue's chest. It never got easier; it seemed at times like this that it only got harder. What could parents know of their adult children? Were someone to ask Minogue for a description of Daithi Minogue, how much would he forget to say, how would he choose the blocks to build the picture?

Seven o'clock. Minogue had been caught in the rain on his way back from his tea in George's Street. The taste of rashers and eggs was thick on his tongue after he had run the last hundred yards.

Kilmartin was holding court in his office. Hoey was back, shaved, and Keating was leaning in Kilmartin's doorway. Doyle had returned from RTE. He sat opposite Kilmartin with a cohort, a prematurely bald detective whom Minogue recognized as one seconded from the Central Detective Unit for the Fine murder.

"Just the man we want," said Kilmartin. "Listen to these lads here."

Minogue collected two yellow phone messages from his desk as he passed. One was from Gallagher, the other from his daughter Iesult. Prompted by Kilmartin, Doyle began.

"Paul Fine used the mainframe computer in RTE for typing and storing some of his work. I met two people who confirmed that; they personally saw him typing away on a terminal. I had them look into his files under his name and there was nothing. Not a sausage. I asked them where it was all gone and they didn't know. Maybe he'd cleared off his stuff a few days ago. Then I found out they have a back-up memory for the stuff they hold on the computer. It's in case

JOHN BRADY

the computer takes a fit or runs amok on account of a
power shortage. I asked them to look at this tape
back-up and see if there was something of Fine's on it.
It took them a while and a good bit of grumbling
because they had to free up the computer so as they
could run the tape back to it."

"Wait for it," said Kilmartin. Minogue recognized
that quickening in Kilmartin, the darting eyes. A happier man, now, in his bloodhound incarnation.

"Your man didn't understand it at first. The tapes, I
mean. They're all buggered up," said Doyle. "Gob-
bledegook."

"You mean erased when they shouldn't have
been?"

"He thinks that someone must have run a bulk
eraser over the week's tapes and that's what turned
them into mush. They started straightaway to make a
new back-up. I was a hero for finding out their back-
up was rubbish."

"Could it have been accidental?" asked Hoey.

"It has happened before, he told me. But it's
unlikely that it was accidental. The staff who are in
that area are wised up to the computer now."

"Would it require some kind of expertise to wipe
the things like that?" Minogue asked.

"No," said Doyle reluctantly. "A bulk eraser is just
a little thing that you wave over the tapes to remove
the data. It's very quick. And there were plenty of
opportunities for a lot of people. It would only take a
few seconds."

"Do you mean that we can't get a reliable access list
for this facility from them, one we could start with
and work up some suspects?" Hoey asked.

Doyle shook his head.

Kilmartin cleared his throat. "So much for that enterprising work. Yours truly here"—he nodded towards Keating still hanging out of the doorway—"finally got a list of things that Fine wanted dug up by their library."

"'Information systems,' if you don't mind," said Keating in a tony South Dublin accent. "He asked for searches of British and Irish newspapers over the past five years. For mention of Ireland in speeches by Arab heads of state. Interception of IRA arms from places other than the U.S. Coverage of conferences concerning Arab and Palestinians in Britain and Ireland; publications arising from those conferences . . ." Keating turned a page and scanned the topics. "Last of all, last Friday afternoon, he put in a request for newspaper, radio and television articles on one Fintan Gorman. Going back for five years."

"The Minister for Defence?" asked Hoey.

"The very man. Fabulous Fintan Gorman," echoed Kilmartin.

"Well. It looks like we had all of those interests already itemized, or we were aware that he was working on them. Did he decide on Gorman because of the work Fitzgerald gave him, the scandal beat?"

"I don't know," Keating replied. "I'm still trying to get in touch with Fitzgerald to see if he knew that Fine wanted to do a piece on Fabulous Fintan. He's left RTE and he's not at home."

"Where did he get the name of Fabulous Fintan, anyway?" Hoey asked.

"This is the man who knows how to solve all our ills," Minogue replied. "The name came from some row in the Dáil when the Opposition called something he was talking about a fable."

"I can see Fitz telling Fine to pick on Gorman because he's a bit too clean looking and deserves a good vetting," Hoey murmured.

"To be sure," Kilmartin snorted, "that's your media mob for you. They go for the dirt and they aim for the biggest scandal they can find. Amn't I right? 'Go for the most upright-looking politician and drag him down into the muck' is the order of the day there, I'm telling you."

"Not that yours is a partisan view or anything like that," Minogue couldn't resist saying.

"Absolutely not," Kilmartin replied hastily. "I don't mind what party the man belongs to. I just think that he should get a fair crack of the whip and not have them hyenas snapping at his heels. I ask you. Looking to see if he ever had a drink or had his maulers on the wrong diddies once in his life. I mean to say, we're all human. That pack of shites out in RTE—they love to show the shots of a Garda defending himself at a demonstration but they never show the gurriers in the crowd provoking us. Lefties. Wife-swapping and cavorting about. As if they didn't do it themselves. Anyway, let's not get bogged down at this point."

"Right," said Hoey. "A bit better news may be just around the corner for us. After the new appeal this evening a fella phoned us—not twenty minutes ago—to say that he saw Paul Fine on Saturday. He remembers Fine's name only. Guess where he works?"

"Radio Telifis Eireann," Minogue tried.

"Good try but no. The National Library above in Kildare Street."

"Paul Fine was in the National Library sometime on Saturday." Minogue declared the question.

"Yep. We should be able to place him for a good

part of the Saturday, during the day anyway. Things are coming together a bit better now, hah?" said Kilmartin as he sat back in his chair.

Minogue did not want to be uncharitable but the gargoyle within was off the leash already. Jimmy Kilmartin had come from a meeting with the Commissioner anxious for any apparent loosening in the investigation. He would read much into the National Library business.

"There's two lads gone out to this man's house and we'll have a statement out of him before the evening is out. Then there are the slips which Fine filled in to get books in the Library," Kilmartin pointed out contentedly.

"So Paul Fine worked on Saturdays too," Minogue speculated aloud. "They mustn't have had what he wanted in RTE, so he went to the National Library instead?"

"That looks like it so far," replied Kilmartin.

Was this why Kilmartin and the others were keen at this hour of the day, the gargoyle asked Minogue.

"Now here's the most interesting thing entirely, the one we've been holding back," said Kilmartin cagily. "We have a match based on the dental work for that poor divil out in Bray. It was Kelly in the car, all right, but the pathologist's report will be saying that Kelly may have been walloped in the head before the fire. There are signs of a very small hairline fracture, but he's not sure about it. It may have been the heat of the fire and his head boiling—but the bone around it is not pressed out enough, he thinks. Kelly could have been knocked out, maybe even badly injured, and shoved into the back of the car. The car was set alight and Bob's your uncle, it was a ball of fire inside of a minute."

Minogue decided that it was indeed time to sit down.

"Meanwhile, back at the ranch," Kilmartin continued. "Kelly's brother is a priest. We got him to go into Kelly's house with us, up in Leopardstown. Naturally the brother is very upset. Kelly was a very good-living man, he says. And sure enough, there's some class of a chapel in the house. One of the bedrooms is like a monk's cell, I'm telling you. 'For prayer and contemplation,' the brother says."

"There are odd people in Leopardstown, I always knew that," Minogue murmured. He was thinking of Kelly's body being consumed in the inferno, the head expl—ughhh. Christ.

"Odd isn't the half of it. Our help-line number from the radio and telly appeals was on a scrap of paper by the phone." Kilmartin leaned forward over his desk, his eyes hooded, and delivered the surprise. Minogue suddenly realized that Kilmartin had probably done this performance for the policemen already. They were all looking at Minogue now.

"Do you know whose name was also on this scrap of paper, but misspelled?"

"Go on," said Minogue, prickly alert now. "Make my day."

"M-I-N-O-G-H. That's how he spelled it. Definitely out of touch with surnames from the County of Clare, I'd say. Wouldn't you?"

# NINE

Minogue chose Keating to work through the tally of calls logged to the Murder Squad's help-line so far. With a copy of that call they could play it back to an acquaintance of Kelly. If it was identified ... Minogue's brain tumbled down mental stairs.

He would have liked to have the nerve to take one of Kilmartin's cigarettes, so fierce was the pleasure and resolution which Kilmartin seemed to be drawing out of them now. Minogue still felt left behind in the excitement which had taken visible hold of the others. He finally waved in a passing Hoey who tried to sort it out for him.

"I know it's not certain," Hoey said. "But why would he have the number at all? You said you remember being told about the call, Keating telling you—a man phoned, asked who was in charge of the Fine case and wanted to talk to you. You alone, right?"

"Right."

"So if and when we find out it was Kelly, there's an obvious connection between two murders."

"But Kelly is a senior civil servant, not a Palestinian or a local gangster. Maybe he was just out in Killiney on Sunday, an ordinary citizen. Maybe he knew Paul Fine somehow."

"Why would he only want to talk to you, so?" said Hoey conclusively as he drifted away from Minogue's desk.

Gallagher phoned Minogue ten minutes after Minogue called Special Branch HQ. Gallagher was co-ordinating the interviews with the people on the list he had drawn up himself. Minogue extricated his copy of the list and placed an X beside five of the thirty-eight names.

"They're the ones you're finished with," said Minogue.

"And they're not in the running. We're still with the rest of them. There's only three that we haven't got a hold of yet. "

Minogue glanced down at the names he had marked with an O. X's and O's, hit and miss. "How do you feel about second interviews with those Arab students before the weekend?"

Gallagher didn't reply directly. "It could be done, if need be."

"Nobody so far knows this group, this League for the . . .?"

"They admit to reading it in the papers reporting on the murder. That's all."

"Well, sooner or later, Pat . . ." Minogue concluded.

"Later, I'd say," Gallagher replied.

Minogue had nearly ten minutes of vacillating

about calling the Fines that night or the next before Hoey waved the phone at him. It was the direct line to the Murder Squad offices, usually marshalled by Eilis. Minogue slid into Eilis's seat.

"Not the Church, Not the State, Women must decide their fate," said the woman's voice.

"I know the air, I'm not sure of the words, though. Or the singer," Minogue said.

"It's the voice of sisterhood everywhere," came the reply.

"Are you actually a paid-up member of the Women's Action Movement now?"

"No, I'm not. But that doesn't mean I sit idly by."

"Sorry, I forgot to phone you back. I don't blame you giving me a speech. Where are you?"

"I'm at home. That's great about Marguerite Ryan, what do you think?"

"How do you know this phone isn't being tapped by my superiors here? I could be out on my ear over what I say to that leading question."

"Don't be so dramatic, Da. I think it's great anyway. I hope they drop the manslaughter charge too," Iesult said. "And let her get on with her life."

"Uh," Minogue said. Iesult paused. Minogue could see her sprawled in the hall, on the floor, most likely.

"When are you going on your holidays anyway?"

Minogue wondered what his daughter was working around to asking. "Now you're talking. A grand idea. I had been thinking of driving across with the ferry to France or something."

"You're a howl. Does Ma know you're planning this caravanserai, or will you just mention it the morning you're going?"

"Your mother likes surprises. Not the kind that your generation deals out, let me add. Something like I think you have in mind to tell me—"

"Get up the yard, Da. Why would you—?"

"You're a bit amateurish at this still. Remember that your father is a Clareman with powers of divination and tricks galore. If you were phoning me just to chew the fat or discuss the weather, I'd be more than happy anyway. I have ready answers and a fund of inconsequential chat. For example: I was rained on unmercifully, and me coming back after me tea in a restaurant. I'm still soggy."

"Soggy? That's an age thing. Poor man, Ma said you had to work late again."

"It's murder, so it is."

"And at your age too. What age are you now?"

"Go 'way with you. I wish you could see me now because I'm turning the other cheek after that slur about me age. I want you to know that parents do in fact survive their children's lack of consideration, you know."

"Your age? Ah, go on. Look at Yves Montand. Clint Eastwood . . ."

"Peter Ustinov?"

"Liz Taylor. They're all getting on . . . No, I phoned you on a whim. I was thinking of going to Clare for the weekend."

"God be praised. A daughter awakening to her inheritance. Are you sure you won't be frightened by the accents down there? It gets very dark at night, you know. There are mighty strange people in Clare."

"Understatement of the century. Ballyvaughan, I was thinking."

"And you want pointers from me, is it?"

"No, I don't. I was just mentioning it. There's a crowd going to rent one of the Irish Cottages there."

Minogue was swayed alternately by what the "crowd" suggested, and his scorn for Irish Cottages. Drawn by a synthetic version of a rural past, Dubliners along with Germans and Dutch and Yanks were booking thatched cottages in Ballyvaughan to savour a quaint past conveniently new. Too full of peasant blood to listen to urbanite guff about peasant virtues, Minogue had no answers to the men he had met in the pubs of Clare over the years defending these Irish Disneylands as "creating employment" and "bringing the tourists." He had realized, with little remorse, that he was, in certain respects, a snob.

"A crowd": said unconcernedly, but heavy with something. Drunken students, up late, farting about and making iijits of themselves—his daughter in the middle of this? Her boyfriend, Pat the Brain, a man of revolutionary theories and humour which carried his ideas easily beyond cant: a dangerous, clever, likeable boy who was mad about Iesult.

"How quaint. Folksy even," said Minogue at last. He upbraided himself instantly when he heard the sneer in his voice. If Iesult wanted to be involved with Pat the Brain any way she liked, she could do it and nothing would prevent her. When Minogue tried to think of his daughter and sex, a numbness and a fog took hold of his brain. Traces of different memories: himself and Kathleen, urgent and whispering to one another, heat and damp bodies, the unnameable arching over, the small sadness later. A feeling that couldn't be accommodated at all. Lying there in the summers with the breeze stirring the curtains wondering how many other couples were making love now. Was there something to the *petite mort*? And why was it all right for Kathleen and Matt, and not all right for Iesult, a woman herself?

So great was their alarming and vigilant love for Iesult as an infant, a child who had been conceived unexpectedly, that Minogue and Kathleen always worried that they had spoiled her. An Iesult who had dug in her heels as an infant; a daughter who had miraculously ended desert years after the Minogues' first child, Eamonn, had died in his sleep.

Minogue had had more dreams about Eamonn these last few years, especially since his own greeting from death when the bomb had gone off under the British Ambassador's car a hundred yards ahead of Minogue. Recovering in hospital, Minogue had discovered that he could safely relinquish much of what had been his former life. Without effort, and with the sense of an untroubled and even humorous presence which could only be his own self, waking up from a long sleep, Minogue had started a new life. His new religion was made up of things divorced before: a cup of coffee in Bewley's where he could be surrounded by people of every ilk; Kathleen's mannerisms when she was pleased about something; a walk on the endless stone pier of Dun Laoghaire—when you were out so far along the walk that you believed it was no longer a pier but that you were surrounded by the sea—with night sneaking in over the sea, water that lapped and kissed the stones in the gloom.

Dug in her heels: the same unwieldy gift as her father. Kathleen's part of Iesult was the more civilizing, Minogue was sure.

"It's not quaint, Da. It's the only place we could get. Everywhere else is booked out, even at this time of year. "

"Fair enough. I understand it's terrible popular with all classes of persons."

He heard her drumming something on the hall table. She had something else in mind. He would have to draw her out.

"Is your mother home?"

"No, she's not. She's over at Costigans'. They have a video-machine there and they rented *Gone with the Wind*."

Minogue laughed this time. "Declare to God, your mother must have seen that a dozen times. She's gone dotty."

"I'll tell her you said that, so."

Minogue pounced. "When you're telling her about going away for the weekend, like?"

"I haven't told her yet. You know how she is."

Minogue firmed up. "You mean you haven't asked her yet. Yes, I do know how she is: that's why I married her. I may be a bit gone in the head but your mother is very much in touch," he said.

"Too much sometimes," said Iesult.

"You want me to intercede for you because your mother suspects a dirty weekend but I'm more 'progressive.' Am I getting warm?"

"Well, you're always standing up for Daithi when he does something iijity," Iesult said petulantly.

"Oh, that man should be getting himself tangled up as a go-between, and him slaving away at the office—"

"Stop it, Da. Be serious for a minute. You know Ma. I wouldn't want her worrying or looking at Pat like he was a roaring divil. Pat's very responsible. He's actually quite conservative behind all the Marxist stuff, but don't tell him I said that, do you hear?"

"I'm getting leery about this 'don't tell so-and-so.' Your mother and yourself should talk man-to-man about this."

"You mean I should sit Ma down and say, 'Ma, Pat and I will not have sex in Ballyvaughan, I promise?'"

"Keep your voice down, would you," Minogue hissed. "Bad enough to be giving me palpitations, but to be scandalizing my colleagues here . . . whatever effect you want to have, you just had it. But this is between you and your mother. I'll certainly reassure her if she has doubts later on, but not before you let her know you're going."

"Very tricky exit there, Da."

"Lookit, the both of us are well past the age where you should be Daddy's little girl. Get to know your mother, would you?"

"But she's so full of what the Church says about this and that, Da," said Iesult, her voice rising with exasperation.

"And I'm easier to get around because I'm supposed to be a pagan or something? Listen for a minute. Did you ever hear me advising you what to do this last while?"

"No. That's what I like—"

"You're missing the point. Did it ever strike you that I may not have any sensible advice to give you? Ye have your own lives and no amount of talk is going to . . . ah, I don't know. Being able to see clearly is what I mean. No gurus. Your mother is not afraid of standing up and saying what she believes is best for you, so you should be glad of knowing her. But face up to her and you'll see something that might be entirely new to you, I'm telling you. She'd leave me in the ha'penny place."

"She has changed a bit, I suppose," Iesult murmured.

"Let me tell you, if Kathleen Minogue, or Kathleen O'Hare to give her her other title, if she ever turns turk on the Church and holy Ireland one morning, it would not surprise me. The Pope and the rest of them had better look out if and when she wants answers. Don't you be worrying about dirty weekends, now."

Minogue was suddenly aware of eyes upon him. Hoey was observing him through threads of cigarette smoke, his curiosity evident, and a small curl of amusement worked at the sides of his mouth. Minogue's glance flickered recognition that that last remark had been overheard and he felt the blush begin immediately at his collar. It would make things worse if he were to plead that he had only been discussing things with his daughter. Only? *Daughter*?

"Hmmm," said Iesult.

"Do you know what I'm saying?" Minogue was conscious of trying to keep his voice down now.

"I'll think about it. Maybe I'll practise that 'Frankly, Mother, I don't give a damn' in case she freaks out. Tell me, anyway, what will you be wearing for the wedding? They all go to registry offices there, I suppose."

"What wedding?"

"When Darling Daithi decides to tie the knot with Curvaceous Cathy, the All-American Girl, in the ol' U.S. of A."

"You have a very sharp tongue, Iesult. I wouldn't care to fall foul of it myself," Minogue mustered. "Remember there's many a man dug his own grave with his tongue, and didn't know he was doing it until it was too late."

After the call Minogue wondered if he had been less than truthful when he had told himself that he would not be jealous of Pat the Brain. It wouldn't take a Freudian to drive this one home, especially when Patient Minogue freely admitted that he loved Iesult immoderately. Hidden in her cutting humour, he knew, was her own concern for Daithi.

Minogue phoned the Fines. The man's voice answering was not Billy Fine's.

"This is Inspector Minogue. Unless it's a major upset to come to the phone, yes—"

Fine sounded like a man talking late at night, unhurried, tired but alert.

"Good man, Inspector. No, it's all right. I had been thinking of phoning you. I wasn't sure how your protocol works. We've had phone calls daily from the Garda Commissioner to tell us where things stand."

"He gets his briefing from us."

"All right. So what there is to know he has told us already," said Fine.

"Now you have it. I was phoning, I think, to say hello. Just so as you know that any minute of the day there are policemen working on this. Everything's done that can be."

"Well, that's reassuring, I suppose," said Fine slowly. Minogue was certain there was no sarcasm under the delivery.

"And if I might inquire further, Justice—"

"You had better start calling me something other than that. Billy will do well enough."

"If I might take a little of your time then, soon? I mean if I might put some questions to you about Paul. Very often the shock hides important facets of a person's life, clues as to what might have happened. Returning to details after the initial shock can often yield up new, er . . ."

"Facts. Yes. I've been thinking, all right. Waiting for something to come to me. I'm fairly familiar with how the Gardai do this. I'm ready, if that's what you want to know, but Rosalie may be out of the running for a little while yet."

"I wouldn't have expected—" Minogue began.

"Oh, don't be too delicate now. Rose is a tough bird. But it'll take a while longer. 'If only' is what comes to mind a lot."

"There's no getting used to it, I believe," said Minogue gently.

"Isn't that a fact. You will probably have realized by now that Paul was not like the other children. We found that we had to do things differently with him, and now of course—"

Neither man spoke for several moments. Minogue wondered if Fine was glad of somebody to chat to, someone outside the people in the house. There'd be plenty of time for weeping in between the stories, and for a lifetime to come after that.

"Ah," said Fine as if concluding a line of thinking. "So you're working away on it. Good. To judge by your Commissioner's reaction to the mention of your name, you have left your mark. Naturally he'd tell me you were the real shemozzle after I made it plain I'd like you to be doing the work," Fine continued. "Seeing as he expected me to be on the warpath on account of who I am on the totem pole in the judiciary."

"Are you on a warpath?" Minogue risked.

"How could I be? If you've ever had any calamity like this happen to you, you'd know that the only anger you can feel for a long time is the anger you feel against yourself and life in general for picking you out to land a tragedy on. You think you could have done better, prevented it. Made your feelings known better, told someone plainly what you thought. Do you know what I'm getting at?"

Minogue said that he did.

"What might begin to annoy me tomorrow, especially if I can't get to sleep again, is the fact that we can't go ahead with the funeral. You may not be familiar with our duty to inter the deceased as soon as possible. There was a time when we insisted that a rabbi, or a relative at least, be with the deceased at all times up until the burial, you know. That used to cause no end of trouble. Johnny Cohen is more upset than I am, actually, but the State has to have its way. Three days, they say, and they'll release Paul to us. It's difficult explaining it to Rosalie without giving her the willies about what goes on in a postmortem."

The resignation was plain in Fine's voice now.

"I may be able to do something," said Minogue.

"I doubt you can, at all."

"Can I come out to your house tomorrow, then? Would you mind me coming out?"

"Come out in the morning if you can. Half-nine would suit," said Fine. "And just knock. We won't be going anywhere."

Hoey looked across to Minogue. The Inspector rested his hand on the cradled receiver.

"Rough. That's the stuff I can't bear to do."

"Rough isn't in it," Minogue murmured. "A terrible thing; the same the whole world over."

For some reason Minogue had images of starving children with swollen bellies before him. Glazed, sickly eyes already empty and marked with the inevitability of death; black children in their parents' arms, themselves impossibly thin, looking fearfully into the television camera. That was death too, his gargoyle said.

"Never having things explained as to why it should be them . . ." Minogue muttered. Meaning, everything has to mean something eventually.

Hoey nodded slowly and dropped his gaze to the reports on his desk. He recovered a cigarette from behind his ear and lit it. An image of Daithi came to Minogue then, the boy's face a mask of puzzlement and resentment; Daithi wanting to ask him a question, to be answered, but no words coming from him. How was it that Minogue's recollection of snapshots of a young Daithi was that of a boy's face always frowning into the camera? Minogue sighed and tried to busy himself so that he might not feel this dead-weight so keenly.

"Anything off the phones, Shea?"

"Four possible sightings in the Park on Sunday afternoon. They're very iffy. The fella from the National Library is our most promising so far, I think. Did you get through yesterday's, the ones from the beach?"

"I did indeed. Not hot at all," said Minogue, sliding further into the trough.

"I was half-ways thinking of putting that car business under the 'scope again. The fella who was necking with his mot in the car-park late Sunday night. Do you know who I'm talking about?"

Minogue nodded.

"There was a car parked there when he arrived and still there when he left. It's a bugger entirely because we can't get him to put a make on the car. I could nearly crucify him for being half-gargled and not noting details, but sure what can you do? At least he phoned us. I'd like to put out an appeal specific to the car-park, though. Anyone who used it at all over the weekend . . ."

"Go ahead," said Minogue. "Add it to tomorrow evening's."

Minogue unearthed his copy of the report on the tides for Sunday night. Hoey shook his head when he saw Minogue reading it.

"They covered themselves for anything there, didn't they? 'If the body was released an insufficient distance from shore between the hours of . . .' What was it?"

"Eleven at night to three in the morning," replied Minogue.

"I forget the exact terminology—"

"'. . . a strong probability of it being washed up south-south-west of the point of release.' They discount the boat thing, that's something. If the body was dumped overboard, I mean."

"But they can't say where the body would have been put into the water. It could have been Coliemore Harbour or even the Forty Foot bathing spot. Even off Killiney Beach itself."

"'Not a steady speed in the nearer offshore currents, speed of drift inshore is indeterminate except for a probable rate of between one and five knots depending on the coastline,'" Minogue quoted.

"Sooner or later we should set up a dummy and try to match the conditions," said Hoey.

Minogue made no reply. He was thinking of Paul Fine's body adrift, the brine dissipating the blood and rinsing the wounds. Water closing over the head, the body sometimes underwater completely. Had someone gazing out on the water early on Monday not seen the gently bobbing body, had they not wondered?

"I must say," Minogue whispered. "I'm damned if I can understand why someone needed to put the body into the sea."

He held his hands up before rubbing his eyes.

"I know, I know. We talked about it. And then we talked about it some more."

Minogue paused and massaged his eyes with his knuckles. "You and me and Jimmy and the scenes-of-the-crime lads," he said. "The idea of getting rid of the body to buy time—dirtying the motive, dirtying the trail. And the fact that the murder site can't have been so well planned in advance. I know. But still..."

"What?" from a distracted Hoey.

Minogue took away his hands, blinked and shook his head.

"Why was he in the sea? If it's a professional killer, this doesn't fit with carrying a body anywhere. No way in the wide world. Pat Gallagher knows that too, I'll bet. If we're chasing an imported, experienced killer, we have the situation of a killer not familiar with the terrain here, who kills his victim and moves off, rapid like. No messing about. It's a lot of trouble to come back after dark, if that's what we're assuming, and carry a grown man to the shore."

"Angle for it being more than the one man," Hoey began. "In the disposal of the body, anyway. Say the killer is a pro. He does his job and confirms it by phone. The person he phones has a fit; says the body has to be moved, hidden."

"Panic, you mean? But we keep on running up against that, Shea: why try to *conceal* the body when the call to the damn newspaper is a run at some kind of publicity? Can't deny that."

"Right. OK. The shooting itself might have been carried out coolly enough. But even the killer'd have the jitters, training or no training."

"Training, you say," Minogue said remotely. "There'd be no lack of familiarity with guns as regards people from the Middle East. Not to speak of our own crop of cowboys here."

Hoey nodded agreement and hoisted his feet onto the desk. Minogue stared at Hoey's shoes. They looked enormous from this angle, at least size thirteens.

"I think I know what you're getting at," said Hoey. "You're thinking the killer and the carrier-awayer are distinct parties, aren't you? The killer tells someone what he's done and they're the ones who do the panicking and decide that the body has to be moved. And we're trying to pin the local connection to the killer if it's a professional assassin thing. I know what you're saying."

"All right, so," said Minogue. "But I don't follow why the body had to be moved at all. Still banging me head over that one."

He looked at Hoey and wondered again if it was not time to return to smoking after fifteen years of irreproachable lungs. Hoey sat up in the chair as if being challenged.

"Let's go through it again, then. Get it out of the running. Scientific and methodical, like. Are you ready?"

"I am, I suppose," said Minogue, glad to have some of Hoey's vigour carry him.

"Number one: the body is moved in an effort to have it disappear entirely—wash it out to sea. Why? Because clues somewhere along the line may incriminate the killer?"

"But the bullets, Shea. Someone went to the trouble of recovering the bullets, even to first picking the types of bullets that could be recovered after going through the victim. I don't see any clues staring me in the face at all either."

"But that might have been the clean-up crowd, the ones who might have carried the body away later. Number two: the body was moved so as to block the investigation in the sense of delaying it or allowing time for leads to run cold. Witnesses who may have seen something, events in Fine's life that might shed light on the murder. The killer may have wanted time to get out of the country. That's why we have to follow the Palestinian thread whether we like it or not."

"OK, Shea. But still and all, Gallagher knows his stuff, we have to admit that. The Branch don't show any names on the list as having left the country in a hurry recently either."

"I know Gallagher is on the ball, and they'd not hold back on something like this. But there's always the possibility of completely new people on the scene. Even the students who have been harmless for years: one of them might be a sleeper. They have worse memories than we have, I hear. They'll carry on a feud or the like to a hundred generations. Maybe that's what Fine found out, that there was some cell which had gone undetected here and was just waiting for the order to do something when the time was right. Maybe we should be looking at a bigger picture, to see if there were any forthcoming events or visits in the offing. Diplomatic things, ambassadors, I don't know. They might have been waiting to get a crack at an American bigwig, knowing that they come here often enough with the Irish-American connection."

Minogue thought about what Hoey was suggesting.

"I'm going to raise that with Gallagher, Shea. That's something we'll have to look at if we're blocked still by the end of the week."

Hoey looked gratified.

"Number three: he or they don't want the victim's last hours connected with Killiney Hill for another reason. Let's assume the killer knows we make public appeals for help in the murder investigations. We'd want to be knowing what Paul Fine was doing there, wouldn't we? Maybe he went there to meet someone."

"So if he met up with someone, a citizen'd call us and tell us that Paul Fine was with someone in the park. And the someone is the one who killed him. We discussed that one already."

"Yes. It may be a little tatty at the moment but we can't be assuming that murderers have a genius intelligence just because we can't put the bits together this very moment," said Hoey with his palms upturned, looking in appeal to Minogue.

"'They make their slips, we make our living,'" Minogue said, repeating one of Kilmartin's favourite maxims, one which he liked to quote at discouraging moments.

"If the killer and the cleaner-upper were two different parties, there could have been a squabble afoot too," said Hoey. "A real fanatic is tired of waiting for action and he gets carried away before his cohorts can stop him. Independent action. I know we talked about it before, but it seems to be creeping back even stronger.

Fine may have met whoever killed him that afternoon. He may even have walked around with the killer for a while. Like we said from the start, if the killer is one of those Arab students he'd have been mighty conspicuous. People would remember him with Fine."

Minogue wished that the phone would ring and Gallagher would announce that he had a strong suspect in custody. He wished he could land in on top of a suspect and give him an aggressive interrogation, in shifts with someone like Kilmartin. Bully him. Anything was better than sitting here, empty. He wished he were not thinking about what the Fines were living through at this minute. He wished that he were not thinking that the body which had floated in and scuffed lightly on the beach at the water's edge on Monday might have been Daithi. Foolish to be thinking this, illogical. But still . . . *At least it wasn't my son that was murdered, no, not mine. It was Billy Fine's boy and I'm sorry for him but it wasn't my son they opened up to see how he had died and if there were still the bullets . . . Death. Sincere regrets, my heart goes out to you; but always happening to someone else, please.*

Kilmartin emerged from his office. Minogue had seen him coming, a shirted bulk approaching the distorting glass on the squad room side of his office. Kilmartin stood in the doorway for a moment, lit a cigarette and resumed his prowl. He reminded Minogue of an illtempered schoolmaster patrolling rows of cowed pupils. There would be chopping and changing tomorrow as Kilmartin took the bit between his teeth on the Kelly case. Would he snatch Keating for that too? Kilmartin paused by Minogue and arched his eyebrows.

"Best so far is the librarian fella for Saturday. He can attest to the fact that Paul Fine was well able to work," said Minogue.

Kilmartin shrugged and moved on, trailing smoke. He fingered an evening newspaper open and blew out a cloud of smoke as he snorted at what he read.

"Fucking yobbos! Legislate them back to work," he said to the headline. He resumed his leonine prowl, a thick-set Mayo-man shaped like one of the innumerable boulders which were strewn about the desolate bog landscapes of his native county. Perhaps a later Ice Age had deposited him, an obdurate lump, on the streets of Dublin and left to him stalk police offices with his shirt-tail dislodged from his trousers, a troglodyte, a bog-man who still hated Dublin after thirty years of policing it.

Minogue had found Dublin different. It had been difficult for him not to melt into its gentle decay when he had first arrived in the capital. The last twenty years had shattered the shabby charm of Dublin. The shards poked out now, gashing even the well-to-do who hid in Foxrock estates. Someone had taken the worst office architecture imaginable and mauled the city with it, rooting out people from the city centre and sending them to gulag garden suburbs where crime flourished. So ugly and widespread was this blight, with its dislocation of Dubliners into suburbs, that many, Minogue included, believed that the ruin of Dublin had been a carefully plotted conspiracy.

Kilmartin slowed after his first lap of the squad room.

"There'll be people who'll have to walk to work with this bloody strike, you know. Bananas is what we should be growing here," he said to no-one, passing Hoey's desk. He stopped abruptly before Minogue.

"Name of Jases, I'm nearly ready to go to this Ard Fheis meself and get up on the shagging podium and give those feckers a piece of my mind. 'Leadership':

that'd be the sum total of me speech. 'All we want is what we're overpaying ye for already: leadership!' We should declare a national emergency and a war on gobshites. People that are dragging their arses around the place, give them a kick-up in the arse and put them to work. 'Here's a shagging job,' I'd say. 'It may not be managing director, but it's a start.' Get the country back up and running again."

"We might all end up working in McDonald's, Jimmy," said Minogue, goaded beyond silence.

"A howl is what you are," Kilmartin snapped. "At least it'd be work, wouldn't it? I don't care if the Russians open a tank factory here, I'd say great, give us jobs. A fella has to start somewhere. This country was once the most civilized nation in Europe, with our monks and our books and our poets and our schools and every-thing—while the mobs beyond in Britain were still painting their faces and lathering the shite out of one another with sticks and stones. Look at us now, for the love of Jases. The best educated young people in Europe, probably the world, and no jobs. As for this European Community stunt, the United States of Europe and that class of bullshit—here, did I tell you this one? If you're an Irishman and you're going into the toilet, and you're an Irishman and you're coming out of the toilet, what are you when you're *in* the toilet?"

"Can't imagine, James."

"You're-a-peein'," said Kilmartin without smiling.

Minogue's lifetime of listening to his fellow-islanders had included countless editions of Kil-martin's perorations on the Land of Saints and Scholars in one guise or another.

"I would not care to have had the career of one of those monks and what-have-you," he baited Kilmartin.

"I would have asked to be excused from the hermit business too. Not to speak of the self-flagellation and the chastity bit. I haven't the heart for one and I haven't the stomach for the other."

Kilmartin fixed a disdaining eye on Minogue. Hoey looked up cautiously from under his eyebrows.

"Now that you're talking about beating yourself up for the greater glory, and all that," said Kilmartin in an unexpectedly low tone. He leaned down with his hands spread on Minogue's desk to confide. "Your man, Kelly, the lad toasted out in Bray. He had some class of a chapel and our resident encyclopaedia, Keating, says it looks like Kelly was one of those Opus Dei crowd."

He leaned further to whisper to Minogue.

"They're so holy that they beat themselves, he told me. No joking. They're like the hermit monks, except they don't run away from the common crowd. But they take sticks to one another and live like the monks in their private lives. Meet them in the street and they're the same as the next man, hail-fellow-well-met. Maybe our Kelly had had enough of it and the pressure got to him. They have very high morals—and you know where that can lead a man. Oh yes, indeed, I wasn't codding when I said earlier on to Keating that poor Kelly might still be a suicide. He might have banged his own head a bit, trying to sort himself out, don't you know."

Minogue remembered the pictures of Buddhist monks burning in the streets of Saigon.

Kilmartin stood to his full height, stretched and growled. "I'll be a happier man when I find out why he had your name and our phone number on a sheet of paper in his house."

# TEN

Wednesday morning brought a break in the ceiling of cloud which had muffled the island for a week. The air was fresh again. Clouds so white as to be patently silly looking to Minogue hung themselves from a sky of Blessed Virgin blue. The good burgher Magritte would have stood at his window for hours today, Minogue believed, so delighted would he have been with a sky like this.

A muzziness from last night's drinking with Kilmartin (who had dragooned Hoey into the pub too) dissipated quickly after breakfast. The worm in his stomach returned when Minogue turned away from his usual route and headed for Fine's house. Crowds stood at the bus stops still, some thumbing. Most cars were full. There were swarms of bicycles on the road. Minogue skirted the beginnings of traffic jams, reversing out of one road near Ranelagh to avoid a bottleneck

and found himself on Fine's street sooner than he had
wanted. Any time would be too soon, he realized.

He parked in front of a light blue Nissan Bluebird.
The passenger had already stepped out on to the footpath and was staring at Minogue. Minogue couldn't
see the man's hands. His back tingled. The driver, a
man with a crew cut and a small mouth, already had
his door open.

"Minogue, Technical Bureau. The Murder Squad,
lads."

The driver nodded. Minogue raised a hand to the
red-haired detective on the footpath who was now
rearranging his jacket. From the corner of his eye he
saw a lightly built man peering around the hedge two
houses down. The driver spoke into a microphone
pinned to his shirt and the man down the street with-
drew into a garden.

Heavy and sweet smells drifted out from the gardens nearby. A wrought-iron gate to the side of the
Fines' house clanked open and Johnny Cohen trudged
toward the main gates where the policemen were
standing. Minogue pocketed his photocard and took
several steps. Cohen nodded curtly. His gaze
searched Minogue's face.

"Morning to you, Mr Cohen," Minogue tried. "I
trust I'm not calling too early on the Fines?"

Cohen squinted hard at Minogue. "He may be
gone already," he said slowly. "Or he may be catching
up on last night. Were you there yourself later on,
then?"

Minogue sensed challenge. The heavy beard
seemed to close Cohen's face. "The investigation, like?
We were at it late, yes. But that's what we do—"

Cohen scratched his eyelids, blinked and frowned.

Then he looked over Minogue's shoulder at the Special Branch car. "You didn't hear, then," Cohen stated the question. "The Museum."

Minogue glanced from Cohen's face toward the front door grinding open. Billy Fine stood in the doorway.

"A petrol bomb was thrown at the doors of the Museum," Cohen said. "The synagogue, I should say. Billy was up all hours. He got a phone call and off he went."

Minogue's wary drowsiness fled. He was acutely aware of details now: the cloying scent from the hedge, the far-off hum of the city centre traffic, Cohen's bloodshot eyes. Fine stood very still in the doorway. Minogue pushed at the gate and strode toward the front door. He heard the gate being closed in his wake, his own feet skipping up the steps.

"I only found out this minute," he said.

Fine's arm moved and the door scuffed over a carpet. The sun escaped from behind a puffy white cloud and the light raced across the garden to the house. Minogue felt a tremor of helplessness when he looked at Fine now. The morning sun, so kind to Minogue already, mercilessly bathed Fine in a harsh light. Fine had lifted his arm above his eyes so as to see Minogue. Cohen was walking toward the steps now. Dazzled by the sun, Billy Fine looked to Minogue as if he were grimacing in agony.

"They, whoever they are, tried to destroy the Museum," said Fine. "Someone spray-painted PLO on the wall and threw a petrol bomb against the door."

Minogue's stomach froze and held tight. Cohen appeared by his side.

"The door held, we're all right," said Cohen. "The door held, that's the main thing." He did not take his eyes off Fine as he spoke.

Fine nodded. Minogue could not stop staring at him. Fine was unshaven, his eyes were reddened and his white shirt, open at the top, seemed to exaggerate the unkempt face. He drew Minogue into the front room.

"What else can happen?" said Fine. "Today's Wednesday? If I don't go to work I forget what day of the week it is. Do you have any cigarettes on you?"

Minogue wondered whether Fine was faltering, close to snapping.

"I don't," Minogue replied. "But I'm sure that . . . Look, I should leave off this interview if you're—"

"It's all right," Fine said firmly. "Rose'll be down in a minute. She has fags." He went on remotely then: "You'll have to persuade her it's all right for her to smoke. She's forever trying to give them up. She's afraid I'll start up again myself, so she won't smoke in front of me, so . . ." The sentence died.

"We're in a bit of a bind, you see." Fine's voice had changed to a monotone. "We can't begin the week of mourning proper until after Paul's burial. It's very trying indeed to have to break custom as regards interring . . . We're in a bit of a limbo, and what with droves of people in here to . . . Then this thing last night—it must be some kind of nightmare, I thought first. Maybe the head is gone on me, and I was dreaming all this."

"It's well in hand now," said Cohen. "Can't you go up and lie down awhile? Get some rest even if you don't sleep."

Fine's face eased. He looked at Cohen with a fleeting

smile. "Ah, Johnny." He clapped Cohen gently on the shoulder and motioned Minogue inside.

"David and Julia are upstairs. Julia flew in from Boston yesterday. She's knackered and very upset. David had to find a locum but he got in yesterday. He sat up most of the night."

"May I ask about Paul's wife?"

"Lily? Ask away. But she's in a state," said Fine as he examined his hands carefully. "She'll only come for the funeral, I'm afraid. Very . . . upset. Bitter, I suppose. I think she feels that his family stole him from her, or Ireland did. Maybe Dublin. She was never gone on the place here," said Fine, rising. "You'll have a bit of coffee, will you?"

"Don't trouble yourself," said Minogue.

"I'm getting a pot for meself. You have a phone call to make before we do anything, anyway. Better do it now, man. It's been hopping off the hook all morning. A Garda Hoey phoned not five minutes before you arrived, apologizing for himself but needing to speak to you."

Cohen, slouched in the chair opposite, looked up as Minogue made for the hall. Minogue's mind was cartwheeling, embarrassed and angry. Here he was, on a delicate enough visit, trying to mine more so that he could fill out a better picture of their murdered son, and this had gone off under him. He should have had a call about this, no matter what time . . . Hoey probably tried him at home.

Cohen touched his arm as he passed. "It doesn't look promising, does it, Inspector?"

Minogue scrambled for words. "Well, it seems to put a strong cast on the murder investigation. I'm just, I don't know how to put it. Shocked. It's . . ."

"PLO. I saw it on the wall, with my own eyes," said Cohen. "Half-two this morning. Someone in a car. There were no witnesses to the actual thing."

"Give me the name of the ranking Gardai you talked to, would you?" said Minogue.

"A Sergeant Hickey. I didn't ask him what station. Then a mob of Guards showed up, just before some of the media. We've been getting calls from all over the world since five o'clock this morning. American television stations. The Taoiseach phoned here at eight o'clock. Archbishops of Dublin, the Lord Mayor. Then your own."

"Commissioner Lally?"

"The very man."

Minogue couldn't decide if Cohen was hinting at his, Minogue's, ignorance of the event. Hoey must have tried him at home, Minogue thought again. He excused himself and went to the phone.

"God Almighty, Shea," he whispered into the receiver. "What the hell is happening? I'm up at the Fines' and I'm looking for a place to hide my face. What broke down?"

"I only happened to be in early," Hoey answered. "I heard it off the radio, and me parking the car."

"Damn and blast it, Shea, we can't be running an investigation like this. We look like iijits. We *are* iijits. This has to stop, man."

Hoey didn't reply immediately.

"It's on your desk, sir," he said finally. "I took the liberty of looking through your morning stuff from Eilis. Timed at four fifteen from Dispatch. They knew to get you, anyway. I tried you at home but you were gone already."

Cohen walked into the hall now, heading for the

kitchen, thereby cutting short Minogue's anger.

"All right, all right." Minogue dug the receiver into his ear. "All right. Was it just this bombing thing, Shea?"

Hoey told him that he was awaiting a call from the National Library with more information. Doyle had gone over to the Library already to see the dockets and give Kearney a good going-over.

"Kearney, the Library assistant who phoned?"

"Yes. He knew Justice Fine's name and figured that the fella looking for books and filling in the request dockets was some relation of Fine's. That's how he remembered. Guess what Paul Fine was interested in?"

"Go on, Shea, for the love of God. I'm in Fine's house here, sitting on their phone."

"Sorry. He signed retrieval slips for nine books. Do you know how the system works there? You ask for books to be brought to you. There are millions of books there, and very valuable ones too. So Kearney is one of the assistants who'd go and get the actual books down off the shelves. Now it doesn't say what time the books were given out and Doyle's going to try and pin Kearney a bit better than that. All the nine books got to him, that is to say that none of the books was missing or anything. Ready for a few titles? *Catholicism and the Franco Regime* by a Norman Cooper. Never heard of any of these meself . . . *Addresses, Essays and Lectures* by J.E. de Balaguer, *Church and Politics of Chile* by a fella called Smith . . ."

"Hold on, hold on there, Shea. What's all this? I'm swimming in detail here and now is not the time."

". . . *Opus Dei: the Call of the World* by—"

"What?"

"That's it, though," said Hoey. "They *all* have something to do with Opus Dei."

"Opus Dei? But Shea, this thing at the Museum. Get Gallagher on to it, or at least confirm he's alerted to it. And is Jimmy Kilmartin on to this already?"

"Yes he is, sir. He fairly pounced, I can tell you."

Minogue stared at a shrouded mirror by the phone. Thoughts flickered and escaped. No order. He realized that he was biting his lip.

"He says he's going to hold off on the separate task force until we sort this out," Hoey continued. "He's hunting down the top dog in Opus Dei, or whatever they call their boss."

"I don't know anything about them, so I don't," Minogue muttered. "All I know is that they're religious."

"Wait now," said Hoey. "More stuff came in, wait'll you hear this. This is what you should have heard before the balls-up about last night."

Minogue stopped chewing his lip.

"Remember we left just after ten last night, didn't we? Well, a woman phoned in at a quarter past, a woman from Dun Laoghaire. She has a young lad in the Scouts. There was a troop of them out on manoeuvres on Killiney Hill sometime on Sunday afternoon. Putting names to trees and counting birds and that sort of diversion. Her young lad was up after his bedtime last night, annoying the heart and soul out of her. He saw a clip from the news, though, our bit on the site up on the Hill. Quick as a flash—so says the mother—the chiseller says: 'I was there.' She asked him about it. There's two detectives dispatched out to the house and the young lad will miss a morning's school over it. Will I call you back there when I have any news?"

Minogue considered the suggestion. A morning with the Fines would be a long morning but Hoey's news had buoyed him.

"No, Shea. Be better if you had some brief on what this Opus Dei is all about."

Minogue remembered Kilmartin's jibes from the previous night. Before they had knocked off for the night, Kilmartin had showed a shrinking Hoey the black-and-white photos of a curled, black mass. It was unrecognizable as the body it was supposed to be, except through the foreknowledge which Kilmartin's expression of grim indulgence brought. "Trial by fire. Burnt offerings," the blasphemous Kilmartin had muttered as he had laid snap after snap of what had been Brian Kelly on Hoey's desk like a ghastly game of cards.

"And try and get a hold of stuff and roll it out for me and Jim Kilmartin," Minogue finished. "And find out what Gallagher and company make of the bombing. Stay put by the phone. I'll get to you within the hour."

Minogue held the receiver while he broke the connection. Phone Gallagher himself? Kilmartin? Drop the interview here and head for the Squad HQ, try and get into the driving seat as the information came in? The phone rang under his stretched fingers.

"Yes," Minogue said, not yet back in the present. A man with a northern accent asked if Justice Fine was available. Minogue recognized the voice from somewhere.

"May I say who's calling?"

"Sean O'Duill from Armagh."

Cohen was already through the kitchen door and he took the receiver from Minogue. Fine emerged, carrying a tray. Minogue trudged after him into the front room.

"John Cohen, Your Eminence," he heard Cohen say. "Very glad of your support . . . I'll pass it on to him."

Fine paused, tray in hand, listening to Cohen. He laid the tray down.

"Look after yourself," he said to Minogue.

Minogue sat down in an armchair. Cohen came in yawning. Through the closing door Minogue heard Fine's voice now, resigned and gentle. "Yes, Sean, we do. We keep on asking ourselves if this is really happening. Shock, yes—"

Cohen closed the door and sat opposite Minogue. The two men remained silent, one staring contemplatively at the tray, the other, a bewildered, middle-aged Clareman.

Rosalie Fine, a compact, stocky woman, entered the room noiselessly. Small patches of colour had gathered high on her cheeks. Her eyes were clear hazel, but they seemed out of focus to Minogue. He rose. She held the limp sleeves of her cardigan as she sat. Billy Fine came in after her and sat next to her on the couch, taking one of her hands in his.

"I'm sorry for your trouble," Minogue said quietly. The words were thick and clumsy in his mouth and they ran back in his mind to taunt him. Rosalie Fine looked at him but Minogue felt she was not seeing him. Different people, these are. His embarrassment flared again. These people didn't use a countryman's stilted words. He dithered with the coffee, grateful for the strong sweet mixture.

"I was just about to apprise your husband of the

investigation so far." He paused to look at Fine. "But I'm far from sure now if this is the time—"

"There's no time," she interrupted. "There's never any proper time. There's no time that's right—"

"With all the people coming to the house," Minogue murmured, trying to recover.

"And last night's—?" She paused, stuck for words, and looked directly at Minogue. Minogue took a quick sip of coffee. He heard Fine's breath exhaled quickly.

"I wanted to reassure you that we're casting the net wide. We have the expertise and the tools at hand to track down the suspects. And the will," Minogue added slowly, returning Rosalie Fine's distracted gaze. "The Special Branch has already conducted an extensive search for extremists who might be even remotely connected with Arab or Islamic causes. We're still not ignoring the possibility of third-party involvement."

"You mean the IRA?" said Fine.

"And groups on the Continent who have links with the IRA," Minogue replied.

Fine nodded. The gesture seemed to wake Rosalie Fine from her detachment. "You don't sound very confident about this," she said abruptly. "We've been hearing these assurances from your Commissioner. I wonder if we're not being reassured a bit too much."

"Rose means that she'd sooner know the truth," said Fine. "Same as myself."

Minogue took a deep breath. He found that Rosalie Fine was still looking at him.

"This group that phoned the paper is not known to the Gardai. We've interviewed a large number of pos- sible suspects already. Now, in the light of what hap- pened last night, we might well be dealing with something involving more than just your own tragedy. I mean, not that . . ." Minogue felt his face redden and prickle.

Then Rosalie Fine spoke as though she had just entered the room. "Billy told me that you were in our Museum in Walworth Road."

Minogue nodded. A faint alarm buzzed behind his thoughts.

"What did you think of it?" she asked. She might be making polite conversation with someone she had just bumped into in the street, Minogue saw. Was this the wavering escapes of mind that grief brings?

"I enjoyed myself," he said. "All new to me. I'm County Clare, you see. Transplanted. I was taken to the altar by a Dublinwoman and I've been here since. It's a tough calling. Our two at home would put the heart crossways in you."

Rosalie Fine's face took on a slightly indulgent cast, with a trace of irony plain in her eyes.

"I'd say you're well able for them," she murmured. Fine seemed glad to let down his load for a moment too. He leaned forward and placed his cup on the table. Rosalie Fine's eyes slid out of focus again.

"I was talking to Lily," she said in a different voice. "Last night, she phoned . . . Paul met Lily here on a holiday. She's cousin of the Greens. Greens the booksellers. Lily is a Londoner, of course. We were happy when Paul fell for her. A nice family and she wasn't your traditional type to stay home and all that. Very modern and Paul liked that, he needed that. She was into the journalism herself, just starting into television. Well, he went to London with her but he couldn't stand it. 'Exile' he called it."

"Lily had every right to say no to living here in

Dublin," Billy Fine took up the conversation. "And to be blunt"—he glanced at his wife before resuming—"they were bitter parting. Lily is a very strong personality, very confident. Of course you'd assume that Paul was the opposite, the one who gave way more . . ."

"With Julia and David it was different," said Rosalie. "They knew early on they'd want to be moving eventually, seeing the world. With the youngest you never know. They say the youngest feels responsible for the parents. And then, who knows, maybe we wanted to hold on to him a bit longer . . ."

Minogue concentrated on part of the pattern on his cup as Rosalie Fine wept. Her husband wept also, sitting upright, clutching his wife's hand until the hands were a jumble of whitened knuckles. A minute passed. The phoned trilled once in the hall before they heard Cohen's bass tones. Then the voice stopped. Cohen opened the door.

"Rose, it's Canada," he said. "If you're up to it."

Rosalie Fine drew in a breath, stood and walked to the door. Fine yawned deep into his palm.

"She has a sister in Toronto," he murmured.

"I won't burden you any longer," said Minogue. "I must get on top of these developments and I don't want to be hanging on your phone."

Fine didn't seem to have heard him. He rubbed at an eyebrow. "I thought we were exempt, you might say," he remarked as he looked at the window. "Irishmen, the same as yourself. Oh, but certainly there's the root in Israel. You know, I must say that the years have me circling back to what I was born into. Being Jews, I mean, having a spiritual homeland. It's no religious fervour. I'm less 'Irish' than I was ten years ago. Than I was yesterday, I must say too.

*Aliyah* looms closer. It would not be a hardship on us."

"I don't follow you there, the last bit," said Minogue.

"*Aliyah*? We've given some thought to emigrating to Israel. Keep that under your hat. I'm a public figure the minute I walk out the door here. I'll tell them when I'm ready to retire and not before. Sure they only gave me the job last year, and me the youngest on the bench."

Fine turned from the window and stared at the policeman. "Look, you don't need to squirm here," Fine said. "I didn't expect you to come here spouting answers. You have to work out what happened at the Museum, same as myself."

Minogue hesitated before deciding to tell Fine. "There's something which came up late last night and again this morning," he said in little more than a whisper. "Something that the Commissioner would not have known to tell you at tea-time yesterday. This may prove important. Please don't read much into it yet until it becomes more substantial. We understand now that Paul may have been researching a group, a topic, which in turn may be linked to the death of a young man very recently."

Fine blinked.

"He may have mentioned this to you? Opus Dei."

Fine shook his head slowly.

"Not a word to me," he replied. "But you can't be in earnest. I heard of them before. They're a Catholic organization, aren't they?"

"Yes, they are."

"To do with lay people, though, religious minded."

"I believe you have it in a nutshell," said Minogue. "I'm awaiting a summary of what Opus Dei is, in Ireland anyway. Paul undertook to read up on them, but we can find no trace of notes he might have made. There was no mention of this until a citizen called last night, a man who works in the National Library. Paul was working there in the Library one day, researching this Opus Dei organization. There are several puzzling things about this. Opus Dei is not an extremist organization in the sense that they'd ever have anything to do with violence. And we don't understand why Paul didn't do his research in RTE, or discuss the topic with the people he worked with there. Then there's the lack of notes. One might suppose that he was making his first pass over the subject reading the books on Friday, so he'd only commit things to paper later on . . ."

Minogue paused but Fine said nothing.

"I'm not suggesting there's anything sinister or conclusive to this. And of course last night's outrage—"

"Friday," Fine interrupted then. "I met Paul Friday for dinner."

"Did he say anything which strikes you as odd, connected with what I've just told you? Was he excited about anything?"

Fine frowned and ran a fingertip around his lips.

"No, no. He made a face at something, though, something that came up in conversation. The journalism tended to make him a bit cynical, I think. Some of the hoi-polloi were in the Gallery for lunch too, some TDs and Ministerial Secs. The luminaries gather there, usually toward the end of the week, to gab and gossip about one another. I recognized a few of them and of course it does them no harm to doff their hats to Mr Justice Fine. Paul thought it was a bit rich. 'Butter wouldn't melt in their mouths,' he said, if I remember.

Yes. Not like him to be cynical, really. That may be more due to working with Mickey Fitzgerald and company. I know that Paul didn't much like digging into the more gritty types of exposés that Fitz and the others like to blow up. Paul said something about the Ard Fheis coming up next week, some comment about 'They'll all be at one another's throats soon.' Always the way, a cynic would answer, I suppose."

"You didn't ask him what he meant?"

"No. I assumed he meant that the Ard Fheis would be planning some strategies for the election. They're always a bit of a circus."

"I suppose," said Minogue. He made for the door. "If you can spare me the time later, could I draw you more toward Paul's personal life? I may be asking awkward questions as to any disputes, shall I say, with family and relations but I believe you'll know that I have only a policeman's interest . . . Could I arrange a time if I phone you later?"

Fine let his breath out and nodded slowly. He sat in the couch again and let himself slump. Minogue thanked Billy Fine and rose to leave. He nodded to Rosalie Fine in the hall. A woman sat next to her, crying.

Through the door and descending the steps, he was grateful to be out in the air again, breathing deeply and trying to loosen the tension in his shoulders. He nodded at the detectives in the surveillance car and headed down the footpath toward his car.

# ELEVEN

**M**inogue sat in the car for a minute before turning on the ignition. The familiar smells of the interior, cooked up stronger by the sunshine, rose around him; sparrows squabbled in the hedges. Kilmartin was nosing into the Opus Dei business. A possible witness, even though it was a child, from the murder site. Minogue had a dim sense of things moving now, gathering momentum, and for the first time in several days he felt excited. The excitement jarred against the anger he still nursed at Cohen's springing the news on him.

The sun's glare off the bonnet of the car prompted Minogue to move at last and he drove off toward Islandbridge. Forty minutes later he had managed to cover three miles. He had turned the engine off but the fan was still running as it worked to cool the engine. The traffic had not moved for five minutes.

Cyclists, many more than Minogue saw on ordinary workdays, swarmed around the jams, skittered over the kerbs, plainly enjoying themselves. Some motorists stood outside their cars, leaning elbows on their roofs. Pedestrians barely hid their smirks and they walked jauntily. Now that the weather was fine for the first day of the strike, the city had a holiday air.

Minogue counted to a hundred. Seeing no move ahead he started the engine and worked the car halfway on to the footpath. He wrote a note which he then placed on the dashboard as he stepped out to join the flow of pedestrians: "*Direct any tickets or tow fees to CDU Investigation Section c/o C. Insp. J. Kilmartin.*" Within a hundred yards of his abandoned car, Minogue was loping along, the motion of his freed body releasing him but slightly from the gloom which he had carried with him from Fine's. He found a working phone booth and told Eilis that he had been shanghaied by traffic but that he'd be in the office within twenty minutes. The shabby streets, the chaos and inertia, this sullen greying town now oppressed him. He began walking faster.

Minogue breezed by Eilis and glanced at the policemen's faces which turned to him. Hoey followed him into Kilmartin's office.

"I'm after coming from the Fines," Minogue muttered.

"How is it with them?" inquired Kilmartin.

"They'd be a lot less upset if they had their son's body," Minogue snapped. "Jews try to bury their dead as soon as they can. It's damned important to them and I wish there was something I could do. As for me, don't ask. I'm fit to be tied. What the hell happened last night?"

"One thing at a time, bucko," Kilmartin snapped back. "PM stipulates a minimum of three days, and well you know it. How would it be if we handed over the remains and then wanted them back for a test we forgot later on?"

"A word in someone's ear," Minogue said acidly, glaring at memos on Kilmartin's desk.

"I'll look into the matter," Kilmartin said slowly.

"To hell and damnation with looking into it, Jamesy," said Minogue. "The point is this: what can we tell Mr and Mrs Fine now?"

Minogue turned to Hoey before Kilmartin could frame an answer. "Shea: what about this child, this Boy Scout fella? Is there anything to hope for?"

"Keating's talking to him. Hasn't phoned in yet."

"Give me what you have on this fire-bombing, then. Or do I have to go out and buy a bloody newspaper to find out what's going on at all? I feel I've been away for a week and I don't know a damn thing that's happening."

"One witness heard the thing go off. Another witness heard a car tearing away down around the corner toward the city centre. She thinks she heard footsteps running fast before that."

"And one in the car, no doubt," Kilmartin slipped in.

"What's Gallagher say?" Minogue asked impatiently. "Is this a planned thing, a campaign? What are we looking at here? Come on, Shea, feed me."

Hoey blinked several times. "I phoned Gallagher: he has detailed a team to pick up a lot of the mob off the lists he drew up for us with the murder. Even ones he has already interviewed. Says the bombing and the murder were hardly the same people. No call to claim responsibility, he kept saying."

"He has all the manpower he needs," said Kilmartin. "We'd do well to leave Gallagher to his own devices on this. His crowd can do the fretting about what might happen next, if this is some campaign about I-don't-know-what."

"Anti-Semitic terror?" Minogue glared up from the desktop at Kilmartin.

Kilmartin didn't rise to the bait. "Lookit, God Almighty was on the phone not ten minutes ago, reminding us to do what we know best and to leave the other matter with the Branch. They have armed detectives outside people's homes and all, already."

"You mean to tell me he's saying or hoping there's no connection between last night and Paul Fine's murder?" Minogue barracked.

"Don't jump the gun, damn you," Kilmartin snarled. "You're in here with a mouth on you, bejases, and you'll know no government. It's all team-work, can't you see? Gallagher's helping us out and we're helping him. He's taking a lot of the weight too. Of course he's not an iijit about whether there's links or not. Don't you start getting foxy with me about it, man. Like it or not, we fall in line with an overall strategy. He said and did nothing to impede us."

"Are we losing staff on the head of this, then?" Minogue shot back. "The staff we were given for the murder?"

Kilmartin looked at Hoey, then swivelled his gaze full onto Minogue. "You're losing your marbles, by the sounds of things." Still staring at Minogue, he said to Hoey: "You didn't hear that, Detective Garda Hoey, did you?"

Hoey shuffled.

"Share and share alike," Kilmartin drawled in a

slow, ominous monotone which Minogue registered as one of his early-warning systems. "We work with them; they're our mates; they have the goods; we need them. If they ask us for breakfast in bed, we'll give it to them and we won't throw it at them. They're doing nearly all the interviewing. Don't be rearing up on me because of it. Are you sure you're not a bit too close to the boy's family to stay cool on the matter?"

Minogue cast around for words. After several moments he felt the loosening of the anger in his throat. "I suppose you could say I'm not cool on the matter, Jimmy. Yes, you could say that, all right."

Kilmartin's brow lifted. He kicked off from the desk and rolled back to the wall before standing up and killing his cigarette. Glad to see me in a flap, Minogue wondered.

"I'll see about the funeral arrangements," said Kilmartin. "Now: about any people that Fine put away in jail."

"We've been through the list of cases he's heard," said Hoey. "Twice, as a matter of fact. There's nothing worth getting excited over."

"What about Brian Kelly and Opus Dei?" Minogue led.

"I'll give you what I have so far. We can't say for certain that this Brian Kelly was actually a member of the outfit but . . ." said Hoey.

Kilmartin nodded. "Go on anyway, man, can't you?"

"Right so. Opus Dei is the Latin for 'God's Work.' It was founded in 1928 by a Spanish priest, a fella called de Balaguer. Hope I'm saying the name right. It was one of his books that Fine looked at on Saturday, if ye remember the dockets. It's an apostolic movement.

Here's a quote on what they do: '. . . *strive to sanctify their daily work and family life, to Christianize society.'* "

"You mean that it was set up to counter the pagan materialistic twentieth century, especially after the Bolsheviks and what have you?" Minogue asked.

Hoey shrugged. "I'd have to know more to agree there. But it's for lay people from any walk of life. Clergy can join up too. The basic idea is so as the church doesn't get to be out of touch with modern society, that's the way I read the aims. Now these Opus Dei people, they want to use whatever social positions they have to renew the faith. Make it more relevant, you see, on the factory floor . . . outside the chapel, like. Very sincere type people. There are ranks in Opus Dei. It's organized like you'd see in any business. The top dogs are called Numeraries. They're about one-tenth of the whole outfit."

"How big is this Opus Dei thing?" Kilmartin asked.

"They don't give out lists of names or tell you the membership in any country. Estimates average about 70,000 world-wide."

"They're not Masons or what have you, running around with funny clothes and doing unnatural things, are they?" Kilmartin pressed.

"I don't know about that, sir. I believe that the church forbids Catholics to become Masons . . . Anyway, the top group are Numeraries. They stay celibate and they have to be highly educated and trained in things like philosophy and theology as well. They usually live in centres, one big house, like. There are at least three centres in Dublin but I'm having a divil of a time getting any facts on this. The next rank is Associate. They can be priests as well. They're supposed to be celibates but they needn't be university grads or professional types. Then there are Supernumeraries. They can marry and so on. The last rank are Co-operators and they're basically sympathizers. I've been talking about the men's branch of Opus Dei. The women's branch has either Numerary Assistants— they're basically skivvies who keep house for the higher-ups—or Numeraries like the men's."

"You mean 'don't like the men' by the sounds of things," said Kilmartin.

"Oh, I get it," said Hoey. "That's a good one. You're probably right there. The women Numeraries are celibates too. Matter of fact the women are encouraged to sleep on a plank until they're forty years of age."

"On a plank?" asked Kilmartin. "Are you in earnest? What the hell for?"

"On a plank. Wait'll you hear this: the men and the women often wear bands with pins stuck on them, stuck into their thighs. So as to mortify themselves. That's not the end of it either."

"Go away out of that, you're codding me," said Kilmartin.

"They flog themselves too," Hoey declared.

"They do not!" said Kilmartin.

Hoey repeated the notes slowly. Kilmartin looked to Minogue. Minogue shrugged. "We're the Island of Saints and Scholars, Jimmy—penance and mortification. The monks did that class of caper too, you know. If that was our Golden Age, I'll take me chances down by the docks after dark."

"Ah, come on now." Kilmartin, the custodian of Irish virtues past, rallied. "They can't all be cracked like that."

"Right, sir. Those details sort of jumped out at me,

though, I must say," said Hoey. "I should tell you the more important stuff—"

"Sleeping on a plank until you're forty sounds pretty important to me," Minogue muttered darkly.

"Like I was saying, I couldn't find out how many Opus Dei there are in Ireland. They're conservative and they consider themselves the knights of the Church. As for people saying they're a secret society, they say they're not. The members take vows in front of a superior but Opus Dei says these vows are not necessarily holy vows. The Pope changed the status of Opus Dei a few years ago and they're now a personal prelature. I'm not sure what the ins and outs of that are but I think it means they are allowed to work more on their own and not have to be telling their local bishop what they're at as much as they used to. They have residences here in Dublin, a few of them near to the university. They have a constitution."

"A constitution?" repeated Minogue. "Sounds like a country. Organized, anyway."

"They have titles like 'President' and divisions like 'Region,' so it doesn't sound very religious, does it?" agreed Hoey. "They don't allow their constitution to be translated out of Latin except with the permission of their brass," he added. Their current President, they call him 'Father,' is another Spaniard. His name is del Portillo. And the constitution is not to be made public at all. That's why people say that Opus Dei is shady."

"No more than shady, though," said Kilmartin.

"Right. Some people say that Opus Dei interferes in politics and what have you. There was a stink a few years ago in Spain because that oul' dictator fella, Franco, liked Opus Dei and some of his Ministers were Opus Dei members. And I seem to remember reading the name Opus Dei in the paper several years ago to do with Chile and Paraguay."

"Well, at least we don't fit into that class of act, do we, men?" said Kilmartin. "It's my opinion that climate has a lot to do with the fanatical temperaments of the races and peoples who make their homes in southern climes. The equator and all that. Latin peoples are very unstable; very tricky with the knife and the gun and full of talk about honour. Sure the men are like bloody cockerels strutting around the place."

"If they only had our brains and our way of life, they'd be sensible enough to lay aside the gun and the knife." Minogue couldn't resist goading his colleague. "Then they could take up the rocket-launchers, I suppose. Do the thing right."

"I could rely on you to come up with something like that," said Kilmartin in the tone of betrayed loyalty. "I know you're only poking fun at me. I was just voicing an opinion. Look at the papers any day of the week and you'll see what I'm talking about."

Look at the papers, Minogue echoed hollowly within. He resisted throwing his eyes to heaven.

"Anyway," Kilmartin continued. "This is very interesting. How did you get your hands on this so fast?"

Hoey looked embarrassed. "Well, actually, Darling—Doyle, I mean, went to the National Library first thing this morning to get the dockets from that fella. He had a look at one of the books and he stuck it in his pocket. He'll take it back, of course. I had a dekko through it this morning for an hour."

"Darling Doyle?" asked Kilmartin.

"Doyle used to be on the whore squad, sir, up outside the Burlington. The girls got to know him rather well."

"The same Doyle is hardly tripping over his mickey in a hurry to join this Opus Dei, I'd say, after some of his work assignments," Kilmartin chuckled. "Maybe we should ask him what he knows about planks in that line of business. Now, no more of this guff: what about our Mr Kelly? Where does he fit in this order of things."

"So far it's not clear, sir. He didn't live in an Opus Dei house, so it's doubtful he was one of their Numeraries. He was university educated. An economist."

"Bejases, he must have seen the state of the nation's finances and realized that prayer was our only hope," said Kilmartin weakly.

"Never married. There was some class of oratory in the house but hardly a stick of furniture. House was his own, bought two years ago and half-way paid already. Kelly had steady advancement in the Civil Service since he joined up eight years ago. He used to go to Brussels quite a lot on EEC business. He was an expert in banking."

"But we haven't actually fitted Kelly in with Opus Dei, have we?" Minogue said.

"Bit of a lemoner there, you're right. Doyle is still on the phone trying to get a name so we can try to plug Kelly in somewhere along the line and see if he has any connections or associates in this group. I'll go out and see if he's having any luck."

Hoey left his notes on Kilmartin's desk and he walked back out to the squad room.

"Has a head on his shoulders, Hoey," said Kilmartin. "That Doyle is handy too, isn't he?"

Minogue nodded. He looked at his watch. "What's Keating doing that he hasn't phoned in? This young lad out in Killiney—"

"Time enough, Matt. He'd phone if there was something we had to jump on right off the bat. You should know how tricky it is getting stuff from kids. Keating might end up having to reconstruct this interview in evidence, so he's probably taking his time and getting it right. Sooner done right than done hasty, man."

Minogue held off a snappy rejoinder.

"You know how the current is taking us, don't you, Matt?"

"Matter of fact, I don't really. I still can't see Paul Fine's killer in my mind. He or she or it or they . . . no profile, really. And I don't even want to think about motives, for fear if I look at one I'll see it can't hold water."

"Jases, man," said Kilmartin. "It's being so cheerful is what keeps us going. Come on now, we're on the road here with this at last, I can feel it in me water. Aren't we, damn it?"

"All roads lead to Rome," Minogue murmured.

"Don't be acting the maggot. We seem to have a bridge from Kelly back to the Fine boy. Leave aside the fire-bomb thing now for a minute. Maybe we had better start thinking out loud so as we know we're on the same track."

"Fair enough," said Minogue, stretching. "We'd like to believe that there's a connection between a reporter and a Civil Servant. A reporter's job is to get information and to present it to his public. To his boss first, to see if it makes sense."

"But Fitzgerald didn't know anything about any interest Fine had in Opus Dei."

"Let's be bold and say that Brian Kelly got in touch with Paul Fine. Recently, very recently. Thursday, Friday, even."

"It couldn't be the other way around, all right," Kilmartin said. "What has Fine got to offer Kelly?"

"Right. Before we start to wonder what it is that Kelly wanted to say to Fine, let's ask why Kelly would want to get in touch with Fine specifically. Assuming he has something to tell him."

"Why Fine? Well, everyone knows everyone in Dublin, Matt. He might have heard Fine's name in conversation or met him socially over a gargle. He might have heard Fine's name on the programme. We can find that out sooner or later, I'm sure."

"But why not get in touch with Mickey Fitz if the same Brian Kelly wanted to air a complaint? Fitzgerald is a tough piece of work. People'd listen to him."

"You have me there, all right." Kilmartin rubbed his hands together as if to summon a genie. "Maybe he wanted to remain anonymous and decided that going through Fine would help him stay that way."

"All right. Now we bump back into the big question as to what it was that Kelly may have wanted to air."

"A gripe about something going on in the Civil Service?"

"Then Paul Fine would have been cramming on the Civil Service. He appears to have been trying to digest what he could about Opus Dei."

"Can't get around it, Matt, you're right. Give me a minute and I'll try and come up with a better one."

After a pause, Kilmartin gave in. "Has to be something about Opus Dei. I can't see around it."

"Fitzgerald has his staff rotating through the scandal department, or whatever name he likes to call muckraking. Paul Fine's turn came, are you with me?"

"I am. But how would Kelly know that Fine was the man who'd like a bit of dirt on Opus Dei?"

214

"Who's to say that he needed to know? Perhaps all he wanted was someone in the media."

"But Jases, why pick *Fine*? He wasn't any tiger, you know, no disrespect intended. And when all is said and done, I can't see what scandal this crowd of Holy Joes in Opus Dei would worry about to the extent of killing someone over. We have to admit that they're motivated by religious principles and all that goes with that. This isn't a dog-eat-dog business, like in Chile or whatever, with the Communists on one side and the Fascist lads waving crucifixes and guns on the other side."

"Umm," said Minogue. "I get the feeling you're a bit shy yet. Are you going to give me the three F's?"

Minogue was referring to what some detectives liked to call the Three Eff-offs. It was something which any astute officer invoked when speculation was getting in the way of police work: facts, forensic information and files. A killer was to be found in one of these three worlds, not in daydreaming police minds.

"Tell you what," said Kilmartin. "By all means we'll go as far as logic takes us with this Opus Dei thing, but I'll have to re-think splitting the team tomorrow. You with the Fine case of course, Gallagher and his big-shots thrown in. What we have of the whole task force will work through what your interviews can point to as well."

"I need Hoey."

"OK," said Kilmartin, less than enthusiastically. "Me, I'll be wanting Keating and Murtagh, then, for a start, to take on Kelly. Lookit, sure, you may have something under your hat this very minute and you not knowing it. That Boy Scout lad—his mother phoned in. There, see?"

Minogue's mind began to wander. *Why* would Kelly get in touch with Fine? Fine's turn at the dirt pile had come around, but he had kept his own project on Arab-IRA links on the side. The help-line number and Minogue's name beside it on the pad—

"Kelly phoning here looking for me the other night," Minogue murmured. "What can we do with that . . . ?"

"I can tell you that one easy enough," Kilmartin said slowly, rubbing the filter end of an unlit cigarette around his lips as an aid to concentration. He slid further into the chair. "You know I have a copy of that call on the day's tape. I'm carrying that copy around with me—here, right inside in me pocket—so as the minute we can latch on to any pal of Kelly that hums and haws about anything, I'll fire the tape at him. We'll get better confirmation it was Kelly's voice, as well as leverage, I'm thinking. There's life in the old dog yet, isn't there?"

"There seems to be," Minogue had to concede.

"Are you sure you don't want a bottle of holy water with you, your honour?" Eilis asked.

Minogue made a face at her. He looked back to Kilmartin's office to see Kilmartin half into the jacket of his suit, like a bear struggling to get a bee out of its armpit.

"Did you see that film *The Exorcist* years ago, did you?" Eilis persisted. "A young one possessed by the divil, spewing up a big spout of pea soup anytime the priest came near her. And then she had an unholy leaping fit when the priest took out the holy water. Cursing and swearing galore."

"I'm not sure it'll be the same effort with us today,

Eilis. This is a Christian country. Pagans have their own way to defend themselves against priests anyway."

"Well, *beir bua*. That tape with that call on it, it's a fright to listen to it."

"I hope it is," said Kilmartin. "We're off to bell the cat. Patch anything important to the car, would you, especially anything from Keating out talking to the Boy Scout and his mammy in Dun Laoghaire."

Kilmartin had used rank where Doyle could not and thus Kilmartin had two names, two men to meet in a house on Churchtown Road. Drumm, Finbar Drumm, was a member of the Opus Dei residence; Father Heher, of order unknown, was from the seminary at Clonliffe College. Kilmartin had had his name from the secretary to the Archbishop of Dublin, as one who had contact with Opus Dei members in the city.

"As for the explanation that the Archbishop's office was not directly responsible for the work of Opus Dei, that didn't thrill the shoes off me, I can tell you," Kilmartin was saying. "Felt like I was getting the brush-off."

"As I understand Church politics, bishops and archbishops want to know about every sparrow that falls in their dioceses," said Minogue.

"Every sparrow . . . what do you mean?"

"The idea is that God knows about and cares about every bird that falls, no matter how tiny. He also keeps track of every molecule and every blade of grass that grows, I understand."

Kilmartin looked across the roof of the car at Minogue, grimacing against the glare. "I hope you're not going to be contrary out here with this priest and the other fella and give me heartburn, for the love of Jases, are you?"

"Of course I am, Jimmy. Isn't that why you're dragging me along? Before you got these two names you were content to let me get on with the Fine investigation."

"Don't be exercising yourself, man dear. The deal was that we hold off splitting the case-work until after we see these Holy Joes. Later on today we'll know better if there's anything real to be working on as regards the two deaths."

Kilmartin swung the tape-recorder on its straps into the back seat of the police car. He drove himself. Minogue signed in on the radio. The traffic seemed to have eased. Kilmartin capitalized on Dublin people's sharp facility for recognizing Gardai in any garb and Garda cars of plain hues, and he stared down drivers beside him at traffic lights. None tried to jam him out of lanes.

"Play it, why don't you?" he said to Minogue.

Minogue listened to the clicks and tones as the voice asked to be put through to the chief officer investigating the Fine murder. *He's not available, would another do?* No. *Could Inspector Minogue return your call? What was that name again? Minogue.* The caller hung up.

Minogue rewound the tape. "Gives me the willies," he said. "I hope there's enough there for one of these fellas to identify it as Kelly's voice."

"Now you're talking—get out of the way, you half-wit—but the thing is . . ." Kilmartin paused to give a withering look at a slow driver he was passing. "Why you're along for the outing is, I want you to watch how they react to the tape. You'll know what I mean if you see it."

"I'm an experienced lie-detector, am I?"

218

"Well, you're always blowing your horn about magic powers from Clare."

"That's only hurling and politics, Jimmy."

"We'll see about that. I could have called Kelly's brother in and he could have given me a confirmation for his brother's voice if that was all we wanted. I'm not saying I expect them to tell me a lie about it, but there's this secrecy thing, the reputation for conniving. Like the shagging Masons. We'll see if us old dogs can pick up a fox here, won't we, begob?"

An old dog. If this Father Heher was sharpish and started playing professor, would Minogue be expected to spring like a loyal wolfhound and do battle with a theological brain?

"Isn't it odd the way everything looks different without buses? You're so used to seeing them all over the place, holding up the traffic. At least there'll be people getting healthy exercise," said Kilmartin as he passed a lorry at speed. "Fire the lot of them, I say. Like Reagan did with the air-traffic crowd. Then they'll know you're serious, so you can give them their jobs back and they won't be so cocky again. I hope to Christ someone stands up this weekend at this bloody Ard Fheis and lays down the law about this strike business. Paralysing the capital city and not caring a damn what havoc they wreak. There's millions of pounds being lost every day, I'm sure. Who's running the country, I ask you? Is it them or is it us?"

Minogue had no reply. He didn't know from one moment of James Kilmartin's hyperbole to the next who the "us" and the "they" were. Paralysis. James Joyce calling the place the centre of paralysis. Should he vex Kilmartin by mentioning Joyce? Bloom, a Jew. Who would these Opus Dei people be then, in this play? All priggish Dedaluses with minds like drawn plans for medieval cathedrals, all edges and God-given certainties?

"Bollocks," said Kilmartin. "Missed the turn."

Kilmartin reversed at speed, the transmission whining, and drew a squeal out of the tyres as he turned onto Churchtown Road. The house was sedate, large even, stolidly middle class.

"Here it is. Read 'em and weep."

# TWELVE

As he stood in the hallway, Minogue forgot that the outside of it had looked like any other along the street. The small front garden had been tidy, the driveway clean. Additions had been made to the back of the house but the annexe could not be seen until one had taken several steps inside the gate. Shrubs and small trees had been well attended to, as though by a gardener.

A replica of an old Irish cross hung on the wall in the hall, the imitation black bog-oak stark and striking. Instead of the clutter of a family—shoes or bags higgeldy-piggeldy next to stairs as unconscious traps for parents, the smells of cooking and carpet and clothes—the hall was a plain vestibule. What was it about the smell of floor wax that reminded Minogue of alien life? Who would take the trouble to wax and polish floors, and why would they want to be doing it? Did they have nothing better to do, like sit around or drink or read or argue?

Finbar Drumm led them to an oversized kitchen: spotless, no pots lying around, all new fixtures. It looked institutional to Minogue, right down to the arrangement of coffee mugs on hooks by the sink. A bearded man with very good teeth and twinkling eyes rose from his seat by the table and greeted the two policemen. He was wearing blue jeans and a short-sleeved shirt. His feet were bare. Father Heher was a man who took exercise, a man who might exert himself in many ways, Minogue believed. He looked into this healthy face as it smiled broadly.

"Joe Heher, how do ye do?" said the sunny, barefoot priest. A tight handshake, the slow vowels of a countryman from the Midlands. Drumm waved them into chairs. Everything about the kitchen and these two men was solid and clean and functional. Drumm smelled faintly of aftershave. His ruddy face and well-groomed hair suggested the same pursuits as Heher. *Mens sana in corpore sano.*

"I hope ye weren't expecting any special regalia," smiled Heher, catching a glimpse of Kilmartin's look of appraisal. They miss nothing, Minogue thought, and they smile so readily. He was not displeased with Kilmartin's discomfort at having to talk to a barefoot mind-reader.

"No bother at all, Father," said Kilmartin, trying to regain a solid ground of titles proper to his Ireland.

Heher was having none of it. "Joe, if you don't mind," he said. "I'm not one for keeping barriers of any kind. There's tea to be had."

"Ah no, thanks," said Kilmartin. Minogue heard in his demur a tone of contest and rebuttal. Kilmartin placed the cassette recorder on the table.

"A plug-in, is it?" said Drumm, ever helpful.

"Batteries, thanks very much."

"It's truly a shock to think of Brian no longer with us," said Heher. He looked intently into Kilmartin's face but then settled on Minogue's. Heher's sad smile faded into an expression which Minogue guessed was to convey a deep understanding.

"Such a tragedy gives us all pause for reflection. I only hope that Brian's death will lead to an enriching of those of us he left behind in this life."

"He may not have headed for the next life willingly," said Minogue. "And that'd make it the more tragic, I'm thinking."

Heher's eyes widened and he looked to Drumm.

"Dear God," Drumm whispered. "Awful."

"Burned to a crisp in the back of his car," said Kilmartin. "Is it something he would have done himself, knowing him as you do?"

"I ask myself every day if we ever know our deeper selves," said the now-contemplative Heher. "What fears and clouds lurk in the back of any man's mind? For myself I had no inkling that Brian wanted to end his life."

"Nor I," added Drumm. "Brian was a gifted and hopeful person. The roots ran deep."

"He was a member of Opus Dei?" said Minogue.

"Indeed," said Heher. The faint signs of a smile returned to flicker around his mouth.

"But he lived on his own. Is that unusual?"

"Not at all," said Drumm. "Our calling accommodates itself to many situations. God calls where he finds you."

Not too early, Minogue wanted to say.

"But, for example, if Brian were one of your Numerary members, he'd very likely have lived in one of your residences. Like this one, for all the world?"

Heher's face showed well-meaning puzzlement. "I see you know a little about our work. Normally we don't disclose information about our members: it's enough to know that they come from all sections of society. Everyone is different, and we all have different needs. It's very difficult to deal in terms of normal and abnormal, as Opus Dei respects everyone's individuality and path to God."

"We tend to think of violent crime as abnormal, even though some incidence of it might seem normal," said Minogue.

"An interesting reflection there. Brian was not a Numerary, he was an Associate. We have no need of secrecy *per se* but we need some measure of privacy to ensure our apostolic effectiveness," said Drumm gently.

"So Brian was well enough known to members of this house, then, such as yourselves?"

"Yes," said Drumm.

"So you live here too," Minogue asked Heher.

"No. I live on the north side. I teach bits of philosophy and French at Clonliffe," said Heher.

"What exactly is your role here, Father?" Kilmartin asked.

"I'm a member of Opus Dei myself. I help with some doctrinal matters, some guidance."

"So the Archbishop's office always turns to you in the event that someone is inquiring about Opus Dei?" asked Minogue.

"Now you have it," said Heher, regaining his smile. "I had the telephone call this morning and that's how I knew to meet ye here with Finbar. They love to load me down with jobs. I think I'll have to learn to complain better."

Which means the exact opposite, Minogue realized. He wondered if complaining was a mortal sin for members of Opus Dei. Did Heher flog himself the odd time too, and take cold showers?

"Form a union, Father," said Kilmartin. "Then you'll be set up nicely."

"Oh, I get it," said Heher, showing his teeth in a broad smile. "You're referring to the bus strike, I take it."

"Did Brian Kelly ever belong to a different rank than Associate?" Minogue asked, rafting in on the pleasantries.

Drumm cleared his throat before answering. "Matter of fact, Brian stayed in this residence for several years."

"Why did he leave?"

"He felt ready for a move," Heher replied easily. "Nobody is shackled here."

"Same rank here, then, as when he left?"

"I was coming to that," said Drumm. He was working to maintain the genial air. "Brian was experiencing difficulties with his calling as a Numerary member. He had demonstrated great effectiveness and faith, but all of us have our clouded days. We all strive to renew our faith and commitment. It would be a poor and unreflective member who didn't experience the anxiety which the deepest and most sincere self-examination can bring."

Drumm looked hopefully into Kilmartin's face.

Heher looked down at the grain on the bare table-top and nodded his head several times. "We're out in the world, you see," he joined in. "We're mortal and fallible, all of us. We meet with the stress of modern living like anyone else. Our apostolic work brings us into tough situations and it's no surprise that we should feel the pressures sometimes, the same as any other thinking men, thinking Christian men. We don't hide in foxholes, metaphorical or otherwise. We don't shun the world. Finbar here is a successful doctor, for example."

Drumm smiled shyly and Minogue thought he saw the first genuine emotion in the group. Praise, nothing more, nothing less: a little praise was the hook when it should always be a pillow. Minogue made a mental note to praise his children to the eyeballs the next time he saw them.

"The other brothers in this house include a solicitor and a town-planner. If you came here at tea-time you'd see plenty of cars parked outside in the driveway. What kind of car does Pierce drive now, Finbar?"

"A Saab," Drumm smiled. An inside joke, Minogue realized.

"There's even a television in nearly everyone's room here. Not to speak of fancy clothes," Heher went on, smiling indulgently at the two policemen.

Minogue felt his unease turn to distaste. "So ye're not Martians, I take it," he said.

"Precisely," said Heher, showing his teeth again.

"Any of the membership work in Radio Telifis Eireann, Father Heher?" Minogue asked quickly, his gaze holding Heher's and watching Heher's smile falter.

"An interesting question, that. Not here, I think, is there, Finbar?"

"No, er, Inspector. We can't boast such glitterati here, I'm afraid."

"Any work on the buses, then?" said Kilmartin, trying to ease the sudden tension. "'Cause if they do, they're not at work today, the rascals. Ha ha."

Undeterred, Minogue went on. "How would I find out if there are any Opus Dei members in, say, advertising companies or factories? Or in the Army, say?"

"Well, you'd ask an Opus Dei member where he or she worked, I suppose," said Heher.

"From the top down, I mean. Working from a membership list."

"Well, now, you have me there, now. I expect you'd have to apply to our President and see if he'd be willing to discuss it."

"The man in Spain, is it?"

"Good for you. In Rome, actually. Our office is in Rome, yes."

Drumm was sitting very still. Heher's smile was a frozen ruin.

"Nobody here in Ireland?"

"The authority to give out the names of members must come from Rome," said Heher.

"Has such been asked of you before, Father?"

"No, it hasn't," said Heher evenly.

"If the civil authorities thought it a matter of great urgency . . ."

"I must confess that I've no experience in this. I'd really need to seek guidance myself if it were a matter of such urgency."

"How about a court order, Father Heher?"

Heher shrugged and worked on the smile again. "If my writing would speed things up, I'll certainly try. But may I ask you then if you'll be candid about why you'd want such information?"

"You certainly may," said Minogue, feeling more

vindictive now that Heher's unctuousness stood out so freakishly in the tense atmosphere. "We'll be investigating the possibility that Brian Kelly's death is connected to his membership in Opus Dei."

Heher's expression changed for an instant and Minogue thought he saw a hostility shimmer in his eyes. In the few seconds of strained silence that followed, Minogue berated himself for dancing so easily to Kilmartin's tune. Here was Minogue, leaping on command. Was he that addicted to his dislike of Heher and what Heher represented?

"You'll be aware that nothing like this has happened before," Heher said coolly. "And I note that you are saying in effect that Brian Kelly may have been a victim of foul play. Not that despondency got the better of him and he took his own life, but that one of our fraternity may know something about the death of his brother?"

"Former brother, I believe," said Minogue.

"Well, now," Kilmartin intervened, scraping his heels on the floor. "Before we go into details about Mr Kelly's tenure here and what you knew of the deceased, I'd like ye to listen to this little tape which myself and the Inspector have with us. The wonders of science. Would ye listen carefully and consider separately whether ye recognize this person's voice?"

Kilmartin pushed Play and sat back in his chair. His eyes flickered to Minogue once. Looking to the intent Heher who seemed as if he might be praying, Minogue believed that Heher had seen Kilmartin's glance.

"Great," said Kilmartin acidly. "Fuckin' great. You're always dragging me in here. Sooner or later God

Almighty or an Assistant Comm will be here and he'll see us and want to know why we're not at work. Where'll we be then, I'd like to know?"

Minogue took the change from the cashier.

"It certainly is," he replied to her observation on the weather. "Me and me boss here are going to mitch off work for the afternoon and go up to the Phoenix Park. Frighten the deer."

"Don't be waiting on the bus," said the girl dryly. She knew Minogue both as a Garda and a large white coffee with a sticky bun, no butter. Minogue grinned. She might even know that he was referring to Garda headquarters in the Park, not the hundreds of acres of parkland where deer ran free.

"Where will we be then?" Kilmartin repeated.

"In good company, if they're here too, I suppose," Minogue replied. "What's it to our legion superiors where we do our thinking, here or back in the squad room? Anyway, you owe me."

"I owe you a kick in the arse if I owe you anything," said Kilmartin.

"You owe me for upping my blood pressure with those two moonies back up on Churchtown Road. You knew I'd see red with the likes of Heher."

Kilmartin had no reply ready. He began shovelling brown sugar into his coffee and looked around at the motley crowd which made up Minogue's congregation in this, his favourite branch of Bewley's Oriental Café.

"See that little shite over there in the corner pretending to be invisible?" said Kilmartin.

Minogue looked toward the corner and picked out a small middle-aged man with the features of a wary cat.

"Yes, him. I shopped him first nigh on twenty years ago. Never forget a face. He was forever breaking into church poor-boxes. As well as that, the bugger could climb anything. A shagging fly, he was. I wonder is he the same now. Take the eye out of your head, he would. Right from under your nose too."

"All God's chillun got wings, Jimmy. That's what I like about this place."

"All God's children, my royal Irish arse. They'll phone God Almighty's office, you know. That Heher fella: bad news if he's vexed, I'd say."

"Do I care, though?" Minogue mumbled, an image of Heher's face still lingering.

Kilmartin lit a cigarette, shook his head and fell to stroking his nose. A tall woman with her hair cut severely, a single sharp-looking earring dangling from her ear over Kilmartin's head, appeared at their table. "This is non-smoking," she announced. Kilmartin looked up into an impassive face. Minogue clamped his jaw muscles in an effort not to smile: she was holding a paperback and he recognized the title as one he had borrowed from Iesult, *The Rights and Wrongs of Women*. The woman left when Kilmartin topped his cigarette.

"Sorry for breathing," he said in a savage undertone.

Minogue could resist the temptation no longer. "See the book? *The Rights and Wrongs of Women*."

"Jesus, Mary and holy Saint Joseph. Everywhere you look there's a fuckin' WAMmer. She knew I was a Guard, too, of course. And she and the likes of her sitting in Bewley's instead of being out at work somewhere. Bad' cess to the bitch, the dying leper's vomit," Kilmartin growled. "If it was a man that was in it, I would have told him where to go and made no bones about it," he added. "Taking advantage of my breeding to be polite to the fair sex."

Minogue did not wish to provoke trouble beyond amusement by noting aloud that Kilmartin's *amour courtois politesse* had gone the way of the cigarette.

"Judo or something, Jimmy. You never know. Smoking is a vice, anyway."

Kilmartin's eyelids narrowed in a glittering contempt. "The niff of her hairy armpits is more of a health hazard as far as I'm concerned. Let's get back to those two Holy Joes above in Churchtown Road."

"All right," said Minogue, bolstered by the first of the coffee. "Not a mention from them of Paul Fine, not a hint: that's the most significant thing that I got out of it."

"Until Drumm asked us how the phone call was taped, like?"

"Right. I think they were genuinely ignorant about it. Drumm turned a bit white at the gills. I don't like them sitting on a possible membership list, though."

"I think you got the message across to them pretty well there. They might work on excommunicating you."

"Too late, Jimmy, I'm the white elephant that fled the circus a long time ago. I had the feeling that Heher was daring me to slap a court order on the organization, knowing damn well I couldn't get one. Even if I could, they could bog me down by giving me a phone number in Rome and telling me to learn Italian very rapid."

"Heher and Drumm," murmured Kilmartin, now in the grip of the coffee. "Sounds like a tobacconist's shop."

"Or a sexual disorder," said Minogue. "Out of Krafft-Ebing."

"Kraft what? Margarine?"

"Interesting idea," said Minogue, mimicking Heher. "Margarine on the wane. No. Krafft-Ebing wrote a compendium of human sexual behaviour. Heavy emphasis on disorders."

"Do you know," Kilmartin said earnestly as he leaned forward, "you seem to have a dirty mind. I hope to God I'm not due for this mental fit that has your brain fried up like an egg. All this talk about sex and the Ryan woman butchering her husband—middle-age crazy, the Yanks call it. With all due respect, you were cracked enough to start out with."

"Jimmy, I've been thinking. Maybe the Women's Action Movement had put something in the coffee here that has us dancing in our heads and being rude to priests."

"Very shagging funny. Do you see me laughing?"

"After all, things are only getting going. First it's Fran Ryan done in by his wife. Maybe there's a secret signal like a dog whistle over the radio that signals women to go out and get the kitchen knife and—"

"Mad. You're barking mad. I don't doubt but that you'll be running up and down O'Connell Street on all fours in a minute, waving your mickey and biting people and lathering at the mouth."

"Remember the thirty-seven, James Kilmartin," Minogue intoned in the most lugubrious West Clare-Transylvanian accent he could muster. "Your number vill be fifty-four—"

"Fifty-three until 7 October, if it's all the same to you. Stop acting the bollocks. There might be someone in here who knows us. Control yourself."

"Don't say I didn't warn you."

"Listen. They didn't make any bones about saying it was Kelly's voice on the tape? No funny stuff there?"

"Right," said Minogue emphatically, launching himself into the bun. "That went a long way toward deciding me too. No humming and hawing. I'm pretty sure they were on the level."

"So what we have out of this"—Kilmartin extended his fingers and held the first—"one, their assistance in tracking down whoever might have been with Kelly this last while. Heher maintains that Kelly didn't come to him for 'guidance,' but he may have gone to someone else if he wanted advice. Two, the names of his acquaintances that had anything to do with Opus Dei. Drumm used to be pally with Kelly up until Kelly left the house last, when was it . . . ?"

"February last year. Over a year and a half ago," said Minogue. "I think we could press more on the business of Kelly being demoted or whatever they call it. Remember? Kelly's commitment changing a bit. 'Such that his work and status better suited the rank of Associate,' said Heher. That's a roundabout way of saying that Brian Kelly had had it with that mob. To my way of thinking, they wouldn't be too happy about losing him from their top rank. Those Numerary fellas seem to be dug in deep and I had the impression that it was a one-way street. They have to have spent years studying, they have to be professionally trained and then devote loads of time to Opus Dei—"

"They don't kill backsliders, Matt. They were giving him a breather to see if he'd renew his whatchamacallit, his vocation."

Minogue tripped on "renew." Renewal, meaningful, communicate, relationship, interaction, share . . . He detested the hijacking of these words. What made it worse was that the Church was devious enough to turn to the new religions of pop psychology to dress up its own vocabulary of salvation. Minogue had been disappointed and then amused to realize that he preferred the Catholic Church to remain flinty and regal, robed majestically in baroque and gilt authoritarianism. He wanted the triumphalist Church of his youth. His pantheism had been thrust upon him, but that older Church would have been the easier to deny. With guitar-wielding priests and personable smilers like Heher and Drumm, Minogue was suspicious. Self-actualization and meaningful communication were all right for Americans. Wouldn't wash in Ireland.

"I didn't like the hint about suicide, even if it was oblique. It felt like they were trying to cut him loose and take no responsibility for him now that he might embarrass them," said Minogue. "All the yapping about pressure and stress of modern society: since when did we have a modern society? As though to say, 'Poor Brian, if only he had stayed with his brothers in Opus Dei, he'd have been all right.'"

Kilmartin stirred his coffee. "You can't deny it, though. We'll never get a definitive from the postmortem saying that Kelly was bashed on the head," he said conclusively. "It's us being pushy because Kelly might have been connected to Fine."

"Come on, now," said Minogue. "I never in all my life saw such a suicide. Even if that crack in the skull is due to the heat and so on. A man empties petrol in his car and sits in the back seat without making a move? We know it's murder."

He returned to his coffee and bun. He would have liked a second cup but did not wish to press Kilmartin to any more complicity in what Kilmartin regarded as truancy here in Bewley's.

"Here's how I see it," Kilmartin began slowly. "We keep the Fine case to ourselves when we're taking statements from Kelly's friends and associates. Say absolutely nothing. Be all ears for even the slightest hint of anything any of *them* say about Fine being murdered. The ones who give any sign of a connection to Fine are the ones we can turn inside out, right?"

"Yep. Leave it for them to trip over and incriminate themselves."

"And we'll hold on to the supposition that Kelly did try to contact or meet with Fine," said Kilmartin with the slow speech of a bargainer. "Remember, we can't dismiss the idea that Kelly might have been involved in Fine's death too and got cold feet afterwards, so that his pals got to him before he decided to spill the beans."

"But how would they know that he was ready to spill the beans? How would they know he phoned up looking for me, for example?"

"Jases, not so many questions, I'm not a fortune teller. Save it for this evening when we have the meeting."

"We could assume that Kelly was being watched, or believed he was being watched. That would account for a few things, like why he went to meet Fine on Killiney Hill last Sunday instead of meeting him in a handier place . . . Maybe if Paul Fine was told by Kelly to keep something under his hat for the time being . . . the need for secrecy, do you get what I'm at?"

"Being watched? By his pals in Opus Dei?"

"Yes. If Kelly had knowledge of, or had participated in, Paul Fine's murder, and that murder was connected to Opus Dei—"

Kilmartin was giving the embossed ceiling his careful consideration. Minogue licked his fingers before taking out his hanky.

"If we could only place the pair of them together," Kilmartin muttered. "That'd be the bee's knees. Then I'd feel a lot easier in myself about taking a flying tackle at this Opus Dei mob."

Suddenly Kilmartin looked down from the ornate ceiling and fixed Minogue with a stare. "I know what you're thinking, you know," he said.

Minogue feigned fright. "I had a fear as a child that adults could read my thoughts," he said. "Being the sinner I was, I had a lot to keep secret—"

"You're thinking that Jimmy Kilmartin is afraid to go nose-to-nose with something to do with the Church, aren't you?"

"I might be."

"You're thinking to yourself that Opus Dei is really a crowd of religious lunatics and they deserve a good house-cleaning but that Jimmy Kilmartin doesn't want to get his wrists slapped by someone wearing a priest's collar."

"The thought had—"

"Feckin' sure it had, and well I know it. Well, I've just thought of something that'll do the trick nicely for us, without us having to ask Heher for the time of day. Are you ready for this? A time-honoured Irish method."

"Prayer? Abstinence? The rhythm method?"

Kilmartin glowered. "I can't get over this. You really are full of dirt today. I don't understand it. It ill becomes you."

Minogue smiled at the reprimand which sounded like a hectoring parent or a teacher.

"I'm on the rebound from those two clean and bright specimens, Jimmy. Go easy on me, I don't meet such angels every day."

"We could look around for an informer. Now." Kilmartin's face shone with the anticipation of praise.

"You mean we should find ourselves a former Opus Dei man and get an insider's view of the outfit?"

Kilmartin nodded, smiling expectantly, but Minogue's gargoyle had broken loose after the coffee.

"Only a Mayo-man would come up with an idea like that."

Kilmartin sat up with a start. "What do you mean by that comment? There was never an informer born in County Mayo. Didn't we take the brunt of the Black and Tans and join up Humbert's Frenchmen in '98 and . . . What does Mayo have to do with the suggestion?"

Minogue was up and scampering to the door. He was unaccountably happy, even in the knowledge that this last quarter of an hour might have been merely an oasis in a day when he'd fall back into brooding about the Fines, about their son, about his own. He saw the closely cropped woman who had tried to add six minutes to Kilmartin's life look up from her paperback treatise at the two heavy, middle-aged policemen hurrying out of the restaurant.

"And as for Clare people, they didn't know what shoes and socks were until the first plane landed in Shannon," he heard Kilmartin in pursuit behind. "And as for sports . . . !"

Minogue winked at the grave face of the woman as he fled. She did not acknowledge his efforts. Perhaps it was not part of her view of the world that two clumsy policemen should be willingly making iijits of themselves.

# THIRTEEN

"The chiseller's name is Patsy O'Malley," said Keating. "He's a godsend, I can tell you. You should have heard him."

"That good?" said Hoey, visibly excited.

Keating widened his eyes and nodded once slowly for effect. "Patsy is nine and a bit. His mother says he only comes into the house to sleep. He's a wild man entirely. If he's not down the end of the pier fishing, he's building forts and hunting boars and tigers in the woods."

"He's in a Boy Scout troop?"

"He is. There was a mob of them up on Killiney Hill last Sunday, all afternoon. They had a picnic up there, then they had little jobs to do like collecting different leaves off the trees and finding out what different types of rocks and stones there are there. Eleven boys and a scoutmaster, a man by the name of Fahy. I haven't been in touch with him yet."

Keating looked down to his notebook.

"It started when Patsy didn't want to go to bed last night. His ma says he's a holy terror when it comes to the bed. He managed to stay up and not be noticed until the news was on. We had our plug about the site up on Killiney Hill and Patsy says—this is his ma's version of it—'I was there on Sunday, I know that place.' She didn't pay a whole lot of notice to that because that reminded her that he was still up. He's a bit of a head-case with his yarns and everything. She asked him later and him going to bed. Himself and another boy were told to go and look for animal signs and to rendezvous with the troop back up on top of the Hill so as they could tell the troop what they'd found. Part of their job was to keep an eye on the time and to be able to lead the troop back to any spot they'd found interesting."

"We ought to give the Russians fair warning that the country is full of Davy Crocketts and wild mountaineers," said Hoey as Keating paused.

"So his ma heard him giving directions as to how to get to the place he saw on the telly and she gave up on him. She thought he was romancing all the detail so he could stay up all night talking to her. I got him to tell me how to get to that part of the Hill and he was right in the general area. He didn't know north and south and that; it was more 'go down these steps' and 'there's a funny tree with a branch sticking out.' So his ma packed him off to bed and she had a little think about it. She decided to phone and that's how it started. I'll tell ye what, lads, this Patsy O'Malley is a ticket. He's his own boss at nine years of age."

"Inspector by the age of twenty," Hoey tried.

Keating flicked forward in his notebook. "Here's the gist of what he saw."

For a moment Minogue imagined the O'Malley household, with the oversized Keating and a Garda by his side sitting in the kitchen with the boy, glad to be excused from school, and a mother both nervous and proud of her nine-year-old woodsman.

"He split up with his pal because the pal was an iijit. They stuck him with the pal for a day so the pal'd learn something from Patsy. Patsy didn't buy that, so he told the pal to shag off somewhere and he'd meet up with him before they had to join the troop again. The pal went off and had a Golly bar on the sly, in a shop in Killiney village. Patsy knows all the paths and the hidey-holes around the Hill and he went off up the path on one of his excursions. He said there does be courting couples up this part of the Hill sometimes and he does have a bit of fun with them."

"I can imagine the fun he means," said Kilmartin dryly.

"He thought he heard someone breaking sticks," Keating went on, looking around at the detectives. Minogue thought of the woman walking the dog: branches breaking, she had thought: the dog nosing into the bushes and barking. A silencer on the pistol?

"Naturally Patsy goes in to see what carry-on there is; if there's some blackguarding going on, well he might be interested. He saw this man down on his knees, poking away at the ground with a penknife—"

"He has the body rolled in under the bushes by then," Kilmartin interrupted.

Keating nodded, licking his lips. "And digging at the ground. The man sees him and stands up all of a sudden. Patsy says the man looked very upset about something, like he was frightened."

"No gun?" said Kilmartin quickly.

"No. They stood there looking at one another for a minute and Patsy sees that this fella is shook. The man is trying to look normal, smiling a bit, but Patsy is not fooled. The man says: 'I've lost something here so I have to look for it.' Patsy says his eyes were huge and he looked like he was very hot or something. That was enough for Patsy and he left the man to it. His ma did a good job of telling him to keep away from quare fellas that acted friendly."

"Trying to find the bullets, or casings from an automatic. That spells out a careful, expert type of assailant," said Minogue. He felt the excitement now as a band around his chest.

"How quick were the shots?" Kilmartin asked.

"Can't get him on that, sir. Could as easily have been a revolver."

Minogue found that he was staring intently at the back of a chair.

"Looks like it, doesn't it?" said Keating hoarsely.

"Does the time fit too?"

Keating nodded vigorously. "The end of the day, sir. The last job of the day for the Scouts. They were on the bus back to Dun Laoghaire about three-quarters of an hour later. It was half-five, a little later."

"All right," said Kilmartin calmly. "Who is this man?"

"He's a cop, sir. That's what Patsy O'Malley said."

Keating's stare switched from Minogue to Hoey and back again to Kilmartin. Everyone in the room was very still. Minogue had the impression that people were holding their breath.

"How does he know?" Kilmartin asked softly.

"'Looked like a cop.' I asked him what that looked like and he says 'Looks like you.' His ma wasn't thrilled about that class of remark and told him to mind his manners. 'The man looked like a rozzer,' Patsy says again. And he meant it. I ended up reassuring his ma that I didn't mind what the boy called Guards, that he sounded truthful and that he was a good, smart lad. You know how people can spot a Guard quick, even if we dressed like the Queen of Sheba? Kids too. He wasn't saying it to get a dig at me, I'm sure. I plugged him several times about skin colour. Very definite no. Consistently."

Keating paused and glanced around to savour the tension.

"Local," Kilmartin murmured.

"Go on," Minogue prompted.

"Right. The man was tall, had short hair and he wore a jacket. Clean-shaven and 'not too old.' Older than me but not as old as Patsy's da, who's forty-four. There was nothing special about him except that he looked scared. Patsy put that down to him being caught up to mischief. Patsy says he didn't see the girlfriend."

Even Kilmartin smiled. "Jases, I hope he joins up the Gardai when he's eighteen, that lad," he said. "But listen: absolutely certain on the complexion, can I call it? Definitely not what the boy would know of Middle Eastern?"

"No. Patsy was sure about that. An ordinary-looking fella, but he didn't look all there on account of Patsy finding him up to no good."

"Did he hear the dog or see that woman at all?"

"He doesn't remember exactly but he saw an oul' wan and a poodle somewhere around at the time. Doesn't know if it was before or after he went in and he isn't sure where exactly. She was putting a lead on the dog, he remembers that."

"There it is," said Hoey slowly. "The woman said she put the lead on because the dog wanted to go back into the bushes."

"But she didn't report seeing a Boy Scout," Kilmartin cautioned. "The boy saw nothing of Fine?"

"No. He stayed back, he told me, because the fella was acting a bit odd. Didn't see any body or notice any blood."

Minogue recalled his visit to the clearing with Kilmartin. It had been choked with high grass, with brambles and weeds. It was possible that even six feet away a child would not have seen blood on the grass.

"Didn't he say anything to Fahy, the General or whatever they call them?"

"No, he didn't. He was mitching, you see. He knew that Fahy was only trying to kill time before they got the bus home. 'Animal tracks!' says Patsy. 'Sure there's only birds and the odd mouse up that hill.' And Fahy didn't get the boys to follow up on what other groups had found, either. Some of them found birds' nests and wanted to bring the troop over to look, but Fahy lowered the boom on that idea. Seems that our Patsy is wise to grown-up trickery. He said nothing about it to anyone."

Of course, thought Minogue. Had the intrepid Patsy mentioned stumbling across a quare fella in the bushes, the full weight of adult worries and injunctions would have fallen upon him as anger and probably as punishment. *Didn't I tell you not to go off on your own like that? Weren't you supposed to be helping your friend on a project? You could have fallen over a cliff and we wouldn't have known . . .* The mountaineer

Patsy O'Malley, ranging far and wide over the vast jungle of Killiney Hill, happy and content, would have learned long ago to protect his freedom with silence. Minogue heard an echo of his own story then, of how he tried to deny the risks he wanted now that he had woken up to life. Maybe the explorer Patsy muttered the same to himself: *Ah, they'd only be worrying if I told them everything—*

"Now," said Minogue. "What I need to know is this—"

Hoey beat him to the line.

"Where was Brian Kelly on Sunday afternoon?" he said.

A cornered Kilmartin was not a happy Kilmartin, but Minogue was forceful. He was ready to insist, even to cite his authority to run the case.

"We can't just initiate this on the basis of what this little gangster said to Keating, Matt."

Initiate, Minogue repeated within. Kilmartin was on the defensive, retreating into formal bureaucratic vocabulary.

"It's strong, Jimmy."

"He's a nine-year-old boy who could be a bit of an imp too. Who's to say he didn't create a bit from what he heard on the news or what he heard adults talking about?"

"He saw the woman with the dog, the woman who put us wise to the murder site."

"Of course I'm not denying things the boy said," Kilmartin agreed wearily. "I'm playing the Devil's advocate. Look at what you're asking, for the love of God. The boy may have an overheated imagination, that's all."

"I think we should broaden the thing, Jimmy." Minogue renewed the attack. "Look: we're not focusing on finding a fella rafted in from the Middle East—if this boy is twenty-four carat. You with me?"

Kilmartin raised his hands in mock surrender. "I know, I know," he said. "Fair enough. But we still need to put these students through the mill. One of them must know about what's beginning to look like a campaign. Yes, call it a campaign. There's a church after being bombed, bejases. There are armed Gardai outside people's houses as we speak. Just because we might begin to think whoever killed Paul Fine need not be a foreigner . . . Think on that."

"I'm not saying ease off on that," Minogue protested. "And I have no problem thinking a local assassin or gunman has been hired or ordered to kill Paul Fine on behalf of this Palestinian organization. But let Pat Gallagher and company steam away at that. What we need to do is take a long hard look at a connection that's staring us in the face: Paul Fine was researching something that Brian Kelly knew about. What are we waiting for?"

Kilmartin pushed back his chair and began examining his knuckles. Then he surveyed his desk-top. "Lookit, all I'm saying is give me some bullet-proof grounds for this search you're proposing. It'd be a mammoth thing entirely."

"All I need from you is advice about shortcuts, Jimmy," said Minogue.

"You want a lot more than that, man dear," said Kilmartin.

"It's not just the boy—look at the other facts. Shot three times. Bullets recovered. High-velocity bullets, fired from a powerful handgun. It's logical to suspect

246

that the bullets were chosen so they'd go through a body. Access to a gun, access to the ammunition: it was someone who is familiar with, or had training in, weapons. Brian Kelly had none of these features. He certainly didn't look like a cop to my eye, anyway. It's hardly a case of Kelly doing the murder and then getting a fit of remorse and phoning me. The way Paul Fine was murdered doesn't indicate a killer who'd opt for much remorse. The someone seems to have been worried that the gun or the bullets could have been traced—the bullets especially. Who'd care about them if the Technical Bureau hadn't a hope in hell of finding the gun?"

"I know, I know, you told me already: 'Because the gun might be traceable.' This is what's giving me grief: that fact doesn't automatically incriminate the Gardai. You saw yourself that the ballistics comments said we don't use that class of ammunition, for one thing."

"He could have used a Garda gun and got his hands on high-velocity stuff himself," argued Minogue.

"But where's the key motive behind all this, I ask? It doesn't hang together very well. Do you know what you're saying? Fine didn't have any friends, or enemies for that matter, that we know of in the Gardai. And why would he, sure?" said Kilmartin.

"But someone could have borrowed or loaned out the gun for the murder and then had to replace it."

"But why, how?"

"If I knew that I'd have the murderer awaiting trial and I'd be at home with me feet up."

Kilmartin drew a deep breath and sighed as he let it out slowly.

"Like I said to you, Matt, I'm only the Devil's advocate, as I said, keeping you honest," he repeated.

"Well, seeing as you're primed for that role, you'd better hear the rest that I'm thinking, then. I still can't fathom this business about the timing of the phone call to the paper on Monday morning, half an hour after the citizen finds the body washed up?"

Kilmartin looked warily at Minogue. "Ah Jases, not that again—"

"Hold your horses a minute, Jimmy. If we had to make our living on coincidences in a murder case, we'd have starved to death a long time ago. What if the killer knew that the body was discovered, and decided it was time to phone up and spin a yarn to buy himself time?"

Kilmartin didn't react as Minogue had expected. He let his eye out of focus and joined his fingers to make a church-and-steeple which he placed under his nose. Minogue sensed victory.

"How did he know when to phone?" asked Kilmartin from behind the finger construction.

"He could have been near the beach and found out. Remember the hotel, and the waiter saying that a barman had seen the Garda cars congregating there?"

Kilmartin nodded noncommittally, eyes still away on an alternative world.

"Anyone around the place might have done the same thing—gone down to see the commotion and seen that the body had not washed out to sea."

"Fair enough," said Kilmartin calmly. "We've caught killers because they returned to the site at some point afterwards. I can go along with that."

Minogue wondered if Kilmartin was buying time, humouring him while he awaited the arrival of the men in the white coats.

"I wasn't getting at that, actually. I was thinking

of something a little different from an eyewitness at the beach."

"You were, were you?" said Kilmartin in a somnambulistic monotone.

"I was thinking that perhaps a member of the Gardai alerted someone to the discovery of the body. Thereupon this someone decided to phone the paper. It may be that our killer is a member of the Gardai."

"Aha. I see."

"Yes," Minogue went on tentatively. "So somewhere between the beach and us here in the squad room, a Garda found out that Paul Fine's body was on Killiney strand and this Garda told someone else. Or else the Garda himself phoned the paper."

"To confuse us," Kilmartin said tonelessly.

"To confuse us," Minogue repeated. "Yes."

"A Garda."

"A Garda," Minogue agreed. Kilmartin was still locked into his reverie. Minogue felt he might be conversing with a person in a trance.

"A Garda took a Garda firearm and shot Fine in the head three times last Sunday afternoon?"

"A Garda may have been involved in the shooting of Paul Fine on Sunday afternoon," Minogue qualified.

"Why would one of our colleagues do that, now?"

"I haven't a clue, Jimmy."

"You haven't a clue," Kilmartin repeated woodenly. He blinked and regained this world, looking blankly at Minogue.

"I'm willing to defend it, Jimmy. After all, I'm the one with the flag in his hand for this."

Kilmartin gave no obvious sign that he read Minogue's defensiveness as insubordination.

"So you'll want an accounting for use of firearms within the Gardai in Dublin, at least?"

"That's what I'm going for, yes. Oh, and the Army too," said Minogue.

"The Army," echoed Kilmartin quietly.

"The Army. Our Army."

"Might as well be hung for a sheep as a lamb?"

"That's right, Jimmy. In for a penny, in for a pound. What do you say?"

Kilmartin looked at his nails.

"Oh, I'm in too. I just wanted to hear how you'd explain turning two extremely large bureaucracies on their bloody heads."

Minogue smiled with the relief.

"Just this, though," continued Kilmartin. "One of us has to phone God Almighty and tell him how you reached this decision."

"Good," Minogue agreed. "I'll do it, so. I want to be sure that the checks are not apparent at all. There must be a way of accounting for firearms and ammunition without the whole Garda Siochana getting to know about it."

Minogue, leaving, heard a strange Americanism from the subdued Kilmartin.

"Have a nice day, Matt."

Minogue ate a scrambled-egg sandwich in between gulps of what the restaurant called consommé soup. He was to meet the Garda Commissioner at half-past one. Kilmartin had agreed with him that for the moment, the fewer people on the task force who knew about this part of the investigation, the better. Hoey was let in on it, as Minogue wanted him along to the meeting in Garda HQ in the Phoenix Park.

Hoey was also the funnel through which all the information coming in from the field on the Fine murder case had flowed.

After Minogue had telephoned the Assistant Commissioner he had waited at his desk to play out the bet he had placed with himself. It had taken the Commissioner less than five minutes to phone Kilmartin. The same Kilmartin must have expected the reaction because his door remained closed. Minogue mentally pocketed his own bet. Kilmartin had emerged from his office with a name written on a sheet of foolscap, had handed it to Minogue and asked him if he had ever met Major-General Seamus O'Tuaime. Minogue had not. Then Minogue would make his acquaintance in the company of the Garda Commissioner. Kilmartin had left the foolscap dangling from Minogue's hand. This was Kilmartin's way of letting him know that he was on his own, Minogue understood.

Minogue checked his clothes for drops of soup. He stood from the chair and flicked at his shirt and jacket to dislodge any globs of scrambled egg which might have hidden themselves in folds while he had been seated. He had been wondering how much he could withhold from O'Tuaime, especially.

"You look like you're thrilled skinny at the prospect of this meeting. If you don't mind me saying so," said Hoey.

"I don't mind you saying so. Army uniforms make me jittery. I must have been an anarchist in me last incarnation."

"I wish we were more like the coppers on the Continent. They can grow their hair and wear their own clobber a lot of the time in Germany," Hoey opined dreamily. "A bit of glamour'd be all right."

He should have driven home to Kilmartin the point
that the real common element was Opus Dei. No, Kilmartin would have insisted on something more tangi-
ble if he, Kilmartin, had had to use it as an
explanation for Minogue's plan. Minogue began to
believe that Kilmartin's diffidence about the plan was
his way of leaving Minogue to await the outcome of
this meeting more or less alone. Right, Matt Minogue,
he might as well have said, you say you're in charge
here, so off you go. Was it that childhood fear of
authority which had filtered through to the adult Kilmartin as an excessive sense of accountability toward
his own superiors now—another cardinal Irish trait,
the constant fear of rebuke?

"So it's really top secret, then," said Hoey.

"That's the way, all right," replied Minogue. "If
we're to get anywhere."

He could avoid telling the Commissioner and
O'Tuaime that he suspected an Opus Dei dimension
by simply calling it a possible conspiracy. God help
him if O'Tuaime asked what motives he could con-
ceivably impute to a conspiracy to murder a radio
journalist who happened to be a Jew.

Hoey looked with distaste across the table as the
waitress swept the plates away. "That was an ugly little sandwich I had. I hope I don't puke on account of
it."

"It would reflect poorly if you were to be sick during this meeting, Shea. After it, perhaps, that might be
all right; during it would be a no-no."

Hoey drove. They waited five minutes at the lights
by Christchurch before getting their chance to turn
down to the quays and the north side of the Liffey.
Minogue knew they could have gone down Thomas

Street but he wanted to borrow a little time. Younger people were holding out their thumbs for lifts. The middle-aged and the elderly stood mutely by the bus stops, with faintly puzzled and embarrassed expressions. Too shy to be so forward as to solicit a lift off a stranger, they hoped drivers would stop and offer. Minogue saw several cars pull over to the kerbs and pick up people. With an acid expansion somewhere in his innards, one which was not due solely to the dinner he had tolerated, he noted that the cars which were stopping were older cars, well used. Big Japanese and German cars sped by the crowds, fighting for ever-shrinking patches of roadways between the ever-lengthening bottlenecks at the traffic lights. He tried not to come out with a cynical remark when he saw that Hoey too had noticed this income-based philanthropy.

"You never know," Hoey observed. "A bit of this self-help might be just the thing to get the place going again. Maybe we don't need the buses at all."

Self-help, Minogue heard, thinking of the tricks of grammar: in these days of the Thatcherite gospel, the number of Audis and Cressidas and Mercedeses suggested that some citizens had helped themselves a great deal.

Once across the Liffey, the traffic thinned. Hoey steered deftly around vehicles and turned down the quay toward Islandbridge and the Phoenix Park beyond. Facades along the quays were for the most part ruined or crumbling. Those which still stood had been transformed into hucksters' shops, headed by oversized plastic signs. Quick tenancies for fly-by-night businesses had left blocked-up windows and boarded doors. The decay was an animate presence hanging over the oily filth of the Liffey at low tide. What could have been an elegant promenade with people living on the banks of Anna Livia was now a series of grimy shattered roadways and empty lots. The blue sky made it look worse, Minogue considered, as the brighter light showed up the mounds of rubble piled in the doorways, the broken railings, the frameless, gaping windows on the upper stories.

"That's where they do their bit, Fianna Eireann," said Hoey as they passed Collins Barracks. They were closing on Islandbridge now. In calling the Army by its official title, as inheritors of the mantle of the Fianna, a legendary band of warriors who had roamed ancient Ireland, Hoey did not need to make the jibe more pointed.

The Barracks, inherited from the British, was a series of grim stone buildings, suggesting a prison more than Army quarters. There were several Land Rovers and Army lorries parked behind the railings.

"And Gorman cooing in their ears, saying that the government can find the money for more equipment, no matter what the cost."

"Did he say that?" asked Minogue.

"They love him, I hear," replied Hoey.

O'Tuaime, Minogue thought. The name suggested a man who obviously preferred to use Irish as his official language. Would he have the other trappings too? Be a devout Catholic for God and Ireland? Minogue began again to wonder why Kilmartin had not seemed interested in coming to this meeting.

The Commissioner had Tynan, one of the Garda's Deputy Commissioners, beside him. Tynan was in charge of B Section at Garda HQ in the Park. Amongst other things, B Section held personal files on every Garda officer. The two of them seemed to have been chatting amiably to O'Tuaime, and, ushered in, Minogue felt that his arrival was an intrusion on polite company. God Almighty had an effusive greeting for him. Minogue could not decide which of the three uniformed men was giving off the smell of old-fashioned shaving soap. It brought back for an instant the scent of his own father's skin, Sundays on the way to Mass. He guessed it was O'Tuaime, a florid-faced but boyish-looking career Army General in his early fifties.

O'Tuaime had the clear eyes of a man who spent time outdoors and he was almost entirely bald. He shook Minogue's hand and greeted him in Irish. His hat lay on an oak table next to a window which overlooked a small grove of deciduous trees, and it somehow amused Minogue to think that this General's hat might have a life of its own . . . might be an awkward item which had to be placed on the head at a correct angle, something which earned a soldier a dressing-down if it were not in place as it should be . . . something which could so easily make one look silly when it blew off or dislodged as one got out of a car . . . Would his wife stand in the hallway every morning, holding the hat for him?

"It's not often I have the pleasure of seeing officers at work in our Garda Siochana," O'Tuaime said in Irish.

Minogue could not think of the Irish for glamorous. "Please God I can make it look showy, then," he replied in Irish, drawing a polite smile in return.

"The matter we're here for is delicate in the extreme. In relation to the need for confidentiality," he went on in English.

"We've already acquainted the Major General with the case you're working on," said the Commissioner encouragingly.

Minogue looked momentarily at his feet so that when crossing his legs as he now wanted to do, he'd not inadvertently kick any furniture. He looked up again, ready to begin, and saw Tynan's limpid gaze on him. Minogue didn't mind Tynan; in fact he had rather liked what he had heard of Tynan's dry humour during the Christmas and retirement parties over the years. He interpreted Tynan's watery look to mean that he, Inspector Minogue, had better make it good. Hoey's shoes squeaked as he drew his feet together. Minogue went straight to details.

"It's not just the expertise and knowledge of firearms alone which suggest that we have to explore these avenues. It's also a question of access to the hardware, in particular the ammunition chosen . . . I'm accepting that for the killer to recover the spent bullets, there had to be planning and premeditation regarding his choice of ammunition. The man was no iijit."

"Or the woman," said O'Tuaime. Cork, Minogue guessed from O'Tuaime's first words to him in English.

"I beg your pardon?"

"Woman, Inspector. The killer. In this day of women's lib, we have to give fair treatment to the girls and the boys."

"Aha," the Commissioner interrupted. "That's the truth, Seamus, and well we know it, don't we?"

He turned to Minogue with a broad smile. "We were just discussing the Ryan business, Matt. The women are getting to be as tough as the men, hah. I said a minute before you arrived that the Army could do with the likes of Mrs Ryan and the WAMmers.

They'd put the fear of God into any hooligans, hah."

So O'Tuaime was interested in the Ryan murder, Minogue mused. Were these men, these nabobs in uniform, having the same dreams that an army of vengeful women was creeping through the fields at night, with bread knives between their molars, eyes gleaming with hatred. Tynan's face shared but the smallest fraction of the joke which O'Tuaime and the Commissioner were enjoying. Minogue exchanged a quick glance with Tynan, and found the same baleful gaze, verging on irony, was fixed on him.

"Our equivalent of the Gurkhas," said O'Tuaime. The Commissioner slapped his knee with merriment. O'Tuaime rubbed his nose and gave a little snort of what could have been laughter.

"Of course, the killer may have had access to the murder weapon through a friend or a colleague in the Army or in a branch of the Gardai," Minogue went on.

"With all due respect to your good work in these difficult circumstances," O'Tuaime said as he nodded toward the Commissioner, "and not to put too fine a point on this issue, but the country is full of guns. "

"And a very sorry state of affairs it is," said the Commissioner hastily. "Lowers the threshold for violent crime. Very pernicious."

Perhaps God Almighty was practising parts of a speech he planned to deliver soon, a more cynical Minogue considered.

"A road once entered upon, impossible to leave," added O'Tuaime in Irish.

Minogue counted to five before continuing. "In any event I need to explore the issues as soon as possible," he said. "And I need your assistance and advice as to how best to do it."

"I'm not sure what exactly you're proposing," said O'Tuaime affably.

"I want the Army to provide me with a list of persons in the ranks who admit to being members of Opus Dei and any other confraternities like that, such as the Knights of Columbus. I want an accounting for the use of Army firearms and expenditure of ammunition in the last while. And a note of missing ammunition, high-velocity ammunition, susceptible of being fired by a handgun."

O'Tuaime's boyish face broke into a smile. Minogue heard feet shuffling behind the Commissioner's desk. Even Tynan was moved to cross his legs and avert his gaze.

"Confraternities?" asked O'Tuaime, the smile a little more indulgent now, as though he was sure he was dealing with a naive child. "Are you telling me that religious associations are particularly suspect?"

"Yes."

"Ah, but Inspector," rejoined O'Tuaime quickly in Irish, "this is a kind of an upside-down thing, isn't it? The more disciplined and honourable are to be heading your list of suspects?"

O'Tuaime's Irish translated "suspects" as "gangsters." Minogue believed that O'Tuaime had chosen that word to add a hint of sarcasm.

"I'm sure that the associations are full of dedicated, honest men, Major-General. It's merely a lead that I cannot ignore. Were this information to be gathered discreetly, as I'm proposing, the men would have no need of feeling slighted. Nobody's saying that these associations harbour criminals. If I were looking for a murderer involved in banking, say, would that mean that I considered all bankers suspect?"

"That's a good one," said the Commissioner. "You picked the right crowd there, I'm telling you. They might be all hooks. I like that."

O'Tuaime's smile had settled.

"Nicely put, Inspector. But we're talking about a group of responsible and dedicated people here. I can tell you that membership of confraternities in the Army is almost exclusively drawn from commissioned officer ranks. These are men who want to serve their country and their people, and hold to the lights of their religion. There's nothing sinister about that—except perhaps in a cynical age. It takes the cynic to see and fear the dedicated, thus to scorn him."

Minogue didn't know what to say. O'Tuaime had kept the tone gentle, so much so that the rhetoric had not grated much on Minogue. O'Tuaime's ease with Irish was so evident that Minogue almost forgot that the man's use of the language was a rebuff to him.

"So the Army knows which of its members belong to confraternities?"

"That is so," replied O'Tuaime. "Our oath obliges us to so inform our commanding officers."

"What about Opus Dei?"

"There are Opus Dei members in the Army too, I'm sure," O'Tuaime replied easily. "But I don't know for certain."

"Do you mean that *they* might not observe their oath and make their membership known?"

"I believe from hearsay that that organization explains to its members that its own membership vows are directed toward a higher Commanding Officer," said O'Tuaime. He glanced briefly at the ceiling. Tynan smiled. "God doesn't have to tell our Chief-of-Staff what's going on, you see," added O'Tuaime.

"Is Opus Dei a problem, then? For you and the High Command, I mean?"

O'Tuaime paused before answering.

"It has been mentioned as a concern before—only on the basis that Opus Dei members don't inform their superiors of their membership. We have tended to be lenient, and given them the benefit of the doubt."

"'Them,' Major-General?"

"Those officers who may be members of Opus Dei. These officers who we believed were members were in every case exemplary soldiers and citizens. There's been nothing to suggest any conflict in loyalties for a man to be in Opus Dei. In fact membership might even add to an officer's value as an indicator of his dedication and service."

"Will you draw up a list of those officers who are members of Opus Dei?"

"I have already said that there *may be* Opus Dei members in the Army."

"You mentioned exemplary officers: you must be thinking of specific men."

"I am guessing."

"Will you give us those names, then?"

"I will not," O'Tuaime replied in English. His tone had not changed. He was looking expectantly to Minogue as if waiting for the next question. Ever ready, Minogue thought sourly. He must have known.

"I have no rational bases for my guesses, you see," O'Tuaime went on, oblivious of the spell which had frozen the other men in place. "It would be irresponsible of me to claim that my guesses mean anything to anyone else, especially to a policeman who must of necessity deal with hard facts. You can see my position and my duties, I'm sure."

O'Tuaime's expression suggested an innocence and a happy readiness to be helpful. Without looking over, Minogue knew that Tynan's eyes had settled on him again. The Commissioner now had a small silver pen doing tricks on his desk.

"Can we move on to the arms and ammunition issue, then?" Minogue said.

"To be sure we can," said O'Tuaime. "I'm a little rusty on small-arms details, but it seems to me that what you're looking for, we won't have. High-velocity ammunition for sidearms makes no sense for Army purposes." He smiled wanly at Minogue. "Nonetheless, I can have a check done on both for you, and I'll give it the highest priority."

"That would be appreciated," said Minogue.

"No bother at all," O'Tuaime continued. "I should tell you, though, that you'll have big holes in the book. I know, for example, that several companies had firearms drill and target practice with small-arms down in Wicklow over the weekend. There was a lot of live ammunition used, maybe fifty rounds a man. I don't know if different stocks of ammunition were used. Naturally we keep track of gross amounts of expenditures there, but accounting for each and every single bullet is impossible. How many are you looking for?" O'Tuaime said guilelessly.

"Three, actually," said Minogue.

"Firing a rifle on automatic is a standard part of practice, so the bullets fairly fly when there are dozens of groups taking their turn. There's some wastage, a small percentage—duds, actual losses we can't put our hands on right away . . ."

Minogue waited before asking: "Could a person take ammunition for his own use off the firing range?"

"Yes," O'Tuaime replied without hesitation. "Nothing is watertight. Ever."

"Could a soldier take a firearm home with him?"

"It is very, very unlikely that he'd get away with that. We're acutely aware of what Army weapons could be used for if they fell into the wrong hands, Inspector. Our security is as tight as a drum."

"Do you know if soldiers who were abroad could have brought home guns illegally?"

"I do. There were two corporals court-martialled several years ago for that offence. It was a matter of grave importance for us. These men had been representing Ireland as members of a UN peace-keeping force. They brought souvenirs home here in the form of an automatic pistol and a Russian-made pistol. Bought on the black market in Beirut. Two fine careers ruined—but that's how we run our ship."

Every avenue covered. Quick accurate answers. Was he born like this, Minogue wondered.

"Tell me this now, Inspector," said O'Tuaime then. He folded his arms and looked genially at Minogue. "Will your investigation be applying the same rigorous checks to the Garda Siochana?"

"It certainly will," Minogue replied quickly.

Tynan showed O'Tuaime out after handshakes all around and Hoey moved with speed when the Commissioner suggested that "Haughey" could meet Minogue outside.

"Hoey," corrected Minogue.

"Right," said the Commissioner, watching the door close behind Hoey. He clasped his hands together and leaned his elbows on to the desk. "About you wanting to run a check on the Gardai, the same as O'Tuaime there in the Army—"

"We can't be asking them to do things that we wouldn't be willing to do ourselves," said Minogue. "We have firearms and dedicated and good-living officers as well."

Whether or not he noticed the irony, the Commissioner did not appear to be mollified.

"I'm not overly interested in what O'Tuaime or any other *Ta Se* thinks," he said ominously. "I'm wondering if uprooting the Gardai is going to help anyone. People need to have confidence in their police, I don't need to tell you that. There has to be a better way."

Minogue was a little surprised at the derogatory term *Ta Se*, especially since the Commissioner and O'Tuaime had seemed to be on the best of terms. The phrase, meaning literally "he is," referred to those who chose to use Irish on the basis that this linguistic sacred cow, which had been the scourge and bane of most schoolchildren's existence, was an official language of the Irish Republic.

"I had to answer him honestly. I didn't want him leaving here thinking we don't apply the same scrutiny to our own officers," Minogue tried. He was very close now to losing his temper.

The Commissioner observed Minogue as though viewing a painting. "Skimpy though, Matt, for all the upset it'll mean, isn't it?"

"If Paul Fine was murdered by a Garda or a soldier, or with the collusion of a Guard or soldier, we'd better go to a lot of trouble and upset ourselves. If the public finds out otherwise, there'll be a damn sight more trouble," said Minogue. He knew already that God Almighty would be on the phone to Kilmartin the minute he, Minogue, left this room. Kilmartin would be wanting to deliver himself of his own bad humour later too.

"I don't want you to think that you're under pressure from Justice Fine here, now," said the Commissioner in a measured tone. "Because you're not working for him. You're working for me and the Minister for Justice and the man in the street. Just because Fine is a bigwig and we took into consideration his request for you to be heading the case, this doesn't mean a free hand to be pulling away at anything. If the investigation is flat, I want to know about it immediately."

Minogue made no reply, but turned aside before the Commissioner could read the anger on his face. The trees outside were alive with the breeze, the sky behind them calm and empty of clouds. No wonder astronauts liked their job, Minogue thought.

"It's easy enough for a man with his own particular loyalties to misunderstand the loyalties of others," said the Commissioner.

"How do you mean?" Minogue snapped. "That I'm contrary enough not to be marching along in step with God and Ireland like the good little men marching around in the Army?"

The Commissioner sat back in his chair, rubbing his cheek as though recovering from a blow. An awkward smile crept over his face. "Hold your horses there, Matt: I was just testing. I'll have John Tynan go to work on this. Just don't be thinking you can ask the world here one morning and expect not to have hard questions thrown at you."

Minogue stood. "It's really imperative to keep the search secret," he said.

"Don't be worrying. The Deputy Comm is well aware of that. And here, look . . . don't be getting in a huff about O'Tuaime. He's the old school. *Pog mo thon.*"

The Commissioner barked his laughter in response to his own suggestion that Major General O'Tuaime should kiss his arse. Minogue had been forgiven, apparently. The price of reassimilation was that he was expected to join in the Commissioner's distaste for Irish-speakers, to join the fray in the rivalry between Gardai and Army.

Minogue met Hoey in the hall and they walked to the car without saying a word. Inside the car, Minogue stretched out with the seat half-way reclined. He breathed in and then out deeply, twice. Hoey was scrabbling for a cigarette. "There goes your promotion," he joked lamely as he drew on the cigarette. "I wouldn't want too many mornings like that. Me knees are still knocking," he added.

"Well, I don't care what they say, Shea," said Minogue. He had regained his cheer.

"What? Who says?"

"All of them: Jimmy Kilmartin, the talking heads on the telly, the ones with the sure solutions and the tough attitudes. The 'dedicated service' lads, the men of high morals. All of them."

"Oh," said Hoey wisely. Minogue thought of Mickey Fitzgerald's biting sarcasm.

"The place isn't Chile or Argentina yet, not by a long shot. Am I right or am I right?"

"Dead on," said Hoey, plainly a talent lost to the diplomatic calling. "We'll get them all yet, so we will."

# FOURTEEN

**H**oey drove through Thomas Street, skirting the fringes of the Liberties. They drove past St Catherine's Church where the body of the hanged Robert Emmet had been decapitated and put on display to dissuade would-be rebels, who were welcome to observe dogs licking up Emmet's blood. The streets were busy and full of a harsher afternoon sunlight which threw cutting shadows and glared off windscreens. Small groups stood by the bus stops looking for lifts here too. The bright light was not kind to Minogue's humour, and he found himself slipping from his morning cheer. The play of the sun on this old part of the city suggested the bare and frightening spaces of de Chirico's and Magritte's more unsettling works.

The city looked tired and over-used. Minogue thought of the pathetic fallacy and he made a half-hearted attempt to notice the schoolchildren skipping by the pedestrians on the footpath. Idly he wondered which parts of Bloom's long day and night had been spent in this part of the city. Should he try harder to read *Ulysses* again? But wouldn't that resolve ruin the reading? It might help if he were to take a keener interest in the place-names and pubs and shops mentioned in the book. Kathleen had heard about walking tours of places mentioned in Joyce's books, and she had suggested that her husband go on one instead of grumbling about not being able to get a handle on the book. There'd be Yanks, he protested, and he'd feel silly. But the man leading the tour is that fella from Trinity, the expert on James Joyce, and he's meant to be a howl . . . Minogue had never taken the tour.

Butchers' shops, hucksters with tables of fruits and vegetables and little plastic whatnots, pubs with their doors open to dark and sepulchral interiors. Two drunken men sat on church steps and swayed as they argued. Without warning, the car in front braked. Hoey was fast, but he had been too close and the police car bounced dully off the back of it. Hoey turned off the engine and stepped out slowly, Minogue following. The other driver was looking down between the two cars. The back bumper of his ancient Cortina had merely collected another minor dent to add to the myriad others. The driver, a fat middle-aged man, unshaven and lumbering, gave the two policemen a disparaging look after he had surveyed the damage.

"We're all right this time," he said conclusively in a broad Dublin accent. Minogue smelled malty breath from the grizzled red face.

"If you had have signalled, we wouldn't be standing around holding up the traffic," said Hoey.

"You don't say. If you hadn't been a half-inch off me arse we wouldn't be standing around," the man retorted. "Didn't yous know there's a fuckin' bus strike? I was pulling in to give these oul' wans a lift."

He nodded in the direction of a clump of bystanders gathered around a bus stop.

"Well, next time turning on your indicator might save you a few bob," said Hoey.

"A few bob, is it? You're a culchie, aren't you? Up outa the bog, with shoes on and everything? Don't you know that the car folleying is supposed to be able to stop, no matter what?"

"Within reason," Hoey said.

"Within reason, me bollicks. Where's the reason of keeping these poor oul' dears waiting on a bus that's never going to come? And the sun boiling down on them?" He turned to the group by the bus stop and shouted. "Hey, missus, are your rashers getting fried there, and you waiting on the bus?"

An older woman with a hair-do like a poodle sticking out from under a head-scarf called back: "Amn't I getting boiled meself here, sure."

"See?" said the driver, turning to Hoey. "This is Dublin, not Ballybejases. We look after one another in this city. And we don't need fuckin' "—he paused to mimic Hoey's accent—" 'indicator lights' to stop at bus stops and give lifts to the elderly that's stuck by the side of the shagging road on account of the fact that yous culchies what are running the country can't get yis'r fuckin' act together—"

Minogue cut short the lecture on the political economy when he saw the barrel-chested man move toward Hoey with his forefinger jabbing the air in front of him.

"Give yourself a shake there," said Minogue, "and don't be making a show of yourself in the street. Do your good deed, and be off with yourself like a good man. There's no damage done."

"Another bog-trotter telling a Dublinman what to do. Be the living Jasus—"

"I'll run you in if you don't shut up," Minogue snapped. He did not like the crowd thickening on the footpath, watching.

"We're Garda officers," said Hoey. "You're talking yourself into court here. Park that car now and go home. You're half-cut already."

"Two coppers!" the man shouted to the crowd. "Two coppers telling me I can't stop me own car to pick up people, with the whole city bollicksed by the bus strike. And all the culchies that are sitting below in the Dáil, running the country and letting the bloody kip fall apart! Did yous ever hear the like of that?"

He stood with his arms spread wide in a theatrical appeal. Heads nodded and bobbed in the crowd. A youth with a crew cut stepped off the footpath.

"Leave the man alone and mind your own fuckin' business," he said to Minogue. "Man is only trying to help people out."

The cry of "culchie" repeated brought Minogue's anger back.

"Listen here to me, now, mister. Get back up on that path there or you'll be in on a breach of the peace."

"You and whose army?" sneered the youth.

Just as Minogue realized that he'd have to collar the youth, a Garda squad car braked noisily beside the crowd. Two Gardai ran over. Minogue showed them his card without taking his eyes from the youth.

"I was just advising this citizen here to hit the trail."

The young man's stare faltered, then turned to a look of disgust before he regained the footpath and walked through the crowd. Minogue watched him stop once, look back and spit purposefully into the gutter.

"Are you going to park it, or do you want to blow in the bag?" asked one Guard.

"Hold on there a minute," the driver began.

"Park it or go off with these two lads now," Hoey repeated. The driver sat in behind the wheel and did a creditable job of parking by the kerb. The younger Garda asked him for his licence and insurance. Minogue nodded his thanks and sat back in the car after Hoey.

"What about the buses?" said the woman with the poodle hair.

"I don't know, missus," said Minogue through the open window. "We could fit two of ye down as far as Dame Street or so. More than that we can't do."

The woman nudged her companion and they stepped down off the footpath. A third elderly woman scurried after them. The three climbed into the car and wrestled their shopping bags over their knees. One giggled.

"Are we right, then, ladies?" asked Hoey.

"Go ahead, driver," one tittered. "And don't spare the horses."

"Yous aren't going to land us in the slammer, are yous?" one piped. All three burst into shrill laughter. Minogue assured them that they would not be chained in the dungeons of Dublin Castle.

"Are yous really pleecemen? Yous must be detectives on account of the gear yous are wearing."

"I'm eighty-two last July," said the one with the

reedy voice, "and I've never been in a police car in me
entire life. I can remember gunfights in the streets of
Dublin with the Black and Tans."

"That must have been terrible," said Hoey.

"It certainly was. It was great," she replied. "Everyone had guns in their pockets them days."

Hoey glanced saucer-eyed to Minogue and then
looked to heaven.

"I hope nobody I know sees me in the back of a
squad car," said the third. "They might think I was
having some excitement."

The trio cackled again. Minogue heard dentures
clacking.

"It's the bloody busmen you should be locking up,
you know," said the poodle hair-do. "I was always
union meself, and me dear Larry—God be good to
him—wouldn't hear a word ag'in the union either.
But this is different, isn't it?"

A chorus of agreement from the back.

"And the pensions might be cut too. Prices going up
every day, it's a holy show. Not to speak of the hooligans that'd rob you in broad daylight. There's no jobs."

Minogue nodded in agreement.

"Ah Jesus, but we showed the Black and Tans,
didn't we? Didn't we, do you hear me talking?" said
the poodle-haired firebrand. "And we'll show the Brits
again if we have to, won't we?" she added vehemently.

The three women launched into a rousing version
of "We're All Off to Dublin in the Green." Minogue
believed that they all very much enjoyed the last line
of the chorus as they leaned into it with gusto. ". . . To
the echo of the Thompson gun!"

They sang the last verse before leaving the car at
the corner of Georges Street.

"Ah, come on now," Hoey protested. "We can't sit here in the car singing."

"One last verse!" cried one, breaking away from the chorus. "Then we're off!"

"... *To the echo of the Thompson gun!*"

Hoey drove quickly away from the kerb. The three waved and laughed from the footpath while passers-by stopped to look at the police car.

Deputy Commissioner Tynan phoned while Minogue was speaking with Kathleen.

"I must go, Kathleen. There's a big-shot on the other line. I want to hold on to my job for a little while yet."

He watched as Eilis tried to look severe, what to him might look Jesuitical, and he frowned at her, but she did not stop. Kilmartin thought that Tynan was a bit stuck up, "too smart for his boots by times, without the common touch." Minogue liked Tynan for those same reasons. Several times during the afternoon he had remembered Tynan's impassive gaze in the Commissioner's office, a gaze that might have been a mute appeal to join in appreciating the humour of life.

"More important than your wife?"

"If you can pay my salary, I'll keep on talking to you."

"You knew she was going away for the weekend."

"I did," replied Minogue. "But she wanted me to, em, tell you about it. I was the messenger to be shot, I think."

"At least she was frank about it. About those others going as well."

"I'm thinking we should leave Iesult do her own bidding, Kathleen, and not have her feeling guilty or that she has to sneak away. Look, I'll phone you if I'm going to be late."

Tynan's voice betrayed no signs of anything but officialdom.

"I have instigated the process. I was obliged to set up a small team here to work on the matter: a team of two, to be precise. Very discreet, and reporting only to me."

"May I ask if there have been any inquiries or reports directed to this concern before?"

"Ask, by all means, do. There have not. That's not to say that there hasn't been mention of officers' membership in such organizations before, merely to say that nothing has been made of the matter. As for accounting for firearms and ammunition, that's a matter for A Branch, as you well know. I'm not high in the firmament there."

Firmament, Minogue thought. Maybe Tynan's humour was so dry that . . . A play on fundament? Tynan had trained for the priesthood as a young man, thirty-odd years ago. Policemen who did not like any mystery to surround their fellows in the job attributed what they saw as Tynan's frostiness to both the training and the native constitution of a fish, a cold fish.

"I have to meet with the Deputy Comm from A Branch within the hour. I propose to run the check as part of a type of secret spot-check, or surprise accounting. This has been done before as an aid to ensuring that care and use of firearms by Garda officers does not become slipshod."

"Great," said Minogue, meaning it.

"I bask in your praise," said Tynan. "There is another matter which you may be interested in, one which we haven't had a chance to discuss so far. Jim

Kilmartin mentioned to the Commissioner that he'd like to find an ex-Opus Dei member so that he and you might have an insider's view of the organization. The Commissioner mentioned it to me in passing. You may or may not know that I was destined for the priesthood many years ago, and at one time I was involved with Opus Dei."

"That's interesting," Minogue fibbed while buying time so another part of his brain might penetrate the fog: why had Tynan called if this was thirty years ago?

"It's not really," said Tynan. "*Ipso facto*, I mean. I was interested in the mention of Opus Dei—surprised, even. I expect you'll find yourself in Bewley's before the afternoon is out, will you?"

"I beg your pardon?" from a flustered Minogue. He glared back at Eilis's amused scrutiny of his embarrassment and felt the prickly heat radiate up to his scalp. Let her think it's hot flushes, for all I care, his gargoyle hissed.

"I've seen you feasting yourself there before of an afternoon. I'll be there in Westmoreland Street, the non-smo part. Will you make a point of being there yourself?"

"I'm not sure I follow the arrangement."

"I can hole up in my office if you want, Minogue, and we can get bored out of our skulls wishing we were out of the bloody place in a restaurant where we could discuss the matter just as thoroughly. Let's do it the easy way. I have some titbits about Opus Dei for you."

Minogue was not pleased to be feeling apprehensive as he walked to Bewley's. He regarded it as a sanctuary, a place where even Kilmartin's company might be tolerable for a short while because the coffee and

the noise and the faces swamped any attempts at
being official. Why had Tynan not taken him aside
after the meeting with the Commissioner? He remembered the steady eyes, not unlike those of a fish
should a fish ever have lazy eyelids.

Tynan was not a policeman's policeman at all. He
had done his time dutifully in uniform and had
worked his way up the ranks steadily, taking his
exams. His superiors couldn't help but notice that
where Tynan went, order followed, and that much of
their own job was made easier by the work of this diligent officer. Tynan didn't seem to mind that others
took the credit for his efforts. He had managed to
reform many bureaucratic areas in the Gardai. "A
mind like a steel trap," Kilmartin had said several
times, usually over pints. Oddly, Tynan had managed
not to antagonize rank-and-file Gardai. He was new
to Garda B Branch, and lately Minogue had heard
quiet compliments being passed about him. B Branch
now seemed to be caught in the grip of some odd efficiency and this efficiency was very quickly noticed by
ordinary Gardai because B Branch dealt with their
bread and butter. As well as each Garda's personal
file, Tynan's dominion included transfers and promo-
tions, leave and gratuities, discipline and training.
Tynan, a man to be suspicious of because he had
turned away from the priesthood, was in danger of
becoming popular. Gardai would never again accept
the dictatorial regime which had only begun to ease
up in the early '70s. An unhappy coincidence of history—the North boiling over, and the aftermath of a
commission of inquiry which had been scathing about
Garda administration—had brought Gardai more say
in their working conditions.

Tynan's reserve had become the springboard for ribald jokes to be pitched out in Garda company. Minogue had heard the jokes but didn't much like them. Tynan had married later than most and his wife was supposed to be very glamorous. Minogue remembered her laughing a lot and smoking American cigarettes at the parties and functions which she attended with Tynan. He thought he had heard Tynan say something to her in Latin once, and recalled the expression on his face while she burst out laughing. Lovely teeth. Jokes about what spoiled priests could do in the line of sexual behaviour were probably signs of an acceptance, Minogue guessed. They had to make him their own because he wouldn't do so himself . . .

He spotted Tynan immediately next to the door in the non-smoking room. Tynan nodded faintly and returned to his newspaper. Minogue, deciding to forgo the bun, carried the coffee slowly and planted it on the marble table-top. Tynan folded the paper and watched as Minogue shoved a spoon and a half of brown sugar into the cup.

"Just the job for this time of the day," said Tynan. Minogue saw that Tynan's civvies were well cut: navy blue, but lightweight, and an ironed white shirt. The tweed tie was to let the discerning know that he wasn't a puritan.

"Do you like it?" Tynan said and looked down at the suit.

"It's all right," Minogue replied boldly.

"Roberta told me to buy it. Rank has its responsibilities. The Emperor has to have his clothes." There was no trace of humour on Tynan's features.

"There's an expression about that, I believe," Minogue hammed.

" 'To lead the people, you must turn your back on the people,' " said Tynan. "You don't want your followers looking at a poorly tailored back, don't you know. If the suit impresses them, they'll be less likely to spoil the cut by sticking a knife between your shoulders."

"I have but the two suits myself," said Minogue. "One is for funerals and the other one is gone too tight for me . . ."

Tynan nodded as if commiserating.

"I prefer to be in the uniform all day. I even have pyjamas done to look like a uniform, I suppose you know that."

Minogue spluttered coffee, still too hot for his greed. Tynan knew of some of the jokes about himself, then.

"I heard that, all right," he said. "I think the blue sits well, though."

Tynan looked off into the middle distance.

"It's the cut," he murmured. "That's why you pay the price. So says Roberta. She's always right in the sartorial line. Those Protestants know how to dress, I tell you."

Tynan sipped from his cup.

Roberta, Minogue echoed within. At least ten years younger than Tynan, so full of life, and she laughing away. American cigarettes, poise. What had Tynan said to her to make her laugh so much that time? A would-be Jesuit marrying a laughing Protestant—no wonder Jimmy Kilmartin was wary.

"Are you a regular here?" Minogue asked.

"No more than yourself. I know that you favour the place an odd time. Even Jim Kilmartin gets dragged in here too. It's not on your file or anything.

Now, about Opus Dei," Tynan said quietly. He leaned over the table. "I told you that I was closely associated with them a long while back. This Brian Kelly, the lad in the car, he was a member?"

"Yes he was; high up in it. He had been a Numerary, but the pair we talked to said he was ranked as an Associate when he died."

"You know that's lower on the totem."

Minogue nodded.

"Well, that doesn't happen often. You're in or you're out of the organization if you've attained that standing. It's usually all or nothing. I'm surprised— unless it was a temporary thing, a punishment."

"They told us that he was going through his period of re-evaluation, his life and aims. That everyone has these . . . spiritual milestones."

"An opportunity to grow in faith and commitment once the dark night is past?"

"You seem to know the tune well."

"Humph. They haven't changed much in that department, anyway. You know they come in for criticism, even from inside the Church?"

"No, I didn't," Minogue replied. "I thought they were just very religious."

" 'Just' is right. There's the charge of brainwashing against them. The way they recruit was the subject of some criticism a few years ago but it seems to have died down. They are very good at recruiting high-minded young people to throw in their lot with them. The initiates are usually very driven types of young men, very sincere, very conscientious and very clever . . . clever isn't everything, is it? . . . the way only young adults can be, before the world announces itself to them in earnest. Hmm. This would be a chat to pass the time, though, if it weren't for the context: Billy Fine's boy."

"Indeed," said Minogue. "It was a cold-blooded murder. Savage. I want the killer very badly indeed, and I have less patience as the days go by."

"That I noticed earlier in the afternoon. Let me ask you, now, what do you think is really going on here?"

"Like I said at the meeting, I'm beginning to think that the murder had something to do with Opus Dei. A youngster has come forward, a boy who had a glimpse of a man who may be the killer. He said the man looked like a copper. You know how it is with kids."

Tynan nodded. "They tend to be a problem insofar as they see things a bit too clearly for our liking. But the claim about the fringe group and the Palestinians?"

"Sergeant Gallagher in the Branch has been banging his head on that one. He's still interviewing but so far he has nothing to lead us with."

"It's cover-up?"

"It might be and it might not. Just because the killer didn't look like an Arab to the young lad who's shaping up to be an excellent witness, that doesn't mean . . ."

Minogue stopped when he saw Tynan nodding his head.

"We believe that Brian Kelly was also murdered and that the forensic will confirm that soon enough. So with those facts, we're starting off with this line of investigation."

"And Kelly was looking to talk to you one night late?"

"He was; we tape the calls to the help-line. We have the sense that Brian Kelly knew something about Paul Fine. I believe he may have arranged to meet Paul Fine just before Paul Fine was murdered."

"Did Kelly kill Paul Fine?"

"No. He didn't match the description we have off that sharp young lad. There's a snapshot of Kelly on its way out to the boy's home so that we can be positive of this."

Tynan looked down into his cup. "The other alternative seems to be that Kelly was killed for the same reason that Paul Fine was killed, and perhaps by the same person or persons," he said.

"Tell me why," said Minogue.

"Kelly gives Fine some information. Kelly has some troubles with Opus Dei."

"Thanks," Minogue said archly. "Now I know how Jimmy Kilmartin feels when it's me talking like that."

"Doesn't work very well when you don't have evidence and facts, does it?" Tynan said quietly.

"I just can't see religious people getting up to this mayhem," said Minogue. "That stops me in my tracks too."

"All right, so. The gist of what's bringing me here is this. I happen to know that Opus Dei has changed over the past few years. The whole character of the organization has changed and so has its membership in Ireland. I know this because I have a personal interest in it. I also know that there are serving members of Gardai in Opus Dei. You may remember what General O'Tuaime said in the meeting," said Tynan ambiguously.

"That the issue of Army members belonging to confraternities has come up before, but that it's of no consequence?"

"Yes. Opus Dei has been around since the '30s. It was a product of the '30s in many ways, when people looked to the Soviet Union and began to get the shivers. Fascism as a counter to Bolshevism, and that sort of mania. Opus Dei never really got near the goal of having a broad base of membership here in Ireland. That's what they realized not too long ago, so the emphasis was put less on recruiting big numbers of young men and more on using the ones they had already, using them more efficiently to do the apostolic work. Quality, not quantity, became the byword for them. I was approached several years ago by a certain party, unnamed, a senior Garda officer. He's retired now. At one of those get-togethers in the Clarence hotel, you can imagine. A few jars after the speeches, and we got down to the real business of gossip and character assassination. I'm sure that a goodly number of people know that I was once well on the way to being a priest and this man did. He suggested to me in the friendliest way—two Gardai having a jar and gabbing—that it would do me no harm if I were to resuscitate an interest in lay apostolic work. I caught on immediately that he meant Opus Dei. If it had been the Knights of Columbus, he would have said so. 'No harm' meant to my career, of course."

Tynan's eyes had taken on a frosty glint.

"This was 1971 when there were deaths every night in the North. The Provos were full of Marxist rhetoric and there was a feeling that anything could happen. I didn't tell him that as regards resuscitating this interest he might as well be asking me to raise the dead. That's none of anyone's business, inside the job or outside of it, except my own. Don't bother trying to think back as to who's senior and who's retired now: he was a harmless fellow, really. With me, you see, and the priestly calling, he would have assumed that once in, I was never 'really' out. It's like being seduced, I suppose. He saw five years in a seminary on my card, and he saw what he wanted."

Was Tynan a pagan too, Minogue wondered. Tynan flicked a glance beyond Minogue as though to address an unseen audience.

"I was told that as a bit of helpful advice. Naturally, as I'm married and the rest of it, I couldn't aspire to the heights of being a Numerary or even an Associate in Opus Dei. My would-be mentor would have known that anyway. What he was saying, I decided, was that someone, some people who mattered in the Gardai, was involved with Opus Dei, even in a minor way. If I was to join, I'd be one of the boys."

"Are we waiting to use the word 'conspiracy' but it sounds too dramatic?"

"Could be. I have no idea if it went anywhere beyond being a few people motivated by piety and a bit of nationalism. I simply said to myself that one day I'd find out more about this. I had put it on hold, and almost forgotten about it."

"When you say 'people who mattered,' do you mean someone senior to you at the time?"

"I was a Chief Super, working in Sligo then. There were three ranks above me. Assistant Comm, Deputy Comm, and the man himself, God Almighty."

Seven in total, Minogue estimated. The noise of Bewley's began to get in on him now. He was dimly aware of some backstage movements but he couldn't focus on them while he had Tynan across the table from him. He watched him finish his coffee. Was he trying to get him tangled up in some messy speculation that could turn out badly? Why would Tynan confide in him like this instead of monitoring the investigation at a distance?

"If you're trying to remember who was in those posts then and where they are now, give yourself a rest. I'll tell you. DC1 was there then, and he's still there. God Almighty used to be DC1 before Quinn. There's only one of us four Assistant Comms who was at that rank back then. But that's not the point, because we're not on a witch-hunt, and I'll tell you why before you get the spyscopes out. You know that Supers and Chief Supers have a lot of say indirectly in who gets promoted above them. In my case, other Chief Supers at the time would have been discreetly asked: 'Is that Tynan worth the money?' or 'Can you work with Tynan?' They even ask Supers and Inspectors, to see how they feel about their masters and their future masters. Not in so many words, of course, but their remarks are noted. So for any of these Opus Dei men to help a fellow along in his career, they wouldn't have to be the dogs with the loudest barks in the house."

Was that how he talked to Roberta after a day's work, talking about the Commissioner as God Almighty or the dog with the loudest bark?

"What I'm saying is this: you should bear in mind that I am interested in what facts might emerge from your investigation that'd tell me about Opus Dei. I told you they're a different organization now, but that doesn't mean they're killers, at all. If there's a 1 per cent chance that there was any Garda involvement in the Fine murder, I want to know about it on the spot."

So this was it, Minogue realized. Tynan was asking that he, Minogue, report to him as well. He was hinting that he need not report more than he needed to to

Kilmartin and the Commissioner because they
wouldn't have the interest to to follow up the consequences in-house.

"I've started a search of the files, but frankly I don't
expect to be able to find the information you need, we
need, on them," said Tynan. "A lot of the men keep
their religion to themselves, me included. You know
yourself that there are plenty of people to laugh at the
Holy Joes these days. It'll be the same story with your
General O'Tuaime and his files too, I'd guess."

He was right, Minogue's sinking stomach repeated:
the same would be true of the Army. The worm burrowed more vigorously into his belly now. If Tynan
was nothing else, he was blunt.

"And you don't need to underline the big gaps in
all this either," said Tynan. Minogue returned his
gaze.

"What was so important that Paul Fine, and perhaps Brian Kelly, were on to that would cause people
to kill them?" Tynan concluded.

They rose to leave. A distracted Minogue sensed
that Tynan's end to the conversation well matched his
decisive moves as he strode away from the table. He
was like a player walking away from a chess game
which was suddenly over. Suddenly over for the loser,
that was, who hadn't seen the checkmate coming.

"I asked the two I met out in the Opus Dei house in
Churchtown for a list of their members who might
have been acquainted with Brian Kelly, you know,"
Minogue said, as they made for the front door on to
Westmoreland Street.

"You did, did you," Tynan said with what could
have been a smile, had it lived. "And what did you
get?"

"A priest by the name of Heher told me he'd be happy to write to Rome on my behalf. Permission has to come from there, he says."

"And what did you think about that?" Tynan asked as he stopped inside the door.

"I thought of trying to get a court order and cause a big commotion. I take a dim view of people thinking they may or may not decide to help the Gardai with information in a murder case."

"The collar didn't frighten you?"

"Heher was dressed in his civvies. I'm not afraid of being sent to hell for impertinence: it's an honourable sin in this country."

Tynan's smile was almost reincarnated but it was his eyebrows only which registered the amusement now.

"You certainly deserve your reputation." He held up one hand. "And don't ask me to explain that remark any further. It'd be more than my job is worth to see you trying to argue the toss with a judge trying to get such a court order, much less enforce it. Tell me, do you think this Heher knew you were bluffing about this?"

"He might have. There wasn't a thing to incriminate them at all in the Fine murder, I have to say. But I want to get to talk to others in that house, ones who might have known Kelly from when he stayed there too."

Tynan scratched his chin lightly. "Let me work on that this evening. I'll see what I can do, at least as regards getting to see the people in this house."

"It'll save me walking through the door on them this evening. I was planning to do just that," said Minogue.

"Hold your fire for the moment, Minogue. We'll see what five years in the seminary thirty years ago can get done, in these pagan times we're living in."

# FIFTEEN

**H**ad Minogue not been brooding, he would have paid more attention to the time. He had briefed the Commissioner with a lengthy telephone call. The Commissioner told Minogue in reply that if asked by a reporter, he would dodge any reference to a link between the deaths of Brian Kelly and Paul Fine. What was more, the Commissioner told him, only if Opus Dei was mentioned by someone else—and it wouldn't be, would it?—would he admit that Brian Kelly was associated with that organization. Minogue agreed that this was "good policy."

In the trough after coffee, Minogue returned to the work of trying to accompany Paul Fine through the last days of his life. Hoey asked him if he wanted tea.

"No thanks. After you get yours, would you come back here and pretend you're somebody else?"

"How do you mean? Do I get to pick who I'd like to be?"

"I'll be Paul Fine. You'll be the all-seeing eye. You can explain everything that goes on, all right?"

Hoey blinked and lit a cigarette. "I don't want tea meself."

Neither Muses nor gods visit policemen. This is particularly true in Ireland because there is but one God there and the Irish Muses are dispersed over many areas and minds. There is a lot of work for both the Muses and God to do on the island, and policemen do not have preferential treatment. So some Garda detectives called their inspirator Murphy, Murphy being a construct born of, and fed by, the detective's hunger for facts to help him solve the problem at hand. Murphy is inserted into criminal situations, and knowledge is attributed to him: it is then a matter of interrogating Murphy to see what has happened, what will happen. Minogue did not need Murphy, he chose Hoey and himself to do the work.

"Right. It's Saturday. I'm in the National Library. I'm reading up on Opus Dei. I am a Jew and I don't know anything about Opus Dei. I spend a good part of the day reading. Do I make notes?"

"Well, it's . . ."

"Do I or don't I?"

"You don't," Hoey blurted.

"Why don't I?"

"Because you're reading for pleasure. It's the weekend."

"Or because . . . ?"

"Or because it's your first look at the subject and you're getting an overall picture: you don't care about details yet. That's the way they train you in the university."

"All right, so. Why am I reading up on a crowd of religious people like this?"

"There might be a story in it."

"Why am I in the National Library?"

"You don't like to be at work on a Saturday."

"That's all? I could be doing a better search over at the television offices, RTE."

"Maybe you like to operate on the quiet. Maybe it's a story you want to keep to yourself."

"Because I want to make a name for myself?"

"Yes. You're a nice lad, but Fitz doubts that you're tough enough for the real thing, whatever that might be."

"Good. I'm sitting on something, keeping it to myself for the moment. I'll land it dramatically on Fitz's desk and I'll be the cat's pyjamas then, won't I? I'll have proved I can do the grind."

"That's right."

"Who or what put me on to this possible story? Why amn't I doing a story on the history of the cocker spaniel?"

"Kelly. Brian Kelly," said Hoey with assurance. "He phoned you."

"Why did he phone me?"

Hoey's confidence collapsed. "It's impo—"

"It's because he knows I'm a reporter, a journalist."

Hoey frowned. "Why you? I mean . . ."

"Exactly," said Minogue. "He knows that I work on a programme with Mickey Fitz, the man that knocks holy statues off their pedestals."

"But why not Fitz himself or other hard-chaw journalists? I mean, you're—Paul Fine, like—you're not the ideal choice. Matter of fact"—Hoey smiled nervously now—"you're a bit of a pussycat, aren't you?"

"I am," said Minogue. "I'm far from being the hit-man that Fitz is."

"Definitely." Hoey smiled broadly. "You're too soft entirely."

"Good, Shea. Because I'm a Jew, I'm circumspect about matters religious. I'm not a bawler or a brawler like the home-grown Christians."

Hoey warmed to his role again. "In actual fact you being a Jew, you probably never even heard of—"

"Exactly, Shea!" Minogue clapped his hands together. "Brian Kelly phoned me *because* I am a Jew!"

"But Opus Dei; they're our crowd," said Hoey in a slightly aggrieved tone. "And what's to Opus Dei that makes a story out of them? I know that Kelly was a bit of a backslider but what would he have to tell Paul, I mean you?"

"Maybe a story about the hold that Opus Dei has on its members. The way they recruit members. Maybe Brian Kelly is soured on the organization."

"But they're Holy Joes. The worst they might do is dress up in women's clothes and whip themselves."

Minogue swivelled around in his chair. Eilis was now standing behind Hoey. Hoey followed Minogue's eyes, craning his neck and twisting to look up at Eilis, who looked down at him with her more sceptical expression.

"Excuse me now if I'm interrupting your plans for your weekend," she said to Hoey. She turned to Minogue. "DC Tynan would want to be talking to you."

Minogue listened to Tynan's brief message.

"Half-past seven? I should pick you up, so. Are you sure I need to be there?"

He thought he heard Tynan snort faintly. "Unless

you're planning to react in some untoward way to the presence of the Archbishop of Dublin," said Tynan.

"Jimmy Kilmartin, I was thinking . . . ?"

"The Archbishop asked for you by name. He knew you were in charge of the case. Tell James, by all means, but it's you that His Grace wants to see, as much as myself."

Minogue wondered if Kathleen would believe him when he got around to telling her. She might regard it as a conversion. He turned back to Hoey.

"Let's go on a bit. We were getting somewhere. I'm Paul Fine and I have Brian Kelly wanting to tell me something."

"That's what I was saying: when you put this against the wall, it doesn't stand up well. Kelly had nothing to tell you that was so scandalous."

"But I'm a Jew. Is that a disadvantage? I wouldn't know the ins and outs of what Catholics do."

"That's it. When you push it to the limit . . ."

"But being a Jew I might have a distinct advantage. I'd know what goes on in Irish heads because I'm Irish, but I'd be bringing a fresh approach to the matter."

"You wouldn't be so cynical about religious Catholics, you mean?"

"Yes. I wouldn't start out spiteful and wanting to go for people's necks. Something else, though, Shea—there's another reason why Brian Kelly picked me. It's something symbolic. Did you ever hear of a fella called Leopold Bloom?"

"I think I did, all right . . . Was it a film?"

Minogue shook his head.

"A symbolic thing . . . because you're a Jew? Like Jesus," Hoey whispered, looking around the squad room to be sure that no one else could see his embarrassment.

"Fabulous, Shea. There's that. Brian Kelly would have been alive to religious symbolism, yes. There's another thing too, something very down-to-earth."

It was Hoey's turn to shake his head. "Can't see it."

"*I couldn't be a member of Opus Dei, Shea,*" Minogue whispered.

Hoey sat back in the chair and drew thoughtfully on his cigarette. "You're saying that Kelly was worried about his pals in Opus Dei finding out that he was none too happy about something to do with the organization? If he had pals left in it."

"You're Brian Kelly now, Shea. Ready?"

Hoey sat up again.

"Why are you not trying to get in touch with Mickey Fitzgerald?" Minogue asked.

Hoey answered in the tone of the hypnotized. "I don't know." He began laughing lightly, unable to hide his embarrassment. "Sorry. I'm not much good in the theatrical line."

"Maybe you're paranoid," said Minogue contemplatively.

"Thanks very much."

"Brian Kelly, I mean. Maybe you're at a pitch of anxiety and you imagine people are spying on you."

"Now you're talking, sir. But does it help us much to find out that Brian Kelly was a nutcase?"

Minogue disliked the term. He had shied from it even before his own brush with the arbitrariness that haunted every life, that you saw if you were able to look beyond "father" and "policeman" and "Irish." Minogue had discovered the hard way that normality was a rather ambiguous accomplishment, something which could backfire, something which involved a lot of work which you hardly knew you were doing or why, until you stopped doing it, or it stopped you.

"Point taken, Shea. We need to get his associates at work to give us a clue as to demeanour and state of mind. Definitely."

Hoey brightened at some remembrance, just as Minogue was about to leave. "I'll tell you one thing: whether or which Kelly was cracked, he certainly seems to have put Paul Fine in the same frame of mind. If you look at events kind of sideways, I mean."

"How do you mean?"

"You might think this a bit odd, but nobody in RTE knew about his interest in Opus Dei, not even the McCutcheon woman, his mot. He kept it to himself. Maybe Kelly told him he had to."

"Ummn."

"And he went to the National Library, not to his own place. He didn't even check what a journalist probably checks first, the newspaper clippings and programmes on tape. And if this notion is still holding together, he's off out to Dalkey or Killiney on the Sunday to meet Kelly. Do you see . . . ?"

Hoey perched up on the front of the chair, slowly waving and pushing at the air with his cigarette.

"Kelly in Killiney Hill?"

"He meets Fine, an arranged meeting. They have a chat and Kelly tells him something—"

"Tell me why Kelly wasn't the one to kill Paul Fine, Shea."

"Like he could have been unbalanced and had some queer thing about Jews? After realizing what he'd done, he might be sick of himself and want to commit . . . ?" Hoey shook his head. "I'm stuck there, really stuck. I'd go along with the business of Kelly trusting a Jew not to treat his information sensationally and muck-rake the organization that he might still have fond memories of. But my belly tells me that the man who shot Paul Fine three times in the back of the head wasn't Kelly. Little Patsy O'Malley will tell us that for certain when we show him a picture of Kelly. I wonder, did Kelly attend a psychiatrist or the like?"

"Good one, Shea. Suggest that to Jimmy Kilmartin, will you? I hope I can come up with names of Opus Dei people who we can grill about Brian Kelly. I'm going to meet a fella tonight who might have something to tell me."

"Great stuff. Who is it, do you mind me asking?"

"The Archbishop of Dublin. Apparently he wants to see me."

"The what?" said Kilmartin.

"None other. Tynan must have been in touch with his office and was able to pull a string. This particular string seems to be attached to a brick . . . or, should I say, a pillar? I hope that it lands softly, now that I've pulled on it. I was trying to chase down an Opus Dei membership list as well as any friends or ex-friends of Brian Kelly. That's what I get for doing a bit of your work for you, Jimmy. I'm meeting more clergy in one day than I've met in years. Maybe I'll get a letter of introduction to the Pope of Rome."

"I'd have it on me conscience if l didn't take it upon meself to warn His Holiness you were planning to drop in," said Kilmartin. "Tynan, now. They stick together, don't they? He's Tynan's age, is the Archbishop. It wouldn't surprise me to find out they've known one another since they were baby priests, before Tynan jumped the wall and came to us. What's the name for baby priests anyway, before they get to be real priests? Scholars, is it?"

Minogue had often thought that calling Ireland's one Cardinal "the Primate of all Ireland" had been an intentional pun. He had seen a cartoon of a simian cardinal on a Women's Action Movement poster near Grafton Street during the summer. The cleric, complete with crozier and pince-nez and hat, had been sitting on oppressed women.

"Novitiates, I think."

"Very clever. That brain of yours is a fright to God entirely. Lookit, though—I'd watch that Tynan, do you know what I mean?"

Minogue used one of the coarse replies which Iesult gave when Kathleen was over-anxious for her daughter to understand what a wise course of action might be. "I know what you mean but the grass is wet," he sighed. "What's there to watch in Deputy Commissioner John Tynan?"

"Exactly. *Deputy*. Deputy always wants to get beyond being deputy anything. He has his eyes set on God Almighty's chair."

"Like your Fabulous Fintan Gorman and the Chief?"

"You can laugh, all right, Matt. Seeing as you're not competing for the job yourself."

Minogue did not bother to confirm Kilmartin's contention here. He turned to the matter of Brian Kelly.

"How do you want the manpower shifted around when we take on Kelly as murder, Jimmy?"

Kilmartin thanked his friend and colleague for reminding him of that headache. In the icy tones of a countryman scorning another countryman, he told

Minogue that he'd be told in good time, most likely tomorrow morning as soon as the forensic reports were delivered in their completeness. Steps were already being taken to get interviews from Kelly's associates at work. Kilmartin then invited Minogue to have the Archbishop bless a non-existent set of rosary beads which he, Kilmartin, pretended to draw out of his pocket. "Ha, ha, ha," Kilmartin laughed, and coughed. "I nearly had you believing me there."

"I'll ask him to say a special prayer for your wife."

"Oh, that's a dirty one there," Kilmartin mocked. "And her the happiest woman in Ireland. Straighten your tie there, so you don't look like an iijit."

Kilmartin called out to him as he reached the doorway. "And ask him what he thinks of Mrs Ryan and the WAMmers running the country and doing away with the men." He collapsed into a phlegmy cough as he laughed after Minogue.

Tynan's clothes still looked sharp after a workday. Minogue felt more nervous the nearer they drove toward the Archbishop's residence.

"Jimmy asked me to get His Grace's opinions on the Ryan case, or rather the Women's Action Movement and their championing of Marguerite Ryan."

"What do you think of it yourself?" asked Tynan absently.

Minogue looked out over the rooftops of College Green where the still-heavy traffic had snared them. The sky was tangerine and russet, like a bloodied egg, making a mockery of the pewter shades on the ground. This Dublin, this time, were just about tolerable, he decided.

"I don't know what to think. I have a daughter at

home and she doesn't take any guff out of anyone. I could never see her getting into a situation like Marguerite Ryan's. Being abused, I mean."

"You are putting a lot of stock in the history of abuse," Tynan said vaguely.

"How can you ignore it? I'd prefer Iesult to be the strap she is rather than be acquiescent or overly obedient," said Minogue.

"With due respect to the Archbishop, I think he'd tend to favour an emphasis on being obedient," mused Tynan. "I studied with him when I was in college, you know. That's how I got to talk to him this afternoon. We swap Christmas cards every year still. There is life after the seminary, I found out."

Tynan looked at the elaborate lamp standards beside the statue of Thomas Moore on the concrete island in the middle of the Green. "Do you know the motto for Dublin? There's a coat of arms there on that lamp, the coat of arms on a blue background."

Minogue looked out but could see only blue patches in the twilight.

"*Obedientia Civium Urbis Felicitas*. That's the kind of obedience we used to take our mental tweezers to when we were in college. I suppose that ideally it's related to the Greek notion of virtue—a citizen who goes along with the correct line, the moral path, being a member of a collective which works together, a collective informed by virtue."

"Virtue is its own reward," said Minogue. "I never much liked the sound of that one. Like, it's all right to get walked on."

"*Virtus. Obedientia*," Tynan murmured. "I hope they meant that a sound civic spirit would make for an agreeable city. Well, they're talking about a city as a group of people, not some abstract institution, and that's something, isn't it?"

Minogue moved with the light and geared into second as they went by the pillars of the Bank of Ireland.

"Obedience is a horse of a different colour, though," said Tynan, awakening with the motion of the car. "I would like to hear the modern-day Opus Dei expound their notion of obedience and virtue. They certainly don't hobble themselves with the 'virtue is its own reward' end of things. Their mandate is to engage the world. Apostolic."

"*Engagé*," said Minogue in a Paris accent diverted through Clare.

"Nice. Someday I can brag to an upstart journalist that some members of the Gardai speak French. They want to be like the early Christians, committed and evangelical. No wonder the man in the street is a bit suspicious of them, if they're working alongside him." Tynan's voice suggested to Minogue that he had a grim smile. "Of course they take private vows and promise obedience to the superior that Rome appoints. That'd be the 'final authority' you were told about by that priest . . ."

"Heher."

"—Heher, over Opus Dei members who work in the Gardai or are enlisted Army men. 'Noble folly,' they called it in my day. The idea of being a knight who did God's bidding."

"Tilting at windmills, is it?"

"They do a lot more than that in places like Guatemala, I suspect," Tynan said. The unexpected edge to his voice startled Minogue. This Tynan was a fish from the depths. Minogue gave his passenger a quick glance.

"Now you're asking yourself if I'm the one, and not you, who might have something abrasive to say to His Grace tonight, aren't you?" said Tynan.

Minogue had to laugh.

"Don't be worrying yourself," Tynan added in a tone heavy with irony. "I was just thinking out loud. It was all a long time ago for me. There's no bitterness. I serve different masters now," he added wryly.

Not for long, if Jimmy Kilmartin is right, thought Minogue.

When they reached the Archbishop's Residence, Minogue searched the glove compartment for a comb and did the best he could with what was left to him of daylight and hair and composure. He recalled that the Residence used to be called the Archbishop's Palace. Vatican II had muted the splendour of titles, at least.

"Ah, you're all right," said Tynan. "An honest face."

"Did he say anything exactly?" Minogue tried again, checking the toes of his shoes for noticeable scuffs.

"He said he wanted to see Inspector Minogue as well as myself. To tell us what can and can't be done about Opus Dei."

"I don't know where he got my name from."

"Heher, whom you saw this morning."

"I'm in for a talking-to, is it?"

"No, no," Tynan smiled wanly. "We're on the threshold of the third millenium. It's not the Church Triumphant any more. Let's look on it as an information session."

# SIXTEEN

The door was answered by a cheerful priest. He was in his thirties and had the look of a happy athlete about him. He was not wearing a jacket and the sleeves of his black shirt were rolled up over his elbows. A farmer's son.

"I'm Pat Sheehy," he said in a Kerry accent. "And you're Gardai."

"Don't tell me," said Minogue, wondering if there was a ban on using the term Father, "we don't look like rock stars."

"Ah no. It's the appointment book that tells all."

Sheehy closed the heavy door behind them. The residence smelled of floor-wax and a chicken boiling somewhere. Minogue and Tynan followed the agile Sheehy across the parquet to a double door that opened into a room with a high ceiling, the proportions of which suggested a Georgian if not a neo-classical plan at work, but in the nineteenth century. Several large portraits hung from the walls. Must be all past Archbishops of Dublin, Minogue concluded after recognizing two. Fresh flowers rested in a Waterford cut-glass bowl atop what Minogue's amateur eye guessed was an antique Irish bog-oak table. In this waiting room the visitor could read *Reader's Digest*, *Time* or *The Word*, a publication of the Oblate Fathers.

Sheehy was back inside of two minutes. Less cheery now, Minogue believed, a lot less. The chicken smell was stronger in the hall: maybe it wasn't chicken but someone's goose getting cooked . . . the fat is in the fire now . . . what's sauce for the goose is—Minogue reined in his flittery thoughts.

Sheehy knocked and entered without awaiting a summons from within the room. Minogue felt quickly that the knot of his tie was in place and brushed over the zipper of his fly. You never know, said his gargoyle within. Was he expected to kiss the ring, or had that gone out too with the Latin Mass? He determined not to do so, anyway.

The Archbishop of Dublin, the Most Reverend Doctor Francis Burke, stood behind his desk and nodded at the two policemen. Minogue heard Sheehy closing the door. Burke was making no attempt to come around the desk to greet the policemen, Minogue realized. Tynan went before him and reached across the desk to shake hands.

"John. How've you been?" said Burke.

Tynan said he was fine. He turned to introduce Minogue.

"Your Grace," said Minogue. Burke nodded as he shook hands briefly. He looked a lot different off the telly, Minogue thought. Maybe it was the light in here.

Or the knobs under the telly to adjust the tint and the— Time to get a new one, Kathleen says, what with the scratchy bit at the bottom of the screen now—

The curtains were dark green and they had been drawn across what could be full-length windows behind the desk. The office was probably thirty feet square, Minogue estimated: there might even be room in here for the Archbishop to have posed for a WAM poster with his foot on the necks of the oppressed women of Ireland. "*Not the Church, Not the State, Women must control their . . .*" One wall was taken up with bookcases whose glass doors reflected the fancy candelabra lights which dangled from the embossed ceiling. There were two hardbacked chairs drawn up on the policemen's side of the desk. A coffee-table stood chairless by the marble fireplace to their right. Business, Minogue knew, otherwise we'd be sitting there at that table by the fire that was probably never lit.

Tynan waited for the Archbishop to sit before he took his chair. Minogue followed suit and stole another glance at Burke. The face fleshy but not unhealthy: tired, anyway. Fifty-four, fifty-five? His mauve shirt was that of an Archbishop. He had piled a series of file folders and one thick book to one side of the desk, leaving plenty of room for the photograph of John Paul II high on the altar in the Phoenix Park with his congregation of over a million of the country's three and a half million souls gathered about in the grass. It might have been taken in the middle of his "Young People of Ireland" speech. Minogue could not classify the smell here in the room yet: it was not pipe tobacco, it was more a medicinal smell. Cough drops?

Burke settled himself and looked to Minogue. "You're a principal officer in investigating Brian Kelly's death?"

"I'm not, Your Grace. I'm merely part of the permanent staff in the Technical Bureau. You'd probably know my department as the Murder Squad."

"I hope I don't get to know it all that well," said Burke humourlessly.

"I spoke with Father Heher this morning," said Minogue.

"Yes, that I know," said Burke. He looked to the closed door behind the two policemen as though to gather inspiration from it. "You'd be the Inspector Minogue who is investigating the murder of Billy Fine's son, Paul Fine, wouldn't you?"

"I am that."

"Tell me, then, Inspector: why do you think he, Billy Fine, asked you to do the job? Do you have some expertise? Before you give me your answer, I should save you the trouble of asking me how I know this—we meet occasionally in the course of our jobs, Billy and I. Yes"—Burke raised both hands off the desk and used them as wands to indicate around the room—"jobs. This is a job as well as a vocation. I am a bureaucrat as well as a shepherd. This is my office. I've met the Fines and many others in the Jewish community in Ireland over the years. My heart goes out to Billy and Rosalie: they are the best that Ireland could hope for in respect of their learning and culture and religion. Billy Fine has the soul of a poet, a writer buried behind those robes. Rosalie Fine is one of the most cultured women I have met in my life. I went to see Billy on Monday night late after I heard the news, and passed on our prayers to them. He asked me then if I knew you. I didn't."

Minogue realized that his nervousness was going now. Something was taking its place, a tension, a feeling of some stretching.

"Your question . . . I'm not sure. It may be a sentimental thing when all is said and done, to be honest with you. I had met Justice Fine in the Jewish Museum here just after it opened. I believe he knew something of my career background in the Murder Squad."

"Modest of you, Inspector. Billy Fine seems to have a lot of faith in you. Tell me, are the policemen who do your line of work very different men from those we see helping the schoolchildren across the street?"

Minogue didn't know whether the talk was toying. "Yes, I believe that we are."

"The job requires a certain flair," Tynan said quietly.

"Flair? Are you very tough, you Gardai here on this work?" asked Burke.

"I don't think so. We're the same as the next man in the street. I can say that my colleagues have a very strong sense of fairness. We try and deal with what people do to other people as best we can. I don't understand certain things about people even after I see them through a trial."

"Not an élite that's used to getting what it wants quickly?"

"I feel very un-élite at the best of times," replied Minogue. "I go home most evenings to my wife. We have two grown children. We read and watch a little bit of telly and do a bit of gardening if the rain holds off and the slugs don't attack the cabbage. Sometimes we go on a holiday."

"Billy Fine said he wanted you. He is no fool."

"I'm flattered. I'll help him out as well as I can, but I work for the State also."

Burke lolled back in his chair. Minogue heard him breathe out slowly as he rubbed his eyes with the heels of his thumbs.

"Anyway, what are we here for? Brian Kelly and Opus Dei. Is that the menu you'd like, John?"

Tynan nodded. "We'd be obliged for your help."

"They told you you'd have to apply to Rome to release the membership rolls, I suppose? You didn't want a list of all the membership in Ireland, did you? You had a sideline interest."

Minogue cleared his throat. Yes, that's what the smell was: cough drops. "Brian Kelly's friends and associates in the organization," he said. "We'd be wanting to interview them. Perhaps the deceased was anxious, under some pressure."

"You mean that it's not certain that Brian Kelly didn't take his own life?"

"Not entirely at all. His is in a category of 'suspected foul play.' It's likely that we'll want to investigate the death as soon as we have gleaned all the information we can from a forensic investigation of the remains. I expect that Brian's death will be a murder investigation by midday tomorrow."

"It's a question of what the books call Forensic Pathology, Frank," said Tynan mildly. "The body was very badly burned."

Burke rubbed his eyes again. "But the gist of what you were wanting this morning was something else, wasn't it, though?" he said laboriously, as though to a duller student.

Minogue's chest was tight with alertness. Something

was forming in his mind, quicker now, but he could not make out the contours.

"If I might know which members of Opus Dei are in the Gardai or the Army," he said.

"And why?"

"There are clues to suggest that Paul Fine's murder may have involved a person who is both an expert in firearms and had access to same. The murderer went to a lot of trouble to remove evidence from the murder site. It's also apparent that the phone call to the newspaper blaming it on Palestinians may have been a hoax."

Burke glared at Minogue with reddened, rheumy eyes. "Do you know anything about Opus Dei, Inspector? You, John"—he turned to Tynan—"you know a bit."

"Little enough," Minogue replied. "I believe that they are not directly accountable to their local dioceses, the local Church hierarchy, I mean. They don't advertise themselves. Naturally one has to be very devout to join—"

"And make no mistake about that," Burke interrupted. His vehemence took Minogue by surprise. "It's not that they're not accountable. They work within their own structure, parallel to our own diocesan work. We're all pulling in the same direction, you know. The Church is involved as a social agency in a huge number of projects, Inspector. God comes to us in Tallaght, in Clondalkin where boys and girls sniff glue from bags in ditches; God is in the employment office where there are men who haven't found work in ten years; God is meals-on-wheels to old people that our consumer society has no more time for. Commitment. Values. Altruism. Service. We're all after the same goals: to serve God by serving our fellow men and women in this world."

Burke pointed a finger at the ceiling. "We're after the will to carry things through, to resist the blandishments of the style of living we seem to have such appetites for now. You won't shock me to tell me we're not the Island of Saints and Scholars, but let me tell you this. The will to persevere amidst Ireland's social upheavals is not the exclusive preserve of the well intentioned. There is a will to do evil too. Our will is allied to and founded upon values we all hold dear, in the Church, in Irish history as a whole, and it's allied to the commitment that Irish people have shown throughout our history."

Saints and scholars, like Kilmartin's dreams. Was everybody in this damn country always ready to deliver a speech at the drop of a hat, Minogue wondered. Perhaps there was some threat in Minogue to which people responded by speechifying. Out of the corner of his eye he knew that Tynan was sitting still, but that it was not a stillness of relaxation. Had Tynan known it would turn out like this?

"Our faith; our culture; our people; our children's future; altruism: where will you find any of that these days, I sometimes ask myself in my most dispirited moments," Burke continued in a low voice. "Short supply, hmm, John?" He darted the remark to Tynan.

Tynan nodded.

"So it troubles me to hear criticism of Opus Dei when I know that its membership shows these qualities. Though they may have any and all the failings which flesh is heir to, and I'll certainly second that," said Burke.

Minogue wanted to protest; to say he was not being

snide about Opus Dei, to say that even policemen could understand context and motives. He saw it would be useless. Any explanation would have the cast of an excuse now. *Qui s'excuse, s'accuse.* What had probably gotten Burke's goat was the suggestion that there was some connection between Opus Dei and Paul Fine's body gently drifting in off the Irish Sea. But why did Burke appear to be resigned now, after starting out so tough?

"You know, I read the paper this morning and I saw something I didn't believe. No, it wasn't the fact that thousands of people, poor people the most of them, are without a way to travel by public transport and carry on their lives in a reasonable manner. No, it was something even more distressing. I had Father Sheehy phone up the *Irish Times* and confirm the sources and I'm afraid the figures seem to be true. There are over 150,000 Irish people, all young men and women, working illegally in the United States."

Daithi. Minogue watched the Archbishop's eyes get bigger. Daithi wanting to be away from this. At least he's resisting in the only way he knows will work. Fled the place.

*"One hundred and fifty thousand people!* Nearly fifty thousand people a year are leaving our shores. We're on the brink of a new millennium: there's no famine any more to excuse us. Except there is a different kind of a famine or a hunger abroad on the land. A blight of a different order, a decay."

Burke's flowing allusions seemed to tire him completely now. His chin sank onto his chest and he stared balefully at the desk-top.

"Do you see what I'm getting at?" he said suddenly to Minogue.

"I think I do. I worry about our two at home," Minogue conceded.

"Scattered," Burke said as though spitting the word out. "Our young people are being scattered all over the world. It's worse than the English ever did to us. It's as bad as when we were persecuted for our faith. The ones that stay are often cynical and they turn inside themselves, they hold on to their jobs and they try to forget about things. Being cynical is a way of containing fear, isn't it? Remember the rows we used to have in the lectures, John? I enjoyed them so much. I always remember you above the others, you were so full of fight."

Burke's features softened at the memory.

"Your Deputy Commissioner Tynan here had a very good understanding of the foundations of religious belief, Inspector. It takes a lot of nerve not to be a cynic. The youth that are leaving, even if they come back from America and the Continent, they've seen that things are not the same. Their faith is tested abroad and doubly so when they return. Few can come through the ordeals of unemployment and emigration unscathed."

Should Minogue tell him that he'd rather see Daithi restless, and even cynical, than have him stay and become a credulous sycophant in Opus Dei? *The authentic over the sincere any day, Burke: I'd pay the price.*

"I suppose policemen'd know more about the drugs and the alcoholism," said Burke. "Contrary to what the media might like to say, the Church does not turn a blind eye to child abuse or wife abuse either. They're symptoms of the same disorder, and what do we have now but further signs of crisis even in rural Ireland, when a married woman with a family of young children kills her husband rather than find another resolution? Making orphans of her children, instead of using the law of the land to get help? Of course there'll always be agitators who can go home to clean, warm homes far from County Tipperary and cheer for murder after breakfast."

That was enough to tip Minogue's gargoyle over the brink.

"Manslaughter, Your Grace."

"Pardon, Inspector?"

"Mrs Ryan is charged with manslaughter."

"She confessed to murdering her husband. Could there be clearer proof of murder?"

Tynan had not moved, Minogue realized.

"Not wishing to contradict you, but the charge against the woman is manslaughter. That means that the Director of Public Prosecutions has looked at the evidence provided by the Gardai and has preferred that charge against her."

"Saying that he knows better than the woman herself, is it?"

"Under duress," said Tynan softly. "She was not her normal self, Frank. She had been abused and she felt her children were in danger. The Constitution obliges the State to look to her interests too, that's the way that the legal opinions see it, I believe."

Burke put on a tight, knowing smile. "Ever the modernist, John," he said.

"I'm holding off on something here," Burke added, after a pause. "It seems to be late in the day to be trying to explain things, I see. You're a policeman, isn't that the way, John?"

Minogue recognized the irony as a light charge of bitterness in Burke's tone.

Tynan nodded. Burke turned to Minogue. "Inspector, I'll be running the risk of offending you now when I ask you to leave myself and my old friend here alone for a few moments."

It was not a question, nor was it an apology. Minogue stood and walked to the door. Behind him he heard a wooden drawer slide open. Closing the door, too confused to be angry at his dismissal, Minogue caught a glimpse of Burke's hand rising from the drawer of his desk. The hand was holding an envelope.

Sheehy was waiting in the hall, a grave Sheehy.

"By all means sit down in the Visitors' Room, er," he said in an apologetic tone.

Minogue began to feel resentful now. He did not sit down but started pacing the room, not caring that Sheehy was looking at him through the doorway.

Minutes passed. Minogue stopped and, not wishing to look at the portraits of Burke's predecessors, stared out of the window at the street-lights. His mind worked around the resentment, the burn in his chest. It struck him that he did not know why he had to be here if all he was to do was to attend a lecture made up of Burke's thoughts aloud and then be told to wait outside. But Burke had asked for him. Just to admonish him for riding rough on Heher and Drumm earlier in the day? Heher's modesty might have prevented him from explaining to Minogue how Opus Dei was tackling the ills of the world and didn't deserve his suspicions but it hadn't bothered the same Heher to phone the Archbishop's Residence and have Minogue receive some leaden advice. Calling in the elephants to trample mice like Minogue? Heher smiling, well spoken, healthy looking, self-effacing—"Call me Joe"—and then phoning Burke to get the system, the selfsame system he seemed to be bashfully abjuring as regards titles like "Father," up to heat.

Sheehy was tapping timidly on the open door to the Visitors' Room. Sheehy too, clean, pleasant manner, with a look of concern and feeling on his face—what made these damned priests look so well washed, so bloody confident? Didn't they have anything like sons and daughters to worry about?

"His Grace would like to say good-bye. I believe the meeting is over," said Sheehy.

Minogue followed him to Burke's office. Burke was standing behind the desk, and Tynan was putting something in the pocket of his jacket. He stood up too. His face had changed, Minogue saw: his cheeks were flushed and his eyes seemed to be more noticeable, bigger perhaps.

"Good night to you, Inspector. I wish you success in your work."

"Thanks," Minogue managed.

"After you leave here I think you may see things a little clearer, Inspector. I think Billy Fine's choice has a lot more to it than a chance meeting in a Museum. Just remember this, if you will: even Billy Fine would agree that it is the people of small grasp, the ones who have a poverty of imagination, who snap at the heels of things too great and profound for them to understand. These people . . . these self-proclaimed messiahs in the media, these cynics, ungenerous minds . . . these do far more damage than their abilities and understanding would ever warrant by themselves. Do you know what I'm saying yet, or are we too far ahead of you here?"

"I don't follow," said Minogue evenly.

Burke scrutinized him for a moment. "You don't follow. I think that somehow I knew that before we met, Inspector."

Burke turned to Tynan and thrust out his hand. "*Tentenda via*, John."

Tynan shook hands. Burke stared into Minogue's face when he shook hands with him. As the two policemen were leaving, Burke called out: "And my regards to Roberta, John."

Minogue thought that Tynan stiffened slightly.

"Thank you," he said.

"I want a drink," said Tynan.

Minogue tried to hide his surprise. He started the engine, set the choke in slightly, and thought what pubs he knew were in the area.

"But not before we stop at the nearest phone," said Tynan.

Tynan slouched in the passenger seat, not looking out of the side windows as Minogue drove, but apparently observing the movement of the needles in the green of the dashboard light. Minogue stopped at a pub, Slattery's. Tynan took the envelope out of his pocket and tapped it distractedly against his knee. Minogue checked his pocket for change.

"Not often you get a night like this," Tynan murmured. "Did you enjoy the lecture?"

"Matter of fact, I didn't," Minogue replied, feeling the sourness rise again in his chest. "I felt I was back in school being told to stand outside the door for being naughty."

Tynan opened the door, and the interior light shone on one side of his head. "I had a notion he'd have something to tell us about our materialist society and the moral chaos of our times. But it's no excuse, and he knew that," Tynan said absent-mindedly.

"You had the advantage of having him as a teacher, I understand," said Minogue grimly.

"I certainly did. Remember me yapping away on the way here, about *virtus* and *obedientia*? Frank Burke did me the great and inadvertent favour of telling me in time that I could expect a lot less philosophical treatment of the notions were I to take Holy Orders, as I was about to. We had good arguments, he and I. He's not a conservative but he has to answer to conservative men. Do you know what I mean?" Tynan asked.

Minogue caught the hint.

"Frank took it worse than I did when I told him I couldn't go through with it. Didn't talk to me for several years after I left the seminary. When he found out that Roberta and I were going to be married I thought he had mellowed a bit, but no. He asked if the usual thing would ensue, that the children would be brought up Catholic, being as Roberta was a heathen. I told him it wouldn't ensue. *Non serviam*, Frank. He said that no priest in his diocese would marry us, so. I told him I had a friend in Kilkenny who had agreed to marry us, but thank you very much anyway. Needn't have been the row as it turns out, but we weren't to know it then . . . one of those things which can't be changed. No children, you see. There were no hard feelings, I told him when I met him later. Maybe he put a curse on me for leaving the tribe, do you think?"

Tynan's tone was a gentler irony now.

"I don't know," said Minogue quietly. "What the Jesuits lost, we pagans have gained. It wasn't all for nothing, I'd say."

Tynan smiled briefly.

"And it seems to be a very curious logic indeed that I have this piece of paper in my fist from Francis Burke. As if we were a nemesis each, one for the other. He assumed it would be a weapon in my hand. After you left he handed me this envelope, what you see here. Then I knew what I was there for, not just you alone. You—I think he just wanted to see what class of a creature you might be, so that if things were to go against him he'd know about the man that'd be doing it."

"Doing what?" asked Minogue. "I have no quarrel with the man. I have me own religion to be going on with, and he has his."

"He got the idea fairly quickly, Minogue. After you canonized Marguerite Ryan."

"Me? All I'm saying is that it takes just a little bit of imagination to see into how terrible her life must have been. We're the race with the big hearts and the big imagination, are we? How is it that we're also so good at applying rules in the abstract? I have nothing to fear from Marguerite Ryan or a hundred Marguerite Ryans, so I don't, or even from a hundred hairy members of the Women's Action Movement. I don't for the life of me understand what the flap is about, unless all the men of Ireland, sitting on their bar stools, are getting premonitions about what a lot of them deserve."

"You should have said that to His Grace," said Tynan drily. "He handed me this envelope and asked me several things before I opened it. I thought it was a few names, colleagues of Brian Kelly; maybe even a good-sized list of Opus Dei members in the Army and the Gardai, something that'd save us a lot of headaches and delays with our own internal investigations. I wasn't hoping for too much."

"What did he ask you? Conditions?"

"No, they weren't conditions. He knew, or he had decided that there couldn't be. Frank is by no means a confused thinker when it comes to deciding what must be done in a crisis. I think he was appealing to a man he thought he knew, a man he'd known thirty years ago: that's why he didn't want you there. He asked me if I could treat the information with discretion, control it in respect of the possible consequences."

Minogue felt the light breeze coming in the open door of the car.

"I looked down the list and I told him I couldn't do it. I think he knew that already," added Tynan.

Minogue's scalp registered something which had yet to reach the parts of his brain that could make sense to him. Tynan stopped tapping the envelope on his knee and he held it at arm's length. The light cast shadows where the envelope had been opened by thumb and by finger. The jagged edges of the paper looked like the serrated edge of a bread knife to Minogue. Knife. List. Names.

"He asked me to think about the repercussions, think would this be justified."

"What repercussions?"

"He didn't outline them, just left them hanging like the better threats that are issued. He didn't need to, because it's quite plain to see. He had led us up to that point, I see now, to load me up so that I'd think twice, considering all the undeniably good work that they do . . . some of them, anyway."

Minogue felt an artery beginning to tick under his jaw.

"Frank thought he could hook me on a weakness. He thought, he hoped, that I could not go through with what we must go through, because it would destroy and impair the work of so many virtuous people. A small sacrifice for the greater good . . . I must say that I hadn't expected that of him. I realized then how much I had fallen by the wayside over the years, so that I couldn't imagine any institution being worth the life of one man. Of two men."

Minogue started in the seat. His thoughts rushed out: Brian Kelly, Paul Fine.

"He knew that too, of course," Tynan continued. "He didn't ask directly. Here he was by some twist of fate handing me something which would harm him and the institutions he represents. Me, the spoiled priest, the one who took up with a Protestant wife. Me, the one he couldn't mould. I didn't tell him that it was because the Fines are Jews. I didn't need to. I'm sure Frank's all too well aware of the significance, and I think that the symbolic side of that actually frightened him. Here"—he thrust the envelope at Minogue—"I can't be sitting around here talking as if I was writing a bloody diary. There's work to be done and quick."

Tynan stepped out and closed the door.

"One more thing, very important, Minogue. Listen to me, carefully. A young man who must remain nameless went to a priest whom he had known in college. This priest was home from a stay in Central America. After listening to the young man, this priest was able to persuade the man to make a confession to him. This young man is undergoing a crisis that has to do with his membership in Opus Dei. He read about the murder out in Bray, and, though he can't finger anyone directly, he was privy to peculiar conversations in an Opus Dei house near Clonskeagh. He flew the coop. Are you following me?"

Minogue nodded.

"Right. This pal of his from years back nearly had a fit, I was told. Radical man, the new generation of missionary. Didn't know what to do with what he had heard, so he wrote down the names he remembered and out he marched to the Archbishop's house, preceded by a few phone calls. Fair play to Burke, he sized up the problem and worked his way around the confessional vow."

"He gave me the distinct impression that he was going to chastise anyone connected with this," said Minogue. "Including servants of the State."

"He's not wild about Opus Dei, believe it or not. But he won't go another inch with us."

"Meaning we'll not know who this rebel Opus Dei fella is? Can't interview him?"

"Just so. What we get from him is a list of persons who may be engaging in a political conspiracy. What we do not get is this: one iota of testimony pertinent to your murder cases," Tynan concluded crisply.

"Run it backwards now," Minogue tried. "Do any of these people know they're on a sheet of paper in our fists?"

"I asked him what the chances were of those on the list knowing that we're on to them. He said that the confessor told the source that it would be a grievous sin for him to alert the people on this list to the Gardai being in possession of this piece of paper. That's as far as he can go. But the person may have told someone after the confession was made. He's unstable, upset. It might be rough."

Minogue frowned at Tynan's face framed in the side window. Someone was singing in or near the pub.

"I'll make my call first and get the thing going from the top. You'll be wanting to talk to Jimmy Kilmartin then, I think."

"Paul Fine?" Minogue called out, alarmed.

"You're the one who built this house of cards, Minogue. You should know. I'd stake my pension on it."

Minogue switched on the interior light and looked at the folded paper he had withdrawn from the envelope. There was no letterhead on the paper and it was addressed to no-one. The door of the lounge-bar banged after Tynan had entered. No remarks, no signature. The car creaked on its suspension. There were only the eleven typed names. Minogue did not recognize the first three but he noted that the ranks had been entered in brackets after them. Colonel Eamonn Gibney. Captain Lawrence Cunningham. The Garda rank was a sergeant: Eoin Morrissey. Garda Sergeant Eoin Morrissey worked in the Technical Bureau and Minogue had met him several times in the company of Shea Hoey at Ryan's pub in Parkgate Street.

Minogue realized that he was still holding his breath. His forehead was pounding now. He looked up from the paper to the windscreen's circus reflections of dashboard and steering wheel. He looked down at the paper again, at the last name. It was still there, still the same. *Fintan Gorman*.

Minogue elbowed himself out of the car and walked hurriedly to the door of Slattery's lounge.

# SEVENTEEN

"This is what we're dealing with," said Gallagher. He turned to the unwieldy tape-recorder on the desk.

It was Friday evening. Kilmartin, Minogue and Hoey were seated in Chief Superintendent Farrell's office. Farrell, who had come from a meeting with the Garda Commissioner and Tynan, seemed impatient, even more than his usual curt and belligerent self.

Kilmartin had said it out loud as the trio were crossing Harcourt Street to Farrell's office. Jimmy would make a lot of his prophecy after they had finished the meeting with Farrell, Minogue knew. After all, Kilmartin had been right . . . again.

"Bet you that God Almighty told him to let us in. And that Tynan told the Commissioner too," Kilmartin had said excitedly. "Bet you any money you like. Go a tenner, Matt? A tenner says that Tynan made him."

Yes, Kilmartin was probably right.

"And you know Farrell, runs the Branch like his own private army. I'd say he's bulling mad. He wanted to go after Heher and get the source who made the confession; squeeze the bejases out of him. What do you think?"

"I wouldn't put it past him," said Minogue.

"I still say it was Drumm who made the confession, and after Heher came down offa the ceiling he knew he'd have to tell the Archbishop about it. Ah, but Farrell'd choke the Pope himself to get at the source," said Kilmartin with relish. He licked a palm and rubbed it back along his crown to settle what was left of his hair.

"I like the sound of that," Minogue conceded.

"Choking the Pope or putting your tenner on the line?"

"The former," said Minogue. "I'd lose my tenner, I'm sure."

"Well, I must say that Tynan sticking up for us is something I don't mind at all, at all," said Kilmartin. "There may be something to him if he stood up to Farrell. Did you hear that Farrell went to the Minister, and all? He wanted the swoop last night even; he thinks this crowd is that dangerous. It was Tynan's doing to put in the phone taps and make Farrell wait for at least twenty-four hours."

"Maybe Farrell didn't believe that the confessional is secret, and thought these—what should we call them—conspirators might have been told of the leak," said Hoey. "But the confessional is still sworn to secrecy, isn't it? So the Branch couldn't have gone any further than ourselves."

"Secrecy, is it?" said Kilmartin in his music-hall

incarnation. "It had bloody well better be, for the love of Jases. I told a few whoppers in confession boxes in my time, and I don't want them broadcast, I can tell you," he added, stepping around the parked police cars.

Tynan's first call from Slattery's pub had been to the Commissioner. A second tenpenny piece had clanged into the phone when he called Farrell at his home in Clontarf. Minogue was in the pub by then and he dearly wanted to eavesdrop on what Tynan was demanding in crisp tones, sentences without verbs, a slow insistent, serious voice, as he stared at the graffiti on the wall in front of him. Minogue had fought off that temptation by giving in to another. He pushed his way to the bar and bought two Jameson's whiskeys with ice in both of them.

Tynan questioned neither the ice nor the whiskey. Minogue phoned Kilmartin at home after Tynan had told him what he had started. To his credit, Kilmartin had not questioned Farrell's involvement. As part of Garda department C3, the Special Branch was expected to see to subversive groups within the State. Nor did Kilmartin pass any remark about Tynan taking the reins. Putting down the telephone, Minogue had then realized that Kilmartin's deferring without complaint was the surest sign of what the list in the envelope could mean. Kilmartin seemed to have been glad to step aside and let the paint-and-powder brigade, as he sometimes called the Special Branch, work it out.

It was not until this morning that Minogue had found out that Tynan had had a District Court judge roused from his telly in Fairview and brought by police car to the Four Courts. No fewer than twenty-seven

phone taps had been operating within ninety minutes
of the two men sipping their Jameson's. By midday
today the number had grown to over fifty. Surveillance
teams had been placed on all the people on the list by
midnight, and had remained in place throughout the
night. They were relieved by shifts of Branch detectives. In the case of the Army ranks on the list, Army
Intelligence had been alerted and was reporting to the
First Secretary of the Minister for Defence.

Gallagher had met the three detectives at the front
desk and directed them to Farrell's office.

"Tommy," said Kilmartin, reaching across the
desk, "how's things?"

"Hot," grunted Farrell, a taciturn policeman with a
reputation for ruthlessness, but a man believed to
have no political debts to service.

"And Matty Minogue himself," said Farrell.

"And Seamus Hoey," Kilmartin added.

There were no preliminaries. Gallagher had the
tape of the telephone calls edited, rewound and
poised to play. He turned the switch and nothing happened.

"Plug?" said Minogue. Hoey checked the socket
behind his chair. Farrell pursed his lips.

"Jimmy," said Farrell. "I told God Almighty a half-
hour ago that leaving things this way was too much of
a risk. We should have jumped last night and worried
about hard evidence and building a case after we got
in the doors."

"Did you play him this tape too?" asked Kilmartin.

"Damn right I did. That's why we're moving
tonight. Yous may have a murder to worry about: we
have several to prevent. As well as lunatics flinging
petrol bombs at Jewish churches."

"Two murders," said Minogue. Farrell glared at him.

"It's nothing to what could happen unless we lift this lot tonight," said Farrell gruffly.

"Well we—that is to say Tynan—had hardly got a start on going through the files for possible associates not mentioned on the list, Tommy," Kilmartin said. "There has to be a lot more than two Army officers and one Garda sergeant."

"And didn't Johnny Tynan tell me the selfsame thing not an hour ago? 'A lot might slip the net if we move too soon,' says he. 'If we don't get the ones on the list to talk, we'll fall short of getting all of them,' says he. Oh, they'll talk, all right, I says to myself, but I couldn't say that to them, now, could I?"

Indeed, Minogue reflected. It was known that Farrell had had a hand in the selection and training of a squad of Special Branch officers whose sole job was to interrogate suspects.

"Well, they've been trying," said Kilmartin. "They've been up all night with the files and they've added possibles to the list."

Gallagher got up off his knees red faced and turned the switch again. This time it worked. After the hiss of the leader portion, a broad Kerry accent announced the time and the names of the persons speaking on the tape.

Gibney's voice was a measured and polite Dublin accent. There were no pauses when he talked. He seemed to have prepared everything he wanted to say to Gorman on the phone. The tone was reasonable, gently persuasive. Minogue watched Kilmartin's face go blank when Gibney mentioned the Ard Fheis.

". . . *We've drawn up a list of proposals for when the Dáil gets back in session. Wait a minute, I dropped something . . .*

*OK. Now you'll have just the one day because the Opposition will go right to work and table the no-confidence. Now there's no way around the business we discussed, you know? You know? We just have to have them so as we can accelerate the thing and—"*

*"—I still say the momentum will carry us through."* Gorman's tone was almost urgent, a palpable effort to stay calm.

Minogue felt a non-existent draught on the back of his neck.

*"But we've talked about this* ad nauseam, *Fintan. Even your own estimates are for four to break ranks and then you—"*

*"Yes, that's what I'm saying. That's more than enough to carry the vote when the Dáil sits. Don't you see what I mean? There's no need for anything more."*

Farrell held his hand up. Gallagher stopped the tape.

"This is toward the end of the call," said Farrell. "The call went through to Gorman's home phone at eight o'clock this morning, just before Gorman was heading off to work. Do you know what these two men are talking about?"

"Gorman's going to jump ship on the Chief," said Kilmartin slowly. "He's going to lead away his supporters at the Ard Fheis next week . . ."

". . . and he's going to bring down the fucking government," said Farrell calmly.

"Four sitting members of the party?" said Hoey. "Who are they?"

"Wouldn't we all like to know that," said Gallagher in his Donegal tones.

"But Gorman," said Kilmartin. "What's he going to get out of this? He's not going to be the next Taoiseach, that's for certain."

"Will we take bets on that?" said Farrell.

"He doesn't need to be," murmured Minogue.

"Smart lad, Matty," said Farrell savagely. "Give the man the rabbit. Gorman needs only four government members to walk out of the party for the government to fall. The next government'll have to be a coalition, and they'll need Gorman. He'll be sitting pretty when they offer him a plum Ministry. Guess which one he'll pick?"

"Defence again," said Kilmartin.

"Top of the class, Jimmy. Gibney and the others will have Gorman in their pockets, then. If they don't have him in their pockets already, they will after they do their bit of 'business' that Gibney's hinting about. Any guesses on what Gibney means there?"

"I don't know why I'm thinking this exactly," Hoey began. "Wouldn't it be to Gibney's advantage to have a bit of disorder in the streets. A general strike, say?"

"How about a bomb in Dublin to get the Army out onto the streets?" said Farrell. "How about shooting someone?"

Farrell looked from face to face in the room. Gallagher rubbed his nose with the side of his hand.

"Name of Jases," said Kilmartin finally.

Farrell leaned lower on his elbows. "What's on here, as I told the Commissioner, is that we have several citizens plotting to destabilize the government of the Irish Republic, and they're willing to use violence to that end."

" 'They,' though," said Minogue. "The 'they' that's trying to do this is an Opus Dei faction. It's not necessarily an Army coup or the likes of that."

"Right," said Kilmartin, recovering with one of his

favourite sayings at hand. "This isn't a banana republic, you know, Tommy. We're a democratic country with troubles, that's all."

"All right," said Farrell quickly. "I've been on the phone to Army Intelligence half the day. I know that O'Tuaime had started a search of Army personnel files for yous, but it was pretty half-hearted. As of half-ten this morning he was relieved of that piddling assignment, and Army Intelligence has launched a real search now that they have two names to start with. Cunningham seems square enough, a follower. This Gibney's a very popular officer all up and down the ranks."

"Like Gorman . . . all things to all men," muttered Kilmartin. Minogue thought of the friendly, open faces of Heher and Drumm.

"They think he might twig to the surveillance. Lookit, if they're jittery, I'm hopping about like a bloody Mexican jumping-bean. The security of the State and its citizens can't be waiting around for any of us to be playing with bits of files and phone lines to gather bullet-proof evidence."

Which is probably exactly what he told the Minister and the Commissioner earlier, thought Minogue.

"So if yous think that your Squad has first dibs on this, you'd be wrong," said Farrell bluntly. He nodded to Gallagher, who restarted the tape.

Farrell looked at his watch after five minutes.

"There you are now. We'd be waiting for ten years before we'd get any mention of the word 'murder' out of them."

"No mention of Paul Fine or Kelly yet. We need to point a finger at a killer, or killers," said Minogue.

"Killers, did I hear you say?" Farrell frowned.

"Murder in the first degree can be charged to more than the actual killer," said Minogue. "If there was a concerted, coherent plan, assistance rendered, weapons secured for—"

"All right, all right," Farrell interrupted. Minogue gave Farrell a level stare across the table.

"Listen," he murmured in the stillness which followed, "we're investigating two murders." He paused and returned Farrell's gaze of impatient scrutiny. "That's where all this stuff flows from, plain and simple. These two victims—and I had better spell it out, that we suspect these two murders are connected—are, or were, individuals. I'm sure we're all entitled to be alarmed by this group, this conspiracy, but I'm in there, and my colleagues are in there, to nail a killer or killers."

Minogue glanced to Kilmartin, who was searching the ceiling, and then to Hoey who nodded once, but kept his eyes on his shoes.

"I hear you, Matty," said Farrell in a tone soft enough for Kilmartin to look at him in some surprise. "Who do you see as the killers here? I mean the ones that actually did the dirty work?"

Minogue exchanged looks with Hoey.

"Out of this list"—he took a deep breath—"my hunch is Gibney." Hoey nodded briefly, and Kilmartin kept his eyes on Minogue. "I see it like this: Brian Kelly hears or overhears chat about this scheme to push Gorman to the top and install a government that leans hard to the Right. You heard the tape yourselves: it'd be nothing for people to make a pretext for getting troops out on the streets these days. You even hear upright citizens who should know better"—Minogue paused briefly to savour Kilmartin's discomfort— "pushing for easy answers. 'Crack the whip' kind of attitudes. We're always looking for the leader, the man on horseback, the hero, in this country. Anyway. Brian Kelly finds out about these plans. He may even have tried to talk people out of it, appealed to them. This kind of talk could have been floating around for years and then it got serious suddenly, so Kelly gets alarmed. He's caught, because he has a loyalty to his pals in Opus Dei too, but it seems that the organization shuns him. So he's torn about the whole thing, he needs to talk to someone. Maybe he tries again with this group, maybe even talks to Gorman. We may never know if he threatens to reveal what he knows, but I can see him doing that, if he's upset. Think about it. Here's a man who has invested so much in this organization. He's sincere, he's responsible, he's devout—"

"He's dead," Kilmartin muttered.

"I wonder what way his mind works. Does he seek out a person from the media? Does he want someone like Paul Fine to do a surface story on Opus Dei, as a way of letting this outfit know that they're now in the public light so they'd better rethink their plans? Does he tell all he knows to Paul Fine? It doesn't seem like that to us, judging by what Fine had dug up. But did Gorman, or whoever, think their whole enterprise was threatened? Did Brian Kelly purposely seek out a journalist who was also a Jew, by way of a symbolic act?"

"Fine and well to be speculating," said Farrell. "But the way you brought it up, you want specifics. Can you link these murders at all, as yet?"

Hoey sat up and intervened.

"The killer may have wanted to make Paul Fine simply disappear," he said quickly. "That would be a stiff warning to Brian Kelly. I doubt that the killer ever planned to kill the two people. It was more a case of 'let's get the more immediately dangerous character out of the way' . . . the journalist, that is . . . and then maybe try to persuade or bully Brian Kelly into keeping his trap shut. Then, when Kelly didn't buckle under, or when it looked like he'd do anything because he was in a panic after hearing about Fine being murdered . . ."

"Killed him," said Farrell and looked around at the faces of the policemen. "All right, I see how your mind is working on it. But lookit, now"—Farrell narrowed his glance when it came to rest on Minogue—"you've had your say. You've stated your priorities. I'm just telling you that it is my duty to bag all these characters as soon as possible. You'll get your man, but you may have to do your digging and burrowing after I have these people in custody. I'm not saying this'll make your job any easier, but that's the story, and that's how it'll have to be."

Before Minogue could say anything, Kilmartin deflected him.

"Do you think Gorman knows about Fine and Kelly?" Kilmartin asked Farrell.

The head of the Special Branch held his palms up.

"I'm no psychologist, Jimmy. He may suspect it, he may know it, he may have been told but turned a deaf ear, he may pretend to himself that he doesn't know it. Christ, there could be any number of things going on. If you ask me, I think Gorman is being led by the nose. By his own bloody ambition. He ran out of patience waiting for the Chief to step down, and now he wants the cake all to himself."

"Well, it appears that the people we've been listening to are not aware of us," said Gallagher quietly.

"Not yet, anyhow." The soft, earnest Donegal accent seemed to soothe the tension.

"And whoever spilled the beans in confession has not alerted this group," added Minogue. That's what Tynan would have argued, he knew.

"That could change at any minute," said Farrell. "If we only knew the source, we could sit on him and make sure he kept quiet until we had all these lunatics in."

Gallagher's finger tapped lightly on the tape spool as he waited for Farrell's instruction.

"So, this evening," said Kilmartin at last.

"Yep," said Farrell decisively. "We just can't wait any longer. Now the, er, Commissioner suggested that we include some representation from your Squad, er, Jimmy—being as you have some business in this line of work."

There was Kilmartin's ten pounds safe, Minogue knew. It was plain that Farrell didn't like offering.

"Not exactly a joint task force, or anything now. No need to be formal after all, is there? We all know one another here," said Farrell.

"Right, Tommy. Good point, that," said Kilmartin with a grave expression on his face.

"Just that, er, you've had valuable input and naturally you'd want to interview persons we pick up tonight. We have the manpower and everything, you understand," Farrell continued in a restrained manner. "And if yous were to talk to a suspect directly upon arrest, you could have him at his most talkative."

"Absolutely," said Kilmartin. "That's decent of you, Tommy."

Minogue was seeing a Kilmartin he knew only too well at work on Farrell. There was no love lost between the two senior policemen. Kilmartin's nose told him that Farrell was under orders to consult the Murder Squad, probably to the extent of having Squad officers present at arrests. A suspect surprised is often glad to talk. Now, Minogue bet an imaginary ten-pound note with his gargoyle, Kilmartin's frown of concern and concentration was the practised foil for what he would come out with the minute they were away from Farrell: *The bollicks, Farrell letting on he was doing us a favour, after Tynan laying down the law with him and telling him to co-operate with us. Oh, we showed him, didn't we?*

"Would there be one suspect, say, that yous'd like to question in particular?" Farrell asked in a strained voice which could not carry the casual flavour he wanted.

Kilmartin put on a face of intense deliberation. Even Hoey knew that Kilmartin was dragging the time across Farrell's patience like nails across a blackboard. Minogue spoiled the fun.

"Gibney. I'd like to have him the minute you lift him."

"Good, so," said Farrell, relieved.

"And I want to be in on the arrest too," said Minogue.

"All right, so, Matty. Do yous want to listen to any more of this? Ah, you probably don't," Farrell said busily. "Top secret, this tape. Gorman'll ride to hell on this little thing yet. Yous heard the best of it, the worst of it. There's work to be done, though."

Gallagher was already rewinding the reel.

# EIGHTEEN

The stars twinkled and the moon rose. A faint breeze that had come in across Dublin Bay exercised itself in blotches of light which wavered on the footpath. Branches stirred slowly beneath the streetlamps. There was nothing left of the earlier russet in the western sky. Minogue thought about the planet turning, shadows creeping over land and water.

He could smell Kilmartin's stale breath. Kilmartin was smoking constantly. Minogue was very nervous. Kilmartin had listened in disbelief when Gallagher had phoned earlier to say Gibney had left his flat on Morehampton Road and driven to Gorman's house in Sandymount. Oblivious of the two teams assigned to watch him, Gibney had gone into Gorman's house almost an hour earlier.

"That's Gorman's home, so it is," Kilmartin said. "What about his missus and kids in there? Why didn't they take Gibney when he left his place?"

Minogue didn't understand it either. Gallagher's explanation was that neither pair of Special Branch detectives knew what to do. They had been awaiting the arrest team proper. The swoop had been set for nine minutes after nine, but at a quarter to nine Gibney had simply walked to his car and driven to Gorman's home in Sandymount.

"It must have been a regular appointment with them, and that's why they didn't mention it on the phone. That's the only charitable excuse I can think of for those fellas to banjax this up," said Kilmartin. "Walked out the front door and they didn't know what to do. Farrell'll eat those boyos . . . if I don't first."

It was now three minutes short of ten o'clock. Kilmartin held the cigarette in his cupped hand by the arm-rest and blew the smoke out of the window in measured puffs. Hoey had the volume on the car radio almost completely down. He was whistling softly, a sign of his nerves too, Minogue remembered, tongue against his upper teeth. Occasionally Hoey rubbed a hand over his chin. Minogue could hear the stubble rasp.

"So Burke wonders if the people in this clique are quite capable of murdering someone," said Kilmartin.

"They may have done it twice already," answered Hoey. "They could do the same and worse, I suppose."

"No wonder Farrell is hopping about the place," Kilmartin added with some satisfaction.

The three policemen fell silent again. Their car was parked nearly eight doors down from Gorman's house. It was a quiet street in the better end of Sandymount, within a quarter mile of Sandymount strand. On bright days, the ebb tide left the strand as a mirror for the sky. Horses galloped and trotted down the sands at low tide every day of the year. Despite the general belief that Dublin Bay was too polluted to be safe, some hardy souls still swam there. The southbound trains of the Dublin Area Rapid Transit system, the DART, shot out from between the hedges of the inner suburbs onto the water's edge at Merrion Gates, almost gratefully leaping out to the open sea and sky all the way to Dun Laoghaire and beyond. James Joyce had walked Sandymount strand and been visited by beauty there . . . Had Gorman walked the same watery emptiness, alone or with these cronies of his, concocting a salvation for Ireland?

Claustrophobia added to Minogue's tension. All but one of the Special Branch cars had been parked in the next street over. One car was parked by Gorman's gate. It would not arouse suspicion, since two armed policemen customarily formed a guard outside the homes of Government Ministers. The two on shift tonight were to help net Gibney as he left the house. Three detectives sat in a Toyota van directly across the street from Gorman's. The van advertised chimney sweeping services and the bodywork was battered and grimy. Minogue had been told that those in the van were monitoring a relayed tap off Gorman's home telephone: Farrell was worried that news of the swoop might reach Gorman by phone from a member of the clique who had evaded detection so far.

Minogue stretched his arms out straight and yawned.

"Didn't I tell you that Tynan is the cute one?" said Kilmartin, breaking off from an interior conversation to let the two detectives know how astute he had been.

Minogue remembered Tynan's expression as he

had knocked back the glass of whiskey last night: regret, and some contentment too, Tynan staring down into the cubes rattling in his empty glass. It had been like a farewell toast to the memory of someone whose funeral he and Minogue had attended.

"You did," said Minogue.

"Ah, but what a waste when all is said and done." Kilmartin dropped into a tone of melancholy. "All that talent. All well educated, and with the best of intentions."

Minogue's anger burst loose. He struggled to get out of the car. "Jesus Christ, Jimmy. I don't want to hear any more about the best of intentions. The damned island is full to the brim with the best of intentions. Loads of genius and no talent. Full of imagination and too damn scarce on ideas that might be in danger of working. The priest who married the Ryans below in Tipperary had the best of intentions, as did the Ryans themselves. Heher has the best of intentions, but he makes my skin crawl. Archbishop bloody Burke has the best of intentions."

"Calm yourself, would you," said Kilmartin.

"What matters is what and who's left after the best of intentions have done their work. Gorman had the best of—"

"That'll do it, Matt," said Kilmartin. The tone was now one of rank, Minogue realized. Kilmartin was sitting still, blinking. What could be excused in private could not be let go in front of Hoey.

Minogue kicked the door open and stepped onto the footpath. The relief was immediate. Kilmartin got out of his side and walked reluctantly around to Minogue. Like fencewire that grows into the bark of a tree, Minogue was thinking: Jimmy Kilmartin and

Matt Minogue. Tied together by a quarter-century of knowing one another as cops.

"Ah, I know how you feel, Matt. You're very involved. When you're in this line of business as long as me, you'll be able to be more objective, you know."

Kilmartin cut short his advice when he saw the unmarked car coming down the street ahead of them. There were three men in it. Minogue saw the short antenna quivering as the car drifted slowly by. A face turned to them from the back seat, Gallagher's. He pointed ahead of the car, beckoning them.

"Come on so, and we'll have a pow-wow," said a cheered Kilmartin. "The brass is here. That was Farrell in the car too, wasn't it?"

Minogue and Kilmartin walked the 200 yards to where the car had stopped. They passed a man standing by a bus stop. He was wearing a three-quarter-length coat, sometimes called a car-coat or a bum-freezer. Minogue recognized it immediately as the trademark of a detective who was carrying a firearm. Kilmartin nodded at the detective in passing, and whispered: "Soon enough."

Minogue wondered if Gorman or his wife or one of their children might look out into the garden and spot one of the half-dozen detectives in position around the house. A shadow by the neighbour's garage, a slight movement by the hedge . . . *Daddy, there's someone in the back garden, I saw a* . . . Minogue forced the groaning door of his imagination shut. Can't think like that now, waiting and worrying. Everyone's doing the best he can . . .

Minogue joined Kilmartin on his hunkers by the back window on Farrell's side of the car. Gallagher was handling the radio traffic from the back seat, the coiled lead from the dashboard stretched almost taut, a handset in his other hand.

"That's the last one brought in just now," growled Farrell. "Except for this Gibney."

"You have the other Army fella, Cunningham?" asked Kilmartin.

"Meek as a lamb, but he's saying nothing."

"Turn up a gun or anything in his place?" Kilmartin persisted.

"No," Gallagher answered. "We found street maps and some kind of an itinerary marked out, though, with times written in on the maps. It looks like a tail on someone who travelled by car over that route. Could have been a planned hit."

"Not a minute too soon," said Farrell sharply. "Tell Johnny Tynan that the next time you see him, Matty."

Minogue said nothing.

"How many in the bag now, so?" said Kilmartin.

"Ten of the eleven on your list . . . twenty-three all told," said Gallagher. "Sorry, it's twenty-four."

"Jases," whispered Kilmartin. "Are there any more Army and Gardai?"

"No," Farrell interrupted. "The ones we fingered, we got them off the phone feeds. Some of them might be duds, though. This last bugger, we had to wait for him since nine. He was visiting his wife in the hospital. She had a baby at seven o'clock this evening. Did you ever hear the like of that for timing? Can you see us going into the maternity ward and clipping his hands in front of his missus?"

Kilmartin snorted. "Great work, Tommy," he said.

"I'll be a lot happier when Gibney's out of that house," replied Farrell harshly. "I don't like this one little bit. You'd think he had a sixth sense the way he left a few minutes before the arrest team showed up at his place."

"Gorman's missus and the three children are in there, all right," said Kilmartin.

Gallagher checked with the radio van. There had been no calls to Gorman's house.

"Looks like it's sealed nicely all the same," said Kilmartin.

"Buy me a pint and a small one on the head of it," grunted Farrell. "What the hell is Gibney doing in there?"

"He may have a lot of persuading to do with Gorman, by the sound of that earlier call we heard off the tape," Minogue observed. "The nearer we get to the Ard Fheis, the more Gorman'll need to be persuaded."

"I suppose so," said Farrell. "We couldn't get into the bloody house all day. The missus was home with one of the kids, so we couldn't get any device inside the house at all. Take too long to rig up an infra-red mike on the windows with all the houses here so higgeldy-piggeldy. Christ, I'd give my right ball to hear what they're saying to one another in there right now."

Kilmartin glanced quickly at Minogue. Both men remembered a recent Special Branch blunder which had involved the use of directional microphones in one of their stake-outs. A Branch specialist had been perched on a wall, headphones on and pointing a dish toward an anchored yacht in Howth harbour one night over the summer. The Gardai had been called by a citizen who was suspicious of such a person pointing what looked like a Martian weapon at the boat. Rather than alert people on the yacht to the surveillance, the Branch man had allowed himself to be arrested. Farrell would not want his officers lampooned in cartoons as they had been after that affair, if neighbours of the Gormans found men perching on their window-sills or in their apple trees pointing things at the Gormans' house.

The car radio came alive with a click and a hiss: *"Phone's ringing in the house, over—"*

"Do it, so," hissed Farrell.

Gallagher squeezed the transmit button on his handset.

"Alert to all units. This is Control. Repeat: alert to all units. Phone is ringing in the house. Repeat: phone is now ringing—"

Gallagher's hand was shaking as he released the button. The radio van began transmitting a patch from the relayed phone-tap. Minogue felt his leg cramping but he ignored it. The familiar double ring of the telephone came eerily from the radio. Farrell had his hand on the door release, body poised to elbow the door open. Minogue moved back on the footpath. The man who had been at the bus stop was now running softly towards Gorman's house. There would be the others poised by the door, by the windows, moving across the grass . . .

The phone was picked up in the middle of a ring.

*"Hello?"*

A woman's voice. Farrell raised his hand as though about to start a race.

Another hello. Minogue stood up and looked down the street.

*"Hello, Finnoula? This is Madeline. Howaryou?"*

*"Madeline! Is it yourself that's in it? How are you doing yourself?"* Mrs Gorman replied. *"Are you up here in Dublin?"*

"I am. I was up today and I met Emer. She said you were confined to barracks."

"Sean is sick, but the other two are grand. It's only a bit of the diarrhoea."

"I hope I'm not calling at a bad . . ."

"Not at all, I'm only delighted to hear you," said Finnoula Gorman. A lovely warm voice, Minogue thought. Welcoming, confident. Does this woman know what her husband is up to?

"Sure they're all packed off to bed. I'm watching a cod of a thing on the telly, an oldie with Cary Grant in it."

The other woman laughed.

"Well, I'll be up in town here until tomorrow, Finnoula. That'll be long enough to spread the word."

Farrell's eyes widened and he sat forward in the seat.

"I'm expecting, so I am."

"Ah, that's just fantastic! Well, tell me the whole story now . . ."

The transmission cut off. Farrell swore and let his hand drop on to his knee. Gallagher squeezed the set.

"Fall back all units. Repeat: fall back. Await further instructions."

"At least she'll keep anyone else from phoning in," said Farrell.

By ten-fifteen Kilmartin could wait no longer.

"I hope there's no-one looking out their windows here tonight. 'Cause if they are, they'll be seeing an important Garda officer by the name of Kilmartin making his pooley up ag'in the wall here. I'm only bursting, I tell you," said Kilmartin.

Kilmartin walked to a shadowed part of the foot-path which was overhung with shrubs tumbling down from a high wall. Minogue strolled back up the foot-path. He was reluctant to get back into the car with Hoey because he knew Kilmartin would follow him. How was it that some people talked even more when they were nervous, while others simply shut up?

Dried leaves had gathered against parts of the walls along the road. Gorman lived in a street of well-to-do people, Minogue saw. A Volvo and a Saab were parked within a few cars of one another. The breeze had died down but Minogue could still sense the sea. If he had the chance he'd take a sick day and walk Sandymount strand before the bitter east wind came in with the Dublin winter. Bring Kathleen. Go for Chinese food on the credit card afterwards. Finish off with a quiet one in Gerry Byrne's over in Galloping Green, he'd have the fire lit in the lounge for sure . . . Anisette. Pernod would do, all right, even if it was a tourist's drink here.

Behind him, Minogue heard the splash and trickle of Kilmartin's urine. A soft sigh from Kilmartin. The States, Daithi . . . what did people his age in the States drink? Cans of beer? Cocktails? Kathleen still considered Parisians snotty. Still. No way in the world would he go for a holiday in the States.

A car drove quickly down the street, heading for Sandymount village. The sharp tattoo of a current pop hit washed over Minogue as the car passed. Kilmartin caught up to him. Minogue had almost forgotten the detective in the shadows by the bus stop. This time he saw the earphone wire snaking up from the coat to the detective's ear. His trained, indifferent eyes followed Minogue and Kilmartin to their car.

Half-ten. Minogue caved in, and got into the car. Hoey had been dozing. Minogue let the seat back and closed his eyes. September, yes. He had woken up early last week and seen that it was still dark at six o'clock. Ireland is on the same latitude as Hudson Bay . . . How many days to Christmas now? New Jersey, that was just a suburb of New York—or was it a State in itself?

Gallagher's voice came softly over the radio. "*Phone call's over.*"

Kilmartin grunted from the back seat. "Jases, how could they find the time to go and get themselves in the family way, these women, and they on the phone half the night?" he grumbled before subsiding into smoky silence again.

Minogue tried to remember the photo of Gibney. A strong, angular face, good looks. An air of assurance, but not the arrogance he had expected. Was this man a killer? Minogue looked all over the face but saw nothing to help him answer the question. Young for his rank, but he'd done it all: seven months in Lebanon with the UN, tours of Border duty here on and off for the last five years. Farrell had raised an eyebrow at the mention of Gibney's father, a retired colonel who counted Major-General O'Tuaime as one of his friends.

Minogue turned his head on the head-rest and opened his eyes. He could see down the footpath to the gates of Gorman's house.

"Maybe they're saying the Rosary," Hoey murmured.

"Hardly knocking back the drink," agreed Kilmartin in a mordant tone. "Where do you want him, Matt? Up in the Bridewell along with the others?"

Minogue wondered what Gibney would be like when they arrested him. A talker? Would he want to explain things, to defend their cause? Or would he be the loyal soldier? "I don't mind," he replied wearily. "We don't have to book a suite in advance, do we?"

*"Front door's opening."*

The voice belonged to one of the detectives in the van. Minogue ratcheted the seat upright. Hoey turned the radio up higher.

*"All units in for the catch now . . . Over. Everybody in. Gibney's in the doorway . . . Gorman too. Make sure that back door's open . . ."*

The detective from the bus stop walked briskly by their car.

The voice on the radio was strained now. *"Gorman's going to the gate with him. They're taking their time. Very slowly now . . ."*

"No sweat, Danno," murmured Kilmartin as he leaned his chin on the back of Minogue's seat. Minogue remembered that Kilmartin had written an anonymous letter to Radio Telifis Eireann complaining about their decision to drop *Hawaii Five-O* re-runs several years previously.

"If Gibney's carrying a gun, it'll be in the car." Kilmartin kept up the commentary in a murmured monotone. "Farrell should have got one of his wizards to pump the lock on his car out there and get inside it for the gun . . . They wouldn't need to be pissing their pants now, I'm telling you . . ."

"Still talking."

Minogue didn't bother to argue with Kilmartin. Farrell hadn't wanted to give any alert to people in the street, but had put his faith in his own arrest-team.

Kilmartin continued his monologue, directing events: "Aisy-daisy and gently Bentley. Gorman'll expect two coppers on guard anyway . . . Let the one walking down the path put it on Gibney, and the two in the car can back him up and get Gorman out of the action . . ."

Minogue imagined the other detectives converging on the two men at the front gate; coming around the side of the house, behind the hedge . . .

"Come on now, boys and girls," murmured Kilmartin in a nursery-school sing-song. "Step up to the citizen and make the arrest. Just like in training—"

"Shaking hands. Gibney's opening the gate."

"How far is Gibney's car down the street, again?" Minogue asked.

"Four or five cars down, sir," said Hoey. "He has to pass the two doing guard duty in the car."

The detective who had walked from the bus stop slowed his pace. Wants Gibney through the gate so Gorman's on the other side of it, Minogue thought. Good training: Gorman could be taken by the detectives who were coming from the side garden. Minogue pressed his head against the glass to see further down the street.

"Get your big head outa me light, would you?" said Kilmartin.

The detective had slowed almost to a halt. If he stops to tie his shoelace that'll be a television cop, Minogue thought wryly. Ahead of the detective Minogue saw a figure step out on to the path. Gibney.

Gibney stood facing the house as he drew the gate closed. The detective picked up his pace again. Further down the road Minogue saw a car door opening. He could not see the driver's side of the car. He heard a clink as the handle of the gate slipped home. Gibney paused before turning toward his car. It's as if he's trying to remember something, Minogue thought neutrally.

"*He's not moving . . . Wait. Gorman's saying something to our two men . . .*"

"Jesus," Kilmartin exclaimed by Minogue's ear, "Gorman's saying good-night to them, or some bloody nonsense. He's going to notice the two are not regulars on this shift! Close in and nab Gibney, can't ye, before he makes them too, for fuck's sakes!"

Minogue watched Gibney's head turn back toward the detective on the footpath. The detective had his pistol out, and he was holding it slightly behind his backside as he advanced on Gibney. There couldn't be more than ten or twelve feet between them now, Minogue guessed. Gorman's upper body appeared in view then, leaning over the waist-high gate as he addressed the two detectives who were getting out of the car. Somewhere behind the detached, observing Minogue's thoughts an alarm was going off. Gorman was in the way: there were two concrete pillars to which the gates were anchored. . . .

The detective had seen it too. He faltered. Gorman leaned further over the gate to see around the pillar. Someone began shouting. Too early yet, Minogue's mind roared. Have to get around Gorman. Where are the rest of them? Gibney had his hand under his jacket even before Minogue's mind could scream: *Gibney knows, he knows now!*

"Jesus!" Kilmartin cried. "They've no angle, with Gorman like that!"

The detective crouched and brought the pistol around in one smooth motion. Minogue did not see the flash. The shot popped like a stone dropped straight into deep water. Gibney had a gun out and was backing on to the gate. Someone was shouting Gorman's name.

*"We have the house, we have the house!"* the voice on the radio shouted.

Minogue saw a flash from Gibney's gun. He shouted for Kilmartin and Hoey to get on the floor and banged his ear as he threw himself across the seat into Hoey's lap. Hoey had the door open already: he reached out onto the roadway and rolled from the car. Kilmartin was tugging at the back door release and swearing. Minogue kicked off against his own door and landed beside Hoey on the roadway. More shots sounded, louder now. Somebody screamed inside the house just as Kilmartin came out of the back door, on his hands and knees. Minogue heard footsteps racing down the footpath opposite.

"He's down!" somebody was shouting. "I'm on him! I'm on him! He's down!" There was an edge of panic to the voice. Kilmartin had crawled around the back of the car. Minogue followed him. They both looked down the road. From nearly fifty feet Minogue could see how tightly a detective was holding his pistol, both arms extended fully. He was back on one foot as though ready to push a stalled car, and his gun was trained on a figure lying against the gate. The figure was not moving. There was another figure closer to Minogue and Kilmartin, that of the detective, leaning against the wheel of a car. Minogue saw him squirm slightly and relax.

Hoey was up first, with Minogue and Kilmartin after him. Gallagher came running down the footpath, the antenna of the handset whipping the air as he ran; he knelt by the seated detective and began fingering the man's clothing. To his relief, Minogue heard the detective whispering to Gallagher. Gallagher's hands moved down to the man's leg. The detective nodded and leaned his head back against the car-wheel.

An elderly man with a newspaper dangling from his hand had opened a hall-door opposite and he was squinting out into near-darkness. Minogue heard another door scraping open as he went by Gallagher. Gibney was lying on his side by the gate. Minogue heard a voice from the front garden asking what had happened, who . . . ? The detective who was training his gun on Gibney was staring intently at Gibney's hands. He kept talking, but quieter now.

"Gill all right there? We need an ambulance, don't we? I don't know if this fella's gone. Where's the ambulance?"

"It's all right now," said Minogue firmly.

"Gill saw him coming up with the gun and he got one off, I saw it happening but I wasn't quick enough—"

"It's all right now," Minogue repeated. "It's over now."

"I had to do it. Gill went down, I saw him shoot Gill!"

Kilmartin was fumbling for a pencil. Minogue looked down at the gun on the footpath near Gibney's outstretched hand. There was a black stain near the gun and it was moving, getting bigger.

"Where's Gorman?" Kilmartin barked. Minogue crouched down by Gibney, well outside the detective's line of fire. Gibney's chest was moving slightly.

"Is Gorman okay?" Kilmartin was saying. He knelt down by Minogue and poked a pencil through the trigger-guard of the automatic pistol. "That's a parabellum, that is. A Beretta, I'll wager," he said.

The stain moving out from Gibney began to creep in a faltering line toward the roadway.

"Is he gone? He looks gone," said the detective overhead.

Minogue heard sirens in the distance. A car burst into the street with its tyres howling. He crouched closer to Gibney and felt for a pulse under the jaw. The stain had emerged on the far side and new lines were branching out across the footpath. Farrell was hunkered down beside Kilmartin now. Kilmartin drew the gun carefully along the tarmac with the pencil.

"That his?" said Farrell quietly.

"Yes, sir," answered the detective from above. "He drew on Gill and shot him, sir. I had to fire then or else . . ."

"It's all right, son. Put that away now," said Farrell gently. "You did what you had to do."

"Where's Gorman, Tommy?" asked Kilmartin.

"We're all right. He's in the garden, they pulled him down when the shooting started."

"He's breathing," said Minogue and leaned his head closer to hear a faint, bubbling whistle that came at short intervals. He tried harder to distinguish the sound but there was shouting nearby. "We have to stop this bleeding," he said then. "Better get him over so we can see it."

As he reached a hand under Gibney, Minogue saw Gibney's eyes open.

"Jesus," whispered Kilmartin.

It was then that Minogue heard the bubbling sound again and he froze: Gibney was in bad trouble, it was a sucking wound from a punctured lung he had been hearing. "I have to turn you over," Minogue said, fighting to keep his voice neutral. "You're bleeding so I have to do something. The ambulance'll be here any second. Can you hear me?"

Gibney blinked once. His eyes strayed from face to

face. His lips moved slackly. He stared at Minogue again.

"I can't hear you," said Minogue. "Don't talk now."

Gibney's face strained with the effort of protest. A whisper escaped him.

"A priest?" said Hoey.

Gibney blinked again. Minogue watched the lips try to shape a P.

"He wants a priest, all right," said Kilmartin. He leaned further in over Gibney.

"I'll say an Act of Contrition with you now while we wait for the priest," said Hoey gently. "If you can't say it, it's OK, just follow along with me in your own mind."

He didn't remember all of the prayer, but Kilmartin carried him over the bits he had forgotten, those parts of the prayer which every Catholic was taught should be recited for the dying. Gibney's lips began to move again half-way through.

Hoey finished the prayer as the approaching sirens became louder. The policemen blessed themselves. Gibney's neck muscles stood out with the effort of trying to raise his head.

"Is it something you'd want to tell us?" whispered Kilmartin.

"Brian," whispered Gibney and his head fell back.

"Brian Kelly, is it?" said Minogue.

Gibney blinked and grimaced. He tried to raise his head again.

"Only me. That's all . . ." he wheezed. Hoey reached his hand under Gibney's head. "Just me. Fine too . . . Only me. Had to . . ." whispered Gibney. His stare was fixed frantically on Minogue. Hoey let the head down slowly. The sirens were tearing open the night on the street now. The blue rotating lights flared off the cars nearby.

"Ambulance," said Farrell, rising. He waved his arms at the glare of the approaching headlights. Minogue turned back to Gibney, whose eyes were closed now. His chin had sunk onto his chest. Hoey had been unable to extricate his hand from under the head and looked up at Minogue, puzzled. Cramp seized Minogue's leg in a spasm then. He stood and hobbled to the gate, stretching and massaging the calf. He watched the ambulance attendant, a young man with a Frank Zappa moustache, roam with the stethoscope over Gibney's chest.

Minogue turned away and saw people from houses on the street walking slowly toward them. The detectives were out of the van now, and sealing off the front of the house. Gorman's voice startled Minogue who looked up from his crouch and saw Gorman's pale face beyond the gate. Gorman looked down then and tried to bless himself, forgetting the handcuffs.

"Will you identify this man for us, Mr Gorman?" Minogue heard Farrell's acid tones.

"This is my friend, Eamonn Gibney," said Gorman slowly. "Will someone please tell me if he's alive?"

Nobody answered Gorman. Minogue stooped to massage his calf again. His chest felt tight and he drew in deep breaths. Farrell's drawl sounded gravelly, mocking.

"Mr Fintan Gorman? I'm Chief Superintendent Farrell of the Garda Special Branch. I'm detaining you under Section 30 of the Offences Against the State Act, as I have reason to believe that you are involved in a criminal conspiracy prejudicial to the good order of . . ."

Minogue watched the mustachioed attendant trying again with the stethoscope, his eyes darting from
side to side with the concentration.

"That Gill's all right," Kilmartin whispered close to
Minogue's ear. "No thanks to the fucking planning
either, but don't quote me here."

Minogue shivered again. The attendant asked
Hoey to help him draw Gibney out from the fence. He
stepped in the blood as he hefted Gibney onto the
footpath. More blood eddied out from under Gibney
as he was moved.

"Jesus," Minogue heard the attendant say in a cutting Dublin accent as he shook his head, "try and get a
line on to him, quick."

Hoey helped lift Gibney onto the stretcher.
Minogue's thoughts gathered around the cramp again.
He imagined the bones in his ankle, his knee, the mus-
culature that held a body upright, the miracle of walking. Gibney saying that it was just him. Then running,
athletes running, that was miraculous too. *Just him*?
Can't believe that. Have to walk more, that'll stop
those cramps. Hoey was standing beside him now.

"Gibney's gone, sir—that's what the man said.
They can't get the blood into him."

How long had he been standing here? Everything
looks so simple until you learn more about what goes
into it. Screams, a woman screaming in the house.
Gorman's wife: one minute chatting with her friend
on the phone, wondering whether her husband was
alive the next.

"He was shot in the chest. There was no hope,"
said Hoey.

Minogue felt the first drop on the back of his hand.
The cramp began to ease. Another drop plinked onto

a car roof nearby. Kilmartin brushed against him as he stepped back onto the road.

"Come on now, lads. Plastic, on the double. Everything counts, now," Kilmartin was saying.

Minogue stepped away from the gate and leaned against a car. Kilmartin backed into him.

"Sorry, Matt. Are you all right now?"

Minogue still felt the emptiness, the raw vacuum of simply being there. Something had taken over and ejected Minogue out of the ferocious present. Several Gardai were going into Gorman's house now and Minogue heard another scream before the front door was closed again.

Kilmartin was poking a pack of cigarettes at him.

"We'll just have to concentrate on Gorman or the others," he was saying. Hoey joined the two by the car, his face pale. He took one of Kilmartin's cigarettes and lit it from the butt of the one he was just finishing. Both his hands were shaking.

"They're taking Gorman to the Bridewell, Farrell says," said Hoey in a small voice. "Told me to tell you . . ."

Kilmartin was still holding the packet of cigarettes out as he observed Hoey. Minogue didn't think about them but took one of the cigarettes and placed it between his dry lips. The rain was still light.

# NINETEEN

In the last week of October Marguerite Ryan was carried through the streets of Cahir, County Tipperary, by a small crowd, almost exclusively women, after receiving a suspended sentence for manslaughter. The State had no immediate plans to appeal the verdict. Minogue saw Marguerite Ryan on the nine o'clock news. She looked proud and embarrassed, but she did not hug the women with the same fervour as they were hugging her. Minogue went to bed early, thereby earning a curious look from Kathleen. He pleaded a light cold. At his age, he argued quietly, a man had to look after himself. He had dug some books out from under the bed and was going to give some of de Maupassant's longer stories a second shot in the French. He also had a dangerous reading experiment in the form of a play next to the bed, too, if de Maupassant didn't go easy on him: *A Long Day's Journey into Night*.

Next to the books Minogue had drawn out a three-week-old copy of the *Irish Times*. It was folded open at the page where the headline announced that a PLO representative in London had disclaimed any responsibility for the firebombing of the Jewish Museum in Dublin, Ireland. The statement, quoted verbatim, included a paragraph referring to Ireland's current post-colonial contradictions and malaise. Another paragraph claimed parallels between the plight of oppressed Irish nationalists and Palestinians. Minogue remembered trying to understand what the paragraphs meant but his thoughts had no bite then. All he fastened on was a statement declaring that it was in nobody's interests to obliterate history.

Iesult—at Kathleen's prompting, Minogue was sure—ferried a hot whiskey to him ten minutes after he retired. He regarded hot whiskey as a frivolous waste of good whiskey for the same reason that Kathleen thought it was a good drink. If a body had to take a drink at all, she would have added. The boiling water in on top of the whiskey burned off much of the alcohol, and the cloves and sugar made a toy of the precious liquid.

"Every broken-down father should have so solicitous a daughter."

"What are you broken-down about? It's only a cold. All Irish men love to complain, did you know that? Even Pat does it. I tell him to shut up. You'll wake up as right as rain tomorrow and you'll have to find some other excuse for feel— What's that book? Eugene O'Neill? That's very depressing. Why are you reading that?"

"Where did you pick up on the notion that art is for comfort?"

"Are you trying to make yourself sicker, is it? You'd better be on your feet when trouble-the-house gets in off the plane tomorrow. His poor little heart will be broken after leaving his Cathy behind in hamburger heaven. I bet he asks you if *you* told the Immigration to raid the shop so as he'd be put out of the place . . ."

Minogue glared at the wolf who had entered as Florence Nightingale.

"I hope you can control your hyperbole when you see him," he said.

Minogue had picked up the cold on the previous Sunday. He and Kathleen had motored up to Sallygap—his choice—and had sat in the car with the Sunday papers and a set of binoculars. Minogue had spotted two hawks before evening. It was chilly and damp in the car, and the flask of tea was soon gone. Minogue hadn't turned on the engine for heat because he saw that Kathleen had fallen asleep across the back seat, with a blanket over her legs.

Minogue surveyed the desolate bog plateau which led into Wicklow proper. He loved the place. It was a brown and grey darkening world, falling away into an early winter. The low clouds covered the television mast on Kippure Mountain high over the empty landscape. Minogue's mind lingered over the view of the bog as he tried to remember the names of the chieftains who had escaped the dungeons of Dublin Castle and fled across these mountain passes in the dead of winter. Red Hugh O'Donnell was one of ours . . . the same year they founded Trinity College was it? Fifteen ninety-two? Them and us.

A few drops of rain were all that had come so far

from the heavy, low cloud. With the light going fast now and Kathleen stirring awake, Minogue gathered his wits and started the engine. As he had a last look at the fading world here—a view of the high boggy plains which he could take to work with him tomorrow—a mile off in the distance, under Kippure Mountain, he spotted a figure moving steadily across the heather. He put the binoculars to his eyes and looked to see what hardy hill-walker was racing the darkness back to whatever spot he had parked his car. The nearest house was four miles in off the pass, in the village of Glencree. The binocular view compressed the scene and crowded the walker into a tighter world. The low clouds seemed to be but feet over his head as he plodded along.

"There's a citizen who's fond of his mountains," he said to Kathleen as he headed for Glencree. Coming down off the plateau, the road snaked and hairpinned under the beginnings of Kippure Mountain, bringing Minogue closer to the figure still striding across the moor. Might have parked his car anywhere along here, thought Minogue, before taking off along one of the sheep tracks. Turning a blind bend, Minogue saw the person more clearly now. Definitely a man, wearing a green anorak and an aran hat. He stopped the car and took up the binoculars again.

"Declare to God, Kathleen, do you know who that looks like? I was thinking about him, maybe that's why I'm imagining it's him."

"A ghost?"

"Not a bit of it. That's Billy Fine."

"You're joking. It'll be pitch black within the hour, lovey. How can you see anything at all?"

"I think it is, you know."

Minogue stepped out of the car and opened the boot. He took out his wellingtons and leaned against the back door as he donned the rubber boots. Kathleen stayed in the back seat, looking down the road toward the valley of Glencree.

"I'll find out soon enough," he said apologetically. "Then I'll hot-foot it back."

"Mind the bog-holes," said Kathleen with irony plain in her caution. "The light is poor already."

Minogue shouldered his binoculars and made off over the heather. Walking, he thought over Paul Fine's funeral. The crowd waiting for the coffin to be carried out of the little house within the Jewish cemetery at Aughavannagh Road. Archbishop Burke, who was there before Minogue and Kilmartin, had worn a yarmulka with no trace of the embarrassment afflicting Kilmartin and the Commissioner, who walked stiff-necked in the fear that theirs might fall from their heads. After Johnny Cohen had slipped him one, Minogue had put it on his head and promptly forgotten it.

As a species (which species or genus Minogue wasn't sure, Gentile or merely policeman), Minogue and Kilmartin found themselves beside Tynan and the Commissioner. The trio of Mickey Fitz, Downey and Mary McCutcheon stood off to the other side of the crowd, nearer to the dignitaries from the government and Dáil. Minogue noted Tynan's almost uninterested attention as Tynan explained parts of the ceremony. The body, taken but an hour previously from the hospital mortuary, had been driven in a Flanagan's hearse to the burial ground. It had been collected and accompanied by three men from what Tynan called the Holy Society.

"They'll wash and dress the body, all under a sheet," Tynan murmured. "All in white. Jews are enjoined to treat the burial of their dead with the greatest respect. All in white, from head to toe. Rich or poor. You don't see any wreaths, do you?"

Minogue looked around. There were none.

"That's how it is with them. Nothing showy. Go to God plain."

They watched the unvarnished coffin being carried to the graveside. The wooden pegs, Tynan explained when the four policemen were seated in the pub afterwards, were supposed to stick out like that. They were not hammered in tightly because God must know that the living were reluctant to part with the dead.

"They'd not be happy burying someone so late after death, you know. Especially with the PM," Tynan had whispered.

Kilmartin had every appearance of being pleased to be in a pub with his own kind after the funeral, Minogue remembered.

"Tell ye something now," Kilmartin had confided. "It wasn't so much the hat falling off me head that had me nervous. When they started to say the prayers and some of them started bowing and waving around . . . But then, to cap it all, when the prayers started up I automatically began with an Our Father and a Hail Mary. Jases, such an iijit, I thought to meself. I hope nobody heard me."

The Commissioner thought that Kilmartin's addition to the Kaddish was very funny. "No fear of anyone overhearing you praying, Jimmy. There's nobody has heard you saying prayers yet."

Kilmartin had felt obliged to laugh, as the Commissioner was happy with his joke.

Minogue stepped around a turf-cut now and found a sheep track which led toward a point where the figure in the gloom ahead would cross his path.

Tynan had described the week of mourning awaiting the Fines after the funeral. The family members shouldn't leave the house before nightfall, but should be together during the day. The prayers they were not expected to join in before the burial could now be uttered by the family members aloud. The bare maintenance of physical needs was to suffice, and even those things would likely be taken care of by friends and relatives. Minogue had wanted to tell Tynan that Fine had mentioned thinking of emigrating to Israel, but Fine would not have people know this. Tynan had not laughed at Kilmartin's wrong prayers either. God, if he was worth his salt as an Omnipotent, had to be multilingual. Minogue remembered the smell of the Commissioner's whiskey breath as they parted outside the pub, the frown of sincerity as he told Minogue that excellent police work had been done, with the minimum fuss over such a major crisis.

Fine had phoned Minogue at home some two weeks after the funeral. He had thanked Minogue for his work and said no more.

Minogue stopped in the heather and used the binoculars. It was Billy Fine. He seemed to know exactly where he was going, and was so intent on his path that he hadn't noticed Minogue yet. Minogue looked back toward the car but it was no longer in sight. The roadway was hidden under a dyke which had been dug as an aid to getting turf out of the bog.

"Hello!" he called out over the bog. Fine did not turn. Minogue adjusted his direction to cross Fine's path, and quickened his pace. Without warning, a fine drizzle began to settle over the bog. Minogue called out again, and this time Fine turned.

"Justice Fine," Minogue shouted, and threaded his way around bog-holes toward the stationary figure.

"I thought it was yourself," Minogue called out.

"We share the same bog, isn't that something?" said Fine as he shook hands. His face was relaxed, suggesting wry amusement at the sight of Minogue. "What are you at?"

"I'm going home for my tea," replied Minogue, pointing toward where he believed Kathleen and the Fiat were. "Here, look, do you want a lift? That rain will be coming in earnest, I'm thinking."

Fine walked alongside Minogue. "I'm parked up above the village. The time ran away on me but I think I could have made it before the dark. I would have stepped out onto the road if it had turned dark on me."

"I didn't know you for a bog-man," said Minogue.

Fine shrugged. "I came up from town to get a bit of space." He stopped and surveyed the desolate land-scape. "Plenty of room up here, and that's a fact," he murmured. He turned to Minogue with a quizzical expression and said: " 'Great hatred and little room...'"

" '... had maimed us from the start,' " Minogue finished.

Fine shook his head and looked down at his wellington boots. "You're a gas man, Minogue. Spouting Yeats and annoying people. I don't think there's a man in Dublin—outside of the Gardai, I mean—that'd believe a Guard is interested in poetry or museums."

"Ah, why ruin a good stereotype," Minogue said. "People depend on them and sure it gives you a good cover to move around under."

Fine began walking again. " 'Great hatred ... little

room,'" he said. "Room in the head and the heart departments, I suppose he was talking about."

"I'd say so, all right," Minogue agreed.

"Rosalie and I have been giving serious consideration to leaving," said Fine then. Minogue was too taken aback to say anything. "It was her saying something that got me to thinking about that poem."

Minogue said awkwardly, "You remember scraps of things, I suppose—"

"She has the feeling that there's not room for us here any more. Odd sort of idea, and I'm not sure what she means."

"If ye get up and leave, there'd be less room for the likes of us, I think," said Minogue. Fine looked over to Minogue and frowned. Then his face relaxed.

"You are one of the oddest people I have ever met, Minogue—and I have lived and worked in a very odd city all my life. How did you ever get stuck into the job of being a Guard?"

Minogue shrugged.

"I don't know. But the reasons I stay at it are different from the reasons I joined up. I was obliged to give up being an iijit a number of years ago . . . and I'm very glad of getting the chance, I can tell you."

Fine smiled briefly and took up the pace again.

"Well, there's a bit more to this place here than meets the eye," said Fine as he looked around the bog. He stopped and wiped drizzle off his forehead, and pointed toward what Minogue guessed was Kippure Mountain, hidden in the cloud.

"I used to come up here for years. That was before they put the television mast up there and then the Army to guard it. You can't be walking up there now because you'd be up for trespassing in a security zone. How would it look if I was up in court in front of myself one fine day, charged with trespass?"

"I'd hope you'd be lenient on yourself," said Minogue. He felt the rain plaster his hair to his forehead.

"I still come up here the odd time," Fine continued as he stared up into the clouds where Kippure was shrouded. "There's something here for us Jews, you see. Did you know?"

"I didn't."

"The story has always affected me more than others I spoke to about it. That comes of being a poet in my spare time, you understand . . . An Irishman, a Dublinman, I believe, went to Spain sometime in the seventeenth century and brought himself home a nice Spanish wife. They lived somewhere near Dublin, I can't find out where. Every year the wife would go missing for a day or two, off on her own. During her lifetime nobody knew what she was at or where she went or why, but it went on year after year. She travelled alone, up into the mountains. Oddly enough, she was never harassed here and you'd know from your history that the O'Tooles and the O'Byrnes didn't care a damn for English rule in the country and did what they could until after the '98 Rebellion, pretty well . . . She came back safe and sound every year after the day's absence. I suspect that her husband must have known what she was about."

"The Wicklowmen are a tough crowd, this is true," Minogue agreed.

The bog road where Kathleen was waiting for them was part of the Military Road which had been built with the aim of moving troops quickly and safely into the mountains of Wicklow to quell rebels and their families in the wake of the 1798 Rebellion.

"Anyway. This woman came up here every year. After she died, it was found out that she came up here to Kippure on the exact day when our Day of Atonement fell."

He looked balefully at Minogue.

"Yom Kippur," Minogue murmured. "Kippure."

"Exactly."

"I'm astounded. I never imagined . . ."

"Hardly anyone knows that," Fine said, beginning his walk again.

"We don't know her name but her life reminds us of Ruth and the whole history of the Diaspora. The woman was a *Marrano*: that's the Spanish for 'pig.' Do I need to remind you of the prohibition against pork? *Marranos* were those who survived the Inquisition only by renouncing their faith. The alternative was to get burned at the stake."

Burned, Minogue's thoughts raced. Kelly in the car. For renouncing? Opus Dei had been founded in Spain and it had flourished under Franco. What did it mean? Was this what history was? Fine had spoken without irony when he uttered the word *marrano*. The facts were simple, the events past and unreachable. Why then did Minogue feel so stricken? Of course Billy Fine would be alive to the connection, this odd echo through time.

"Apparently people liked this woman very much, and they named the mountain after her," said Fine quietly, picking his way around a turf cut already filling with water.

"That was a terrible thing that she should have to—"

"Worse has happened," said Fine simply. "And we're still here. Let's avoid this survivalist stuff. There's more to Judaism than what some Austrian crackpot or the Spanish Inquisition tried to do."

The two men were now in sight of the car. Minogue's mind groped for the connection between Paul Fine and the woman who had come up here every year of her exile, centuries before. He wanted to go to Burke's Residence and tell him that there could be no excuse, that people like Gibney would always follow because of the way the Church throttled Irish minds. But no: Burke and Heher and the rest of them would simply ask him for proof of causation . . . direct causes . . . necessary and sufficient cause. They'd tie Minogue up with sophistry.

"Who's in the car?"

"Kathleen, my wife."

Fine turned and took a look at where Kippure Mountain should be.

"Rosalie's at home, packing. We're off in the morning to London for a few days. We'll stay with David and give him a rest from looking down people's gobs to make a living. Then we'll be off to Jerusalem."

"For a while, is it?"

"A nice ambiguous question from a nice ambiguous Garda," Fine smiled slowly. "We'll stay a couple of weeks but then we'll be back."

Minogue nodded. "That's great," he said.

"I thought about it a lot. I don't think I could keep quiet about the distaste I have for the way Israeli politics are going at the moment. It's a very different country from what it was before 1967. I don't do very well with extremists: that may be a Dubliner's trademark, that. As well as that, I think I might make an injudicious remark there a bit too often. Johnny Cohen says I'm not religious enough to ignore things, but I know he's codding me. Then I was thinking about those Opus Dei people. There are extremists everywhere, aren't there? It's that simple."

"I wouldn't be so quick to acquit certain institutions here," said Minogue.

"You're a tough nut but you are an insider, you see."

"They've done nothing right for the people," said Minogue. "Excepting for the odd priest, the rest of them have been sitting on us for too long."

"I believe Gorman. That may shock you," said Fine.

"It does."

"He was just a kind of an icon for them as I see it. These people really wanted to install some kind of a government that'd suit their brand of Irish: Catholic, Nationalist, conservative. Gorman's no Peron: he was the one they chose to push for, and I don't think he understood how far they were prepared to go. I don't believe he would have thought of murder for a moment."

"Don't you think he must have known, have felt some inkling?"

"I don't. Gorman wanted power. He wanted it enough so that he paid no attention to events that were happening. He wanted to believe that things were unfolding naturally, and that he was the man to deliver the country. A man with a mission, was Gorman. He saw what his ambition permitted him to see. I've met hundreds of people like him in court. Tell me, how many do you think would have rallied to Gorman if he had made his break at the Ard Fheis?"

Minogue thought of Kilmartin's anger, the widespread grumbling about leadership, the simple solutions.

"I don't know. There's nobody admitting to even

knowing the man now, of course. Not one member of the Dáil or Senate," he said.

"I expected as much. An Opus Dei member has testified that Gibney argued with poor Kelly a few weeks back. And that was how Kelly knew of the plan to bring down the government, I expect."

"It was bred into Gibney to be ruthless, that's what I keep thinking," said Minogue. "And he had any amount of help he wanted, it seems. Our fella, Morrissey, actually fed him a telephone bug for Kelly's home phone."

"I'm a Jew, remember. I'm not supposed to be privy to the depths of the Irish Catholic Nationalist mind and what it can hold. What about the others in this group?"

"Well," Minogue began, "it may well prove that everything leads back to Gibney. Morrissey is in more serious trouble than the others: he's an accessory because he concealed knowledge of a crime. I maintain he abetted it. Gibney even got Morrissey to phone him if he heard anything about a body being washed up on the beaches. Morrissey heard it on the South Dublin Garda frequency first thing on Monday morning, and he admits to phoning Gibney. Gibney decided at some point he'd have to kill Brian Kelly, too. Best we estimate now is that he got into Kelly's house and killed him there. The day your son was found."

"Thus the peculiar timing of this fake call from the Palestinian outfit to the newspaper."

"Gibney wanted to buy time as well as dirty up the motive. The Ard Fheis was only a week away then. There was the chance that your son would not be found at all—that's why Gibney went to the trouble of putting him in the sea, I think."

Fine's eyes wandered past Minogue and slipped out of focus.

"Yes," Minogue went on, "we have yet to get anything definitive from Gibney's cohorts and it may be that he didn't disclose to them what he was up to. It looks like he found some pretext to lure Paul out to Killiney. He might have used Brian Kelly's name to set it up. Wily, organized—I think he had them all mesmerized. Leadership is an odd business. But Gibney's associates are beginning to let slip that Gibney was obsessed with the way the country was being governed. Half of it is hindsight, I'm sure, patching up recollections to fit what has transpired. It's possible that Gibney dithered over killing Brian Kelly. He may have thought or hoped that Kelly could be frightened off or brought back into the fold. . . ."

"Had a row with Mr Kelly prior to murdering him, perhaps?" said Fine. Minogue shrugged.

"What I still can't get around is the fact that Gibney had such an effect," said Fine. "How could he influence educated people to go along with this sort of thing? They were ready, before the weekend, to gun down the union man who's leading the strike, weren't they?"

"That's what's coming out, all right," said Minogue. "They had a plan to cause as much chaos as they needed to."

Fine turned up the collar of his anorak.

"The ground-work was done years ago," Minogue said. "Not directly, of course. But the whole process took its toll, that's how Gibney was able to persuade all those people: the fella out in Radio Telifis Eireann to monitor what Paul did on the computer and then wipe it out when we came looking for Paul's stuff, those civil servants, Gorman, even. They had been readied years ago."

"You're talking about something I can't comment on, you know," said Fine. "I know piety and fervour in very different forms when they're planted onto politics. That's why I'll be keeping my comments to myself when we're in Israel."

The drizzle was turning to rain now. Kathleen rubbed the window inside.

"The charges will stick, you know," Minogue said. "We'll get them all on conspiracy, if not accessory to."

"It was hardly a conspiracy at all," said Fine in a resigned tone. "They were simply afraid of Gibney after a while, by the sound of things. I suppose we have Archbishop Burke to thank for getting to these people before they did worse."

"And whoever it was who broke ranks and made that confession," said Minogue.

Fine stepped over the ditch and climbed up toward the road. Minogue walked around to the driver's side. The rain was drumming on the roof now.

"Has the Commissioner kept you up on the evidence as it comes in?"

"The whole bit," said Fine. He seemed to Minogue to be concentrating on the rain as it hopped off the roof.

"Yes. Court martials, the investigation tribunals in the Gardai—I believe the panel appointed by the Civil Service Commission is like the Inquisition all over again. Nobody has asked my opinion on the whole business yet, do you know that? It's as if they're going at it so ferociously to prove something."

"It may be the guilt. Atonement."

Fine took a lingering look back up into the rain and

the gloom. Night was coming in with the rain clouds over the bog.

"For Paul too, for not knowing him as well as I could have. I don't think he'd like to see us run out of Ireland by this. Do you know what finally decided me, though? I remembered this afternoon. It was something Johnny Cohen said to me afterwards. We all carry a spare yarmulka or two in our fobs at funerals, so as Gentiles can wear them. Johnny was complaining that he had run out of them and he had borrowed every spare one he could find, but that there'd be people in the burial ground without a covering over them. Catastrophe in Johnny's mind, of course. There were that many at the funeral. We were very glad of that."

Again the image of the funeral circled in Minogue's head. From a distance he heard his own voice, odd in the gloom. "Not a part of the world or a season that a man could afford to be without some class of a covering over his head, is it?"

Minogue opened the door of the Fiat.

"Hop in there like a good man and introduce yourself. We'll be down off this place before the night."

John Brady was born in Dublin, Ireland, and attended Trinity College, Dublin. He emigrated to Canada in 1975. His first book, *A Stone of the Heart*, won the 1989 Arthur Ellis Award from the Crime Writers of Canada for Best First Novel. His second book, *Unholy Ground*, was published to rave reviews. Brady lives in Bradford, Ontario, with his wife, Hanna Wagner, and their two children.